brenda novak

one perfect summer

mira

mira™

ISBN-13: 978-0-7783-8634-6

One Perfect Summer

First published in 2020. This edition published in 2022.

Recycling programs
for this product may
not exist in your area.

Mira
22 Adelaide St. West, 41st Floor
Toronto, Ontario M5H 4E3, Canada
www.Harlequin.com

Printed in U.S.A.

Also by Brenda Novak

For a full list of Brenda's books,
visit www.brendanovak.com.

To my sisters.
One of the best gifts Mother ever gave me
was the three of you.

one perfect
summer

1

serenity

Gripping the steering wheel tightly, Serenity Alston navigated the winding freeway heading east toward Donner Summit. Dark, ominous clouds hung low on the horizon. Although she was driving a BMW X5, which had 4-wheel drive, if it started to snow, the highway patrol could close the road before she could get over the pass. This was California, where even a little bad weather was cause for panic.

The Lumineers' "Ho Hey," a song that had been popular when she'd first married Sean eight years ago, came over the sound system, bringing to mind the way he'd been back then—handsome, charming and so earnest and true.

Or so it had seemed...

She told Siri to delete it, but the next song—Jason Mraz's "I Won't Give Up"—brought painful memories of how committed she'd been to him, and what it had cost her.

Unwilling to go through her entire playlist right now,

for fear she'd be tempted to delete most of her collection—and lose too much of her focus—she turned off the music. Snow didn't often come to the Sierra Nevada Mountains after April. But here it was nearing the end of May and those dark clouds loomed ahead. She needed to beat the storm, just in case. The two women she was meeting at the cabin were relative strangers; only she had a key. If she got caught on the road, how would they get in?

Although...

She eased off the gas pedal. Maybe it would be better if she *didn't* make it through. She'd been experiencing some regret since she first set this up. Sean's trial was over. She could finally close that chapter of her life, put it behind her and move on. Why ask for a whole new problem? One that could easily create more wreckage in her life? Right now her family was strong, functional, happy. They could stay that way if she ignored what she'd found, just let it go.

Part of her was tempted to do that. She could head back right now. But another part—her natural compulsion to reach the truth at any cost—won out. She'd never been able to turn a blind eye to anything, which was why, she supposed, she'd become a true-crime writer.

At any rate, she couldn't ask two people to come clear across the country to meet her and then stand them up.

Her phone rang and Bluetooth announced that it was her mother.

Damn.

After taking a deep breath to steady her nerves, she told it to answer. For the sake of everyone involved, she had to continue to act as though nothing had changed. "Hello?"

"Hi, honey!" her mother chirped, as breezy as ever.

Serenity winced at the sound of her voice. Hiding anything from Charlotte was difficult. But if she hadn't answered, her mother would've just called back. And if she didn't behave normally, Charlotte might begin to suspect something was wrong, which would only make the next days and weeks, maybe months, while she was trying to figure this thing out, that much harder to navigate. "Hi, Mom."

"What are you up to?" she asked.

Serenity adjusted the heat, increasing the warmth inside the car. "I'm heading to the cabin." She spoke casually, as though this trip was just like every other, even though it wasn't remotely the same.

"Again?"

"Sure, why not?" Serenity couldn't see why her mother would mind, not if she didn't know what Serenity had planned. Ever since her parents had moved away from Berkeley, where she lived, to San Diego, the place sat empty. With the rest of the family nowhere near Tahoe, it wasn't as if anyone else could drive to the cabin for just a couple of days. Serenity had a brother and two sisters, but her brother, the youngest at twenty-four, was getting his master's at UCLA, and her twin sisters, who were twenty-eight, both lived in San Antonio. One had married a man who was from there, and the other had married a man who was flexible enough to move to Texas so the twins wouldn't have to live too far apart.

"It's just… I don't know," her mother said. "You've been going to Tahoe almost every weekend."

"I love Tahoe." The cabin had become a refuge for her. As soon as Sean had been sentenced, and she no longer had to worry about his smarmy lawyers getting him released on probation with time served, she'd started trading the rat race of the Bay Area for the peace and tranquility of the mountains whenever she could. Heading up the hill gave her something to do, somewhere to go when she'd normally be with the man she'd married.

It also gave her a break from researching the gruesome facts behind the Maynard murders that were the subject of her latest book—about Frank "Coop" Maynard, a pharmacist who killed his whole family, fled the state, married again and started anew. She used to be able to maintain a sort of clinical separation from the crimes she wrote about, but she seemed to be losing that. Ever since she found those files on Sean's computer, the fact that a person could be a monster down deep troubled her more and more. And that made her fear, at some point, she wouldn't be able to continue writing.

What would she do then?

"We all love it up there," Charlotte was saying. "But do you have to go every weekend? You're still so young."

Although she was only thirty-five, Serenity felt older. Having to testify against her own husband seemed to have aged her by a decade or more. "What does my age have to do with anything?" she asked.

"You should be out meeting people. It's not as though you socialize during the week. You write at home and never get out."

She had to work. She had deadlines. And now that

she was no longer planning to take a break to have a baby while Sean supported them—thank God she'd found those files before they'd gotten that far—she had to be extra careful to maintain her career, or she could wind up without an income. That was one of the reasons she went to Tahoe so often; the beauty and isolation helped clear her mind. "Are you talking about another man? Another relationship?"

"Of course."

Irritation made Serenity tense up even more—until she felt as though she'd shatter at the slightest touch. "I'm not interested in another man, Mom."

"You need to move on at some point, Serenity. You're only getting older."

"You just said I was too young to closet myself away at the cabin every weekend. Now you're saying I'm too old?"

"I'm saying if you want to have a family, you can't wait forever."

"I'd like a family one day. But if it isn't meant to be, it isn't meant to be."

"You can't take such a passive approach—or it *won't* be. Not all men are like Sean. Look at your father."

Her mother was using her father as an example of integrity? When he might be in on the lie they'd been living? Serenity was no longer sure she was even related to him or to the rest of the family. The Facebook message she'd received six months ago, after taking a DNA test mostly on a lark—just to see how it all worked for the sake of her writing—had upended everything she'd ever believed she could rely on. "I'm not ready to start dating," she reiterated.

"What about Sawyer?" her mother asked. "I suspect he's always been attracted to you."

Where had that come from? Sawyer had never shown any romantic interest in her. "Sean's *brother*?"

"Oh, stop! You don't look at him like a brother. He was in the military most of the time you were married. You barely ever saw him."

She pictured Sawyer. At six foot four, he was taller than most men, had a sturdy warrior's build, thick sandy-blond hair and stormy green eyes that had probably seen too much. "He was raised with Sean."

"So? He's not really related to him. He didn't even live with him for very long."

He was still *connected* to Sean. "Sawyer should be glad he's not actually related to him," she grumbled.

"Except that now Sawyer has *no* family."

Serenity felt bad for him. He hadn't had an easy childhood. When his mother died shortly after she married Sean's father, Sean's father was kind enough to finish raising him. So when Sean went to trial and the whole Alston clan rallied behind him, they considered Sawyer an ungrateful traitor when he wouldn't join forces with them. "The way they treated him once the trial started wasn't fair. He was just trying to stand up for what's right. But as far as the two of us ever getting together, there's no way. We've always butted heads on everything. No matter what the issue is, we're on opposite sides."

"You were on the same side when it came to Sean," her mother pointed out.

"Because Sawyer was able to put his head above his heart, something the rest of the family couldn't do—or refused to do." The way Sawyer had handled the situation showed emotional maturity. Serenity had been impressed but not all that surprised. He was incredibly smart, which was why it bugged her so much whenever he disagreed with her. Not only did he think faster than anyone she'd ever met, he was the only person she couldn't beat, regardless of the game they played—even games of complete chance.

When the entire family got together for a reunion two years ago, they challenged each other at everything they could think of—horseshoes, volleyball, chess, backgammon, trivia. She'd won at backgammon once or twice but lost at all the rest. She'd never forget the enraging smile that had tugged at his lips when she insisted he give her another chance.

"Sean put up a pretty convincing front. He had me fooled for a long time. You, too," her mother added.

Serenity didn't need to be reminded of that. She'd fallen hard, planned her whole life around him. "He was a good liar," she admitted. "And his lawyers were even better." So good, in fact, there were moments Serenity had wondered if she was crazy for trusting her instincts above what she heard from his counsel in court—moments when she'd asked herself if she was not only being a bad wife, but ruining an innocent man's life.

If she hadn't been the one to find the proof and confront Sean before he had time to concoct the slick lies he and his lawyers presented afterward, they might've swayed her. Maybe she shouldn't be so shocked that his family went the other way and only Sawyer could figure out the truth.

"He almost got off," her mother said. "He would have, if not for your testimony. You were great on the stand. So poised. And Sawyer was right there to support you through it all. I love the way he stood by you. That had to have taken a great deal of courage when the rest of his family was glaring daggers at him, day in and day out."

Large drops of rain began to splatter on her windshield. Serenity scowled as she glanced up at the foreboding sky. "He only did that because he believed Sean was guilty." She switched on her wipers. "Anyway, I'm sure he was glad when the trial ended and he could go on with his life and forget all about me."

Although, oddly enough, she'd heard from Sawyer recently. He'd called her, out of the blue, just to check in—not that she was going to tell her mother. Her conversation with him had been awkward, and he didn't say much before hurrying off the phone.

"You should reach out to him, see how he's doing," Charlotte said.

Serenity wished she'd been friendlier during their brief conversation. But she hadn't expected to ever hear from him again. And she was still so disillusioned after what'd happened with Sean she was off men in general—and anyone who was associated with Sean in particular. She didn't need the memories Sawyer evoked. She preferred to forget the past eighteen months, start over.

"If I get the chance," she said, and before her mother could press the issue any further, she asked how her brother was doing in school. He'd been struggling with his grades lately, which was unusual for him.

Her mother said she thought he was improving, at which point Serenity said the weather was getting bad and she needed to go.

Within ten minutes of hanging up, the rain turned

to heavy snow, making the road slick and the traffic slow until she was sitting in place, staring at a sea of red taillights.

"Come on, come on," she muttered impatiently. She'd been hoping to arrive at the cabin before Lorelei and Reagan. To get settled in, walk around and acclimate. To become anchored in the familiar before having to meet the two strangers who were her half sisters.

But at this rate, they'd beat her there.

2

lorelei

Lorelei Cipriano read the latest text from her husband: Are you kidding me? You left for an entire week right in the middle of everything we're going through? I thought you'd agreed to try to work things out!

She hadn't agreed to anything. Her husband had been trying to convince her, had been pleading with her to forgive him ever since the ugly truth came out. And she'd been walking around in a shocked daze, going through the motions of life for the past three weeks like some sort of automaton.

But she'd made no commitments, and wasn't even sure she was capable of letting this one go…

She was itching to reply to his text and tell him that. He was acting as though *she* was doing something wrong. But she'd already met up with Reagan at the Reno, Nevada, airport, where they'd rented a car to drive to Serenity's cabin, and she didn't want to get caught up fighting with Mark, didn't want Reagan, who was driving, asking questions. She was so humiliated by what Mark had done she wished *no one* had to find out.

But, sadly, there'd be no hiding, at least not from her friends and family back home. As the weeks wore on and the proof became more apparent, she'd become an object of everyone's pity, whether she liked it or not.

"Mommy, I want to get out," her daughter said, a whine in her voice.

Poor Lucy. At only four, she'd found it difficult to sit on a plane for most of the day. Buckling her into the back seat of a car for another hour and a half as soon as they landed was almost more than the child could bear. And the weather was making the drive take forever. "Soon," she promised.

Had she made a mistake coming here in the middle of everything that was going on at home? Lorelei wondered as she gazed out at the onslaught of white flakes pummeling the windshield and sticking to the road.

That was possible. But she'd needed an escape, some time to think about what she was going to do. And the hope that she might have support from family—something she'd never been able to count on before—had been too tempting to resist. Even if she ultimately chose not to share her situation with Serenity and Reagan, it was nice to have a neutral place to go while she figured things out. A safe haven where no one really knew her and she wouldn't have to field all the questions she'd face at home as soon as word began to spread.

It was possible she'd *never* go back. To Mark, anyway.

Stifling a sigh, she shoved her phone in her purse. "Look at this traffic," she murmured as though she wasn't under so much pressure she felt she might start sweating diamonds.

Lines of concentration creased Reagan's forehead. "It's ugly, all right."

Lorelei had been so curious about her newly discovered half sisters. For the sake of comparison, they'd exchanged pictures and provided their heights and weights months ago. All three of them had dark hair and blue eyes, which was unusual, given how rare that combination was. Like Serenity, Lorelei wore her hair long. Reagan's had been buzzed into a dramatic yet stylish cut that fit her more assertive and gregarious personality. They were all three close to the same height, at five foot nine to ten inches, and weighed within twenty pounds of each other—she being the heaviest, thanks to the baby weight she'd never quite lost, and Reagan being the skinniest. If they were to walk through a mall together, most people would guess they were sisters, because of their lanky builds. But Lorelei wondered if there were other, less obvious similarities. How would her new siblings behave? Would they have the same likes and dislikes? The same mannerisms?

As a child who'd never had any real family, who'd been alone and adrift for so long, Lorelei had been beyond excited to find Reagan and Serenity. The wondering and waiting, the painstaking research and the hope that had driven her through it all had paid off. *Finally*. Now she had not one but *two* other human beings, besides her daughter, who shared her DNA. She'd thought having these connections, being more like other people, might eventually fill that terrible void inside her.

But her thrill over finding Reagan and Serenity had dissolved the instant her husband had blindsided her with such a painful admission that she no longer cared about anything else. She'd lost the very foundation of her life, and she hadn't seen it coming.

"Should we call Serenity?" Reagan asked. "Let her know we landed?"

"Good idea." Lorelei pulled up her contacts and tried the number she'd been given but couldn't get the call to go through. "I guess I don't have enough service."

Being careful not to take her eyes off the road for too long, Reagan fumbled around in her oversized bag situated between them, and eventually located her own cell. "Do I?" she asked as she handed it to Lorelei.

Lorelei checked the signal. Reagan had a different carrier, but her coverage didn't seem to be any better. "No more than I do."

"Damn." She hunched forward to gaze up at the mountains towering on either side of them. "Maybe it's because we're in this narrow gorge. Let's try again in a few minutes."

"I might be able to get a text to go through," Lorelei suggested, giving Reagan back her phone. "Sometimes that'll work even when you can't make a call."

Lorelei sent Serenity a message to tell her they were caught in the storm and to see if she was having the same problem.

It seemed to deliver, so she dropped her phone in her lap and once again frowned at the weather. "Looks like it went through, but we're going to need GPS, so I hope we get a stronger signal before too long. How else will we find the cabin?"

"For now, I'm following the signs to King's Beach, which Serenity said will take us to Incline Village."

"Okay." Lorelei smiled as though she believed everything was under control. But it was hard to trust a total stranger to drive in these conditions, especially with Lucy in the car. Since Lorelei lived in Florida, she wasn't used to snow. That was the logic Reagan had used for taking the wheel, but that wasn't the reason Lorelei had agreed. Once again, she'd sacrificed her own best judgment because of her past. She'd been shuffled around to so many homes when she was a child, had grown up with the harsh knowledge that if she wasn't always sweet and compliant her foster parents could decide at any moment that they no longer wanted her. And even though she was now an adult and didn't have to worry about being returned to a group home to await the next foster placement, she couldn't get past the deeply rooted fears that situation had created. So she spent her life trying to build what she'd been missing, which meant she'd probably compromised too often, and now she was riding in the passenger seat while Reagan, who worked as an ad executive and came from New York City, drove.

Reagan didn't even own a car! How long had it been since she'd driven before today?

Lorelei's phone buzzed, signaling a new message.

"Is that Serenity?" Reagan asked.

Unfortunately, it wasn't. "No, it's my husband."

I wish I'd never given you that DNA kit, he'd written. But it was too late for regrets. He *had* given it to her—last summer—so she could possibly discover where she came from.

After she'd taken that test and received her results, there was no one on the list of matches they'd sent her who could be her mother or her father. But she'd never forget the email letting her know there was someone designated a "close match" at 1957cM named Reagan Sands. When she logged on to the company website, there was a link to Reagan and they'd been in touch ever since. That was last August.

Then, in November, she was surprised by another notice from the DNA company showing a small, circular picture of someone named Serenity Alston, who looked very much like her and Reagan, under that same "closely related" category. Serenity didn't respond to the message feature—she'd since said that she never even opened the many emails the DNA company sent her—so Lorelei had checked Facebook and found her there. And right after that, she brought Serenity and Reagan together, and they began a group chat in Messenger.

What a year. Would she one day discover other siblings? That was the thing about sperm. It went pretty far when it was from a donor—and since she, Reagan and Serenity were all born within two years of each other but came from such different situations, Lorelei could only assume that was how they'd been conceived.

Reagan seemed completely engaged in navigating the storm, so this time Lorelei allowed herself to respond to Mark, who had ruined her wonderful, momentous year by dragging her into the depths of sorrow.

That DNA kit isn't the problem, and you know it, she wrote back.

He messaged her again, but she didn't bother to read it. He wouldn't want to talk about what *he* did. He'd just go on about her leaving and how inopportune a time it was right now, given the situation at home. He didn't see what she had to gain by meeting Reagan and Serenity. He'd already told her how foolish she was for opening herself up to whatever problems they might bring with them.

Relationships aren't all fun and games, Lorelei. They come with responsibility, he'd said when she'd first broached the subject of meeting her new sisters in person.

She could only laugh about his comment now that everything had come out and she knew he'd let her down more than anyone else ever had. Chances were far better that he wasn't excited about Reagan and Serenity because he didn't want to share her and was worried about what having them in her life might change.

What if one or both of these women are like Osha and Mercedes? Don't you have enough dysfunctional people in your life?

Mark had said that, too, and even if the comment was selfishly motivated, she couldn't argue with the fact that she did have too many dysfunctional people in her life. She wouldn't want another Osha. The youngest of the children Lorelei had known at her last foster home was so extremely narcissistic she couldn't get along with anyone. After two impulsive marriages and two acrimonious divorces, she was working in the porn industry and was absolutely defiant if anyone questioned it. Because of the things she said and did, and the people she associated with, Lorelei couldn't let Lucy be around her—not that Osha had ever shown any interest in Lucy in the first place.

Mercedes, two years older, who'd also been in the same foster home just as Lorelei started high school, had gone in the opposite direction. She'd joined a cult and wouldn't speak to anyone outside of it because she was so afraid she'd be led "astray." The cult's leader had warned his followers that Satan lurked around every corner, effectively inoculating them against anything an outsider might say. For a brief time, Mercedes had shown much more interest in Lucy, but Lorelei worried she might be even more dangerous than Osha.

"Osha and Mercedes are the reason I want to meet Reagan and Serenity," she'd argued. "I don't have any real family. You grew up with seven brothers and sisters, so you don't know what that's like."

"Some of my siblings can be difficult," had been his response. "Reagan and Serenity could make your life worse instead of better. That's what I'm saying. Maybe they're related genetically, but you have no idea how they were raised, what kind of people they might be."

He'd presented such a convincing argument that she had, at first, tried to listen to him. She'd told Serenity she couldn't come to the cabin and, for a brief time, she'd even backed away from having any contact with them.

But that was before Mark had mowed down all her previously held beliefs—as well as her sense of well-being, her trust in him and her hope for the future. After he sat her down and broke the news about what he'd done, she'd decided she didn't want to shut out Serenity and Reagan. Maybe he was wrong about them. Maybe they would offer joy and friendship and support when she needed it most.

"Still nothing from Serenity?" Reagan asked.

Lorelei checked again. "Not yet."

The car in front of them slid on the ice. Lorelei caught her breath until the driver managed to recover— only inches from slamming into the guardrail and possibly hurtling over the edge into a deep ravine.

Reagan's knuckles turned white on the steering wheel, but she didn't acknowledge the close call. Instead, she seemed intent on talking, probably to distract herself. "What's your husband saying? He's worried about you in this weather?"

In Lorelei's mind, if Mark cared about her as much as he claimed, he wouldn't have done what he did. But that wasn't what she said. "I'm sure he is," she replied, hoping the expected response would steer the conversation away from him that much sooner. "What about Drew? Did he have any problem with you flying across the country to spend a week with two sisters you've never met?"

Reagan didn't respond.

"Reagan?" Lorelei prodded.

"I had the vacation time," she said shortly.

"I wasn't talking about leaving work," Lorelei clarified. "I was wondering if he was afraid you were making a mistake by getting to know us, or wished he could come, too, or—"

"I didn't discuss it with him," she said. "He doesn't really have any say over what I do."

Lorelei blinked in surprise. "He's your boyfriend, isn't he?"

Again, no answer.

"I'm sorry if you two have hit a rough patch. When you mentioned him on Messenger I got the impression things were going great between you, that you were in love."

"I *am* in love," she said. "That's the problem."

"Why is that a problem?" Lorelei asked.

Reagan bit her lip as she glanced over. "Because he's married."

Lorelei felt her jaw drop. "You're in a relationship with a married man?" *Why?* she wanted to scream. Reagan wasn't just moderately pretty, she was beautiful. Successful, too. She could have almost any man she wanted. She didn't need to steal anyone's husband.

"Mom, are we there yet?" Lucy asked from the back seat.

Lorelei was so thrown by what she'd heard she didn't answer until Lucy started crying.

"We'll be there soon, honey," she replied as her daughter's distress finally cut into her thoughts. Problem was she'd been saying the same thing for the past three hours, so it had no effect.

When Lucy wouldn't stop crying, Lorelei got a sucker out of her purse. She hated to ply her child with sugar, but it was about the only thing that would keep Lucy happy until they could reach the cabin, and with the storm and what she'd just learned about Reagan, the situation was stressful enough. "Here, I'll give you this. Will that help?"

Her daughter sniffed but brightened as she accepted the bribe, and Lorelei managed what she hoped was a pleasant expression even though she felt close to tears herself. She'd been hoping her two sisters would be the kind of people she needed. That the time, effort, money—plus navigating this damn storm—would be worth it. But she had no desire to invest in someone no better than Francine. Her best friend had turned out to be an even bigger disappointment than Osha and Mercedes.

Reagan shot her a sheepish look. "I know what you're thinking."

Lorelei doubted she did, doubted she could possibly

guess how repulsive she found this revelation. She said nothing, just turned to stare out the window.

"Lorelei, please don't judge me so fast," Reagan said. "As a stay-at-home mom, you probably don't come into contact with temptation very often. But when you're out in the workforce, like me, you spend a lot of time with your coworkers and…and sometimes you begin to have feelings you shouldn't. It wasn't as if I *planned* on this happening. It wasn't as if I've ever done anything even remotely like it before. I'm telling you…it came out of nowhere."

"I don't care what your excuse is," she said. "That's a line you don't cross."

Reagan's face turned bright red. Lorelei was overreacting, and she knew it. This wasn't *her* husband they were talking about. But it hit so close to home, and she'd put so much hope into her sisters being people she could admire—*and count on*—that she was bitterly disappointed.

Reagan had already proven herself unreliable in one of the most important ways.

"Thanks for your understanding," Reagan said tightly.

Lorelei rubbed her temples. "I'm sorry. What you do is none of my business. But so you know, I'm not unsophisticated. I have a degree in marketing. I was a digital marketing manager for a great company and made decent money. It's just that…when Mark and I discussed having children, we felt it would be best for me to be at home instead of shuttling our kids to and from day care every day."

"Why is it always the woman who makes that sacrifice?" Reagan grumbled. "Why couldn't *he* have been the one to stay at home?"

"It's not always the woman. More and more men are doing it and—"

"A small fraction."

Lorelei ignored the interruption. "And by the time we paid for day care, I wouldn't have earned enough to warrant being away from our child, let alone been able to support us if Mark had stayed home." Letting go of her career had been difficult. But she'd felt it was the right thing to do, the practical thing.

Or had she, once again, compromised when she shouldn't have? Given up her job to keep Mark happy?

Now that she was possibly staring down a divorce, she felt it might've been smarter to push back.

"Yeah, well, we'll see what you think of that decision when Lucy's out of the house and on her own."

"*What* did you say?" Lorelei asked.

Reagan sent her a scowl. "What will you have then?"

"Hopefully, I'll have a happy, well-adjusted child. Mark was making more than I was, so…"

"*So?*" Reagan challenged when she let her words trail off.

"It made sense," Lorelei insisted. She hated that she hadn't finished her sentence to begin with, that Reagan had to call her out. It revealed that she *was* concerned she'd made a mistake—one that might cost her dearly in the long run.

But Reagan was so caught up in attempting to justify her own actions, she didn't capitalize on Lorelei's uncertainty. "I've been trying really hard to cut it off with Drew," she said. "But it's not as easy as you think. He's one of the senior partners at the agency. I'll lose him *and* my job, and I've worked my ass off for ten years to get where I am at Edison & Curry. It's so competitive in advertising."

"If he's vindictive enough to fire you because you won't sleep with him—especially when he's already married—he's an asshole, and you need to get away from him as soon as possible, no matter what it costs," Lorelei blurted out.

Lucy gasped. "Mommy, did you say *asshole*?"

Lorelei squeezed her forehead. "No, I said... I said..."

"She said, 'He's on the last hole.'"

Small point for Reagan for jumping in to help, even though Lucy wouldn't understand the golf reference. Lorelei was about to mouth a polite thank you but what Reagan said next quelled the impulse.

"Your saintly mother would never use such language."

"What's *saintly*?" Lucy asked.

Reagan had spoken in a sulky mumble, but that hadn't stopped Lorelei's bright daughter from picking up on every word.

When no one answered, Lucy seemed to catch on that it hadn't been meant as a compliment. "Mommy, are you and Aunt Reagan having a fight?"

Lorelei held the strap of her seat belt away from her body so she could glance back to reassure her daughter. "No, honey. We're just...tired. We all had a long flight today, right? Aren't *you* tired?"

"No," Lucy said immediately.

Drawing a deep breath, Lorelei faced forward. "Well, I am."

"Now you regret coming," Reagan said. "I can tell."

"I don't regret it," Lorelei lied, but she was hoping Serenity wouldn't be the terrible disappointment Reagan was turning out to be. She'd committed to staying for an entire week, and it wouldn't be easy to leave sooner, not unless she was willing to spend a lot of extra money on two last-minute plane tickets.

Actually, that wasn't even an option. There was hardly any money in the bank account she shared with Mark, and her credit card was maxed out from their recent kitchen remodel. He'd started paying the bills from a separate account, and she thought she could guess why. He was trying to protect his assets in the event that she left him.

If that happened, until the court divided their property and ordered him to pay child support, which could be months away, she'd be left with little or nothing.

Just in case the worst did happen, she'd have to be very careful when it came to expenses.

Which meant she and Lucy were stuck in Tahoe until her return flight.

3

reagan

Reagan mentally kicked herself as she continued to fight through the storm and the traffic to reach the cabin. What had she been thinking? She'd known better than to announce she was the other woman in a romantic triangle. That was the quickest way to destroy her credibility as a decent person, the quickest way to be shunned. Poor Lorelei hadn't even had a chance to get to know her first.

Good job making sure your half sister never has any respect for you, she told herself. But she was lugging around so much guilt even she didn't feel she deserved respect. And holding back that information would make her feel dishonest on top of everything else. She wasn't a liar, wasn't one to pretend she had any claim on the man she was seeing if she didn't, especially to people she was hoping to have a lifelong relationship with. What was the point of coming here to meet her sisters if she was only hiding who she really was?

Truth be told, she was probably also looking for

someone who'd understand, who'd believe she hadn't meant for anything like that to happen. She'd felt exactly as Lorelei did—a married man was simply off-limits. But somehow Drew had worked his way through her defenses. She still wasn't sure how.

"What, you've never done anything you regret?" she asked Lorelei. She couldn't keep the accusing tone from her voice, although she knew *she* was the one in the wrong, that Lorelei had every right to think the worst.

"Nothing like *that*," Lorelei responded.

"Your situation is vastly different from mine. Your husband is probably the only man you see on a daily basis." It was a weak defense, something she'd already pointed out, but it was the best she could muster.

"I wish you'd quit painting me as being so insulated and out of touch with the rest of the world. I have neighbors, male friends and associates. I could find someone to…to—" she checked her daughter to see if she was paying attention before finishing with a euphemistic "—be with if I wanted to."

No doubt Lorelei assumed Reagan had been having sex with Drew on a regular basis. But they'd only been together—like that—once. A week ago they'd been working late when the feelings they had for each other had somehow boiled over.

Reagan had been devastated afterward. She'd worked from home the next few days, so she wouldn't have to see him before leaving on this trip. Because she cared about Drew, because she wanted him more than anyone she'd ever known, she knew she had to stay away until she could overcome her emotions or it would only happen again.

"Except that you're deeply in love with your husband.

Why would you want to?" she asked Lorelei. "You've told me how wonderful Mark is. Not all of us are as lucky as you."

"Yeah, I'm lucky, all right," she snapped. "About as lucky as Drew's wife."

Reagan felt her eyebrows jerk together. "What are you talking about?"

She pinched the bridge of her nose before dropping her hand. "Nothing."

"Tell me," Reagan insisted.

Lorelei twisted around to look at her daughter again. "I can't. Not right now."

"What, Mommy?" Lucy said.

She faced front. "Nothing, honey."

Reagan studied her new sister as much as driving through this terrible weather would allow. "Is something going on between the two of you?"

She nodded.

"Since when?"

"Two weeks, six days and—" she screwed up her face as though struggling to get the timing correct "— three hours ago."

"Don't tell me he's seeing someone else…"

Once more, she glanced back at her daughter, but she must've felt Lucy was no longer paying attention because Lorelei nodded.

"You're kidding me!"

"I wish I was," she said bitterly.

A sign listing the mileage to Incline Village came up on the right, but the numbers were partially covered with snow. Reagan hoped they were getting close. "Let me guess, it was someone at his work."

Lorelei shot her a sullen glance. "No."

"A neighbor?"

"Worse."

"What could be worse than that?"

"My best friend would be worse."

Reagan gaped at her.

"She's my *ex*-best friend now, of course."

No wonder Lorelei had reacted so badly when Reagan confessed her own situation. "I'm sorry."

Lorelei said nothing.

"How did you find out?" Reagan asked.

"He told me."

"Right when we were planning this trip?"

"Just after."

Reagan's phone chimed, but she ignored it. She was pretty sure it would be Drew. He was dying to get hold of her, had called and messaged her many times since that night in his office. "I'm surprised you still came."

"I *had* to come. I felt like I was suffocating in that house with him."

Lowering her voice, Reagan tried to choose her words carefully. "Did you have any clue something like that might be going on?"

"None."

"I see." She used the rearview mirror to check on Lucy. Lorelei's daughter seemed completely preoccupied with her sucker, but Reagan turned up the music, just in case. "Are you going to stay with him?"

"I don't know. He claims he's sorry. Is begging me not to leave."

Doubt concerning a man she'd never even met made Reagan hesitate. "Do you believe he'll be true to you in the future?"

Lorelei raked her fingers through her long, dark hair.

"I don't know anymore. I don't seem to have any confidence in a love I would've staked my life on less than a month ago. But I have a child to think about. And I'm not sure I want to step out of the way so my best friend can replace me. I'm not even sure I'd be able to make a living on my own. As you've already pointed out, I've been out of the job market for six years, ever since we moved to the house we're living in now. Who'll hire me?"

Reagan cringed. "Sounds like you need to get that so-called best friend out of your lives. Start there. Then maybe you'll have a chance of repairing your relationship and…and putting it all behind you."

"I wish we *could* get her out of our lives," she said.

The wipers could barely keep up with the snow. The rhythmic swishing, the long day and being strapped into the car seat Lorelei had carried all the way from Florida seemed to be putting Lucy to sleep, which came as a relief to Reagan. The sucker had fallen against her shirt and would probably stick there, but at least she wouldn't start crying again. "Why can't you?" Reagan asked. "You don't owe her anything."

Lorelei caught her eye and mouthed, "She's pregnant."

Reagan felt her jaw drop. "Oh, my God."

Lorelei said nothing.

"Is she going to have the child?" Reagan whispered.

"Says she is," Lorelei replied.

"And she's going to keep it?"

"Of course. Because then she'll have exactly what she wanted—a claim on my husband."

"He'll be financially responsible for the care of the child, you mean."

"Yes. We'll be writing a check to Francine every month."

That would be hell, Reagan decided. The three of them would be entangled in a tight little dance—one that was as awkward as it was painful.

Then she thought of something else. "What about visitation?"

"I'd have to allow that, too. It isn't the child's fault. He or she deserves to have a father."

This was getting worse and worse. "That's true, but..." Reagan let go of a long sigh. "Wow. If you forgive him, you'll have to deal with this 'best friend' of yours, a person who betrayed you, indefinitely. And you'll also have to associate with the kid?"

Lorelei lowered her voice even further. "Yes. But if I don't forgive him, Francine will be the one who'll have Mark living in her home, helping raise *her* child. And *my* child? She'll be packing her bags each weekend to go stay with him and someone I no longer want her to have any contact with."

"Me, Mommy? Are you talking about me?" Lucy suddenly piped up.

Reagan bit back a curse.

"No, honey," Lorelei said. "I was just talking to Aunt Reagan about a friend."

"Francine?"

Lorelei paused briefly before confirming. "Yes."

"Are you mad at her?"

"I am," she admitted.

"Why?"

"Because she's...made Mommy very sad."

"How?"

"She took something that belonged to me."

"Without asking?" Lucy was struggling to understand, but Reagan could tell Lorelei was counting on her inability to do so.

"Yes, without asking."

Lorelei's phone began to ring and she snapped it up. "It's Serenity," she said. "We have signal at last."

Reagan listened as Lorelei answered. "I think we're getting close… No, we can finally use our GPS. Where are you?… Us, too. It's a mess out… We will. Glad you're safe… See you soon."

"What'd she say?" Reagan asked when Lorelei ended the call.

"Apparently, the weather's even worse coming from the opposite direction, but she just arrived. Wanted to check on us."

"I have to go to the bathroom," Lucy announced.

"Oh, no," Lorelei muttered.

That explained why Lucy hadn't finished drifting off to sleep. "What should I do?" Reagan asked. "There's nowhere to stop."

Lorelei checked behind her. "Can you hold it, honey? For a little while?"

"No!" Lucy insisted, growing instantly distraught. "I have to go!"

Lorelei cast Reagan a pained look. "Is there any way you could pull over? We'll have to let her go on the side of the road."

"We can't do that," Reagan said. "It's too dangerous. We could get hit. Or get stuck in the snow."

Lorelei spent the next fifteen minutes trying to cajole her daughter, which proved so difficult Reagan was relieved she didn't plan on having any children of her own.

That effectively ended their conversation about Mark

and Francine. But as they drew closer to the cabin, the story about Lorelei's husband and best friend played over and over in Reagan's mind, and she began to fear that her involvement with Drew might cost her far more than she'd even realized, including a meaningful relationship with her new sister.

4

serenity

Serenity stood in front of the wall of photographs at her family's cabin. She'd seen these pictures so many times she scarcely looked at them anymore. There were several of the lake itself. Tahoe straddled the border between California and Nevada and was the largest alpine lake in North America. Behind only the Great Lakes by volume, and with mountains on every side, it was a popular subject for photographers and painters. She had several representations in her house in Berkeley, purchased mostly from the local vendors and galleries that capitalized on the unique beauty of the area. Emerald Bay was particularly gorgeous. A spectacular shot of it—showing Fannette, the lake's only island, with touches of snow contrasting with the vivid blue of the water—hung right before her, in the center of everything.

But Serenity was more interested in the many family pictures surrounding it. There was one of her and her three siblings in front of the Christmas tree when they were children, shortly after her parents purchased the cabin. One was of her father holding her in front of him while they sledded down a hill, and there was one of her with her brother, two sisters and mother stretched out on the narrow strip of rocky sand that served as the closest beach, white-capped mountains in the background. The temperature in summer ranged from the low forties to the midseventies, and Serenity remembered that day as being too chilly to get in the water, but it had been warm by Tahoe standards, so there'd been a lot of sunbathers and swimmers who didn't care.

Normally, Serenity would've smiled at the pleasant memories associated with these pictures. She and her family had spent so much time at the lake. The smell of tree sap that hit her the moment she opened the door made her feel as though she'd come home even though she'd grown up in the Bay Area, not far from where she lived now.

But after learning she had two half sisters, neither of whom had ever been mentioned, she couldn't view these photos with the same blissful ignorance she once had. They looked almost fake to her, staged. And that brought so many questions to mind, as well as a profound sense of loss.

"Damn it," she muttered, peering closer at a small picture of her parents laughing at a casino on the south side of the lake, from back in the eighties. They'd always been elegant and, thanks to the money they'd inherited from her father's parents shortly after they married, they'd also been well-to-do—the quintessential, upwardly mobile California couple. Both were in their fifties now, but they hadn't changed much. Her father was a successful real estate attorney who'd worked in

San Francisco's financial district until they moved to San Diego. Her mother was an organic gardener who sold her produce and flowers to local restaurants looking for "farm to fork" produce. Charlotte had also supported a lot of charities while Serenity was growing up, focused mostly on raising money for cancer research, since Beau had once battled leukemia. Serenity had always considered her parents to be young for their age, hip, open-minded and smart.

So what reason would people like that have to hide the details of her birth? Knowing her parents as well as she did—what they believed in, what they stood for—she felt they would've been up front with her if it was simply a matter of being unable to get pregnant. It had to be something else.

"What happened back then?" she asked their still images. "Why do I have two half sisters you've never mentioned or acknowledged? And why did I have to find out about them the way I did?"

She nibbled at her bottom lip as she tried to remember any telltale signs—whispering, the sense that her parents were holding back or hiding something important, any strangers in her life—from when she was a child. She'd been racking her brain ever since she'd learned about Reagan and Lorelei, but she couldn't come up with a single thing that seemed odd or unusual.

Maybe her parents were superior actors. Or they'd simply forgotten anything they didn't care to remember, put it behind them and moved on. After all, when she was born there'd been no internet, no smartphones, no DNA companies like 23andMe. Her parents probably never dreamed that technology would eventually reveal what they'd hidden, even if they both kept their mouths shut.

That was another thing. Were they *both* in on the secret? Had they made a pact between them? Or was it something only one knew and the other might not be pleased to find out?

There were so many possibilities. Maybe she wasn't related to either one of them. But if she was adopted, where did she come from and how did she wind up in their family?

The sound of a car outside sent a prickle down Serenity's spine. When the engine went off, she cast a final glance at the photos of her parents and the siblings she'd grown up with and squared her shoulders. This was the point of no return. By welcoming Reagan, Lorelei and Lucy into her life, she could wreck relationships that were dearer to her than any others, especially because she was doing it without consulting her parents.

But she didn't feel she *could* consult them—not until she had a clearer understanding of what might have happened. She was afraid it might split them up or send one of her siblings into an emotional free fall. And yet, turning a blind eye to what she'd discovered wasn't an option. Ignoring what she'd learned wasn't sustainable, not for someone like her who had to face the truth head-on. She made a living uncovering dark secrets.

So, for better or for worse, she, Lorelei and Reagan were going to get to know each other and try to figure out how they were related. Maybe once they started to delve into the past they'd find a string they could tug on that would unravel the whole story.

Before she could reach the main entrance downstairs,

she heard the distressed voice of someone trying to console a crying child.

The child had to be Lucy.

Bracing herself—as much to meet her new family members as against the cold—Serenity opened the door just as Lorelei and her daughter came hurrying up the steps, gripping the railing tightly so they wouldn't fall while sheltering their faces from the wind and snow.

"Lucy has to go to the bathroom," Lorelei announced without preamble.

Serenity drew a steadying breath. Based on the photographs she'd seen, she wasn't surprised but Lorelei looked just like her. It was uncanny, unsettling. "Down the hall, on the right," she said, quickly stepping to the side.

Reagan took longer to reach the porch because she'd grabbed some of the luggage, which was smart. It would only be harder to go out later, when it was colder and darker and the vehicle could be buried in snow.

"I'm glad you made it safely." Feeling awkward at finally facing someone who was closely related to her—and yet a complete stranger—Serenity reached out to take one of the suitcases Reagan carried.

"That one's Lucy's," Reagan told her. "Lorelei will have to go out and get her own. This was all I could carry."

"No problem." Serenity had known that coming face-to-face with these two people might be difficult, but she hadn't anticipated that this moment would feel quite so surreal. Although she didn't want to be obvious, she let her gaze sweep over Reagan several times. The visual proof made everything in the DNA report undeniable. "How was your flight?"

Reagan seemed reticent. Was she feeling the same emotions? The shock and betrayal, as well as the excitement engendered by such a strange situation? Serenity couldn't have felt more odd if she'd come face to face with an alien from outer space.

"Better than the drive here," she replied.

Serenity got the impression Lucy had significantly contributed to the difficulty, so she didn't press any further. "Well, fortunately, that's behind you, and I've got a fire going in the living room upstairs." Hoping to cover nervousness with politeness, she waved Reagan in ahead of her and managed to wrestle the door shut despite the howling wind. "Whew! I can't believe it's storming like this in *May*."

Small talk. When there's so much more to say...

"Just my luck." Reagan dropped her own luggage, which looked far more expensive than what Serenity had seen of Lorelei's so far. "Wouldn't you know it, the weather in New York was nearly eighty degrees when I took off from La Guardia."

"Hopefully this will blow through. The weather this time of year is normally beautiful." Serenity couldn't stop watching her and noticed that Reagan couldn't quit staring, either. "Are you hungry? Did you have a chance to eat after you landed?"

It took Reagan a moment to respond. They were both transfixed. "Yeah, um, sorry. It's just...well, you know. You look so much like me. So does Lorelei."

"The situation is definitely...unique."

"Right. We knew that coming into it. But you asked if we've eaten. Lorelei had a meal packed for Lucy, and she and I just grabbed something out of a vending machine."

"Then you must be ready for something more. I brought groceries. I thought I'd make broccoli cheddar soup for dinner."

"Sounds delicious."

The conversation once again fell by the wayside as they stood and gaped at each other.

"I can't believe I'm related to you," Reagan said, her voice barely a whisper. "But I have to admit—it's like looking in a mirror."

Serenity didn't know whether to hug her or not. It hadn't been a possibility when she'd walked through the door carrying so much luggage, but now they were both empty-handed. "Except that my hair's a lot longer than yours."

Another meaningless statement made because of nerves and self-consciousness...

"Are we doing the right thing?" Reagan asked with a degree of trepidation. "I mean...this is kind of a risk, isn't it?"

That answered the hugging question. They were going to be open and honest with each other, not pretend to feel emotions they didn't yet feel. "I have no idea," Serenity replied. "But even if we aren't, I have to know how this happened. *Why* it happened. And why no one ever told me. Don't you?"

Reagan continued to study her closely—and ultimately nodded.

"I'm glad you came," Serenity said. "That we'll... that we'll have a chance to get to know each other."

"I should warn you that Lorelei and I haven't started off on the best foot," she said, but then the door to the bathroom opened.

As Lorelei led Lucy out, Reagan added a softly spoken, "Never mind."

Serenity wasn't sure what that meant. She hoped it was just the result of jangled nerves from having a four-year-old who was tired of being restrained in the car. "Lorelei," she said, turning to greet her other half sister. "Thanks for coming."

Lorelei didn't seem happy, either. She certainly didn't step up for an embrace. She seemed gun-shy, like an animal who stands back and watches warily, making sure it's safe before venturing closer.

Considering what Serenity knew about her background, that made sense. She probably wasn't someone who could trust easily.

"Thank you," she said. "This is…this is *really* a nice place."

Serenity quickly sized up both sisters, now that they were all standing close. They were both pretty. Lorelei had a softer, more full-figured look. Well-dressed Reagan seemed to be on the cutting edge of fashion, which made sense, since her mother was a designer. Her features were a bit more angular and she came off as decisive and in charge.

"It is. But you should see the other 'cabins' they have up here. Some are even called chalets," she said with a laugh that she hoped would at least partially conceal her discomfort. "They're owned by very wealthy people and go for millions of dollars."

Lorelei's eyes were wide as she looked around. "This one can't be cheap."

The comment reminded Serenity that they all came from such different backgrounds, and Lorelei had very little in the way of creature comforts growing up. "It didn't cost a whole lot when my parents bought it, but that was thirty years ago. They've added on and improved it quite a bit since. And real estate values have gone up."

Serenity gestured at the suitcase she'd taken from Reagan and left inside the doorway. "Reagan was nice enough to bring in Lucy's bag, but that was all she could carry along with her own. Do you want to grab your luggage while I show Reagan to her room?"

"Sure." She looked from Serenity to Reagan and back again, as though she, too, thought they might've fallen into an alternate universe. Obviously, Serenity wasn't the only one struggling with this moment.

"I left it unlocked," Reagan volunteered.

Finally, Lorelei turned to her daughter. "Sit right here, where it's warm," she told Lucy, gesturing to the soft leather couch. "Mommy will be right back."

After Lorelei had buttoned her coat and headed back into the storm, Reagan lowered her voice. "This might be harder than we initially imagined," she confided.

"Because of…" Serenity didn't say Lucy's name, but jerked her head in the child's direction.

"No, that wouldn't be a problem by itself. I'm referring to the fact that we were all raised by different families, have different backgrounds and experiences, and come with a different emotional makeup—maybe even a few scars. Will we be able to get along for an entire week?"

"Of course. All we have to do is remain open-minded and understanding."

"A very California thing to say."

"That isn't how a New Yorker would handle it?"

"A New Yorker would be less euphemistic about the whole situation."

Serenity glanced at Lucy, who was sitting dutifully in the small family room that formed the hub of the lowest level of the cabin, watching them with red, swollen eyes. This little person was her *niece*. Her first niece, since none of her siblings had any children, which only made the whole thing more bizarre. "What about a Floridian?" she asked.

Reagan shrugged as if to indicate it was anyone's guess. "As I said—three different perspectives."

Serenity went over to say hello to Lucy and introduce herself. She couldn't get the little girl to respond—Lucy just kept ducking her head shyly—but Serenity couldn't blame her. This was an unusual experience for her, too.

Straightening, she drew on the familiarity they'd gained interacting online to try and establish some normalcy. They'd all been rather guarded so far, but they did have *some* frame of reference. "It's only a week, Reagan."

Reagan didn't seem convinced. "A week can feel like an eternity."

"It should be enough to tell us if we ever want to do this again." Serenity laughed, this time in an attempt to encourage Reagan to relax. She understood having second thoughts; she'd had a few of her own.

"If you say so." Reagan stood back and gazed up the stairs. "How many bedrooms does this place have?"

Grateful that she'd no longer be standing there, feeling out of place despite the fact that this was *her* cabin, Serenity grabbed Reagan's suitcase. "Five. Plus a library in the loft." She didn't bother to add that the fifth bedroom was off the loft, and that it was stuffed with boxes her parents hadn't bothered to haul down to San Diego with them. It didn't matter; they weren't going to need that room, anyway.

"Wow. Five bedrooms *and* a library? You could have an army of siblings come stay with you—all at once."

"Don't say that," she muttered ruefully.

"After what's happened with us, you never know."

"Exactly."

This time they both laughed, and Serenity felt a wave of relief. Maybe a shared joke wasn't a huge connection, but it was a start.

5

reagan

Reagan's bedroom was spacious by New York standards, where hotel rooms were often the size of broom closets. Planning to take her time to unpack and settle in, she wandered over to the window.

Due to low visibility, all she could see were pine trees dusted with snow and more of the white stuff swirling through the air, buffeted by strong winds. But even if it hadn't been storming, she doubted she'd see much more. Perhaps some granite outcroppings, bear or raccoon tracks or a small woodshed. Her window faced the forest, not the lake.

Still, the room was nice—not lavish but tasteful. Whoever had decorated the cabin seemed interested in making it comfortable above all else. With its overstuffed furniture, thick rugs covering hardwood floors, yellow, white and blue–colored linens and draperies—even a worn leather chair in the corner, situated next to a small bookcase—this place was obviously intended to be a retreat from the world, a safe haven from which to enjoy nature, rest, read and recuperate.

She wasn't sure she'd find her visit too relaxing, however. Afraid that coming to Tahoe would only further complicate her situation, she hadn't been keen on opening her life to two sisters. She grew up the only child of a workaholic mother; she was so used to being on her own she didn't know how to interact with them. And she certainly didn't need someone else to disapprove of what she'd done, someone who would never understand how she could make the mistake she had. She was hard enough on herself.

She dragged her fingers along the heavy log walls, which were slick with varnish, before rolling her shoulders and stretching her neck in an attempt to ward off the headache that was starting behind her eyes. She would've gone down to the kitchen to help Serenity cook, even though she never cooked, never had time to bother and wasn't very good at it.

But she could hear Lorelei and Lucy talking to Serenity and decided it was more important to take a break from them both. She doubted Lucy would allow herself to be confined, so once Serenity finished showing them to their rooms, they'd likely venture right back out. What else was there for a four-year-old to do except explore the cabin? Lucy couldn't go outside, not in this weather, although the big deck on the middle story overlooking the lake would be a temptation.

Grabbing her phone from her purse, Reagan dropped onto the thick feather comforter that covered the bed and shoved a couple of pillows behind her back as she pulled up her recent calls. So many people had tried to reach her. Drew, of course. He'd been calling and texting for days. She'd expected to see his name. There were several others from Edison & Curry, too. Everyone at work was freaking out, wondering why she wasn't checking in or responding to her email.

She needed to get back to them. This was unlike her. She was usually on top of everything. But it was almost as if the life she'd known had simply…imploded. She'd screwed up so badly that she couldn't find a way to fix it, and she couldn't deal with failure.

At the back of her mind she saw her mother, frowning in disgust and disappointment, and the pain in her head increased. If she didn't quit thinking of how Rosalind would react if she found out about Drew—how she reacted whenever she was disappointed in Reagan—she was going to have a full-blown panic attack. How many times had her therapist told her not to measure herself through her mother's eyes?

Speak of the devil, she thought when she saw that her mother had tried to call.

Unable to face speaking to Rosalind right now, she kept scrolling until she spotted a name that stood out from the rest. Rally McKnight, an architect she'd met at an AIDS fund-raiser a month ago, had tried to reach her while she was on the plane. He seemed a little old for her, but he wasn't unhandsome. And he had a solid career—a sign that he was functional. So many of the men she'd met on various dating sites had more excuses than they did accomplishments. One guy she'd agreed to have dinner with had *three* different baby mamas, none of whom he'd ever married.

Rally stood out among that whole group. She'd been attracted to him from the beginning, which was why she'd given him her number, but he seemed too good to be true and that scared her. She'd been single long enough that she could spot a man's flaws from the get-go—and yet she couldn't figure out what was wrong with *him*.

That made her so uneasy she hadn't agreed to go out with him even though he'd called her several times since to ask.

Pressing the button that would play his message, she put the phone to her ear. "Reagan, this is Rally McKnight. Sorry to bother you again. I told you last time that if you'd rather not hear from me to send me a text, but I haven't received anything, so… I was hoping no news is good news. I'm also hoping you might be willing to have dinner with me this weekend. I know of a great place in SoHo, and I thought we could visit a speakeasy afterward. There's one called The Last Word I bet you'd enjoy. Or Fig 19 has some great art. Give me a call if you're interested."

He ended with his number even though she didn't need it. It was the same number he'd called her from, which was stored in her phone.

Feeling particularly angry with herself—that she hadn't been more receptive to *this* man, who seemed decent, instead of sabotaging her life and her career by getting involved with her married boss—she almost erased the message. She didn't deserve someone like Rally. She had no business dating *anyone* right now, when her life was such a mess.

But something about the fact that he'd been so patient made her text him.

Thanks for the invitation, Rally, but I'm out of town. Will reach out when I get back.

She planned to leave it at that, but then she saw the three dots that indicated he was replying to her message.

Hey, I'm moving up in the world, he wrote back.

She had no idea what that meant, which prompted a further comment. Moving up?

This is the first time you've acknowledged me. I must be a glutton for punishment to keep trying.

She couldn't help smiling at his message. Or too confident to assume a lack of response means no.

So you're a spin-doctor as well as an account manager?

"I'm a fool," she wanted to write. Instead she kept it light. I thought they were one and the same.

That worries me a little. ;)

I'm joking.

Good. When will you be back?

In a week.

Vacay?

Meeting two half sisters I never knew existed.

She wasn't sure why she'd volunteered that information. She hadn't told anyone else.

Interesting. How'd you find out about them?

DNA testing. One of those ancestry sites.

What made you get your DNA tested?

My mother was having heart trouble, and several of my coworkers were doing it. They suggested I do it with them so I could learn more about my genetic endowment—what health risks I might face, etc.

And? Did the results reveal anything particularly worrisome?

No health issues. Just two new sisters.

Better that than discovering you carry the heart attack gene—or that you have a relative who's a serial killer police have been trying to catch for years.

With the luck I'm having, that could still crop up...

Are you nervous about meeting your sisters?

Already met them, but I'm nervous to learn more. Whether my mother knows about them and, if so, why I was never told that I have siblings. Whether I'm truly related to the man who was my dad. If my new sisters are, too. How I'll feel after I learn. That sort of thing.

Have you asked either of your parents?

My father died when I wasn't quite two, so I can't ask him. There's just my mother and I, and I haven't mentioned it to her.

Because...

Because Rosalind rarely talked about the past, seemed eager to forget it entirely.

Besides, there was something daunting about that kind of secret—one that struck at the very heart of Reagan's identity and could possibly reveal a side of her mother she never knew existed.

Reagan wanted to figure out a few things first, feel confident that she had some answers of her own. She had open-heart surgery a month ago. Is still recovering.

I'm sorry to hear that. But maybe she's been carrying this secret around for a long time and will find it a bit of a relief that you know.

That was a wise and balanced thing to say. She was impressed. But he had no idea how difficult her mother could be.

Why was she discussing this with him in the first place?

She supposed she needed someone to talk to who didn't know her family or friends. That way, if he had loose lips it couldn't be a threat to her. If it would be a relief, I think she would've told me.

I'll take your word for it.

My life is complicated, she wrote, out of nowhere. In her current situation, basic honesty demanded it.

Are you trying to warn me away?

Maybe. Is it working?

Everyone's life is complicated.

Is yours?

Would you ghost me if I said yes?

She frowned at his response. Although she wouldn't have believed a denial, she would've preferred one. That depends on how complicated.

Fair enough. Before you count me out, let's have a meal together, see if my imperfect meshes with your imperfect.

Why haven't you given up on me?

Because I haven't been able to forget the beautiful brunette I saw at the gala a few weeks ago.

She allowed herself a reluctant smile. She had to give him points for flattery and persistence. Okay. You ARE a glutton for punishment.

No. Just too confident to believe you won't ultimately like me.

She laughed when she saw that after she'd thrown a version of his words back at him, he'd done the same to her.

So will you really contact me when you get back? he asked.

If you'll tell me a little about your situation, I can answer that more honestly.

Ask away.

Do you still have a job?

Yes. Still an architect. Since I own the company and have been in business for twenty years, I think I'm going to stick it out. ;)

Twenty years? That meant he was probably in his forties... Are you married? Divorced?

Married?

You never know...

You make saying I'm divorced feel good.

:) Any kids?

One teenage son—a junior in high school. I hope kids are allowed because he's nonnegotiable.

Exactly what I would expect of a good dad. I have nothing against kids.

What about you? What's your situation?

Never been married. No children.

Do you want a family? he asked.

I don't know. Are you done having kids?

Some days I think yes. Other days I'd like a second chance to have a family that will last. So I'll go with undecided.

She wanted to ask why his first marriage hadn't survived, but it was too soon for that. He'd probably just blame his ex. That was what most people did.

Besides, her phone started beeping. Drew was trying to call in.

She stared at the picture she'd connected to his number—his handsome face, his Hollywood smile—which was covering her texts with Rally.

She desperately wanted to let Drew tell her they could undo what they'd done and continue working together, somehow pretend it had never happened.

But even if he said the words, she'd know they weren't true. Sex with Drew had been one of the most all-consuming, enjoyable experiences of her life. They'd *finally* acted on what they'd been feeling for so long, and it had been an unparalleled release.

"Reagan, would you like a drink?" Serenity asked, calling up from below.

She'd stayed in her room for too long. She needed to go downstairs and be social, or at least help with dinner. She couldn't withdraw and sleep for the next seven days, even if it was what she felt like doing.

"Sure. I'm coming," she called back. But then her eyes returned to her phone and that incoming call from Drew.

Undecided will work. I have to go. We'll talk more later, she texted to Rally.

By then, Drew's call had transferred to her voice mail. She experienced a wave of relief when it did—

but also a sharp jab of remorse. So when he called right back, she couldn't resist answering. She *had* to hear his voice.

"Hello?... Hello?... Reagan, would you please answer? We need to talk."

His name was on the tip of her tongue—along with so many other comments and questions.

But she forced herself to hit the End button without saying anything at all.

6

lorelei

No matter what Reagan and Serenity were doing—chatting, laughing, moving about the cabin or smiling at Lucy—Lorelei couldn't help surreptitiously watching them. She felt like a sponge, soaking in every possible detail. She memorized their facial expressions, the sounds of their voices, their body movements. They were the only people she'd ever found who were genetically connected to her—besides Lucy, of course—and after seeking that familial connection for so long, it felt strange to be in their presence at last.

After Mark's litany about how some people—a lot of people, at least the ones she'd met so far in her life—could be more of a curse than a blessing, however, and with what she'd learned about Reagan so far, she was hesitant to fully embrace them. She wasn't resilient enough to take much of a risk right now, and she knew it. Not only had Mark destroyed the foundation on which she'd built her life, he'd destroyed any confidence she had in her ability to be loved.

So she was afraid—of loving the wrong person, of being rejected again, of being sorry she'd taken this risk.

Would coming here turn out to be a good thing or a bad thing?

She'd had enough bad things happen lately...

"Would you mind helping Reagan set the table?" Serenity asked, motioning to a drawer where Lorelei supposed she'd find the silverware.

"Of course not," she said. Lucy was up on her knees at the kitchen table, putting together a puzzle Serenity had found in a box of old toys stored in the extra bedroom, which left Lorelei free to contribute. She was actually tempted to take over making the soup. Judging by the awkward way her sisters chopped the vegetables, she could tell that neither Serenity nor Reagan had much skill in the kitchen.

She, on the other hand, cooked often and loved developing recipes. At times, she even toyed with the idea of creating her own cookbook. Whenever she was bored or lonely, and she wasn't thinking about finding her birth mother or father, she was dreaming about what she'd put in a cookbook if she were ever to publish one.

But this wasn't her cabin; it wasn't her role to take over the cooking as soon as she walked through the door. So she merely did as Serenity asked.

"Well, here we are," Serenity said after the ready-to-bake rolls were in the oven, the soup was simmering on the stove and they were sitting around the dining table sharing a bottle of wine.

"Yes, here we are." Reagan held her glass loosely in her long fingers as though she was at some high-powered lunch in a swanky café. Reagan's good looks, direct manner and striking confidence could be intimidating. That was another reason Lorelei had a hard time getting over the fact that Reagan was sleeping with a married man. Lorelei wanted to believe that someone with that much personal power couldn't possibly be so fallible.

"Fortunately, we made it in spite of the weather," Serenity said.

Serenity seemed like more of an intellectual—someone everyone would want to talk to at a dinner party. She was measured, reasonable, well-read and interesting. Right now she was obviously trying to make conversation. But Lorelei got the impression her sisters were frightened of what they might learn and what it could do to their lives.

She was the lone exception, in that she hadn't been reluctant in the beginning. Because she'd known her background, she hadn't been devastated by the news that she had surprise siblings; she'd been elated. After being passed around so much as a child—in and out of one foster home after another until she headed to college—she'd thought she was *finally* going to have the family she'd craved since she could remember.

Or a portion of it, anyway.

Be careful what you wish for, she thought as she sipped the Napa Valley Chardonnay Serenity had pulled from a cute metal wine holder on the counter.

When no one chimed in, Serenity began to turn the stem of her glass around. "So, I knew this might be awkward, but it seems we're already facing something a little more difficult than just meeting for the first time."

Lorelei felt her eyes widen as she looked up.

Reagan merely frowned.

"I hate to put you both on the spot," Serenity went

on, "but it's important that we be able to trust each other and feel comfortable here this week. And the fact that the ride from the airport didn't go so well is disappointing. What happened? We all seemed to get along online."

Lorelei resisted the urge to shift in her seat. "Reagan and I simply…disagree on some fundamental issues, I guess."

"Fundamental issues?" Serenity said.

"I wouldn't say we *disagree* on those issues," Reagan volunteered. "I screwed up, okay? I feel terrible about it. But at least I was honest. What more do you want from me? I could've lied, kept it to myself."

"Maybe you should have," Lorelei grumbled.

"Except I prefer to be real—and not some impossibly perfect version of myself. If you can't accept me for who I am, what good is building a relationship with you in the first place?"

"Whoa! Wait." Serenity lifted both hands. "What are you two talking about?"

Lorelei didn't want to be the one to tell Serenity that Reagan was involved with a married man, but when she remained silent, Reagan went on the offensive.

"Lorelei found out her husband's been having an a-f-f-a-i-r with her best friend, who is now p-r-e-g-n-a-n-t," she said.

The spelling caught Lucy's attention. She understood adults did that when they were trying to exclude her from the conversation. But she was so happy to be off the plane and out of the car she simply glanced around the table before going back to her puzzle.

"I can't believe you just blurted that out." Although

she tried, Lorelei couldn't keep the pique out of her voice.

Hearing it caused Lucy to look up again.

"I didn't blurt it out," Reagan responded. "I was careful to spell the more upsetting points."

Lorelei folded her arms. "I shouldn't have told you. It's none of your business."

"What's wrong, Mommy?"

"Nothing, honey. Do your puzzle," Lorelei said softly.

"I'm glad you did," Reagan said. "Otherwise, I wouldn't understand why you reacted the way you did to what's going on in *my* life."

"You mean, what you've *done*?" Lorelei cried.

Serenity interrupted. "What am I missing?"

After the information Reagan had revealed about Mark, Lorelei no longer felt any compunction about sharing Reagan's situation. "She's having an affair with her married boss."

"You could've spelled some of that," Reagan complained.

Lorelei gestured toward her daughter. "She doesn't understand what an affair is."

"That's lucky for you, then, isn't it?" Reagan snapped.

"I hope this is a joke," Serenity said. "What we're here for—what we might find out—could be difficult enough without all this drama."

"It's not a joke." Lorelei glared at Reagan. "You shouldn't have told Serenity about Mark. That was up to me."

Reagan scowled. "Well, you weren't stepping up. Were you planning to keep it a secret from Serenity?"

Lorelei clenched her jaw. "No, of course not. I just—That isn't the point."

"Then what is? Because as bad as your life might be right now, at least you're not to blame for it!" She shoved away from the table and stood. "I'm not hungry. Don't worry about me for dinner," she said and walked out.

"Wow," Serenity said. "I definitely wasn't expecting that."

"Mommy?" Lucy blinked up at them with her wide, innocent blue eyes. "Is Aunt Reagan mad?"

Lorelei rubbed her temples. "I guess she is."

Serenity lowered her voice. "Is it true?"

"About Reagan?" Lorelei said. "Yes."

Serenity glanced over her shoulder in the direction of the stairs, where Reagan had gone. "I could tell that part was true. I meant about your best friend and your..." Her eyes darted to Lucy. "You know."

Lorelei took a big gulp of wine. "Yes. That's true, too."

Serenity didn't speak for several seconds, but then she asked, "Why didn't you say anything to us about it online?"

"I only found out three weeks ago. And then... I haven't wanted to tell anyone, to be honest. I haven't fully processed it myself."

Suddenly Lucy scrambled off the chair. "I have to go potty."

"You know where it is," Lorelei said. "Or do you need me to show you again?"

She didn't answer. She just hurried out of the room and was heading in the right direction, so Lorelei let her go on her own.

"I can see why you might not have wanted to say

anything about…about your situation," Serenity said as she refilled Lorelei's glass. "What you're going through has to be excruciating. But the fact that Reagan told me isn't a big deal. If your best friend is really pregnant, the news is going to get out eventually, isn't it?"

Lorelei stared at the liquid in her glass. "Unfortunately."

"So…has Mark moved out? Is it over between you?" She shook her head.

"You're staying in the marriage?"

"I'm still trying to decide. Sometimes I think I could forgive him—*if* she wasn't pregnant. But every time I imagine seeing their son or daughter…" Lorelei winced as she pictured Francine carrying Mark's baby in her arms. What would the child look like? Would he or she have his brown eyes and sandy-blond hair? Or Francine's lighter eyes and fairer complexion?

"Holy shit." Serenity scrubbed a hand over her face, smearing her mascara. She didn't seem to care that she was wearing makeup.

Lorelei gave her a weak smile. It didn't make things any easier that she thought Francine was beautiful. That only made the jagged edge of jealousy cut deeper. "Sorry to start the trip off on such a downer."

Serenity peered more closely at her. "Reagan didn't say whether the man she's seeing has—"

"You mean her boss?" Lorelei broke in.

"Yes. Has he told his wife? Does *she* know what's going on?"

"Reagan didn't say. I think we both realized it wouldn't be smart to continue talking about it."

"I see." Serenity tucked her hair behind her ears. "So

I guess the question is…are you both going to be okay staying here this week?"

Lorelei hated feeling as though she was the least successful of the three of them but all the talk about Mark and Francine had definitely reminded her of the situation she was in. She'd been a good mom, a great homemaker. Her house was beautifully decorated, and it was spotless. Every day she spent quality time with her daughter—reading to her, teaching her, helping out at the preschool she attended, which required quite a bit of parental interaction. And she provided a warm, wonderful atmosphere for her husband to come home to at night, as well as a delicious meal. She'd once prided herself on those things.

But now her contributions of the past several years felt like nothing, as if no one valued them, including Mark. While Reagan and Serenity both had successful careers and their own money—total control over their lives—*she* had to worry about Mark ferreting away what he was making so he wouldn't have to share it with her.

Or so that she wouldn't have the funds to be able to leave him in the first place.

"I'm not going home early."

Serenity peered closer at her. "You're sure?"

She nodded. Besides the fact that she couldn't really afford to change her travel plans, Lucy couldn't face spending another day on a plane, not so soon after this one, and Lorelei wasn't ready to go home to Mark and Francine, couldn't tolerate more of Mark's entreaties and inadequate excuses.

"Then I'll talk to Reagan and…and see if we can't

get beyond this so that we can have a chance to get to know each other and share our childhood memories as we'd planned. One of us *has* to remember something that might offer a clue as to how we got here—and why things happened the way they did."

Lorelei watched her daughter hurry back to the table. "Is that all you're interested in?" she asked Serenity as she helped Lucy into her seat.

Serenity had just gotten up to stir the soup. "Is what all I'm interested in?"

"Figuring out how, why?"

The lid clanked on the pot. "What do you mean?"

"Are you even interested in having another sister? From what you've said, you're hurt and angry to think you've been deceived, and you're curious about the truth. Where you come from. Who knows the real story. Why no one spoke up. But I don't get the impression you're excited about adding to your family. You have enough siblings."

"No," Serenity cried. "I'm sorry if I gave you that impression. I'm happy to have more sisters. For one thing, the twins are seven years younger than I am, and they're completely caught up in their husbands and each other. There's *definitely* room in my life. I'm just worried about what the past will reveal about my parents. That's all."

"Right." Lorelei forced a smile. "I understand," she said, but she'd definitely been hoping for more. Now that she'd *finally* found some blood relatives—not one but two sisters—neither of them seemed very excited to have found *her.*

* * *

reagan

A soft knock sounded. Curled up in bed, Reagan called, "Come in," and Serenity walked inside with a tray that held a bowl of soup, a roll and a glass of wine, which she put on the small desk by the wall.

"You've had a long day," she said as she sat at the foot of the bed. "You need to eat something."

Reagan hesitated before propping herself against the headboard. Food was the last thing on her mind. She wanted to pull the covers over her head and pretend that what she'd done was just a nightmare, that she'd be able to go back to Edison & Curry when she returned to New York and all would be well.

She eyed the tray dubiously. "I don't think I can."

Serenity leaned to one side. "Lorelei didn't mean to offend you. She's angry with the friend who betrayed her, and she's taking it out on you. You realize that, right? You're just a proxy."

"Of course I realize that. I'm not mad at her. I would loathe me, too, if I were in her shoes. I can't believe *I'm* that woman, you know? The one everyone hates for being so stupid and selfish."

Serenity's eyes were sympathetic. "Everyone screws up—"

"Not like this," Reagan broke in. She wasn't willing to accept such an easy excuse. "There are enough regular setbacks in life, setbacks you can't avoid. I'm furious at myself for causing my own downfall."

"Downfall?" Serenity echoed. "Isn't that a little... extreme?"

"Hardly. I can't continue to work with Drew. I'll have to quit my job, and I love what I do. Love where I work." She'd had her eye on achieving partner from the beginning, and she was so close! She didn't want to start over. It was much harder for a woman to climb that corporate ladder than a man. She'd had to do a great deal more to prove herself.

She shook her head in disgust as she remembered some of the partners in the agency mentioning how detrimental it would be if she were to get married, because she might lose her focus. Or, God forbid, have a baby, which would require the death sentence of maternity leave.

"You might find something even better," Serenity said.

It was hard to be optimistic, given the situation, but she made herself say, "Maybe. I just wish I'd been smarter."

As she shoved more pillows behind her back, she remembered Drew catching her hand as she started to walk out of his office. The next thing she knew, they were kissing and touching and, at some point, he kicked the door shut.

That had merely been a safety precaution, though. Everyone else had already left the building, except maybe a couple of accountants who worked on another floor.

If only those accountants had been closer, she and Drew would've *had* to stop...

"I should've quit my job as soon as I could tell he was beginning to have feelings for me—and that I reciprocated them," she went on. "I'd still have to start over at another firm, but at least my dignity would be intact. And my reputation. I never dreamed we'd *act* on what we felt. He's been a devoted family man ever since I met him. That's partly what I love about him."

"Does he feel as bad as you do?"

She thought of the many calls and texts she'd ignored. "I have no idea. I haven't talked to him."

"Since…"

"Since it happened," she clarified.

Serenity sat forward. "Then this isn't an ongoing affair?"

"No. It's brand-new. I haven't been back to work since."

"Does his wife know?"

Reagan pictured Sally, whom she'd met along with their three boys, seven, nine and twelve, at various work functions. Had Drew gone straight home and confessed? Or was he keeping it from Sally until he could discuss it with Reagan?

And what about his other associates—her associates, too? Had they guessed what was going on?

"Who can say? Like I said, I haven't talked to him."

Serenity raised her eyebrows. "Wow."

Letting her head fall back, Reagan stared up at the ceiling. "I was too confident, you know?" she said, looking at Serenity again. "I believed I had the self-control to avoid going that far. And then…"

When she let her words fade away, Serenity finished for her. "And then you made a mistake. It happened, and you can't take it back. But punishing yourself by going hungry won't help."

Reagan frowned at the soup and bread. "I'm not punishing myself. I have no appetite."

"Well, you're already the skinniest one of the three of us, and we don't like that, so we've both decided you must eat."

Reagan couldn't even make herself laugh. But when Serenity got up to retrieve the tray and place it on her lap, she picked up the spoon.

Serenity sat back down on the bed. "How do you like the room?"

"It's great. The whole cabin is."

"Wait until you see the lake."

"Believe me, I'm anxious for this storm to pass so that I can." She took a bite, found the soup much tastier than it looked and realized she was hungry, after all. She ate half of it before she asked, "Where's Lorelei?"

"Putting Lucy to bed."

She tore off a piece of the roll and crammed it in her mouth, so depressed she didn't care about her manners. "Can you believe her best friend is pregnant with her husband's child?" she asked as she chewed.

"I can't. An affair is bad enough. You have to wonder—how did the two of them let something like *that* happen?"

Reagan had no idea. A baby made everything so much worse. It affected the future, not just the past, making it that much harder for Lorelei to forgive and forget. Harder for her to stay in the marriage, too. A child was a lifetime commitment. In nine months or less, she'd have a constant reminder of her husband's philandering.

Reagan opened her mouth to say as much—then nearly choked on the bread she was trying to swallow as a memory flashed through her mind. She and Drew hadn't used any birth control. She'd been so busy the past few months she hadn't been sexually active, so she wasn't on the pill. And he was married. It wasn't as if he was walking around with a condom in his pocket.

A curious expression came over Serenity's face. "What is it?"

Surely *she* wasn't—

Reagan tried to cut off the thought before she could fully think it. She'd been so worried about all the other ramifications of what she'd done that she hadn't even considered this one. But now the possibility had burst onto the stage of her mind, and she couldn't chase it away, no matter how hard she tried.

And that put the fear of God in her.

Somehow she managed to finish swallowing before pushing aside the tray. "That was good, but I've had enough."

"Are you okay?" Serenity's voice was filled with concern.

The chance of pregnancy had to be slight. They'd had only one encounter, and Drew had pulled out.

"I—I'm fine," she replied, but she could barely force out those two words, and the food she'd eaten sat heavy on her stomach. The situation with Lorelei and Francine proved that the worst *could* happen.

And she had to acknowledge that it could happen to her.

7

lorelei

The familiar nightmare woke Lorelei, the one where she was lost and wandering around in the dark on a cold, rainy street she didn't recognize. She couldn't find a single thing that looked familiar, no one she knew or trusted. Figures seemed to skulk in the shadows, following her, and yet, when she turned around, there was no one there. Her surroundings, those strange people—*everything*—felt menacing, but she couldn't say exactly why, couldn't identify the danger.

Clammy with sweat, she pushed off the heavy comforter she'd found so welcoming when she went to bed and hauled in a gulp of clean, cool air. She'd been having that dream since she was a child, and she hated it. Her various foster parents used to tell her caseworker that she'd wake up in the night, kicking and screaming, and couldn't be consoled.

Lorelei was convinced that was why she'd never been adopted. She should've had a good chance, especially with her first placement, when she was so young. But those foster parents had taken her back to the receiving home after only nine months. Somehow, following years of infertility, they'd managed to get pregnant, but they were having a baby with Down Syndrome, so they said they weren't up to the challenge of raising *two* children with special needs.

Lorelei had always believed they would've kept her had she been an easier child—a *normal* child. Even with the unexpected pregnancy. But they were afraid she'd never get over whatever trauma she'd endured. And, sadly, she'd proven them right. The nightmares had plagued her throughout adolescence. They'd eventually gone away, once she'd been married to Mark for several years. But now they were back. Mark's confession must've triggered a memory she'd buried deep inside her brain, because this was her fourth nightmare in the past three weeks.

"Bastard," she muttered. She could call him that when Lucy wasn't around. Not only was it liberating, it reflected her pain and anger better than anything else she could say, even though it didn't change the situation.

Restless, she climbed out of bed and crossed over to the window.

The storm had died down. Shafts of moonlight struck a glistening blanket of new-fallen snow. Evergreen trees jutted through it, standing tall and straight, like sentinels watching over the pristine landscape. She could see why Serenity loved this place. It was beautiful— a winter wonderland even though it was spring—and nothing like anything she'd ever experienced in hot and humid Florida.

Closing her eyes, she tried to regulate her breathing in an effort to slow her heart rate. Although the fire

Serenity had built earlier must have gone out by now, the smell of wood smoke lingered in the cabin. Lorelei found it oddly comforting.

That's it. Just breathe.

She rested her forehead against the glass as she continued to gaze out at the snow-globe-like scene. If she didn't calm down she wouldn't be able to go back to sleep. And caring for a four-year-old wasn't easy even when she was well rested.

Instead of going back to bed, however, she went into the room next door to check on her daughter.

Curled into a ball, her long medium-brown hair streaming across the pillow, Lucy seemed to be sleeping soundly.

A wave of tenderness drove Lorelei to drop a kiss on her soft, round cheek before pulling the covers higher. That Mark hadn't considered what his actions might mean for Lucy when he'd gotten involved with Francine rattled Lorelei's faith in him more than anything else. She'd believed his love for their daughter would be strong enough to preclude him from ever doing anything that would harm their family.

Too bad he'd proven her wrong. By damaging their marriage, he'd left Lucy vulnerable to a huge upheaval, one that could gouge deep emotional scars.

The insidious images Lorelei had been holding at bay ever since she'd learned the truth began to steal into her mind like a poisonous gas. The thought of Mark cheating was painful enough—but with *Francine*?

Lorelei had known Francine since college, had trusted her like the sister she never had—which only doubled the betrayal, outrage and pain. It sickened her to picture them together, which was why she struggled so hard to avoid it. But she knew them both so well, could all too easily imagine how their affair had played out—

Stop torturing yourself!

She curved her fingernails into her palms, hoping a jolt of physical pain might distract her. She hadn't spoken to her best friend since Mark broke the news. Francine had attempted to call her a few times. She'd even come over once, shouting from outside that they needed to talk. But Lorelei had refused to accept her calls or answer the door.

That night, Mark, trying to play the arbitrator, had suggested the three of them sit down together, which let her know he and Francine had spoken that day. Lorelei remembered wondering bitterly if they'd managed to squeeze in a quickie. She hadn't accused Mark of it— he was too busy acting remorseful—but Lorelei had refused to let him arrange the meeting with Francine, told him she wasn't ready yet.

Yet, she repeated to herself with a mirthless chuckle. She doubted she'd *ever* be ready, wasn't sure she could be civil, even though there was a time she would've given Francine anything.

When they were roommates in college and Francine lost her job, it was Lorelei who'd paid Francine's share of the rent, saved her car from repossession and made sure she had food. And she'd done it while living on a shoestring budget herself. She didn't have family she could fall back on, unlike most other people. And yet she'd tried to be there for Francine, even when Francine's own family wasn't.

It was Lorelei who'd nursed her through mono. Lorelei who, when Francine's mother died, helped make the funeral arrangements. And Lorelei who'd tutored

Francine during the depression that had ensued later so that she wouldn't flunk out of school.

Lorelei had helped out much more recently, too. Francine hadn't been happy with her husband for a long time, so Lorelei had allowed her to hang out at the house whenever she needed an escape, made her a bed on the couch so she could stay over if she and Allen were fighting and gave her a shoulder to cry on when they finally split up for good six months ago.

Of all people to betray her! Letting Francine come over so often had probably contributed to the problem, which made her feel even worse.

But Lorelei wouldn't—*couldn't*—allow what Francine and Mark had done to destroy her. She had to hang on for Lucy's sake, no matter what kind of determination and sacrifice it required.

What other choice did she have?

She refused to let Lucy down the way Mark had.

She was determined to be the kind of mother she'd always wanted but never had.

* * *

serenity

"Serenity?"

At the sound of her name, Serenity rolled over and lifted her head. It was morning—maybe even late morning—but she'd never been one to drag herself out of bed early. She preferred to work late, when telephones and emails weren't bombarding her from her publisher, readers and people who were providing research or documentation on the case she was currently writing about.

At night, she wasn't as tempted by social media, either, which had become an important part of her promotion process. Without a following, she couldn't continue to publish.

So she blogged once a week and maintained a Facebook page, an Instagram account and a Twitter presence. Increasing engagement on each of those could be taxing—Sean used to complain about the amount of time she spent trying to cover every base—but she felt it was necessary.

And now she was glad she'd made the effort. Her career could've crashed right along with her personal life if she hadn't maintained a relationship with her readers. Since Sean's trial ended, and she suddenly found herself with hours and hours and nothing besides work to fill them, she'd been happy to have something she could devote herself to. Something that helped build her career but didn't require the same level of mental acuity as writing. She didn't have the focus and concentration she'd had before, hadn't been able to make much progress on her latest book.

Although she hadn't made her ordeal public, there were certainly people who knew what had happened, especially if they lived in her area. It hadn't been reported in the news, but word quickly spread through the firm where Sean worked and leaked out from there. A couple of friends and neighbors had posted well wishes or questions on her social media pages that had sparked a bit of conversation, but she'd managed to minimize all of that by hiding those comments and ignoring those who posted them. Most of her followers had no idea what Sean had done and how his actions had impacted her life.

She was planning to let them know, however. She'd kept it as quiet as possible, but now that she was through the worst of it, it was time to address the scandal openly and honestly and then put it behind her. She hoped that would act as a purge of sorts, help her get back to writing.

But every time she sat down to tackle that particular blog, she came up with another excuse to procrastinate. What Sean had done was so despicable, so humiliating and embarrassing she didn't even want to *think* about it let alone tear the scab off the wound.

"Serenity?"

Her name again. Pushing her hair out of her eyes, she blinked and then squinted, trying to bring the world into focus.

Lorelei was standing over her. "Someone's at the door asking to borrow a shovel."

"Who?"

"Says he's your neighbor."

"My *neighbor*?" She struggled to clear the cobwebs from her mind. "There's only one other cabin near this one, and the owners are in Europe."

"Maybe they rented the place out while they were gone."

Serenity supposed that was possible. No one had been there last weekend, but someone could've come since. A lot of cabin owners used Airbnb and other services if they weren't going to be in town. "Okay." She covered a yawn. "Tell him I'm coming."

After Lorelei left and Serenity heard her say, "It'll be just a minute," she rolled out of bed and pulled on some yoga pants, a Berkeley Cheeseboard sweatshirt and her favorite fleece-lined slippers.

She didn't take time to brush her teeth or comb her hair. She planned to find the shovel, hand it over and be done.

But once she finally located the thing—in the garage, where it had fallen down behind her ski equipment—and brought it to the door, she wished she'd taken a little more care with her appearance.

At first glance, she thought the man at the door might be Kevin Love.

Celebrities did appear in Tahoe quite often, so it wouldn't be outside the realm of possibility. The cabin next door had cost a fortune and would rent for one, as well.

Then he smiled and she realized he wasn't the famous basketball player. It was only his overall body type and the shape of his face and nose that reminded her of him. But he wasn't quite as tall as Kevin Love, and he had light brown hair with amber-colored eyes.

"Sorry if I woke you." There was a hint of chagrin in his expression.

Afraid she had a waffle-like pattern on her cheek from the blankets on her bed, she raked the fingers of her free hand through her tangled hair. "No problem. Anything for a neighbor. You're staying next door, then? Are you related to the owners?"

"Just renting for the summer."

She hadn't realized the McClouds would be gone that long. But she'd been walking around in a fog for months. Maybe they'd told her and she didn't remember. "I doubt the snow we got yesterday will stick, so you've all but missed ski season. Are you a backpacker or…"

"I mountain bike now and then, but that's not why I'm here."

He didn't explain any further, and although she wondered why he'd come to Tahoe, she felt it would be too nosy to ask. "Well, there are a lot of great trails in these mountains, if you get the time." She handed him the shovel. "Here you go."

"Thank you. I'll bring it back as soon as I'm done."

She peered out at the snow covering the walkways, the cars and much of the street. She and her new sisters had their share of shoveling to do, too, or they wouldn't be able to get out. "No rush. We aren't going anywhere today."

A sexy grin curved his lips—or maybe she only thought it was sexy because it had been eighteen months since she'd made love, and her body was beginning to notify her of the neglect.

"Thanks," he said. "You'd think there'd be a shovel where I'm staying."

"I'm sure there was one," she said. "Somebody probably left it out and now it's buried under the snow. That's happened to me. Start digging around the back door—or near the woodpile if you're hoping to find it."

"Good advice. I'll give that a try."

When he turned to go, she shut the door instead of watching him walk away like she wanted to.

"Nice-looking neighbor." Lorelei spoke from the stairs behind her. She'd followed her back down to the front door. "I wonder if he's married."

"I didn't see a ring."

"You noticed?"

"Didn't you?"

They exchanged a sly smile. "A woman would have to be dead *not* to notice."

When Lorelei laughed, Serenity was impressed by the way it transformed her face. She'd thought Lorelei was pretty from the first moment she met her, but her new sister seemed a lot less tired and stressed today, which made her even prettier.

They climbed to the second floor together, after which Lorelei went to the kitchen.

Serenity was planning to go back to bed, but when she smelled coffee and saw that Lucy was up, she followed Lorelei.

Lucy sat at the table with a bowl of oatmeal.

"Good morning," Serenity said.

Lucy gave her a sweet smile. "Good morning."

"How old do you think that guy is—the one staying next door?" Lorelei asked as Serenity poured herself a cup of coffee.

"Younger than we are."

Lorelei had just opened the fridge. At Serenity's response, she twisted around, a skeptical expression on her face. "Really? I didn't get that impression."

"Maybe it only feels that way. After what I've been through in the past eighteen months, I feel ancient."

"You mean the trial?"

Serenity immediately regretted bringing that up. She'd told her sisters that she'd found something that shouldn't have been on her husband's computer and, as a result, she'd reported him. But that was all she'd said. Although she knew they wondered about the specifics, she'd promised herself she wouldn't tell anyone she didn't absolutely have to, wouldn't force herself to hash and rehash the terrible details. When she was ready, she'd put it in her blog, let everyone read what would constitute her official statement on the ordeal and be done with it. That blog would be the period— or the exclamation point—at the end of the nightmare. "All of it," she said simply.

Fortunately, Lorelei didn't press her. "Want some oatmeal?" she asked as she put a glass of milk on the table for Lucy.

"Not right now. Coffee's enough for me. But…" She sent Lorelei a teasing glance. "You seem pretty interested in the man who borrowed my shovel."

"I guess the one thing I haven't considered in everything I'm going through is…what else is out there, you know? My heart was sealed off. I thought I'd never have any reason to look at another man."

"And now…"

"That hasn't *officially* changed."

Serenity arched her eyebrows. "Interesting."

Lorelei blushed. "Stop. You're the one who's available. I thought he was cute. That's all."

"He *was* cute," Serenity admitted. "But I'm not ready to start dating."

"I don't want to bring up a touchy subject or anything, but do you ever hear from Sean?"

Obviously, Lorelei was still thinking of Serenity's offhand comment about the past eighteen months having aged her. She'd already brought the conversation back to Sean. "I've received a few letters."

"Letters or email?"

"Letters."

"And? What do they say? Does he apologize? Try to convince you that he's innocent? Blame you for turning him in? What?"

"I don't know. I've thrown most of them away without reading them." She saw Lucy sneak more brown sugar into her hot cereal and grinned despite the topic of conversation.

"You have?" Lorelei persisted. "You're not curious enough to open them?"

After adding a dash of cream to her coffee, Serenity took a tentative sip. "I'd rather forget him. I definitely don't want to become pen pals."

"I know but—"

"He's probably just asking for money," Serenity explained. "During the trial, he yelled out that he got ripped off in the divorce, since I got the house. But he spent everything in our retirement accounts on his legal defense, and that amount was equal to the equity in the house. So he got a fair deal."

Lorelei wrinkled her nose in distaste. "I'm sorry."

"Thanks." Serenity jerked her head toward Lucy. "Let's not discuss it right now." She took another sip of coffee. "Where's Reagan? Any word from her this morning?"

Before Lorelei could respond, Serenity heard her other sister say, "Right here."

Reagan was just coming down the stairs.

"You sleep okay?" Serenity raised her voice so it would carry. The kitchen was open to the living room; she could see Reagan but received no response.

Reagan had paused before the wall of windows that looked out on the deck and the snow-covered landscape and trees beyond the deck to the lake.

"Reagan?" Serenity prompted.

Pulling her gaze away from the view, she finished crossing the living room to reach the kitchen. She was wearing sweats, her face was freshly scrubbed, and she'd taken the time to put some product in her hair, but she wasn't wearing any makeup. "What?"

"Did you sleep okay?"

"Yeah." The dark circles under her eyes contradicted her, but Serenity chose not to mention it.

"Would you like some breakfast?" Lorelei asked. "I made oatmeal."

Reagan seemed vaguely surprised that Lorelei would be the one to offer her something to eat. "No, thanks. I'm just going to have a cup of coffee."

"Any word from Drew?" Serenity asked.

After a slight hesitation, Reagan poured herself some coffee and carried her mug to the table. "He tried to call again last night."

Serenity slid the cream and sugar in her direction. "Did you take it?"

When Reagan didn't answer right away, Serenity sensed Lorelei going rigid at the sink behind them and wondered if Reagan was aware of the tension in her, too.

"What'd he say?" she asked, assuming the answer was yes or Reagan would've said no.

"I didn't give him the chance to say anything. I answered, but then I panicked and hung up."

"Why?"

"Because I'm afraid," Reagan admitted.

Serenity scooted her chair closer to the table. "That he's going to stick with his wife?"

After testing her coffee, Reagan glanced over. "No, that he'll offer to leave her. I don't want to be responsible for breaking up the family."

Serenity let her breath seep slowly out. She liked Reagan, in spite of what she'd done. Reagan had made a big mistake, but she obviously regretted getting involved with Drew and wasn't using their attraction to her advantage—wasn't out to steal Drew from his wife or get a leg up at the agency, even though her career was clearly very important to her. "What are you going to do?"

"I told you. I have to quit. I can't be trusted around him." She rubbed her temples. "Do you have any painkillers? I have a terrible headache."

Serenity got up to get some for her.

"I'll look for another job online while we're here." She swallowed the two tablets Serenity handed her. "I doubt I'll be able to get anything that pays what I'm making now. Along with a pay cut, I'll have to start over and work my way back up. But…"

"But…" Serenity echoed, sitting down again.

"Those are the consequences of my actions, right? If I cut it off with Drew and leave Edison & Curry, at least I'll be able to look myself in the face again."

Lorelei put a bowl of oatmeal in front of her. "Just in case you can take a few bites," she said softly.

8

serenity

After breakfast, Reagan went to her room to answer a few work emails. She said too many people—both coworkers and clients—were waiting for something from her, and she had to take care of those responsibilities.

Serenity felt bad for her. Reagan had said that ever since she'd slunk away from the office a week ago, disheveled and ashamed, she'd been too upset to interact with anyone connected with the agency. She was afraid her coworkers would somehow guess, and she was embarrassed as well as humiliated. But Serenity had encouraged her to keep her head up and finish strong. All Reagan could do at this point was show her contrition by taking steps to get out of Drew's life.

After Reagan went upstairs, Serenity helped Lorelei clean the kitchen and then Lorelei sent Lucy to put on her boots and coat. Lucy wanted to go outside to play in the snow. Later, when she was having a nap and Reagan was finished taking care of her business, they'd sit down together and begin to hash out possible scenarios for how they could be related.

They were all supposed to bring pictures of their parents and other close relatives, as well as anything else that might be pertinent—although Serenity didn't expect Lorelei to have anything. Lorelei had grown up in the foster care system. She didn't know who her parents were.

"Found my coat, Mommy!" Lucy called down.

Lorelei was standing in the living room, examining the pictures on the wall while Serenity sat on the couch, using her phone to respond to an email from her editor. Serenity had been working with a woman named Nikkita Woods for about two years, ever since her first editor resigned and moved to a different publisher. But despite the number of business emails they'd exchanged, they didn't know each other all that well. That was partly why Serenity was pretending to be further along in her current work-in-progress than she really was. She wasn't sure her editor would stand by her, couldn't risk spooking her by admitting the truth—that she was still struggling to become productive again. If she didn't get going soon and send in some sample chapters, she was afraid her publisher would contract someone else to write about the Maynard Murders.

"Good job, honey," Lorelei called back. "Don't forget your boots."

"Boots?" Lucy echoed as if the word was foreign to her.

"What we bought right before we left home—with Elsa on them."

"Oh! My Elsa shoes."

As Serenity hit Send, she was amused by the fact

that Lucy had very likely never owned a pair of boots. Watching Lorelei with her little girl made Serenity a trifle envious. She'd expected to have a child this year. She and Sean had just decided to go off birth control so they could start a family when she found those files. And now that she was thirty-five, divorced and disillusioned, who could say if she'd ever become a mother?

"This is a *great* picture," Lorelei said.

Serenity put down her phone and walked over to gaze at the painting of the lake that had captured her own attention yesterday, right before Lorelei and Reagan arrived. "That's Emerald Bay."

"Is the water really that blue?"

"It is. The lake is nicknamed Big Blue. I can't wait to take you down there, but we'll wait for Reagan to join us, if that's okay."

"Of course we can wait. Lucy will have a blast just playing outside. Yesterday was the first time she'd ever seen snow." She pointed to the photograph of Serenity's parents at the casino. "These are your parents?"

"Yes. Meet Chuck and Charlotte Currington."

"They're a handsome couple."

"I've always thought so."

"And these are your siblings?" She pointed to a different picture now, the one with the Christmas tree.

"Yes. That's Beau, my brother, who's getting his master's in aerospace engineering at UCLA. And these are the twins, Tara and Tia."

"They're all younger than you. I remember you telling us that."

"Yeah—Beau's twenty-four and the twins are twenty-eight."

"So you were seven when the twins were born."

"Yes." She'd been old enough that she could remember her father taking her to the hospital to meet them and how excited she'd been to have not one but *two* baby sisters.

Serenity hadn't thought much about the age gap while she was growing up. She'd figured her parents had simply decided to wait. Or Mother Nature hadn't, at first, cooperated. Charlotte had always said Serenity was her "right hand," as if she felt lucky to have had so much time alone with her oldest daughter.

But knowing what she knew now, the fact that she was seven years older than her twin sisters seemed a little suspect. Was there a bigger reason than she'd supposed?

Lorelei didn't say anything for several seconds, but she studied that Christmas picture as though she wished she could climb inside it.

Finally, she moved on to another one. "Is this you?"

"Yes—sledding with my dad."

She indicated the beach shot. "At this elevation, it's hard to imagine it gets warm enough to swim. But it must. Look at all those people in the water behind you."

"The air warms up in the summer, but the water stays cold because the lake is so deep." Feeling a bit nostalgic, Serenity touched the photo. "That's Sand Harbor, one of the most popular beaches in Tahoe."

"Was your dad taking the picture?"

"No, I'm sure that was my uncle Vance or his girlfriend. They were visiting."

"Where was your dad?"

"That particular day?" Serenity shook her head. "I don't remember."

"Did he usually come up with you?"

"If it was on a weekend. Maybe he had to meet a client in San Francisco, where he worked at the time."

Lorelei studied the photo more closely. "Where is Sand Harbor? Will I be able to see it while I'm in town?"

"Sure. It's right here at Incline Village. You can even walk to it."

"And the casinos?"

"Those are at South Shore, about a thirty-minute drive. Emerald Bay's over there, too. South Shore has more of a party vibe. North Shore, where we are now, is made up mostly of nature lovers. There's a very different feel."

"I see." Lorelei examined yet another picture, one in which Serenity's father was lounging on the boat they'd owned back then. "Did you do a lot of boating growing up?"

"A decent amount. My dad loves both types of skiing."

"Looks like you had a fun childhood."

The wistfulness in her voice made Serenity feel slightly ungrateful for not appreciating—or appreciating enough—how good she'd always had it. Did it really matter whether she'd been adopted without ever being told? She'd been loved, hadn't she?

She'd never doubted that. And her parents had provided everything she needed and then some. She'd certainly had a lot better life than Lorelei—

"Serenity?"

Lorelei had said something Serenity had missed. "What?"

"Do you still have the boat?"

"Not that one, but we have another one. Sean and I used to take it out all the time."

"Do you ever take it out by yourself now that Sean's… um…out of the picture?"

"No, I haven't yet. The trial was still going on last summer, and I didn't feel like boating on my own. When I go down to the lake, I usually kayak."

"I've never been kayaking. Is it fun?"

"I love it. At sunrise or sunset it's a little cooler than at midday, of course, but it's so calm and peaceful." She'd spent hours and hours paddling through the glassy water, with the call of the California Gulls filling her ears—and had done a lot of thinking while gazing at the mountains rising majestically around her.

"Is it something we could do with Lucy while we're here?" Lorelei asked.

"If it warms up enough by the end of the week, maybe. Does she know how to swim?"

"She does. There are so many pools in Florida, I started her in swimming lessons when she was two."

"Still, we'll put her in a life vest. We have all sizes down in the garage."

"You do?" she said in surprise.

"My parents were hoping for grandkids, so they never got rid of the ones we had when we were little."

"Why didn't you and Sean have any children?" she asked. "You were married for what…ten years?"

"Eight."

"That's certainly long enough to begin a family."

"We decided to wait until we'd established our careers."

"You said he was an accountant?"

"Yes."

"Mom, I'm ready."

They both turned to see Lucy wearing her coat and

boots, although the coat was buttoned unevenly and the boots were on the wrong feet.

Serenity laughed at the sight. "Here, let me help you, sweetheart," she said and fixed Lucy's coat before squatting down to switch her boots to the right feet.

"Are you going outside to play with us?" Lucy asked.

"I have to do a few things first. But then I'll join you. It might be chilly. Is that okay?"

"My mom says I can build a snowman."

Serenity straightened. "Well, if you're going to build a snowman, you're going to need a carrot."

"A carrot?" she echoed.

"Of course. Your snowman's got to have a nose, doesn't he?"

She considered that for a moment before nodding decisively—yes, Mr. Snowman would need a nose.

"And what are you going to use for his eyes?"

"I don't know," she said, her mouth dropping open as though she'd suddenly been made aware of a serious problem.

"Come on." Serenity held out her hand. "I bet we can find something in the kitchen that'll work."

As Lucy's small fingers curled through hers, Serenity felt lucky for the first time since learning about Lorelei and Reagan. She'd been angry at the thought of being deceived, frightened at what she might discover, curious to know the truth, worried about how this might affect her life and a bit shell-shocked to have something like this happen on the heels of her ex-husband's trial. That was a lot of emotion to deal with—all of it negative.

But in this one moment, as she led her niece in to find some accoutrements for a snowman, she felt a touch of gratitude simply for having more people to love.

* * *

lorelei

Lorelei tried not to bite her nails. Usually, she purchased acrylics to prevent what she was doing now. When she was young, she wouldn't quit until she'd made her fingers bleed, and since she'd been too busy to get a manicure before coming to Tahoe—too upset to go out or spend the money on something that had suddenly become a very low priority—she found herself reverting to her old habits.

"You okay?"

Serenity's voice was soft and reassuring. Lorelei wanted to respond to her kindness, but trust didn't come easily for her. There'd been a lot of people in her life who'd seemed reliable—but weren't. Mark and Francine were just the latest.

Folding her hands in her lap, Lorelei nodded. After running around in the snow for two hours, and having a sandwich and some celery and carrot sticks for lunch, Lucy was asleep upstairs. Reagan and Serenity sat at the kitchen table across from her, each with a pile of photographs from when they were children, along with various other scrapbook items.

Lorelei had nothing, of course. Which was why she felt this meeting was more important to her than either of them. She was hoping to finally forge a connection with her past. That need had dimmed slightly after she'd married Mark. She'd been able to bury it for a while, give it less thought and attention.

Lucy's birth and the love and devotion she lavished on her child helped, too.

But now, with her trust in her husband destroyed and the future uncertain, she felt as though she was tumbling down the long hill she'd so painstakingly climbed since meeting him—or, more accurately, that he'd *pushed* her down it.

She could've brought a few pictures from when she was older, of course. Birthday cards she'd received from friends. School pictures her foster parents had kept for her. A teddy bear—worn out because it had stuck with her longer than any human. Some early examples of her schoolwork. A nice note from a teacher.

Some years were spottier than others as far as these types of items were concerned, depending on what had been happening with her housing situation at the time. Even when she was old enough to save things herself, they often got lost in the shuffle. She had nothing that could shed any light on where she was born, or to whom, so there hadn't been anything to bring.

"Before we go through this stuff, why don't we each share our earliest memories?" Serenity said. "Where we thought we were when various events took place, who we were with, whether those people stayed in our lives... I've found in researching the cases I write about, sometimes it's the most innocuous detail that leads to something bigger and more revealing."

Reagan rubbed her face. "Okay. Do you want to go first?"

"Yeah, let's start with you," Lorelei chimed in, looking at Serenity. As fragile as she felt, she didn't want to go first. Talking about her childhood could be difficult even when she was in a better state of mind.

Serenity spread out the items she had with her. "I admit I don't have much to complain about. I had a wonderful childhood. So good, in fact, that I couldn't help thinking there must be some mistake with…with what we've learned. I didn't tell you both this, but I was so convinced this had to be the result of a false positive or whatever, I had my DNA retested."

Reagan crossed one long leg over the other. Although she was casually dressed in sweats, she appeared to be taking a professional approach to this. Lorelei couldn't see her acting any differently if they were all sitting around a conference table wearing skirts and heels. "And?"

"The results were right to begin with." Serenity glanced at Lorelei before quickly continuing, "But so you know, I didn't double-check because I don't want you both as my sisters. It's just that everything I've ever believed about the rest of my family has broken down, and depending on how this happened, I'm afraid of what it'll do to them. I don't want to push people— loved ones—who are otherwise happy, off an emotional cliff." She paused. "Reconstructing our history, our relationships, won't be easy."

Reagan stared into her wineglass as she swirled the liquid inside it. "You're assuming they'll react negatively."

"Isn't that why you haven't told your mother?"

"Yes, but your family seems much better adjusted than mine. My mother is all I've got. If she reacts negatively, there's no one left."

Then maybe you'll know how I feel, Lorelei almost said but managed to bite it back.

Serenity toyed with a picture of the siblings she'd

been raised with. "I tried to subtly suggest to my brother and sisters that they get their DNA tested—told them I'd done mine to see how it all worked for my writing—but none of them seemed particularly interested. They're content with their lives. I was, too—before Sean, of course. I didn't want to raise suspicion or risk having them mention anything about DNA to our parents, so I didn't push, but I may try again later."

Despite all the tension Lorelei was feeling, she was distracted by Serenity's mention of her ex-husband. What, exactly, had Sean done? Serenity had been so tight-lipped about him. "Your parents don't know that you had your DNA tested?"

"No, but I would've mentioned the results if they hadn't been so…unexpected. It's interesting that I have 3 percent Neanderthal DNA, for example. My dad would get a kick out of that. He's always been interested in evolution, watches all kinds of documentaries about early hominid species before *Homo sapiens*. But when I received the notice that I had a close living relative I knew nothing about, it spun me in a completely different direction. Then Lorelei reached out on Facebook and the rest is history."

"Do you think you're related to your siblings?" Reagan asked. "Do you think *we* are?"

"I don't think you are," Serenity said. "You don't look anything like them."

Lorelei's mind went to the pictures she'd studied so closely on the living room wall. She doubted Serenity would want to hear it, but she didn't see a lot of resemblance between her and her siblings, or even between her and her parents. "Judging from the ones on the wall—"

"Wait." Serenity pulled some more pictures of herself, her brother and her twin sisters at various ages from a box at her feet and put them on top of those already on the table. "Here are some more."

Lorelei picked up a photograph of the twins at about ten years old. They had lighter hair and darker eyes. And they were more petite, didn't have the same tall, lanky build that Serenity had in common with her and Reagan. "The younger three resemble each other more than any of them resembles you."

Reagan considered a photograph of Beau before setting it aside to examine a picture of Serenity's parents. "Yeah, I guess I'd have to agree with Lorelei. Your coloring is different."

"But I still look like them, don't I?" A defensive note had crept into Serenity's voice.

Reagan continued to sift through pictures. "A little," she allowed. "How old were you when your mother had the twins?"

"She was seven."

It was Lorelei who answered, but Reagan kept her focus on Serenity. "For twins to follow such a long gap suggests your parents might've been undergoing some sort of fertility treatment. Do you remember them talking about anything like that?"

"No. But I'm not sure I would've picked up on it. Do seven-year-olds understand what fertility means? I just remember how excited I was when my mother told me I was going to be a big sister. I'd asked Santa Claus for a baby sister for two years in a row, so I thought he was finally answering my request." She chuckled as she shook her head, obviously lost in the memory. "You can imagine how grateful I was when I learned

I was getting two sisters and not just one. I thought he was making up for being late."

Resentment hit Lorelei like a sledgehammer. *She'd* begged Santa for a mother—something she never got. She'd never been given many presents, either, but she wasn't upset about that. She was grateful for the few she *had* received. No one was technically obligated to provide her with a Christmas.

"How many more years was it before Beau came along?" Reagan asked.

Lorelei could've answered that question, too, but she didn't. She was still grappling with the way Serenity's story was making her feel.

"Four."

"So you would've been eleven," Reagan mused. "Old enough to understand a bit more."

"I guess, but, again, I only remember being excited. Especially when the ultrasound revealed it was a boy." Serenity pulled back her hair, twisted it into a knot at her nape and then let it fall free again. "I had my two sisters—I was eager for a little brother."

"And of course you got him," Lorelei piped up. "You got *everything* you wanted."

Reagan and Serenity stared at her in surprise. "What are you talking about?" Reagan asked.

A warning light started to flash in Lorelei's head. She needed to reel in her emotions. She didn't lose her composure very often, and when she did, she almost always regretted it. But she didn't seem to have any reserves to draw from. This conversation was churning up too many hurtful memories. "I guess it's hard for me to feel a lot of sympathy for Serenity when I would've given *anything* to have it even half as good."

Serenity rocked back as though she'd been slapped. To her, this had to be coming out of nowhere. But it was Reagan who rallied first.

"She hasn't had a perfect life, Lorelei. Her husband just went to prison, for God's sake. Not only did Serenity have to turn him in, she had to testify against him."

There was an edge to Reagan's voice, telling her that she needed to stop, but that only pushed Lorelei further down the path she was already on. "So?" she cried. "At least she was an adult when she went through that. At least she had her family to offer support. She also had a viable career to fall back on."

Lorelei hated the things she was saying, and she hated herself for saying them. Serenity had done nothing to deserve this. But once she started to speak, the harsh words seemed to come out almost involuntarily. "And he only got five years," she couldn't keep herself from continuing. "Which means he couldn't have done anything *too* terrible. With good behavior, he'll be out in two. She's said so herself."

Serenity's face had grown mottled and her lips were tightly compressed. "He deserves a lot more than he got."

"Why? Because he dared to disrupt your beautiful life?"

The chair squealed against the floor as Serenity shoved away from the table and stood. "*Disrupt* it?"

Reagan tried, once again, to intervene, but Serenity didn't so much as look at her and neither did Lorelei.

"Yes! God knows you wouldn't have expected a shocker like marrying a crook," Lorelei said. "What'd he do? Embezzle from the firm where he worked? And did that humiliate and embarrass you?" She'd tried to look it up online but hadn't been able to find anything. The fact that it wasn't even reported in the news supported what she was saying.

"What he did is none of our business." Reagan stood, too, spreading her hands out as if that might stop the argument. She was still trying to act as mediator, but no one was listening to her anymore. Serenity had been pushed too far. Lorelei could see the anger sparking in her eyes, but wasn't willing to back down or apologize. She wanted to fight and fight hard—with Serenity, with anyone.

"He was involved in a child pornography ring, okay?" Serenity snapped. "Are you happy now? He was buying and selling pictures of innocent little boys and girls being defiled, which I can only assume must have excited him. Those are the kinds of pictures I found on his computer—the kind that make you want to vomit and then cut off his junk with a dull pair of scissors!" With that, she stomped out of the kitchen and up the stairs, and a few seconds later the whole cabin reverberated with the force she put behind slamming her bedroom door.

Lorelei sat in stunned silence. Serenity's husband was a *pedophile*? Just thinking of anyone owning kiddie porn made her shudder with revulsion.

"What's *wrong* with you?" Reagan whispered, her eyebrows knitted as though she was mortified—and she probably was.

The threat of tears suddenly made it impossible to speak.

"Lorelei?"

Oh, God. What had she done? "I don't know," she admitted, managing to force a few words past the tightness in her throat. "I—" She swallowed hard. "These days my emotions are all over the place. One minute I'm angry and looking for a target, the next I'm crying and feeling sorry for myself." She squeezed her eyes closed. "I can't seem to function normally."

Lorelei expected Reagan to stomp off the way Serenity had. After this episode, and the problem she'd had with Reagan in the car yesterday, she expected them *both* to decide she was too insufferable to have around and ask her to leave.

Maybe she was even *inviting* them to do that—forcing them to reject her now so they couldn't reject her later, after she'd begun to care.

She was so sure that was what would happen next she was already thinking of where she and Lucy might stay in Reno until their plane left on Friday—and how she'd pay for the unexpected expense—when Reagan reached across the table to squeeze her arm. "It's okay," she said.

Lorelei opened her eyes. "What?"

"It's going to be okay. None of us are perfect. We all have some pretty crappy problems right now. We'll get through this."

"But Serenity did nothing to deserve that or…or provoke it."

"I know. Still, it couldn't have been easy for you, sitting there while she went through all that memorabilia and talked about the kind of childhood you wish you could've had."

"That's no excuse." She refused to let herself off that easily, but Reagan kept talking.

"You must've been feeling left out and…and unlucky and who knows what else, especially now that you've lost your faith in Mark. But remember what we're trying to achieve." She sat back down and leaned forward, her expression earnest. "If only we can figure out how we're related, you might be able to find your real parents—or at least learn something about them and the circumstances of your birth. You want that, don't you?"

Lorelei cleared her throat so her voice wouldn't wobble. The fact that Reagan could be so understanding, could forgive her before she'd even asked, was so unexpected. It made her think of the unconditional love families often gave each other—something she'd always yearned for but never had. "Of course I do. More than anything. I used to lie awake for hours as a child, hoping that one day I'd learn what happened and why. But I owe Serenity a sincere apology," she said. "And I owe you one, too."

"You don't owe me anything," Reagan insisted. "And I know Serenity will feel the same. Just give her some time to cool off—and then let her know you're sorry."

9

reagan

Reagan expected Lorelei's daughter to appear at any moment. She doubted Lucy would sleep through the slamming of Serenity's door. But all the travel, the change in altitude and playing so hard in the snow must've worn the little girl out because five minutes turned into ten, and she didn't come down.

Lorelei had been pacing in the kitchen ever since Serenity left. "Should I go up and talk to her now?" she asked.

"Not yet." Reagan had distanced herself from Lorelei at first. She didn't need Lorelei's judgment and condemnation coming down on her when she was already so angry with herself. But as she'd gazed at Lorelei, sitting across from her and Serenity with no baby pictures or other memorabilia, she'd felt such empathy.

She and Serenity had both had so much more than Lorelei, at least until Lorelei got married. And maybe after. Reagan had no idea what Lorelei and Mark's financial picture had been like, but she could easily guess that if the marriage ended, Lorelei wouldn't be too comfortable. Not if she didn't have a good job to help cover the bills—and good jobs were difficult to come by after being out of the workforce for even a few years.

That Lorelei's husband could do what he'd done, to someone who'd already been through so much, made Reagan angry. She'd always been high-spirited, and her mother had trained her to be a fighter, someone who'd dig in and, if she wanted something badly enough, keep slugging no matter what. She could never have survived her first few years at Edison & Curry without that rock-hard determination. The atmosphere had been competitive there from the start. Some of the people she'd worked with had done everything possible to undermine her, or get her to quit because they felt threatened by her.

She'd persevered, but she was used to being in the right. She could stand fast because she believed in herself and what she was hoping to achieve, which was why getting involved with Drew had thrown her for such a loop. While she'd met with obstacles before, her mother being the biggest at times, she'd never been pitted against *herself.* To be in the same boat as Mark—to be one of those people for whom she had no respect— made her wonder if she was really who she'd always aspired to be.

As much as she was tempted, she couldn't completely condemn him. She refused to be that big a hypocrite.

"I feel so bad," Lorelei said, pivoting once again at the counter.

"I know. But you're going to get through this, just like you've gotten through everything else, okay?"

She sighed audibly. "If you say so."

"What're some of your earliest memories?" she asked

as she picked up the photographs and other things to get them out of Lorelei's sight.

"They all deal with foster homes. Parents who were briefly part of my life and then gone. Other children who passed through like ships sailing on the same ocean but going in different directions. It didn't feel as though I could hang on to anything, to anyone, you know? Everyone seemed transient. Until Mark."

Reagan winced at Lorelei's words. "I'm sorry—on behalf of cheaters everywhere. I can't believe I'm one of them. It's humiliating."

Instead of narrowing her eyes and pursing her lips, as she'd done in the car when this subject first came up, Lorelei's expression revealed a hint of confusion and vulnerability. "Maybe you can help me understand why he did it," she said. "I keep going around and around it in my head, trying to figure out what I did or didn't do that made him want to cheat on me. But I can't come up with anything, except letting Francine stay over so often. I wasn't perfect, but I tried to be everything he could want in a woman. Our sex life was great—maybe not off the charts but certainly robust. Our house was always clean. I'm a good cook and had dinner waiting every night. I didn't go out and spend a lot of money. I'm a caring mom. Isn't that enough?"

Reagan hated seeing the tears in her eyes, hated knowing she was causing someone—a wife, like Lorelei—the same kind of pain. "I'm betting it had almost nothing to do with you."

"How can that be? I'm the one who's supposed to fulfill him. I'm the one he sleeps with at night, the mother of his child."

Reagan slid her wineglass out of the way so she

wouldn't inadvertently knock it over. "Drew's wife is probably a wonderful person, too, Lorelei. She didn't deserve what happened to her any more than you did. I've met Sally. I liked her. And I have no doubt Drew cares about her. So why'd he get involved with me? It was just an inexplicable attraction—a few minutes of selfishness we couldn't overcome."

"You told me you love him."

"I do."

"Does he love you?"

"He said so."

"Do you think it's possible to love two people at once?"

"I do. Could that be why Mark did what he did? Is he also in love with Francine?"

Lorelei's shoulders slumped as she considered the question. "It would make my decision easier if he was. Then I'd *have* to leave him. But he claims he's not. He says he loves me, wants to keep our marriage together."

"You don't believe he's sincere?"

"I've never trusted words. Actions are the only way to determine what someone is truly thinking and feeling, and his actions suggest the opposite."

"I hate to say this, because I don't want you to get the impression I'm minimizing what I did, or what Mark's done, but it's possible he just made a mistake. That he was confronted with something that…that got the best of him for a short time. That's what happened to me."

"How short a time? That's the question. Was it only one encounter? More?"

Reagan felt so bad for Lorelei. As strange as it was to think of anyone as a sibling—after growing up with no siblings at all—she had two sisters now and wanted to connect with them in a meaningful way, even though they'd lost all their childhood years and it was much harder and more awkward now. "Has he said?"

"He claims it was an isolated incident, but now that I know the truth I can point to other things—comments, times when neither of them was available—that indicate it's been going on for some time. A month, at least."

"So he's *still* lying."

"I think so."

Once again, Reagan suppressed the urge to get angry with Mark. "What does *she* say?"

"I haven't spoken to Francine. I don't want to speak to her. This is all too fresh. And if it *has* been going on for a while, I have to wonder if the only reason Mark told me is because of the baby."

To Reagan's mind, that didn't make him seem too contrite. "He would have no reason to lie about who he wants to be with, though," she said, trying to remain positive.

"I guess not," Lorelei agreed. "But he could always change his mind. That's the problem. It's not just the baby that's making it hard for me to forgive him. I'll wonder from here on out, especially once the baby is born, if he'd rather be with Francine and his other child. I don't know if I can live with that constantly hanging over my head. It's soul-crushing. I had to put up with that sort of thing my entire childhood—feeling as though, if I wasn't the greatest kid ever, my foster parents would take me back and exchange me for a better child. I can't face that as an adult."

Despite the irony of the impulse given what *she'd* done recently, Reagan wanted to slug Mark. "I don't blame you."

"And yet I have to do what's best for Lucy. If he's really as sorry as he says, I don't want to rip our marriage apart. Before all of this happened, we were happy. At least, *I* thought we were."

Once again, Reagan tried to come up with a way to make the situation less upsetting. "Is there any chance the baby could be someone else's?"

She shook her head. "From what he's told me, there isn't. Once the baby's born, we'll get a paternity test before we start paying child support, of course. But when Francine and her husband Allen split up six months ago, he moved to Arizona, where he's from. I doubt she's been with anyone else. As her best friend, I think she would've told me."

"How does Mark explain what happened? What kinds of words does he use?"

"He says it didn't mean anything to him. That being a father can be a heavy responsibility, and coming home to the same woman every night can seem confining. He was bored with his life and intrigued by having a 'different' experience—and she was there to provide it."

"Bored?" This came from out in the living room.

They both looked over to see Serenity returning to the kitchen, and Lorelei immediately approached her. "I'm sorry," she said.

Serenity waved her words away. "I overreacted earlier. It's not a big deal. Let's just forget it."

"I can't. What I did was completely uncalled for. I don't even know why I picked that fight. I was just… angry and wanting to strike out."

"I can understand why. Once I got upstairs and started to calm down I realized how much what we were doing here—" she gestured at what was left of the memorabilia Reagan hadn't yet packed away "—must've stung. I'm sure it was a trigger for you. Like I said, let's just forget it."

Lorelei's troubled expression didn't ease. "Are you sure you wouldn't rather Lucy and I left?"

"And go back to Mark early?" Serenity said. "No! It's bad enough that he said he was bored with his life. Even if there's some way he could spin that to make it sympathetic, why didn't he wear a damn condom when he was with your best friend?"

Reagan caught her breath at the mention of birth control. If *she* was pregnant, everyone would say the same thing—they would marvel at her stupidity and carelessness.

She was tempted to explain how an accident could occur, wanted to say that maybe the encounter was completely unexpected and happened too fast. But she was afraid that would reveal too much about her own situation.

"Claims he did," Lorelei said. "He doesn't know how she wound up pregnant. But that's another reason I think they've been together more than once. I don't see it as very likely that she got pregnant the first time they had sex, not if they were using a condom."

Reminded of her encounter with Drew, Reagan's stomach muscles tightened. Once was all it took, especially without birth control—which was what frightened her.

"Did *she* supply it?" Serenity asked drily, intimating that Francine might've *wanted* to sabotage Lorelei's marriage by getting pregnant.

Lorelei grimaced. "I don't know. Those were details I didn't want to hear so I didn't ask."

"Well, I heard what you said to Reagan as I was coming down the stairs, and I'll be honest. I don't like what he's had to say so far. There's been nothing to make me believe he's truly repentant."

Reagan jumped back into the conversation before it could seem strange that she'd fallen silent for so long. "I agree. I feel like absolute shit for doing what I did. Where's *his* contrition?"

"His explanation sounds like he's only thinking of himself and not accepting any responsibility for what he did," Serenity agreed.

"So I should leave him."

Reagan was afraid to go that far. "If you do split up, does he have a good job? You once mentioned—in a text or something—that he works for a defense contractor, but I have no idea how much that pays."

"He's a propulsion engineer for an aerospace company. He has a good salary."

"Then you'll get enough child support?" Serenity cut in.

"Who knows? If we divorce he'll also have another family to support."

Serenity picked up the wineglasses and started to wash them. "He'll have to support the new baby either way. It's not worth staying with him if you're going to be unhappy."

"I'm not convinced I'll be any happier if I leave him," Lorelei said with a frown. "That might only make my life worse—because anything that hurts Lucy hurts me."

A knock sounded at the front door.

When Serenity looked as though she couldn't imagine who it could be, Lorelei said, "I bet that's your neighbor, bringing back the shovel. I saw him clearing the walks earlier when I was out with Lucy."

"Oh, right. Of course. Thank God I've showered," Serenity muttered and, after setting the wet glasses on a dish towel, went to the door, leaving Reagan alone with Lorelei.

"I know you're sorry for what you said to Serenity—"

"I am," Lorelei broke in, but Reagan lifted a hand, indicating that she wanted to finish.

"But I owe *you* an apology. I feel terrible that, like Mark, I've given you a reason to distrust me."

Lorelei seemed taken aback by her apology. "That's really nice. Especially because I believe you."

As they exchanged a smile, Reagan felt better than she had in over a week. Maybe everything was going to hell back home, but Lorelei's response gave her hope that she might have the chance to redeem herself in her new sister's eyes. As unpracticed a sibling as she was, she might still get the hang of it.

When Serenity came back into the kitchen, she had a funny look on her face—one that suggested she was both surprised and amused.

"Was it him?" Lorelei asked. "Was he bringing back the shovel?"

"Yeah. I left it by the front door, in case he needs it again."

"So…what's up?"

"He wanted to clear our walks, too, but by the time he finished his, he was too exhausted." She smiled. "He obviously comes from warmer weather. If you're not used to snow and haven't done a lot of shoveling, you think it's going to be much easier than it is. Just with what he's done so far, he'll probably be too sore to walk tomorrow. But he feels guilty about not being Superman and helping out the ladies next door so he's invited us over for dinner."

"*All* of us?" Lorelei asked. "Or is this a date?"

"It's not a date. I told him I had my two sisters and my niece staying with me, and he said to bring you."

"Is he over there alone?" Reagan asked.

"He was expecting his brothers to arrive today, so he made a huge pot of chili before he started to shovel. But something came up and now they won't be able to get here for a few days."

Reagan hadn't seen the neighbor, but from the way her two sisters were acting, he had to be more than mildly handsome. "You mean he needs our help eating all that chili."

Serenity winked at her. "Exactly. I didn't tell him I'm a vegetarian. I'll just eat the corn bread and anything else that doesn't have meat."

"So you agreed?" Lorelei asked.

"I did." She gave them both a mock scowl. "We're neighbors. I didn't want to be rude."

Reagan gestured at what was left of the memorabilia. "Should we talk about this later?"

"There's no reason we have to stop," Serenity replied. "We have a couple of hours before we're supposed to go over. Dinner isn't until six."

"Actually, I'd like to take a little nap myself before Lucy wakes up."

Lorelei could probably use the break. After that little blow-up and then the reconciliation, they all could. "We're here for a week," Reagan said. "Can't we talk about it later, after Lucy's in bed for the night?"

Lorelei's face filled with relief. "That's what I was thinking."

"Of course," Serenity said. She was the hard-nosed investigator, the most eager to find answers so that she could right her world, but Reagan was glad she could leave it alone, for now.

Once Lorelei left the kitchen, Reagan exchanged an uncertain glance with Serenity. "Are you okay?"

"Yeah. I'm fine. She's been through a lot. I shouldn't have been so sensitive."

"You've been through a lot, too."

"But, like she said, I've also had a lot to be grateful for. She had it rough when she was a kid, and now she's married to a bastard."

Reagan sighed. "I was trying to give Mark the benefit of the doubt, for obvious reasons, but…"

"But he's using her insecurities against her. He's got complete control because she obviously cares more about their child than he does. That's why I couldn't stay mad at her. She's going through hell. I can't blame her for acting out a little."

Considering what she'd heard, Reagan had to agree. "Yeah, I got that impression, too. But we're defensive of her, which makes us prone to assume the worst. We have to be careful. We could be wrong about Mark."

Serenity pursed her lips as she weighed Reagan's response. "I guess that's true."

10

lorelei

Not only was the neighbor tall and broad-shouldered, he had thick sandy-colored hair and beautiful amber eyes. They reminded Lorelei of Jason Momoa's eyes in *Aquaman*. He was so handsome he made her feel… frumpy. After all, she was the only married sister, the only one with a child and she was twenty pounds heavier than Serenity or Reagan.

Since she didn't expect him to pay her much attention, she crouched down to talk to Lucy about the snow and how fast it was melting, while Serenity took the lead at the door. But when Serenity turned to introduce her and Lorelei stood and shook their host's large hand, she was slightly embarrassed that the warmth of his touch lingered in her mind long after he'd said hello.

"It's very nice to meet you," he said to Lucy.

Lorelei smiled as her daughter ducked shyly behind her, and he stepped back so they could come in.

"How can you even call this a *cabin*?" Lorelei muttered to Serenity as soon as she saw the floor-to-ceiling windows overlooking the lake.

Serenity's cabin had a similar view and almost as many windows. It, too, was beautiful and expensive. But the ceiling wasn't quite as high and dramatic, and the furnishings weren't nearly as formal. Lorelei was certain the owners of this place had used a professional decorator, but in her opinion, that decorator had lost all grasp of what most people wanted out of a lake house.

Because Lorelei's comment had been directed at Serenity, she was surprised when Finley Hatch—or "Finn" as he'd told them to call him at the door—responded. "It's a bit much, isn't it? The owners are friends of my father's, and gave me and my brothers a steal of a deal, or I would've chosen something else."

Reagan whistled softly as she gazed around. "On the plus side, you could do a lot worse. It's certainly not cramped."

"That's true, I guess," he said. "But who puts white furniture and carpet in a *ski* cabin?"

Lorelei eyed the large chandelier dangling above them. "This isn't a ski cabin—it's a mansion."

It had been an offhand comment, one that didn't really require a response, so she was surprised again when he singled her out. "Where are you from?"

"Me?" She pressed a hand to her chest. "Florida."

"That's a long ways off. Do you come to California very often?"

"This is the first time I've ever left Florida," she told him.

"What about you?" Reagan asked, turning the question back on him. "Where are you from?"

When his eyes shifted to her half sister, Lorelei slowly let her breath go.

"LA, born and raised. My whole family lives there." He gestured at the grouping of furniture around a spectacular rock fireplace, offering them a seat before continuing on to the gourmet kitchen.

They could hear him digging through the drawers behind a large, granite-topped island. Eventually, he came up with a wine opener for one of the bottles Serenity had given him.

Reagan chose a high-backed white leather chair, and Serenity perched on the ottoman, which looked as though it had never been used.

Lorelei tossed a throw over the couch to protect the upholstery before pulling Lucy onto her lap, since they'd just come in from the snow.

"What brings you to Tahoe?" Serenity asked as he took some wineglasses from a rack overhead.

"My older brother was released from the hospital a week ago. Lost his arm in a motorcycle accident. So my other brother and I decided we'd get him out of the heat and the crowds of LA. We're hoping a summer spent up here might encourage him, keep his spirits high, help him recover."

"I'm sorry about his arm," Reagan said.

"He's taking it pretty hard," he admitted as he popped the cork. "He's always been capable, active. Loves to play almost any sport, which he'll have to relearn now, if he can. And he was an actor, so losing his arm impacts a lot of what he had planned for his future."

"That's tragic," Serenity said. "Has he appeared in anything we might know?"

"He's only gotten a few bit parts so far. He was working for our father, managing one of the car dealerships to cover the rent. But he signed with a reputable agent two months ago and felt that was going to make a big difference."

"Is he married?" Lorelei asked. It sounded as though their father was wealthy, so maybe Finn's brother didn't have to worry about his living expenses while he recovered. But the emotional support of having someone who loved him and was committed to him would probably be invaluable.

Finn started to pour the wine. "Not anymore. He went through a divorce last summer. Thank goodness they didn't have any kids, or it would've been even harder."

Since Lorelei was potentially facing a divorce, and she did have a kid, she could easily sympathize.

"Sounds like he's had one hell of a year," Reagan said. "I guess I can quit feeling sorry for myself now."

Before he could respond to Reagan's comment, Serenity said, "It's great that you and your younger brother can take the summer off to be with him through his recovery."

"We won't technically be *off*." He came toward them carrying two glasses. "I'm an artist, so I can work from anywhere. That's partly why this place sounded appealing. There's plenty of room for me to set up my studio. And Nolan, my younger brother, just finished his BA in business at UC Santa Barbara. He's managed to get a part-time job bartending in Truckee, so he'll have to go to work whenever they schedule him. But the commute will take only twenty-five minutes. Then he'll start at one of the dealerships in the fall, once we all go home."

"You don't have anything to do with the dealerships?" Lorelei asked.

"No. I'm sort of the odd man out. I've never been interested in the car business. But you know what they say about struggling artists." He gave them a wry grin. "We'll see if I wind up selling cars for my dad in the end."

Lorelei avoided Finn's gaze when he offered her the first glass. For some reason, he threw her off balance. She figured it was the beauty and appeal of youth. She'd decided that Serenity was right—he was younger than she was, probably by as many as five years.

"What do you paint?" Reagan asked as he went back for the other two glasses.

"Skyscrapers. Cars. Diners. Houses. Inner-city stuff. But it's so gorgeous up here, the lake might tempt me into doing my first nature scene."

"There's a nude beach not far away called Hidden Cove. That might give you some inspiration," Serenity joked.

"Is that where you three ladies will be hanging out?" he joked in return.

"If I didn't have Lucy with me, maybe I would," Lorelei piped up. "I've never been to a nude beach, so at least it would be an experience."

Her response had been impulsive, born of a desire to do something others might *not* agree with just to be that bold, to rebel and flip off the rest of the world for a change. But she wished she'd kept her mouth shut when they all turned to stare at her.

"I'll watch Lucy if you really want to go," Serenity said.

"And I'll go with you," Reagan told her. "If you can't

do something daring with your sister, who can you do it with?"

Lorelei had begun to like Reagan, despite their rocky start. "Okay," she said with a bit more conviction.

"Okay?" Finn echoed in surprise. "Definitely let me know when you do that. I wouldn't want you two to go alone."

They all laughed except Lorelei. "I need to live a little," she said.

The raw honesty in her voice must've given away the fact that she wasn't joking, because he sobered instantly. "What's the riskiest thing you've ever done?"

She thought back over all the years of struggling to walk the high wire that was her life—of how hard she'd always tried not to lose her balance for fear she'd plummet to the ground. "I can't think of anything." She smoothed back Lucy's hair. Just living had been hard enough; she'd always been careful not to do anything that might make it worse. "That's kind of pathetic, isn't it?"

"My mother would say it's better to be safe than sorry," he said.

But his mother didn't know how careful she'd been. "What would *you* say?"

His grin turned slightly devilish. "I'd say you only live once."

Going to a nude beach with a new friend and her sister wasn't any big deal. It wasn't illegal. It wasn't dangerous. And it wasn't immoral—at least according to most people. Not like cheating, anyway. Mark wouldn't approve, but that was partly why it appealed to her. If he could have an affair, certainly she could be audacious enough to visit a nude beach with a neighbor and a half sister. "We'll have to see what the weather does."

"Then I'll hope for sunshine," he said, but she could tell he was teasing.

Reagan changed the subject. "Do you have any samples of your work you could show us? I'd love to see it."

Lorelei was interested, too, but he shook his head. "I only brought the piece I'm working on. And that's nowhere close to being ready to show anyone."

Serenity took a sip of wine. "You must have a website."

"I do." He got the other two glasses from the kitchen. "It's RealArtByFinn.com. Double *n*."

Setting the wine he'd just handed her on a side table, Reagan took out her phone and typed in the URL.

After exclaiming that he was very talented, she passed her phone to Serenity and Lorelei so they could have a look.

His work was good—so good that Lorelei took several minutes to study the pink-and-black small-town diner he'd depicted. It had an old-fashioned neon sign with a giant arrow and a 1950s convertible sitting out front.

It was all so lifelike, so real. At first she thought it had to be a photograph. "This is called photorealism, isn't it?"

He came over to view the screen with her. "Yeah. That diner's in Palm Springs. I took a picture of it once when I was there and decided to paint it. I love the palm trees."

"Me, too." Lorelei hoped he never wound up working for his father; it would be a travesty for him to give up art.

"Thank you."

She used the excuse of returning Reagan's phone to be able to get up and move away from him. When she sat back down, he asked if Lucy would like some lemonade. Lorelei requested water instead and, fortunately, Lucy didn't complain. She seemed a little awed by Finn, too. She'd been uncharacteristically quiet since they arrived and gave him a shy smile when he brought the water.

"I hope you won't be too sore tomorrow after all the shoveling you did this morning," Serenity said. "Especially since it looks like it's going to warm up, which means it'll melt quickly on its own."

"I thought my brothers were coming, so I had to do it. Davis would never allow me to help him into the cabin like some kind of invalid. He'd insist on walking in on his own even if he'd lost a leg instead of an arm. And with all the ice and snow on the front steps, I was afraid he'd fall."

"He sounds stubborn," Serenity said.

"He is." Finn rolled his eyes in exasperation. "And right now he's angry, which makes him a bear to deal with. But once he gets over the anger, I'm hoping that fighting spirit of his will give him the determination he needs to rebuild his life."

Lorelei could hear the affection behind those words. "You seem close to your brothers."

"We fought a lot when we were younger, which is probably typical. But we're close now. We're still not too thrilled with our stepmother, though..."

"What's wrong with her?" Reagan asked.

"She's only six years older than me, for one. The rest, you can probably guess. But our real mom is great.

She's a nurse. Matter of fact, she was on duty the night the ambulance brought Davis in."

As a mother herself, Lorelei couldn't help cringing. "They took him to *her* hospital?"

"That was the closest one."

"It would be so hard to see your child like that!"

"I'm sure it was, but she's a professional. She keeps saying it could've been much worse, that we should be grateful." He went back to the kitchen, poured a bag of tortilla chips into a bowl and put them in the middle of the large dining table. "*I* can look at it that way, and so can Nolan," he said. "I mean, Davis is alive, and he could've died. But Davis isn't capable of that perspective quite yet. Right now, he feels he'd rather have died."

"Will it be possible for him to get an artificial limb?" Reagan asked.

He went back into the kitchen. "Should be, but his doctor wants to wait until the residual limb heals fully from the surgery. That could be anywhere from two to six months. So we figure, if all goes well and Davis doesn't develop any infection, he should be ready by fall." He waved them over to the table, where he had some guacamole and salsa waiting with the chips. Lorelei was glad there was something Serenity could eat.

She helped Lucy put some chips on her plate. "Why didn't Davis come up this weekend?"

"Couldn't. His temperature climbed a few degrees, so the doctor asked him to wait." He gestured toward them with the chip he was about to dip. "So what about the three of you? Serenity told me you're half sisters, but I can't figure out who's the oldest."

"That would be Serenity," Reagan said. "She and I are only six months apart. Lorelei's two years younger."

"*Six* months apart?" he echoed in confusion. "So… you're related through your father?"

"We don't know," Serenity said. "We met for the first time yesterday."

"You're not all from Florida?"

"Just Lorelei," Reagan said. "I was born in Ohio but live in New York City now, and Serenity's from Berkeley."

He ran his free hand over the beard growth on his jaw as he considered this information. "Sounds like an interesting story. Do I get to hear more?"

Lorelei tensed. Talking about her childhood was like reopening an old wound. She didn't like the questions it elicited, since she didn't have any answers, and she didn't like the pity that it engendered. She wanted Finn to like her, to admire her the way she admired him.

But she didn't know how to avoid going down that road tonight. Reagan and Serenity would have no reason *not* to. They didn't have anything to be embarrassed about, so they didn't understand what being abandoned at such a young age did to a person. How it made her believe she was so flawed even her own mother couldn't love her, and made her afraid that others would see the same unforgivable imperfections—whatever they were.

So when Serenity started to explain, Lorelei got up and led Lucy over to the windows, where she tried to tune out the other voices in the room. "We're going to go on the lake in small little boats with paddles if it's warm enough by the end of our trip," she told her daughter. "Would you like that?"

Lucy pointed at the water. "Out there?"

Lorelei kissed her soft, round cheek. "Yep."

"Can we do it tomorrow?" she asked, jumping up and down.

"Probably not while there's snow on the ground, but maybe in a few days."

"I like it here," she said. "Don't you?"

Lorelei gazed out at the spectacular view. She could see why Finn would want to bring his injured brother to Tahoe. There was a magical quality about the lake—about this whole area. The peace and beauty reminded her to be more grateful for the simple things in life: her health, having good people around her, having enough food to eat and clean air to breathe. It also encouraged her to have the determination to push forward regardless of anything that stood in her way—not only to survive but *thrive*. "I do," she said.

Lucy's little arms slipped around her neck. "Can we stay forever?"

Surprised by the question, Lorelei studied her daughter's face. "Daddy would never be able to leave his job to join us," she said at length.

But if her marriage ended in divorce, who could say where she might live or what she might do?

New adventures could be waiting just around the corner.

Certainly, those adventures wouldn't include anything as drastic as moving to Tahoe permanently. Lorelei doubted she'd be legally permitted to take Lucy so far from her father, even if she wanted to. But she would no longer have to live her life with Mark at the center of it—like a planet orbiting the sun. She wouldn't have to stop what she was doing the minute he got off work. Wouldn't have to cook and clean with the goal of pleasing him in mind. Wouldn't have to live where he wanted to live.

She would have a second chance to choose what *she* wanted to do with her life and what she wanted to be.

The possibility of positive change instead of negative change made her feel something she hadn't felt since she'd learned about Francine.

She was pretty sure it was a trace of hope—and maybe even a little excitement.

11

reagan

Reagan wanted this night to be like any other evening spent enjoying a drink with friends. But every time she started to reach for her wine, she'd think about the possibility of being pregnant and hold off, just in case.

"What a story," Finn said after she and Serenity had explained why they'd had their DNA tested. "I can see why you might not want to tell your parents that you've found each other, but that's a pretty big secret. Could you really keep your mouths shut indefinitely?"

"I don't know," Serenity said. "Secrets don't come naturally to me, which is why I've made a profession of unearthing them. Would *you* be able to stay quiet?"

"I guess that would depend on what I found," he replied.

Reagan could hear Lorelei talking to Lucy. She had moved to the couch with her daughter and taken an iPad out of her bag. They were playing some sort of learning game. But Lorelei could do that with her daughter anytime. Reagan found it odd that she wasn't more engaged in the conversation.

Finn must've wondered about that, too, because he gestured toward her and Lucy as he leaned back in his chair, lifting it off its front legs. "So Lorelei's the one who contacted you both? Why did she get her DNA tested?"

Thinking of what had transpired earlier, when they'd had all their pictures and other memorabilia scattered on the table, Reagan turned to see if Lorelei had heard the question and would answer.

When she didn't even look back at them, Serenity jumped in. "Her childhood was…considerably more difficult than ours."

"She grew up in foster care, and took the test hoping to find her parents." Reagan assumed answering his question would be the quickest way to move on, so when Serenity shot her a warning look, she lifted her palms. "It's not a secret. And there's no shame in it."

"I was two years old when I was found wandering a busy street in downtown Orlando."

This came from Lorelei. They all turned to her, surprised that she'd finally spoken up. She stood so stiffly as she faced them that Reagan wondered if Finn could tell how much her background still affected her.

"My parents abandoned me," she added, in a tone even more forthright than the one Reagan had used.

"You don't know that," Serenity said.

Lorelei attempted a shrug, but it hardly came off as careless. "That's the assumption."

"Disney is in Orlando, isn't it?" Finn said. "Are you sure you didn't just wander away while your family was on vacation?"

"If that'd happened, wouldn't someone have gone to the police?" she asked.

He put his chair back down. "No one reported you missing?"

"No."

Reagan could tell he was at a loss for words. "I'm sorry" was so inadequate. It also smacked of pity, and she doubted Lorelei would appreciate that—especially coming from him. Reagan was glad when he didn't go in that direction.

"Maybe you weren't at Disney World. Maybe you were being raised by your grandmother and she had a heart attack and died, and you somehow got outside," he suggested.

Lorelei's eyebrows slid up.

After squirming a bit, he tried to retract the idea. "Sorry. That's not a happy scenario. I'm just saying that anything's possible."

"You were only trying to be nice," Reagan murmured to him. "Most possibilities aren't very pleasant. That's the problem."

"You're married now, though, right?" Finn asked Lorelei.

He must've seen the ring on her finger.

"Yes."

Reagan sent Serenity a guarded glance. Finn was heading toward another dangerous subject.

"Is your husband here, too, or—"

"He's back in Florida, working."

"He didn't mind that you were coming out here?"

"He wasn't thrilled about it, but not because he was opposed to it, exactly. It just wasn't a good time for me to be away."

Finn hesitated as though he wanted to ask why. That was the next logical question. But when Lorelei didn't volunteer the information, he probably figured it would be too intrusive. "How long will you be staying?" he asked instead.

"Lucy and I go home on Friday."

Finn turned to Serenity and Reagan. "What about you two?"

"I'm leaving at the same time," Reagan replied. "We arranged it so we could drive to the airport together."

"And I'll be going back to the Bay Area once they've left," Serenity said.

"Damn." He scowled at them. "I was hoping you'd all be here when Davis arrived, and I'm not sure he'll make it before then."

"I wish we could be," Reagan said. "I'd love to meet him."

"Do you have to go back so soon?" he asked. "For work, or whatever?"

Reagan almost said yes. But then she realized that wasn't strictly accurate. If she quit her job, there'd be no reason to return right away. "Not for the job I have now," she hedged.

"Then you should stay longer. You, too," he said to Serenity.

"I could put off going home for a few days, since I can work out of the cabin. I'm here a lot, anyway, especially during the warmer months. We could even take Davis out on my parents' boat one Saturday, if you think he'd enjoy it."

"I bet he'd love it," Finn said. "I'm sure he'd really like all of you, and he could certainly use some friends. Because he didn't know you from before, there'd be no awkwardness, no sense of him being less than he was, no need to try to act like his old self. He could just be the dude he is right now—a man trying to recover from the loss of his arm. If that makes any sense."

"It makes perfect sense," Lorelei said. "I think they should stay longer, too. I wish I could."

Was she serious? Reagan exchanged another glance with Serenity.

"You'd both be welcome," Serenity said, sounding completely sincere. "You could even stay for the whole summer."

Lorelei seemed hesitant, but when Serenity continued to encourage her, she finally smiled more brightly. "Another week or two probably wouldn't hurt."

Reagan couldn't believe her ears. "Really?"

Lorelei bent to kiss the top of her daughter's head. "Why not? I think having a little more time to myself would be a good thing, given…given my situation. Don't you?"

"*I* do," Serenity said. "As long as my parents aren't planning to come up—and they'd tell me if they were—there's no reason we can't stay as long as we want. So…" She turned to Reagan. "Does that mean you'll stay longer, too?"

Reagan's mind raced. They could reschedule their flights. There might be some cost involved, but it shouldn't be too much. What about her job situation, though? "Even if I quit at Edison & Curry, like I plan to, I'll have to apply somewhere else."

"Right away?" Serenity pressed.

"Not right away, I guess." Reagan had always been conservative with her finances. Although it worried her to use her reserves, she figured she could survive without an income for several months, if necessary.

"When will you ever get another chance to stay in Tahoe?" Lorelei asked.

Reagan twisted around to look at her and Lucy. "That's true. I could stay for a little longer, but I'd feel lazy or self-indulgent if I stayed the whole summer."

Lorelei left Lucy playing her game on the couch and returned to the table. "Maybe you owe it to yourself to take a good long break. Maybe that would be just the thing. Think of what it would be like to spend three whole months here—what we could make of it."

"And that is…" Reagan prompted.

"A perfect summer," she answered.

A slight smile curved Serenity's lips. "Wow. You could knock me over with a feather."

"I can't believe it myself," Lorelei said with a self-conscious laugh. "But staying doesn't have to be an ironclad commitment. If we aren't getting along or enjoying ourselves, or your parents or other siblings want to use the cabin, we could leave earlier rather than later."

"That's true," Finn said, obviously hoping to persuade them.

Serenity scooped some more guacamole onto her plate. "Then we'll leave that open as a possibility and see how things go."

* * *

reagan

"That was really enjoyable." Reagan was the only one who wasn't slightly tipsy as they walked back to Serenity's cabin. After they'd eaten dinner, they'd stayed late and Serenity, Lorelei and Finn had finished off a third bottle of wine. Reagan wished she could've had a glass with them, but she didn't regret one minute of the time they'd spent laughing and talking. She couldn't remember ever feeling so relaxed or having more fun. For once, she hadn't been trying to pull away early to get some work done, hadn't been more concerned with emptying her inbox or the fact that she had to manage some sleep so she could beat everyone into the office in the morning.

It was a nice change to be relieved of the constant pressure. She'd always had something to do, ever since she was a child. First it was her school assignments and swim meets and debate team. Then it was tackling the working world and fighting her way up the corporate ladder.

Tonight reminded her that maybe there might be other things out there, things that would prove far more meaningful to her in the end.

She wondered why her driven and creative mother had never been concerned about balance. Maybe it was because she was so bad at it. She had only one gear and that was to push as hard as she could—*always*. And she expected her daughter to do the same. Rosalind had only been proud of Reagan when Reagan out-competed everyone else—set the record at her high school for the hundred-meter butterfly, raised the curve in English class or obtained an academic scholarship for college.

Reagan felt they'd both been missing out on the kinds of relationships that enriched everything else—even when it came to each other. Their conversations were so superficial. When was the last time they'd really talked? *Really* connected?

Maybe they never had. Her mother wasn't an easy person to connect with. She was too stoic, driven and goal-oriented. And Reagan had turned out just like her. There'd been periods when Reagan had tried to remind herself to slow down, so she wouldn't miss out on the best years of her life. But before she knew it she was once again canceling lunch with her friends, skipping their calls and even forgetting to eat dinner in pursuit of being the best in her chosen field.

Inevitably, she'd allowed her life to be narrowed down to one primary focus. Edison & Curry.

And Drew.

If nothing else, she hoped what'd happened would serve as a wake-up call that she had to do more than work twenty-four/seven. Maybe now that she had the support of two sisters, they'd remind her, act as a counterbalance.

But if she was going to have a baby, that would force the issue...

"Spending more time in Tahoe might help me gain a better perspective," she said as Serenity let them in.

"So you're really considering staying?" Serenity asked. "I wasn't sure."

What would it be like, Reagan wondered, to spend more than a week with Lorelei and Serenity? So far, everything hadn't been *completely* smooth between them, but there were characteristics about each that made her like them, admire them or at least sympathize.

And if she *was* pregnant she'd have some tough decisions to make. She could see herself working that out better here than when she was back in New York, starting a new job and facing the prospect of telling her bosses that she'd soon need maternity leave.

"I am," she said. "Preparing my resume and going through the application process feels like too steep a mountain to climb at the moment, anyway. Maybe I should step back and examine whether I want to continue in the direction I'm currently headed before I do anything else."

"That's how I feel," Lorelei said. "I need to decide what I really want out of life. We're all at a crossroads in one way or another. We missed out on growing up together, but maybe we were meant to find each other at this particular stage of our lives. Maybe everything will change from here on. Maybe we will all reinvent ourselves."

That was an appealing thought. Reagan liked it. She was surprised it was Lorelei who was talking that way, though. She'd gotten the impression that Lorelei had also allowed her life to be distilled into only one focus—Mark. And her daughter, of course, who'd fallen asleep on Finn's couch much earlier and was currently in her mother's arms.

"You go in first," Serenity said to Lorelei, in deference to her heavy load as she swung open the door.

At four years old, Lucy wasn't outrageously heavy, but she couldn't be easy to carry, even if it was just from next door. Finn had tried to get Lorelei to let him bring Lucy home for her, but she'd insisted on doing it, said she'd be fine. Since Reagan could tell Lorelei really liked Finn, she wasn't sure why she hadn't let him help.

Brushing past them, Lorelei climbed the first flight of stairs and then the second to put her daughter to bed. Reagan could hear her footsteps as she moved briskly upward.

"I can't believe Lorelei's thinking about staying longer," Reagan said when she was out of earshot. "I never saw that coming."

"Neither did I," Serenity agreed. "But she's never had any family, so, in a way, it makes sense. Even if she stays all summer, three months can't replace a whole childhood, but it would be *something*. I'm glad she wants to be with us."

"I agree. I'd love to help Finn by befriending Davis this summer, but I'm staying for you and her more than I am him." After being so independent and comfortable on her own, Reagan found it surprising that she was warming up to the idea of having sisters. But Serenity and Lorelei could offer her something her mother couldn't—family that wasn't quite so difficult to get along with, family who came from her own generation and understood life in that context, family members that were willing to be more vulnerable, and therefore more accessible, than her strict mother.

"I bet Mark thinks he's all she's got, that he could never lose her," Serenity mused.

Reagan let her lips curve into a devilish smile. "But we're going to show him she's got sisters now."

As soon as they reached the main floor, they both dropped onto the soft leather couch.

"Do you think your mother will be okay with you staying here longer?" Serenity asked. "It's only been a month since her surgery. Isn't she still recovering?"

"She's recovering in the sense that it was fairly recent. But she's already back at work, which means I'd hardly see her even if I was closer. She works long hours and never misses a day." Reagan pictured her mother, who was almost as tall as she was and always so well turned-out, so in command of herself and all those around her.

"You live within twenty miles of each other and don't see her very often?"

"She's busy. I'm busy. I go to her place in the Hamptons for dinner the first Sunday of each month. So, depending on how long I stay here, I'll miss up to three visits. She'd never admit this, but she'll probably be relieved that she doesn't have to reserve that time for me and can use it to get caught up on email and other things before the new workweek starts."

"I'm a little shocked that you're not closer. You're all she has."

"She should never have had children. It's her job she loves." That statement made Reagan wonder if maybe she wasn't cut out for kids, either. What kind of mother would *she* be? And would she soon find out?

She couldn't help touching her stomach. She desperately hoped she *wasn't* pregnant. How would she face a pregnancy on top of having to look for a new job?

Serenity propped her feet on the coffee table. "Surely your mother loves you."

"In her own way," Reagan allowed. "She loves me a lot more when I do what she wants. Otherwise, she criticizes every decision I make. I swear, when we eat together I can't even hold my fork right—according to her, anyway."

"She's a very successful woman who's made something of herself and wants you to do the same, I guess."

Which meant she'd be *so* disappointed if Reagan had to tell her she was pregnant as well as jobless. "She wants me to be a reflection of her. But I could use a break from trying to match what she's accomplished.

I've always tried to be a good daughter, but I'm tired of feeling like I'll never measure up."

"What will she say when she learns you're quitting your job—and not coming home on Friday?"

"She'll go quiet. Then she'll say something like, 'That's a long time to be off work. Shouldn't you get back and start applying right away? You know how difficult it is in your industry. You've told me that yourself.'"

"Sounds…polite."

"It won't feel that way. It'll feel as though she's screaming, 'That's the stupidest decision you've ever made!'"

"Is there any chance she'll change your mind?" Serenity asked.

"There's *always* a chance," Reagan replied with a mirthless laugh. "After all, her tactics have worked on me for thirty-five years. And we *are* making the decision to stay here awfully fast. We've only known each other for two days."

"No, we met months ago—online, anyway. And as Lorelei said at Finn's, it doesn't have to be an ironclad commitment that we stay all summer. You can play it by ear and leave whenever you want to."

"True. But we'll have to take the rental back to Reno even if we don't catch our flight. We can't pay for it all summer."

"There's no need to. One car for three of us should be enough. For the few times more than one person needs to use it, we can Uber. And I can take you to the airport whenever you want to leave."

"Staying would be a fabulous escape from what we're each going through at the moment."

"Yes, a time-out. One we could all use." Serenity pulled a lap blanket onto their legs. "Your mother should be able to understand the need for you to get away."

"Don't count on it."

Serenity sighed. "It's almost impossible to escape the beliefs our parents instill in us, isn't it?"

"It is. For some, those beliefs can amount to a prison."

"So by quitting your job and staying here, you'll be breaking out of that prison and establishing your independence. You need to remember that when you talk to your mom."

She needed to remember a lot of things. Staying in Tahoe would give her up to three months during which she couldn't break down and see Drew. That was a positive. Maybe she'd be able to figure out how to stop her mother's disapproval from shoving her around like a playground bully. Another positive.

She was so much more decisive and confident with everyone else…

But quitting her job without a clear plan seemed foolish. She could see why her mother would view it that way, too, which left her on unsteady ground.

"Maybe I'll stay for just a month," she mused. By then she'd know if she was pregnant. She planned to buy a test as soon as she could get to a store.

Lorelei came down the stairs.

"Lucy all set for the night?" Serenity asked.

"Yeah."

Reagan scooted over so that Lorelei could join them on the couch. There were other chairs in the room, but Serenity shared her lap blanket with the two of them, and they sat side by side, staring out at the stars, which shone far more brightly away from city lights than any

Reagan had ever seen. She loved New York, but she was going to enjoy being here for a while longer. "When are you telling Mark that you're not coming home on Friday?" she asked Lorelei.

"Maybe tomorrow," Lorelei said.

"He hasn't tried to call you tonight?" Serenity asked.

"He's tried. Many times."

Reagan couldn't remember ever seeing her step out of the room or talk on her phone. "You didn't pick up?"

Lorelei combed her fingers through her hair but never shifted her gaze from the large windows that showcased such a spectacular chunk of sky. "We were having too much fun."

Because of Finn. Reagan hid a smile. Lorelei liked him, all right. Reagan didn't expect that to go anywhere. But she couldn't help taking a little joy in the fact that being ignored must've come as a terrible shock to Mark.

12

serenity

Everyone else in the cabin was asleep as Serenity tried to compose a text to her mother. Despite Charlotte's concerns about Serenity "closeting herself away" and not getting right back into the dating scene, she doubted her mother would mind if she spent the entire summer at the cabin. Her parents had made it clear the cabin was hers to use as often as she wanted. And if that didn't make her feel free enough—if she wanted even more of her mother's support—all she had to do was mention Finn and his brothers staying next door. Charlotte had such a soft heart—she would sympathize with what had happened to Davis and be all for Serenity staying to befriend him.

Of course, she'd also hope that something romantic might spring up between Serenity and one of the Hatch brothers. Her mother wouldn't be able to relax until Serenity found another mate.

But secretly meeting her new half sisters already

smacked of deceit. Would entertaining Reagan and Lorelei at the cabin all summer be going too far?

Serenity preferred to tell the truth and get her mother's blessing. They'd always been honest with each other, which was why she still couldn't believe that Charlotte had hidden such a big secret for so long.

Mom, I need to talk to you about something. It's a touchy subject, one that might upset you, which is why I haven't said anything so far. To be honest, I'm sort of confused and upset myself. I couldn't believe it when...

Puffing out her cheeks, she deleted all of that before blowing her breath out and starting over.

Mom, you know that a lot of people are getting their DNA tested these days, right? Well, they're finding family members they never knew existed. The police are even using ancestry sites to locate suspects about whom they've been storing biological evidence. You heard about The Golden State killer and how they finally captured him. Anyway, I decided to get my profile done, to see how it all works so I could depict it accurately in my writing and...

She stopped, read it over and deleted it again. That wasn't what she wanted to say. What she really wanted to say, from her heart, was simply, Mom, why didn't you tell me?

She typed that but knew she couldn't send it, either. If she could've gone to her mother, she would've done it already. She couldn't have Charlotte working to cover up what she was hoping to find—which Charlotte might do, if having Serenity learn the truth really scared her.

And what if Charlotte freaked out and didn't want her to have anything to do with Lorelei and Reagan? They had just decided to prolong their trip, possibly for the whole summer. She couldn't suddenly kick them out after encouraging them to stay.

She went to delete that text—and her heart jumped into her throat. Instead of selecting all the content to delete it, her thumb accidentally hit the Send button.

Shit!

She covered her mouth for several minutes as she stared at her phone, eyes wide, to see if her mother was going to respond. She'd still been a little tipsy, which was why her errant thumb hit the wrong spot in the first place, but she was feeling completely sober now.

No response.

She hadn't awakened her mother, but that text would be there, waiting for Charlotte in the morning. There was no way to un-send it.

Damn it! What have I done?

She climbed out of bed and began to pace in her room. What was she going to say when her mother called to ask about it?

She couldn't think of an appropriate response. She couldn't tell her mother the truth, not yet.

Her pulse raced as she struggled to come up with some way to neutralize what she'd just done.

Another text?

Forget that...

Never mind...

That was intended for someone else...

None of those things would be believable. She'd obviously known who she was texting. She'd started the text with, "Mom."

She was still pacing, trying to come up with something that would appease her mother when she heard crying.

Stopping, she held her breath so she could listen more carefully.

Sure enough, someone was awake.

Taking her phone with her, just in case Charlotte called, she left the room to find Lucy in the hall, frightened and disoriented in the unfamiliar, dark house. "I don't know where my mom is," she said in a distressed whimper.

The wine had probably put Lorelei into a deeper sleep than usual. There was no need to disturb her. After sending that text, Serenity was afraid she'd be up for the rest of the night, anyway.

"Her room is right here next to yours." Serenity walked her to the door to show her just how close. "This one," she said, pointing. "But she's very tired and sleeping. Would it be okay if I lie down with you and we read a few books until you're ready to go back to sleep?"

Lucy seemed skeptical as she wiped her cheeks. "I have to go potty."

Serenity glanced at her phone. Still no response from Charlotte. "Okay. I can take you. Come on."

She led her new niece to the bathroom and helped her pull up her panties and straighten her pajamas when she was finished. "Feel better?"

Although her face was still streaked with tears, Lucy nodded. "What books do you have?" she asked, sounding more amenable to Serenity's suggestion.

"I got some Dr. Seuss books out of storage." Serenity snapped on the lamp in Lucy's room. "Some others, as well." She gestured at the stack on the nightstand. "Let's have a look."

With a sniff, Lucy wiped her face again and chose *Where the Wild Things Are* before allowing Serenity to lift her into bed.

Serenity climbed beneath the covers, too, and read one book after another—all while keeping a frequent, worried eye on her phone.

"Is someone going to call you?" Lucy asked with a yawn.

The question alone caused the knots in Serenity's stomach to tighten.

"I'm thinking I might hear from my mother," she said ruefully.

"You have a mother, too?"

The question surprised Serenity. Everyone had a mother—except Lorelei, she realized. Lucy was so young. Maybe she thought that once you became an adult you no longer had one. "I do. Your mother had a mother, too. But we don't know what happened to her."

"Will I ever get to see her?"

Serenity wasn't sure how to answer that. "I don't know. Does your father have a mom?"

"Yes."

"Do you ever get to see your grandma and grandpa?"

"We go there sometimes."

"Do you also have aunts and uncles?"

She nodded. "Lots."

All of that was on her father's side. Her mother had had no parents or siblings, until recently. No wonder Lorelei wanted to stay in Tahoe, wanted to connect with her past and the people who shared her DNA.

Once again, Serenity considered just how difficult it would be to grow up as Lorelei had. And hearing that Mark still had his parents, as well as many brothers and sisters, only made her more upset with him for letting Lorelei down.

For their next book, Serenity chose *Are You My Mother?* and couldn't help wondering if Lorelei had ever read this book—it would likely have a sad echo for her. But it seemed to be Lucy's favorite. Serenity had to read it three times before her niece finally nodded off.

Once Lucy had fallen asleep, Serenity slipped out from under the covers, trying not to jiggle the mattress. But she paused to look back at the sleeping little girl before turning off the light. "Good night," she whispered and checked her phone once again.

Still nothing from Charlotte, but Serenity went back to her room determined to come up with something to correct the mistake she'd made by sending that text—even if her explanation was a lie. She had to make her mother believe that her simple, heartfelt question meant something completely innocuous, had to protect Lorelei and Reagan long enough to get the answers they sought.

* * *

lorelei

It was bright and early, before even Lucy got up, when banging on the door woke Lorelei. She gazed at the ceiling for a few seconds, trying to orient herself, then jumped out of bed. She'd been hoping to sleep in, didn't want whoever was so rudely interrupting the household to disturb Lucy before she woke up on her own.

"Damn it," she muttered, and yanked on a pair of yoga pants and a sweatshirt.

She flew down the stairs as Reagan and Serenity both appeared on the landing looking as disheveled from sleep and irritated by the noise as she was.

"What's going on?" Reagan asked. "We've only been in bed for, what, four hours?"

"I can't imagine it's Finn," Lorelei said. "He went to bed late, too."

"Who else could it be?" Reagan asked.

Lorelei reached for the knob, but the mystery was solved before she could even turn it. After the door rattled with another solid knock, a deep voice called out, "Washoe County Sheriff's Office."

Lorelei whipped around to look up at Serenity.

"Go ahead and open it," Serenity said, clearly concerned as she started to descend.

Lorelei did as she was told and soon found herself facing a stocky deputy, about six feet tall, in a dark green uniform. "What can I do for you, Officer?"

He glanced down at a paper he held in his hands. "Are you Lorelei Cipriano?"

"I am," she said in confusion. "How—"

"And do you have your daughter with you?" he broke in.

"Of course." She gestured behind her. "She's upstairs sleeping. Is there a problem?" She craned her neck to see what was on the paper he held. "Why do you have a picture of me?"

"Your husband emailed it to us. He's been worried

about you. Said he hasn't been able to reach you for more than twenty-four hours."

Reagan's footsteps sounded on the stairs as she hurried to join them. "Mark called the cops?"

"Apparently," Lorelei muttered.

"He wanted us to do a wellness check, said you're away from home for the first time and haven't been answering your phone," the officer explained. "We're just making sure you're safe."

"Yes, I'm fine," she assured him. "Lucy is, too. We were out to dinner last night, so I had my phone turned off—that's all. I'll contact my husband today."

"I'm sure he'll be happy to hear from you."

"Thanks for going to the trouble of…of coming out here, especially so early on a Sunday morning," she said.

The deputy must've been satisfied with what he saw, because he angled his head to acknowledge her comment, wished them a good day and left.

After closing the door, Lorelei leaned against it. "What was Mark thinking? It's three hours later in Florida, almost nine, but still. It's not as if I've been out of touch for *days*."

"If you typically respond right away, I could see where he'd worry."

She got the impression Serenity was trying to be diplomatic. "Enough to bother the cops?"

Reagan covered a yawn. "He's not used to being ignored."

"True. I've let him be the center of my universe for too long. He's gotten a little too comfortable there."

"Are you going to call him?" Serenity asked.

"I'll text him," she said. "Then I'm going back to bed."

She shoved away from the door and shuffled wearily to the stairs when she heard her daughter's small voice.

"Mommy, is it morning time?"

Lorelei's heart sank as she looked up to see Lucy peeking through the bars of the banister. She'd been awakened, after all. Because of Mark, Lorelei wasn't going to get the chance to sleep any more this morning.

She wanted to tell her daughter to go back to bed, but she knew that wouldn't be easy for Lucy, who was wide-awake and ready for the day.

"Yes, it's morning," she said with a sigh. "Are you hungry?"

Lucy clung tightly to the railing as she started down. "Yes. Can I have eggs?"

"You bet." Lorelei waited for her daughter to reach the bottom of the stairs before leading her into the kitchen. She assumed her sisters would both go back to bed. They were tired, too. But Reagan joined her and put on a pot of coffee.

"You're not going to get some sleep?" Lorelei asked.

"I'll hang out with you," she replied. "Or why don't you grab a few more hours? I'll make Lucy's eggs. Having breakfast together will give us a chance to get to know each other better, won't it, Lucy?"

"I want them sunny-side up," Lucy said.

Reagan cringed. "What about some good old-fashioned scrambled eggs? I don't think I could go wrong with those."

Lorelei chuckled. It was obvious that Reagan had never had kids. "She likes them with a soft yolk and a piece of toast for dipping."

Reagan wrinkled her nose as if she didn't quite know

where to start. "I'm not much of a cook. But I should be able to manage that. Or a bowl of cold cereal. Or a bagel."

"It's okay. I'll do it," Lorelei said. But after she slid the eggs onto Lucy's plate, Reagan prevailed on her to go back to bed.

"I've got it now," she said. "Once I'm awake, I can't go back to sleep, anyway. So Lucy and I will play a game. Everything will be fine. Go! Sleep!"

Lorelei walked toward the stairs, but before she got there, she doubled back to give Reagan an impulsive hug for her thoughtfulness. "Thank you."

"That's what sisters are for," Reagan said with a smile.

* * *

reagan

"Aunt Reagan?"

Reagan's stomach was a ball of nerves, and she had a tinny taste in her mouth from having drunk too much coffee without eating. She'd just finished typing her resignation, had been staring at her computer screen for the last five minutes, trying to work up the nerve to send it. But the impatience in Lucy's voice told her this wasn't the first time the little girl had tried to get her attention.

"What?" She spoke mildly, despite the angst inside her. She had too many memories of her mother responding in a harsh, irritated voice when she'd been interrupted to want to perpetuate that behavior with another child.

Lorelei's daughter held up a sheet of the paper Reagan had given her. "Do you like it?"

After rubbing her eyes to help ease her tiredness, Reagan made a show of studying the picture Lucy had drawn with some colored markers Reagan had found in a kitchen "catch-all" drawer. "I love it," she said. "It's *very* pretty. What is it?"

"It's *you*!" She sounded slightly offended that Reagan couldn't immediately see the likeness.

"Oh, right," Reagan said. "Of course. The big head. The pointy nose. The purple mouth." She noted the stick figure body Lucy had given her. "At least you made me skinny."

"Yeah," Lucy said as if she understood what that meant and had done it intentionally.

"Who are you going to draw next? Aunt Serenity?" Reagan imagined posting their humbling portraits on the fridge so they could joke about them throughout the summer.

Lucy pushed the picture of Reagan out of the way so she could start on her next masterpiece. "No, Mommy."

Resting her chin on her fist, Reagan watched as Lucy drew another giant circle for the head. "Hmm. I get the feeling Mommy and I will look a lot alike."

"Yeah," she said again, without glancing up.

"What's that?" Reagan pointed at some squiggly lines around Lorelei's mouth. It appeared as though Lucy was giving Lorelei a beard.

"That's ice cream," Lucy explained.

Reagan hid a smile. The fact that she could feel like cracking up at this particular moment surprised her. She'd been on the verge of tears a few seconds ago. But this little girl's innocence and honesty, and her wide-open heart, were endearing.

"Hey, how are you two doing?"

Reagan twisted around. Lorelei had entered the kitchen in a robe.

"Great. Look what Lucy's drawn."

"I like it," she said.

"That's *me*," Reagan pointed out.

Lorelei paused at the table to take a closer look. "Of course. I recognized you instantly."

When Lorelei managed to keep a straight face, Reagan arched her eyebrows. "Oh, yeah? Well, this is you. You have ice cream on your face."

They exchanged a grin. Then Lorelei kissed her daughter's head and moved to the counter to pour herself a cup of coffee. "Where's Serenity?"

"Still sleeping, I guess. We haven't heard from her."

"I don't blame her. I was out in seconds, could've slept all day."

"Then you should've stayed in bed. We were doing okay down here."

"I didn't want to strand you for too long. Not when you were doing such a nice thing." She used the cup in her hand to indicate the computer. "What have you been doing while Lucy draws? Getting caught up on work?"

Just being reminded of her resignation made Reagan's stomach churn again. "Not exactly." She angled her computer so Lorelei could read the subject line.

"Oh. I see." Suddenly very serious, she sat down next to Reagan. "How are you feeling about it?"

She felt like shit, but she didn't say so. How could she complain to Lorelei? "It is what it is."

Lorelei leaned closer to the computer, reading.

"You're not sending it to Drew? I thought he was your boss."

"He is, in a way. He's one of the four partners, but he's not the managing partner. I'm afraid he'd just kick it back to me, refuse to accept it or use it as an excuse to get me involved with him again. I need to send it to Gary in order to put a quick end to...to everything."

"I admire you," Lorelei said.

Reagan scoffed. "How could you, of all people, admire me?"

"I do. For the way you're handling the situation. But—" Lorelei squeezed her arm "—are you *positive* this is how you want to proceed? It makes it all feel very...permanent."

Reagan swallowed against a dry throat. "That's why I haven't been able to bring myself to send it yet. But it's what I need to do, right?"

"You're the only one who can answer that question."

She nodded. "Yeah, it's what I need to do."

Compassion filled Lorelei's eyes. "I'm sorry."

"It's my own fault," she said and slid the computer back in front of her. "Like you said last night, maybe this will be a good thing. Maybe we're all meant to go in a different direction from here."

"Maybe. But that probably depends on what you want most out of life."

"I honestly couldn't tell you what I want because so much of what I've done has been to please my mother." She watched Lucy change from the purple marker to the blue one. "I'm about to quit my job, which could damage my entire career, and yet the biggest concern I have is telling her. There's something wrong with that, right?"

"I don't know. I've never had a mother. But I have

plenty of experience with trying to meet everyone's expectations so they won't reject me. It's easy to become a slave to that—to lose yourself in it."

Reagan could only imagine how much heavier the burden she carried would be if she were trying to please everyone and not just her mother. "I agree. This is where I draw the line, regardless of what my mother will think. Drew doesn't belong to me. I need to stay away from him," she said and, fixing a picture of Sally—and Drew's three children—firmly in her mind, she pressed Send.

13

serenity

Although she'd been up most of the night, Serenity had crashed hard after the police came by. When she finally woke, she saw that she'd missed three calls from her mother.

With a groan, Serenity got up to use the bathroom, procrastinating, for just a little while, the moment when she'd call her mother back. She needed a few seconds to prepare for what was coming.

Then, as she sagged back onto the bed, she hit the button that would return her mother's call.

Charlotte answered on the first ring. "Serenity, there you are! What's going on? I've been so worried about you."

"Everything's fine, Mom. Sorry for the scare. I met a new friend last night, and we had a little too much to drink." She laughed awkwardly. "Otherwise, I wouldn't have bothered you in the middle of the night."

"It's okay. I didn't see your text until this morning, anyway."

At which point she'd called immediately. Serenity had such a loving, caring mother—and Lorelei had no one playing that role for her.

"So what's wrong?" her mother asked. "Who did you meet?"

Fortunately, those questions had come rapid-fire, allowing Serenity to answer the second one instead of the first. "A guy, actually."

"A guy?" her mother echoed, showing a bit of excitement. "Is he cute?"

"Very. And he's renting the cabin next door."

"How lucky! What's his name?"

"Finley Hatch."

"And you like him?"

"He seems nice, yes."

"I'm so happy to hear this. After what Sean did… Well, you deserve better."

Serenity winced at the compliment. She hated being deceitful, especially with her mother. She also hated to make last night sound like more than it was. Although she really liked Finn, she didn't feel anything romantic toward him. She was too numb, had been too burned, to even venture in that direction.

She didn't know if he was available, anyway. "It is."

"How long will he be in town?"

"The whole summer."

"That's fortunate," her mother said, her voice growing even warmer.

"His brother lost an arm in a motorcycle accident, so Finn is bringing him to Tahoe for a few months to heal."

"Did you say his brother has lost an arm? How sad!"

"It *is* sad, which is why I'm considering spending the summer here in Tahoe, too. So I can befriend Davis and try to…you know, encourage him. He's in a very dark place right now."

"Of course you should do that. You can work from anywhere—the cabin's as good a place as any."

Serenity grimaced at her reflection in the mirror over the dresser. *Liar*, she thought as she studied her flushed face. Her mother was going exactly where Serenity was leading her—and it was all because of love.

She was taking advantage of that love.

"By the way. What were you referring to in your text? What haven't I told you?"

Serenity tried to detect some guilt in her mother's voice, a hint of fear that suggested she'd caught on, but she couldn't determine if there was any. Slightly relieved, and yet more curious than ever, she pressed three fingers to her forehead while forcing herself to say what she'd devised before falling asleep last night. "That Uncle Vance has a new girlfriend. I went on Facebook after I got home and noticed that he's changed his profile to 'in a relationship.'"

"Oh, is that all?"

Her mother acted as though she'd let herself get worked up over nothing. That was what Serenity had hoped she'd do. But a lot would depend on the next few minutes. Would she question what Serenity was saying? Try to clarify? And would Serenity be able to convince her?

"Yeah. Like I said, I'd had a little too much to drink and wasn't paying attention to the time," Serenity said, putting some effort toward making the lie believable.

"Well, the news, such as it is, about your uncle Vance is nothing to be *too* shocked about. He's always in a new relationship. I don't even pay attention anymore.

He's never been with the same woman for more than three years."

"Why is that?" Serenity asked, purposely leading her mother even further into a discussion that had nothing to do with the problem she'd texted about last night. "He's handsome and charming."

"He's also superficial and can't keep a job," her mother stated flatly. "If he doesn't get fired, he finds an excuse to quit. I used to admire him. He's quite handsome, which is why women are attracted to him, but after seeing what he's done with his life, I'm disgusted, to be honest with you. He's not half the man your father is. Hard to believe they're even related."

"Nature versus nurture is an interesting study." She held her breath as soon as those words came out of her mouth. She'd been thinking of her, Lorelei and Reagan—not her father and his derelict brother—but if her mother had suspected that she might've discovered the secret of her birth, this could lead her right back to it.

"It is," her mother said. "But they were raised in the same household and have the same genes. Who can say why your father turned out so well, and Vance didn't?"

Her mother's strident voice suggested she wasn't second-guessing the conversation. But the comment about Uncle Vance and her father having the same genes made Serenity briefly wonder if *Vance* could have fathered Lorelei and Reagan.

No. If that were the case, they would've come up as first cousins, not half sisters, on her family tree. "Where does he live now?"

"I think he's in Vegas. Shows up here in San Diego every once in a while—whenever he needs something. He called your father just last week, asking for a loan."

"Did Daddy give it to him?"

"Probably. I didn't ask, didn't want to know. It galls me to give Vance money. He received as much of an inheritance as your father did, but he blew through his in record time. Now he has nothing. If there's a new woman in his life, it's probably someone who hasn't figured out yet that he's using her to pay the bills. I doubt it'll last."

"That's disappointing."

"It is. I don't know how your father copes with having such a useless brother. But enough about Vance. What do you have planned for the day? Have you been able to get anything done on your book?"

"A little." Serenity rolled her eyes at the image staring back at her in the mirror. This was another lie.

"That's great, honey. You can pull out of the funk you've been in. No one's a better writer than you are."

"You're always so good to me, Mom. So supportive. Thank you."

"Of course. I love you and your brother and sisters more than anything in the world."

"I know you do," she said and prayed that her mother would be able to forgive her when she learned that Uncle Vance had nothing to do with what was really going on.

* * *

lorelei

"So *now* you call me?" Mark said. "I finally gave up waiting to hear back from you. I'm at the hardware store."

The pique in her husband's voice put Lorelei on edge. He was lucky she'd called him at all. Dialing his number hadn't been easy for her. She didn't even want to hear his voice.

But she didn't say that. Although she'd left Lucy inside the cabin with Serenity and Reagan so she could talk without feeling inhibited, she wouldn't make this call any more difficult than it had to be. "I've been busy."

"Doing what, for God's sake? You're on vacation."

She kicked at a clump of snow. "While you're slaving away at home, fixing things around the house, you mean?"

"Well, I'm sure as hell not having any fun."

Lorelei moved farther from the cabin, into the thicket of trees surrounding it. "Is that the problem? Is that why you had an affair with my best friend? You're looking for more *fun*?"

"Please tell me Lucy isn't overhearing this," he said flatly.

Lorelei let her head fall back so she could stare up at the clear blue sky. "She isn't."

"Where is she?"

"In the house, making brownies with Serenity."

"So you're free to make cutting remarks."

"I think most women would make cutting remarks under the circumstances, don't you? Besides, all I said was that you had an affair with my best friend, and it's true."

She could see part of the roof of the cabin where Finn was staying. As she gazed in that direction, she remembered his engaging smile and tried to cling to the memory of the evening they'd shared as a group of friends getting to know each other.

"Right. I'll give you that. I've ruined our lives, and I'm as upset about it as you are. Do you think that I'm happy Francine's pregnant? Do you think I *intended* this problem? No! But it happened and now we have no choice but to try to move past it."

"I can't imagine why I can't get with the program," she said.

"Sarcasm isn't going to help, Lorelei. Please, can we just…put it behind us?"

"Why not? After all, it's been so long since I found out."

"More sarcasm? *Really?*"

"Okay, I'll play it straight. I'm not sure I can," she admitted. When he screwed up, he never wanted to talk about it, didn't want to suffer through her disappointment. It was frustrating not to be able to express herself, not to be able to thoroughly discuss their problems and get beyond them. She'd gotten used to the way he was and could let most things go. But this fell into an entirely different category, and yet he was trying to treat it the same.

"I'll give you time," he said, obviously realizing that he was being unreasonable.

"I think you're going to have to give me a better understanding as to why it happened. You said you were bored with your life. Were you really saying you were bored with me?"

"No, of course not."

"Then is it your job? Do you want to quit and do something else?"

"No, it's not my job."

"But if your job isn't to blame, and I'm not to blame, what's left?"

Her question met with silence. Then he said, "I'm at the hardware store, trying to buy some parts to fix the mower, which broke down this morning. I can't have an emotional blowout right now."

"Okay. I'll give you a call tomorrow. Or maybe the next day," she added as an afterthought.

Seemingly shocked that she was willing to put an end to the conversation that quickly, and that the promise of another call was such a loose one, he said, "Wait! Don't go yet. Tell me…tell me about your trip."

She swatted at what little snow was left clinging to the boughs of the closest tree and watched as it showered down on the ground. "I'm having a good time. I'm really glad I came."

"You are."

"Yes."

He didn't sound pleased despite the fact that she was trying to be positive. "What have you been doing?"

"Taking care of our daughter and visiting with my sisters."

"What are they like?"

"Nothing like Mercedes or Osha." She loved being able to throw that back in his face. He'd been so convinced she'd be disappointed and regret the trip to Tahoe.

"You probably wouldn't know it yet, even if they were," he pointed out.

In his mind, he was always right. So of course he wouldn't concede the point that easily. "I'd have some inkling," she said stubbornly. "Serenity is a successful writer, and Reagan is a successful advertising executive. I admire them both."

She purposely didn't mention that Reagan had just quit her job—or the reason behind it.

"So you love them? *Instantly?*"

He sounded catty, jealous. "I'm growing to respect them as I come to know them. Is that a problem? Are you disappointed that it's working out for me despite your dire predictions?"

She was never snippy with him. If anything, she was usually the one trying to cajole him out of a bad mood. But she couldn't seem to help herself today. The anger and hurt kept welling up and as hard as she tried to hold them back, they came oozing out in everything she said.

"No," he finally replied. "I'm just afraid I'm going to lose you."

Tears welled up, causing her to blink quickly. "Maybe you deserve that."

"Wow. If this is how you act around your new sisters, I can't believe they're good influences."

"Well, they aren't very big fans of yours, either."

"Damn it, Lorelei! Is that what's going on?" he asked, getting angry himself. "You're clear across the country, telling two total strangers what a terrible husband I am?"

She spotted Lucy through the window, laughing and talking as she stood on a chair to reach the counter. "I haven't said anything that isn't true," she told Mark.

He seemed at a loss. "I don't even know how to react. I've never seen you like this."

"I've never been like this." She rubbed her left temple.

"I'm sorry. How many more times do I need to say it?"

"I don't know. I can't seem to stop myself from…

from wanting to strike out at you. Maybe it'd be better if we talked later."

"I'd rather not have the conversation end on such a sour note, especially because, with the way you're acting, I have no idea if you'll call me back."

"Neither do I."

She heard him haul in a heavy breath. "Since you're in such a dark place anyway, we might as well talk about Francine. This isn't all my fault, you know. She had a hand in it."

"I'm sure she did."

"Have you heard from her yet?"

"I haven't talked to her. I don't know if she tried to call because I haven't looked through my call record since I got here."

"You're just going to write her off? Never speak to her again?"

Lorelei wished she could—possibly with both of them. "I'm considering it."

"Lorelei, please. Come home. This trip is obviously making things worse instead of better."

She peeled off a piece of tree bark. "Do you honestly think it's the trip?"

"Look." His voice dropped lower. "I've admitted that I'm to blame. And I've said I'm sorry at least a dozen times. What more can I do? Tell me, and I'll do it. If I could go back and change the past, I would. I'm not happy about the baby. I wish Francine would… I wish she'd get an abortion. There, I've said it."

"Have you told her that?"

"You want me to be that cruel?"

"To her? Yes. I hate knowing that she's happy about what she's done to me."

"She's *not* happy. Francine is just as upset as you are. She loves you, hopes to salvage your relationship."

"That will never happen," she said vehemently. "At this point, I'm not even sure we can salvage *our* relationship."

"Don't say that, babe. We can get through this."

She gripped the phone tighter, remembering Reagan sending in her resignation despite how badly it hurt. "Maybe, maybe not. I'll decide in September."

"Why September?"

She could hear the fresh alarm in his reaction. "Because I'm staying here for the rest of the summer."

"*What?* The summer hasn't even started yet!"

"I know, but June is close, and I like it here. I need some time to think, to find myself. And this place... you should see it. Being here is almost like a religious experience."

"Lorelei, please. You can find yourself here at home, where you belong."

"No, I can't," she stated firmly. "Not when I'm around you. I've tried to be everything you could want for so long it's a habit now. And I'm even wondering if it's the fact that I've always tried so hard that's making you stray. You don't respect me enough to treat me fairly in return."

"You did nothing that made me stray. I was an idiot, that's all. But I was a good husband before that, wasn't I? Does none of that matter? It was...it was a one-time thing—a simple mistake!"

His words sounded desperate, but they lacked conviction. "Are you really going to stick by that story?"

"What do you mean? We've talked about this!"

"Yes, and I've tried to believe it. But I can't. You're

lying about your…affair being a one-time thing, aren't you?"

Silence.

Lorelei's chest grew ever tighter, so tight she could barely breathe. "Right. I knew it. I just didn't want to face it."

"It was a short, whirlwind kind of affair, which is almost the same thing," he explained. "I just got…swept away for a while. But the pregnancy has woken me up, Lorelei. I mean it. Nothing like that will ever happen again. I *swear* it."

"The way you swore to be faithful to me in our wedding vows?"

Silence.

"We'll talk about it in September," she went on. "When I return."

"What about Lucy?" he asked.

"She likes it here, too."

"But I have the right to see her."

"You can visit whenever you'd like. There are cabins you can rent all over the area, but it's a popular place, so be sure to book well in advance."

"Visit. Rent a cabin to see my own wife and child. This is crazy. I should never have let you leave in the first place."

"*Let* me?" she echoed. "It wasn't up to you."

"You wouldn't have been able to go if I hadn't paid for it."

Stunned, Lorelei steadied herself by putting one hand against the tree she'd been picking at. "How *dare* you. You *wanted* me to quit my job. You preferred I stay home with Lucy. You understood what that would mean financially. And yet…now you resent me for not earn-ing money of my own?"

He was obviously struggling to reel in his emotions. "I don't resent you, no," he said. "I'm just trying to hang on to you—with everything I've got."

"And you think siphoning money from our joint ac-count is the answer?"

"I don't want you to leave!"

"You don't want me to leave? Or you want to be sure *you* get the bulk of the money if we split?"

"If we don't split, we won't have to worry about it."

"You know what?"

He waited.

"You should move in with Francine while I'm gone, or have her move into our house. Just throw all of my stuff in boxes and shove it in the garage. That's what she'd like, isn't it? To take my place? She'll be happier, and maybe you will be, too. It's certainly worth a try."

"Oh, God," he said. "This is going too far. I don't want to be with Francine!"

"Yeah, well, maybe you should've thought of that before," she said and disconnected.

Because she had to be so stoic in front of Lucy and, for once, Lucy couldn't see or hear her, Lorelei allowed herself to cry out and slug the tree.

It felt so good, she hit it again. But once she'd started venting the anguish inside her, she couldn't seem to stop. She punched the tree until she was sobbing un-controllably, her knuckles were scraped and she was so exhausted she could hardly stay on her feet.

"Hey, what's going on? Are you okay?"

As soon as she heard the voice behind her, she turned, blinked rapidly and sniffed, trying to pull all that emotion back inside. But it was too late. She could see the concern on Finn's face as he hurried over.

"What is it?" he asked. "What's happened?"

"It—it's nothing," she tried to say, but she choked on the words before she could get them out, and the next thing she knew he was holding her as she cried, rubbing her back and telling her everything was going to be okay.

* * *

finn

Finn could feel Lorelei trembling in his arms. "What is it?" he murmured. "Has someone been hurt?"

Eventually, she managed to pull herself together enough to step away and wipe her face. "No. I'm sorry. I… I don't know what got into me."

He was surprised she'd allowed him to comfort her. The way she'd behaved yesterday suggested she wasn't someone who opened up about her problems. "Obviously, something's happened."

"It's nothing for you to worry about. With your brother's accident, you have enough to deal with. What Davis is going through—that's a real problem. This is… this is just a cliché." She tried to laugh as she wiped her nose with her forearm. "Have you heard from Davis today? Is his temperature back to normal?"

He noticed her attempt to swing the conversation back to him and his interests and suspected it was her way of dodging uncomfortable questions. "What kind of cliché?" he asked instead of answering.

When her smile wobbled, he could tell she'd expected him to take advantage of the opportunity to talk about himself instead. "Oh, you know, the typical cheating husband. Mine happened to have an affair with my best friend, which is even more of a cliché."

He immediately felt protective of her. There was a fragile quality about Lorelei. She seemed determined not to lower her guard, not to let herself be hurt, which was why he felt so bad that her husband had managed to hurt her so deeply. "Whether it's a cliché or not doesn't make it any less painful. Is this the first time your husband's been unfaithful?"

"I don't know. I'd like to say yes, but it's possible he only told me about Francine because she's pregnant."

"Holy shit." Finn had been able to tell that something wasn't right in Lorelei's marriage. He'd caught on to that yesterday when they'd all been talking about staying for the summer. Now he understood the extent of it.

"It'll be okay." She attempted a shrug. "I can't believe you caught me throwing a tantrum like a child. It's embarrassing."

He bent his head to catch her eye. "You don't have anything to apologize for. Life is messy. For all of us. And you would've had the privacy you thought you did, except I was coming over to see if you, your sisters and Lucy would like to go sledding before all the snow melts. I came across some sleds in the storage under the cabin and figured we could enjoy a few hours before it's too late."

She infused her voice with more energy. "Thank you. That sounds like fun."

He scowled at her.

"What?"

"Will you stop being so polite? Makes it hard to get to know you."

"Yeah, well, I don't know myself right now."

Considering her background, he could understand why. "It's okay that you feel like shit. We don't have to go sledding. So we miss the snow for this season—no big deal."

"Not going sledding won't fix anything," she said. "Besides, I have a daughter to think about. And she'd love to do that."

Hoping to cheer her up, he grinned. "Great. Let's go see if everyone else is interested."

She'd just started to trudge to the cabin alongside him when he said, "Has your friend decided what she's going to do with the baby?"

"She's keeping it, of course. She made that clear from the start. Her ex refused to entertain even the possibility of children, which was what caused a lot of the fights between them. So... I guess this is her way of getting a child."

Catching her left hand, he lifted it to look at her hurt knuckles and noticed that she'd been doing a bit of damage to her cuticles, too. "When did you find out?"

She pulled her hand away. "I've known for about three weeks."

"Then it was time you let loose and really vented. Maybe now you'll give your poor hands a break."

They walked in silence for a few minutes and rounded the cabin before she spoke again. "I just told Mark that I'm staying for the whole summer."

He studied the thick fringe of her eyelashes as she watched the ground ahead of them, since she wouldn't look up. "And? How'd that go?"

"He's not happy about it."

Finn felt kind of bad since *he* was the one who'd suggested they all stay longer. "Can he force you to come back?"

"I doubt it. We're not divorced, so there's no legal agreement between us—you know, as far as custody and visitation. And I've told him he can come see Lucy whenever he wants. He'll hate spending his vacation days traipsing across the country because I won't come home, but…"

"What would he rather be doing?" Finn asked.

"Hunting or fishing with his friends."

They were almost at the front door when she grabbed his arm, pulled him to a stop and gave him an earnest look. "Am I being unreasonable? Should I go back to Florida, so he doesn't have to spend the time or money to come here?"

"It sounds like he has the money and time to visit, if it's important enough to him. What about you? Do you feel better here? Happier?"

"I do. I've never had any siblings—or parents, for that matter, so having a chance to get to know my sisters means a lot to me."

"Then I think you have every right to stay," he said, and was rewarded with the first genuine smile he'd seen on her face today.

They climbed the steps to the porch, but as she reached for the door handle, Reagan came charging out.

"There you are!" she said as soon as she saw Lorelei. "I was just coming to see if everything was okay."

"It's fine," Lorelei said.

Reagan shot him a tentative look. Obviously, she could tell Lorelei had been crying. Although Lorelei was careful to keep Reagan from seeing her hands, there was nothing she could do to hide the puffiness of her eyes.

Finn suspected Lorelei would not want to be questioned, however, so he was glad Reagan chose not to mention it. "I see you're out causing trouble already," she said to him.

"That's what I do," he said with a lazy smile.

"Any word on Davis? Do you know when he'll be able to come up and join us?"

Finn tried to keep his manner casual, but the fact that his brother's temperature hadn't dropped back to normal was a real concern. If infection set in, the doctor might have to remove more of Davis's arm, and he knew how his brother would react to that. "He'll be here in a few days," he said as though it would all be fine, which was what he wanted to believe.

"I can't wait to meet him," Reagan said.

Finn was about to suggest they go sledding but decided he might not have a better opportunity to prep Lorelei and Reagan for when they finally met Davis. "Just so you know, I haven't mentioned you to him. I don't want him to think I'm suggesting that meeting three beautiful women will make a big difference to what he's going through. He'll get angry if he interprets it that way, which means he'll wall himself off, won't give you a chance. But friends and a good dose of laughter make every struggle easier, right?"

"I'm just learning that myself," Reagan said.

"I want to be smart in how we approach him. I think we should act as though I'm bringing you around for no particular reason except that we're already friends. Otherwise, if he feels you're trying to help him, he'll close himself off from you, like I said, just as he has with other well-meaning people."

"He doesn't want to be pitied," Lorelei supplied.

"Exactly."

"Got it. We'll treat him the same way we treat you and Nolan." Reagan turned to Lorelei. "So...did you tell Mark that you're staying for the summer?"

Lorelei nodded.

"I'm guessing he didn't take it well."

"You'd be guessing right," she said with some chagrin.

Motioning for Finn to follow them, Reagan drew her sister into the house. "Oh, well. Forget Mark. Forget my job, too. We're going to have fun."

"Speaking of fun, I think we should start by going sledding," Finn said. "Not many people can say they've been sledding in California at the end of May."

14

serenity

A full day had passed since they'd dragged out their pictures and other memorabilia and yet they hadn't even attempted to get back to their discussion on how they might be related. As Serenity sat in the living room with her computer in front of her, she couldn't help counting the hours. She was anxious to find answers, but she kept telling herself there wasn't any huge hurry. Not if they had all summer. The most important thing was that they take some time for themselves—to become happier, healthier people. She was glad she could provide a place for her sisters to spend a few months, especially because they seemed to appreciate it.

Even if nothing momentous happened, at least they were getting a break from their normal lives. They'd had a blast sledding with Finn. Serenity had never laughed so hard in her life as when he decided to tackle a much steeper hill than the one they were doing because it had a lot more snow, then hit a dip at the bottom and went flying off his sled. He was willing to take more risks than they were, so his antics had kept them entertained. Fortunately, he wasn't hurt.

They'd decided to stop for Mexican food on the way home, and she'd seen him step off to the side to accept a call on his cell while they were waiting for a table. He hadn't been smiling then, but when she asked if he'd received an update on Davis, he glided over her question by saying nothing had really changed.

After dinner, they'd returned home, showered and Finn had come over to watch a movie. He'd seemed quieter than earlier in the day, which concerned her.

"What are you doing?"

Since the house was dark and everyone had gone to bed, Serenity was startled by the sound of Reagan's voice. She turned to see her holding a reusable water bottle and assumed she was going to the kitchen to fill it.

"Trying to get my weekly blog written," she replied but she hadn't come up with more than the title so far. Every time she tried to get started, all she could do was drift off into memories of Sean. His kindness and his patience, especially toward children, was one of the things that had first attracted her to him. She'd always believed he'd make a great father.

Now she saw him in an entirely different light, of course. The way he'd gravitated toward children and tried to gain their trust turned her stomach. And she'd come *so* close to having a family with him, still couldn't believe they'd been married for eight years and, in all that time, she'd never suspected that his love for children was based on the wrong kind of interest.

"Serenity?"

She blinked. Apparently, Reagan hadn't continued on to the kitchen. "Sorry. What'd you say?"

"I said...we've been in touch for several months, and yet you've never mentioned you have a blog?"

"It didn't really come up."

Reagan ran her free hand through her short hair. "I guess that's true. We didn't talk about our daily routines. We were all shocked to have found new family members and were too busy wondering what it might mean."

Leave it to Reagan to go straight to the bottom line. "We were for sure tiptoeing around. But if you'd ever looked me up online, you'd know I have a blog," she teased. "I followed you on social media."

"I was sort of in denial. Although, after we decided to meet, I did buy and read one of your books. It was the one where the neighbor murdered the wife of the young couple next door, and it took the police ten years to solve the case even though the murderer kept inserting himself into the investigation."

"What happened there was so sad. The woman he killed was sweet and loved by everyone."

"I'm glad they finally got him. You did a great job covering it, by the way."

Serenity smiled. "Thanks."

"So what's the name of your blog?"

"Serenity Alston Investigates."

"Good idea to use your name—for branding purposes."

"I'm glad an advertising expert approves." Serenity was tempted to close her laptop. She wanted to give up and go to bed. Her blinking cursor mocked her feeble efforts. But she refused to let that blank screen win. She *had* to get back on top of her writing and the business side that went along with it. "Any word from Edison & Curry on your resignation?"

"Haven't checked. I'm too afraid to see how Gary will react."

"Is it possible he'll demand you return and give him two weeks' notice?"

"No. Once you're fired or you quit at Edison & Curry, they have you clear out immediately. It's almost as if they suddenly can't stand the sight of you. First thing tomorrow, they'll probably dump the contents of my office in boxes and shove them in the storage room."

"What if you're wrong? Don't you think you should check your email, just in case?"

Reagan's water bottle made a popping sound as she opened and closed it again and again. "Tomorrow morning will be soon enough. Otherwise, I might be too upset to sleep."

"Makes sense. Any calls or texts from Drew?"

"No. My phone's been quiet since I turned in my resignation."

Serenity tried to read Reagan's expression, but it was difficult in the mostly dark room. The only light came from the kitchen and the glow of her computer screen. "That's good, right?"

"Doesn't feel like it."

"You said you didn't want to talk to Drew."

"I do and I don't. It was weirdly reassuring that he wanted to talk to *me*. Now that he's gone silent, I feel… I don't know…worse. But for different reasons, of course." She seemed to manufacture a shrug. "I knew giving him up wouldn't be easy."

Serenity felt bad for her. It was painful to fall in

love with the wrong person. There were times when she still missed Sean—things he did or said, even the way he touched her. And that only made her feel more cheated and duped, which angered her all over again. Her mother expected her to relegate it to the past, pick herself up and get married again, but she'd honestly loved her husband.

She still did, in many ways. That was probably the saddest part of all. "Will you ever speak to him again?"

"I'd like to say goodbye, gain some type of closure. But I'll wait to see how everyone reacts to my resignation first." She perched on the arm of the love seat that was at a ninety-degree angle to the couch. "Anyway, enough about me. We were talking about your blog. Do you sell advertising on it?"

Of course Reagan would be interested in that aspect. "No. I have about fifteen thousand followers, and they're quite active, but I haven't pursued any advertisers."

"Why not? You could make some extra money."

"I'm more concerned with staying in touch with my readers so they'll buy my next book. If I don't sell enough copies, I won't get another contract."

Reagan set her bottle aside. "And? Are you seeing the carryover you were hoping to see?"

"I think so. My books bring me more followers for my blog and my blog brings me more buyers for my books. The only problem is the constant need for content—and the fact that I haven't been able to write much lately."

Concern entered Reagan's voice. "How long has it been since your last post?"

"Three weeks," she replied but didn't mention that

she hadn't been making much progress on her book, either.

"I hope it isn't because of me and Lorelei."

"No, definitely not." Serenity shifted to get more comfortable. "I've struggled ever since I found that garbage on Sean's computer."

"But you found those files eighteen months ago. The writing's not getting any easier after this much time?"

The ticking clock in Serenity's head seemed to grow louder. Knowing that she should be back at work, that it *had* been long enough, only made the frustration worse. "No. If anything, it's getting harder."

"Why?"

"It's as if Sean blew a huge hole through me. I've lost part of myself. My innocence. My security. My trust in others. Something. And I can't seem to get it back. A year and a half may sound like a long time, but it went by so fast." She let her head fall back on the couch. "When you were a kid, did you ever go on The Rotor at an amusement park?"

"Is that a ride?"

"Yeah. It spins faster and faster until the floor drops out and the centrifugal force pins you to the wall."

"Oh. I *did* try that ride once or twice. I think it's still around."

"If it is, they probably call it something else now. Anyway, what I've been through reminds me of that ride. When I realized my husband was such a monster, my life started spinning in circles, going so fast I was pinned to the wall, couldn't even move. Sean was so vocal about the people who perpetrated the crimes I've written about, calling them scum and other names. The sheer disconnect it would require to say what he said while doing what he was doing…" She shook her head; she'd all but given up trying to understand Sean's actions.

"I can't even imagine what that must've been like."

"It was hell. And after the initial shock, I got caught up in the fight to make sure Sean didn't get away with what he'd done or get off with a slap on the wrist. Every waking moment was consumed with his trial—preparing for it, participating in it, watching it. I couldn't think about anything else. It was as though it became my personal mission to segregate him from the rest of society."

"Was that a form of revenge for hurting you, or was it fear for the children he was victimizing?"

"Both," she admitted. "At that point, the ride was spinning faster than ever and the floor had dropped out. I wanted to climb off, but was pinned to the wall. And then, when he was finally found guilty, it was over so suddenly. The ride had stopped but the bottom hadn't come back up to save me from the fall. I didn't want to leave my house, didn't want to see my neighbors, didn't want to talk to my friends. It didn't help he only received a five-year sentence. He'll probably be out before I quit wondering how I could miss the fact that my husband was not only a danger to society but never really loved me."

"He wouldn't have married you if he didn't love you."

"I provided someone to come home to, a social network, a degree of status because of my job and easy access to sex—although it makes my skin crawl to think that when I was feeling closest to him he was probably imagining me as a prepubescent child." Squeezing her eyes closed, she once again willed away the images she'd found on his computer. "He might have liked my company. But he didn't love *me*. How could a man who victimizes children care about anyone but himself?"

"Okay, I concede that point. But you can't let what you've been through—what he put you through—ruin your career."

Serenity's gaze moved back to her screen. After an hour of sitting on the couch, she should've finished this week's blog. "I'm trying to fight for it."

"How can I help?" Reagan asked. "Maybe Lorelei and I shouldn't stay for the summer. Won't that be too distracting for you?"

"No. I like having you both here. It does distract me, but in a good way. It makes me stop obsessing, at least for brief periods of time, about the fact that I can't seem to pull my life back together."

"Then we'll stay, as long as you can get going on your writing again." Reagan gestured at her computer. "What's your latest blog about?"

"Sean."

"No wonder you're struggling," Reagan said with a grimace. "Why would you write about him?"

"Because I've been avoiding the elephant in the room, and I can't keep running and hiding, can't shy away from this case just because it happened to me instead of someone else. That actually gives me greater insight—something deeper I should share."

"I don't agree," Reagan said. "*Why* should you share it?"

"I have to take ownership of it at some point, don't I?"

"No! It wasn't your fault. Why not let it go?"

"Because I'm afraid there are people out there who think I must've known what he was up to and didn't report him right away—or that I could've caught him sooner if I'd been paying attention."

"No one thinks that."

Serenity wasn't nearly so confident. "You'd be surprised. I watched a show about BTK recently. You know, that serial killer?"

"The nickname sounds familiar, but I can't really remember him or his crimes."

"His name was Dennis Rader. Lived in Kansas and killed ten people in the seventies and eighties. BTK was a name he gave himself—stands for Bind, Torture, Kill."

Reagan made a face. "How gruesome."

"And would you believe he was a devoted husband and father? It's a crazy story. Anyway, he kept his kill kit in a duffel bag right in his closet."

"Is that how he was eventually caught?"

"No. That's the thing. You'd *think* that's how he would've been caught, but it wasn't. He liked to interact with the police, kept taunting them and the media, and finally gave himself away by sending in a floppy disk from which the police were able to extract the name of his church, where he'd been using the computer."

"He was *religious*?"

"He was the president of his Lutheran church, if I remember right."

"Now there's some irony for you."

"He *still* talks about being forgiven. Anyway, in this documentary, one of the commentators scoffed at the fact that his wife claimed she didn't know he was harming people. 'What wife doesn't go through her husband's closet?' the woman cried." Serenity shook her head. "But the answer is *me*! *I* was that kind of wife. I trusted him, and I was too busy with my own life and keeping track of my deadlines and responsibilities. I never snooped in Sean's closet, his drawers, his car or his phone. Even his computer—*especially* his computer."

"So you're blaming yourself?"

"I'm just saying that if I'd been more aware, maybe I *would've* caught him sooner."

"Hindsight is always 20/20, as they say. What was he doing with the pornography, anyway? Was he using it for his own personal gratification or was he—"

"He claims he *wasn't* using it for that." Serenity cut her off before her words could conjure up the images Serenity tried so hard to keep out of her brain. "He said he didn't even know those pictures were there. That his computer must've gotten a virus or something when he went onto the dark web to see what it was like. But the police proved that he was buying and selling them on the dark web, not that they were somehow accidental."

"What tipped you off?"

"It was actually a fluke. One night, when he wasn't home, my computer was out of battery, and I couldn't find my cord. So I got his laptop out of his briefcase. He has a PC and I have a Mac. We don't normally use each other's computers—I find it too frustrating that everything is so different. But I just needed to download some notes my editor had sent me via email and print them out."

"His laptop wasn't password protected? I'd be damn sure mine was, especially if I was hiding creepy things like that."

"It was, but he was so used to me minding my own business—and being prejudiced about using a PC—that he'd grown a bit lax. I knew what passwords he used for his ATM cards and bank accounts and was able to break it quite easily. That's when I found the files he'd downloaded, because when I downloaded what I needed to print out, they came up in the same folder."

At first, Reagan seemed speechless. Then she rallied and said, "That must've been the worst moment of your life."

Even after eighteen months, Serenity could feel the revulsion that had welled up then as strongly as if it had just happened. "It was, especially because we were planning to start a family."

"No kidding? I'm sorry. You're lucky you found that crap when you did. But you can't blog about that. Even if most people will sympathize with what you went through, there'll always be those internet trolls and agitators who try to cause problems—or think like that commentator who said what she did about BTK's wife—and, at the very least, make you feel like shit."

"But I write about criminal cases involving other people. How can I be such a coward as to skip myself?".

"Easily. You come up with another topic, and you keep posting about other topics until you're whole and healthy again and what Sean did has been forgotten. Trust me. I'm in advertising." She frowned as she corrected herself. "Or I was. Advertising isn't quite public relations, but it's close, and I'm telling you, it would be a mistake to give others a forum in which to criticize you."

Serenity thought about how thin-skinned she'd become, how sensitive. "Maybe you're right."

"I am. You'd be so busy trying to deal with the blowback you wouldn't be able to write for months."

The idea of scrapping such a daunting blog post—

of giving herself permission to do that—brought relief. She deleted the title to make it official. "Okay. So what should I write about?"

"Write about discovering two sisters you never knew you had. Most people will find that interesting."

"I can't. My other siblings follow my blog."

"Then write about BTK."

"BTK is old news."

"What about the dark web? I can't be the only one who doesn't understand much about it."

"If I do, someone will bring up how Sean used it—and who knows where the conversation will go from there."

"True." She paced to the windows and back. "What's your next book about? That guy who killed his wife and kids, right? Isn't that what you told me on Facebook?"

"That's what it's supposed to be about."

"What do you mean? Are you changing cases?"

"No, I've done a lot of the research, gathered a ton of information and made notes. But…"

"But?"

"I haven't actually started the book."

Reagan stopped walking. "When is it due?"

The panic Serenity had been trying to hold at bay rose a little higher, as though she was marching steadily into the deep end of a pool and the water was now nearly over her head. "It was due last month."

"Shit."

"Yeah. If I don't get started soon, you might not be the only one who's unemployed." And since Sean had used all their reserves on attorneys, she didn't have the financial depth she needed to last very long, not without going to her folks for help—which was something she didn't want to do at thirty-five.

"Then you're going to get started," Reagan said firmly. "You're not only going to get started, you're going to finish that book and turn it in by the end of the summer. Can you write it that fast?"

"If I was the old me. But I'm not, Reagan. I can't seem to find that capable person."

"You still have the skills. That hasn't changed. Just forget about blogging or doing anything else besides writing the book."

"I can't drop my blog. I'll lose all the momentum I've gained there."

"Then I'll write it while you focus on your book. I'll pick subjects that relate to your work—like why parents sometimes kill their children. There's a name for that, isn't there? What's it called?"

"Filicide."

"Fine, filicide. Most people will never have heard that term, even if they've read stories in the media about parents murdering their children. It's such an unnatural act, so horrifying that they'll be curious about the reasons. You can edit what I write, or simply name me as a guest blogger while you're on deadline."

Serenity couldn't believe Reagan would volunteer to help that much. "But…why would you do this?"

"Because you need it, and I don't mind. I don't have a job right now. This will be new, it'll be interesting and it'll free you up to put your energy and creativity where it needs to be. You'll write for four hours every morning when you first wake up and you're fresh. After you take a break to hang out with us and Finn and his brothers, you'll read what you've written to Lorelei and me once Lucy goes to bed at night. Hopefully, you'll be able to get rolling, and we'll march steadily forward through the summer."

Dumbfounded, Serenity stared at her. "You're planning to hold my hand all summer?"

"You're damn right I am. You're too good a writer to fall into an abyss of doubt and shock. We're here to pull you out." She took Serenity's laptop and closed it before handing it back. "So we'd better get some sleep, because we start early in the morning."

15

lorelei

Lorelei woke up thinking about Finn. She'd gone to sleep thinking about him, too. She'd found him attractive from the start, but now she knew he was much more than a handsome face. He was kind and funny and warmhearted. And Lucy seemed to love him.

Yesterday when they were sledding, he took Lucy down the hill with him dozens of times. After he'd coaxed her into trying one run, she'd become absolutely enamored of him and had stuck by his side for the rest of the day.

"Mommy, it's time to get up. It's morning."

Lorelei stretched and lifted her head to see her daughter standing inside the doorway. "Come give Mommy a kiss," she said and threw back the covers.

Lucy was usually too eager to start playing to lie in bed, but they occasionally snuggled together in the mornings, after Mark left for work.

Today, she hurried over and climbed in, letting Lorelei pull her close.

"You're smiling!" Lucy said.

The hint of surprise in her daughter's voice told Lorelei that she hadn't been doing nearly enough of that lately. "I feel good. How about you?"

"I feel good, too. The sun is shining."

The light gleaming around the blinds indicated as much. "I can see that."

"Can we go sledding again?"

"'Fraid not, kiddo." Lorelei covered a yawn. "There was barely enough snow to do it yesterday. Remember how the rocks were poking through in some places and we had to be careful to stay away from them?"

"Yes…"

"There'd be even more rocks poking through today."

"Why?"

"Because the snow is melting. It's turning into summer."

She scowled. "I wish it *wasn't*."

Lorelei caught her little hand and kissed it. "I thought you wanted to go kayaking."

When Lucy didn't seem to recall the term, Lorelei clarified. "You know, riding in those little boats I told you about?"

"On the water?"

"Yes, on the lake."

"I do!"

"Then we need the weather to warm up."

Lucy seemed to consider this as Lorelei smoothed her hair back. "Can Finn go in the little boats with us?" she asked once she seemed to decide that would be an okay substitute, after all.

Lorelei had to admit she was hoping to see more of Finn herself. "Maybe."

Her phone buzzed on the nightstand, where she'd plugged it in to charge for the night.

Eager to see who it was, Lucy squirmed out of her arms. "It's Daddy!" she announced when she saw her father's picture on the screen.

While Lorelei kept her outer smile firmly in place, she felt her inner smile fade. "You can answer it," she told her daughter.

Lucy pushed the button. "Hi, Daddy!"

Lorelei could hear the deep rumble of Mark's voice, but she couldn't make out what he said. And that suited her fine. She didn't want to hear anything from him.

With her daughter occupied for a few minutes, she allowed her eyes to close and her mind to wander, remembering what it had felt like to have Finn pull her into his arms when she was crying.

But then she heard Lucy say something that made her eyes snap open.

"I said Finn… No, *Finn*, Daddy…" She giggled. "That's his name!… No, he's not a fish… You're silly… He went sledding with us yesterday… Mmm-hmm. He has a *big* sled… He's nice… Yeah, Mommy likes him, too…"

Mommy likes him?

Holding her breath, Lorelei shoved herself up on one elbow.

"She's here… Yeah… Okay…" Lucy held out the phone. "Daddy wants to talk to you."

Although she was cringing inside, Lorelei put the phone to her ear. "Hello?"

"Who's Finn?" Mark demanded without preamble.

Lorelei was trying to decide which response would sound more innocuous—"the neighbor next door" or "a friend"—when Mark spoke again, the volume of his voice rising.

"Hello? Did you hear me?"

"I heard." Obviously, this wasn't going to be an easy call. She gave Lucy a nudge. "Why don't you run and get dressed, honey? We'll go down and make you some breakfast when I get off the phone."

"Okay," she said and bounced off.

"Who's Finn?" Mark sounded like a time bomb about to detonate, but the irony of his anger, combined with the way their daughter had described Finn, made Lorelei start to laugh. "Just a guy with a big sled," she said, unable to resist the metaphor.

"Aren't you hilarious," Mark growled. "What's going on, Lorelei? You've been so odd since you left. Are you seeing someone else? Is that why you aren't coming home?"

Sobering, Lorelei drew a deep breath. "No, *you're* the reason I'm not coming home, Mark. You and Francine and the whole nasty affair."

He backed down when he heard that. "I know the situation isn't ideal, but we can wade through it. Just come back to Florida, so we can get some counseling or something and figure this out."

Figure it out? Or do everything in his power to convince her to live with the consequences of his affair for the rest of her life?

Lorelei thought of Serenity and Reagan—and Finn. She'd mentioned a therapist when Mark had first told her about Francine, and he'd been unreceptive, made it clear that he didn't think counseling had anything to offer him. He said there were far too many other places their money would have to go, given the new baby and trying to continue building their own lives. So why was he suggesting it now? Was it that he thought *she* was the one who needed a psychologist?

Considering her background, she figured professional help couldn't hurt. But if he was only willing to go in order to change *her*, it wouldn't save their marriage. And she could get counseling whether she remained in the marriage or not.

Feeling more resolute than ever, she said, "I'll be home in September."

"You're sticking to that."

"I am."

"You're really going to leave me here with Francine…"

She swung her legs over the side of the bed and got up. "Is that a threat?"

"No." He backed off immediately, but she could tell it *had* been an attempt to manipulate her through her jealousy, and that galled her after everything he'd done.

"I should tolerate you having a baby with my best friend, but you can't give me three months to spend with my new sisters?"

"I'm not saying… I didn't mean… I miss you, that's all."

Too bad he hadn't led with that, because it was too late now. "I'm sorry, Mark. I need this time. It's possible you do, too. If I can't fulfill you, maybe Francine can."

"Damn it! Will you stop throwing your best friend at me?"

"*I* didn't throw her at you! And she's not my best friend. She'll never be my friend again. *You* cost me that."

He seemed to be at a loss for words. But then he

said, "I'm sorry. Please, Lorelei. Will you...will you just come home?"

"I'll be back in September. In the meantime, I'm giving you permission to see whoever you want."

Silence. This time, she didn't sense anger, as she had when she'd been talking to him outside yesterday; she sensed panic. "Are you saying that because *you* want to see other people? This *Finn* guy?"

"No," she said. But only because she couldn't imagine she'd ever really have a chance with Finn.

A guy like Finn could have anybody.

* * *

reagan

There it was—her response from Gary at Edison & Curry.

Reagan could hear her sisters downstairs in the kitchen with Lucy, but she hadn't joined them. She first had to deal with whatever she was about to find in this email.

She took a quick shower, to put off reading Gary's response a little longer. But with only ten minutes to spare before she had to be downstairs to adhere to the new schedule she'd given Serenity, she finally perched on the edge of the chair near the bookcase, pulled her computer onto her lap and clicked Open.

Dear Reagan:
I'm sorry to hear that you're moving on. I feel as though the many opportunities we provided for the advance-

ment of your career should have been rewarded with more loyalty than having you suddenly call in sick for several days and then quit without so much as a conversation between us.

But since you've already made up your mind, I'll wish you well and will remind you of the non-compete clause you signed when you started working here, in which you expressly agreed "not to enter into or start a similar trade or profession in competition with Edison & Curry."

Just so you know, I plan to rigorously enforce that agreement, so best of luck getting started in a new industry.

Sincerely, Gary Rincon

Feeling like a balloon someone had poked with a pin, Reagan slumped over, completely deflated. So there it was. The culmination of years of hard work and dedication, dogged focus and creative energy. Nights. Weekends. Lunches. The sacrifice of almost all her personal time. She'd received no "thank you." No "please reconsider." Just "You'd better not do anything to threaten my business or I'll come after you."

"Wow." Stunned in spite of having seen others leave the firm with a similarly cold send-off, she felt slightly nauseous. Although she'd been aware of the non-compete clause, she'd signed it ten years ago, when she was fresh out of college and so happy to land a good job. She hadn't thought much about it since. Because she didn't plan on starting her own advertising firm, she certainly hadn't expected it to be much of a stumbling block.

But now that Gary had quoted the actual language,

she wondered if simply going to work for another advertising agency would be considered an infringement.

If so, what was she going to do?

"You think you did so much for *me*," she murmured. "What about everything I did for you? Not just anyone could've come up with the campaigns I created. I brought in—and managed—a lot of business."

Shaking her head in disbelief, she checked her phone to see if Drew had tried to reach her this morning. Since it was three hours later in New York, it was almost lunchtime—late enough for him to be in the office and to have heard about her resignation.

She'd received nothing from him, though, not so much as a text in the past twenty-four hours.

Was she compounding the mistake she'd made with Drew by quitting her job? With that non-compete clause, there was a chance she wouldn't able to stay in the industry.

Maybe Gary was bluffing, trying to punish her for displeasing him. He didn't take disappointment well, which was partly why she felt she deserved a thank you, at the very least. Not just anyone could put up with the pressure he exerted, let alone excel in spite of it.

Putting her phone and computer aside, she went to the railing, where her sisters' and Lucy's voices floated up to her, to see if she could tell whether they were finished with breakfast.

Lorelei: "Want some toast?"

Serenity: "Sure. I haven't had dip eggs in forever."

Lorelei: "Or, if you can wait an hour, I'll make a goat cheese, spinach and sun-dried tomato quiche."

Serenity: "Do we have all the ingredients?"

Lorelei: "I saw some spinach in the fridge, which is

what gave me the idea. But I may have to drive over to the store to get a couple of other things. I'll do that while you're writing, and we can have the quiche tomorrow morning. And maybe I'll make a pesto pasta for lunch."

Serenity: "You like to cook, huh?"

Lorelei: "I love it."

Serenity: "Hopefully, that'll rub off on me."

Lucy: "What's quiche, Mommy?"

Lorelei: "It's like an egg pie."

Lucy: "Pie is yummy."

After deliberating for a couple of minutes, Reagan went back into her bedroom, quietly shut the door and called Drew.

Too nervous to sit down, she paced at the end of the bed while the phone rang.

"Hello?"

Her heart began to race at the sound of his voice. She missed him so much, missed her former life, too. Now that she knew she wasn't going back to Edison & Curry, she felt as though she'd lost her anchor and was drifting, rudderless, out into the squalls of the open sea.

"Drew?" She hated feeling so shaky and uncertain. She wasn't used to being in such a weak position. Generally forthright and decisive, she knew her own mind—when dealing with everyone except her mother.

"There you are!" he said.

"Can you talk?"

"For a few minutes. God, I'm glad you finally called. I've been trying to reach you."

"I know. I'm sorry. I… I needed some time to myself to do some soul-searching."

"About…"

About you. About what they'd done. About how she

could be a good person and still make such a terrible mistake.

The fact that he'd even asked seemed strange. Didn't he feel as out of sorts as she did? "What I most want out of life, I guess."

"So are you back from Tahoe? Because if you are, we should meet up, have lunch together."

And then what…go back to her place? He was acting so casual, as if nothing had changed. She couldn't help bristling, especially after the avalanche of guilt that had nearly destroyed her this past week. "No, I'm not back yet. I'm—" She was about to tell him she'd very likely be spending the whole summer at the lake, but he cut her off.

"Oh, that's right. Your flight isn't until Friday. It was on the company calendar until Gary deleted it."

"That was quick," she said dryly.

"He sent an email to the whole company this morning, notifying everyone that you'd quit."

"How nice of him."

He didn't respond to her sarcasm. "I hope it wasn't because of me."

She stopped pacing. Of course it was because of him! What other reason could there be?

But he didn't sound too broken up by what they'd done—that he'd hurt his wife so deeply, if he even planned to tell her, or that Reagan wouldn't be coming into the office each day. "We can't continue to work together after…after what happened, Drew."

"Give me a minute."

Assuming he was closing his office door, she gripped the phone tighter as she waited for him to return.

"Listen, I'm afraid you're taking what we did far too

seriously," he said when he came back on the line. "I was afraid of this."

"Afraid of what?"

"That you'd freak out and turn it into a big deal. Don't ruin your career over fifteen minutes of panting and one good climax, Reagan."

Fifteen minutes of panting? One good climax? Was that how he characterized what they'd done together?

She'd thought he might try to minimize the incident, tell her they could forget about it so they could continue working together. But she'd imagined he'd do that because he cared about her and wanted to remain in close contact. The throwaway tone he'd just used made her wonder if she had meant anything to him at all. "We had sex on your desk," she said.

"Believe me, I remember."

The satisfaction in his voice irritated her. She couldn't detect a hint of remorse. "You're married!"

"You knew that before it happened."

"I did. Which is why I feel so bad."

"Don't feel bad. I'll always be there for Sally and the kids."

What did he mean by that? "Isn't having sex with another woman the opposite of being there for Sally and the kids?" she asked. "Doesn't that strike a blow at the very structure of your family—I mean, if word were to get out?"

"Are you threatening to tell her?" This was the first thing that seemed to trigger an emotional response. She could tell it upset him.

"No! I'm pointing out how serious what we did is."

"Look, you can beat yourself up over it all you want. But I'm not going to do the same." Now that she'd said she wasn't going to tell his wife, the tone of his voice had evened out, indicating that he'd relaxed again. "We've worked together for a long time, and you're a beautiful, intelligent woman. Of course I'd want you. Any man would."

"Even if he was married."

"Sally is happy, Reagan. I work hard and bring home a lot of money. I help out around the house. I go to everything she and the kids ask me to. I grilled burgers for some people she wanted to have over for a barbecue just yesterday. I deserve to have a little fun on my own now and then."

Reagan couldn't believe her ears. "A little *fun*?"

"I won't lie. You're all I've been able to think about— for months. So I'm glad you quit. Now that we don't work for the same firm anymore, it'll be easier for us to see each other. We won't have to worry about someone here telling Sally, because no one will have any idea. We could travel. Attend the theater or the opera. Go out to eat. As long as we don't frequent the same places everyone else around here does, we could do a lot of fun things. And I'd make sure you were well taken care of."

She felt as though he'd just slugged her. "You mean carry on a secret affair, where I'd be the other woman."

"You've never mentioned wanting a family. So does it matter what our relationship is *technically* called as long as we both enjoy spending time together?"

Her legs suddenly didn't seem capable of supporting her. "Oh, my God," she whispered as she sank down on the bed.

"Wait. Hear me out. You have no idea how great it could be. And after the way you quit this job, you're going to need some help getting another one. I can smooth the way with Gary, so he doesn't sue if you sign on with someone else. I can even put in a good word for you with our competitors. I bet you'll be able to land something in the next two weeks. And if you don't? If it takes a while to find what you're looking for and you need help?" He lowered his voice even further. "I can be there for you, pay a few of your bills, keep you on top on things."

Fire seemed to be consuming her from the inside out. "You told me you loved me."

"I *do* love you," he whispered. "But I love Sally, too. And my kids. You know that. I can't blow up everything I've established in my life because of your guilty conscience."

He wasn't making any sense to her. He wasn't the man she'd thought he was. Where was the Drew who'd been sensitive and kind? Funny? The most congenial of the partners? Apparently, he'd only shown her what she'd wanted to see in order to gain her interest—and now she was getting a taste of the man behind the front. "You love me, your wife and your family."

"I do."

"Like you love the latest hit song, or a certain flavor of ice cream or sushi at Blue Fin."

"What are you talking about?"

Feeling slightly dizzy, Reagan put her head between her knees so she wouldn't pass out. "Loving something and being devoted to it are two different things," she said dully.

"*Devoted* to it? Come on, Reagan. Lighten up. You're a realist. I know you are. How much devotion does one fuck deserve? Granted, it was a good fuck. A great fuck. But still."

And if she was pregnant?

Sitting back up, she closed her eyes and told herself to breathe.

"Hello?" he said when she didn't respond.

She was tempted to educate him on what love was all about. How loyalty and compassion and sacrifice were integral. But what was the point? If he was married with three kids and didn't get that by now, he probably never would.

How had she been so blind? *How* had she missed seeing what a shallow, selfish man he was? He came off so good-natured, so smart, so driven—until he felt he could drop that mask.

"I'm still here," she said.

"What are you thinking?"

"I feel sorry for Sally."

"What?"

"She deserves better. We both do," she added and pressed the End button.

16

serenity

Serenity bent her head to peer through the French doors leading into the cabin, trying to see if Lorelei and Lucy were back from the store. Reagan, who sat across from her, had dried the dew off the metal table and two of the chairs and persuaded Serenity to set up her computer on the deck. After that brief, unexpected storm when they first arrived, the weather was now a glorious sixty-five degrees, which was why Reagan had insisted they work outside. She'd said it would be good for them both to be out in the fresh air and sunshine, that they might find the view inspiring.

Since the overhang on the cabin blocked the glare of the sun on their computer screens, Serenity had decided to give it a try. And she was glad she had. She'd written the first five pages of her new book.

Once she was no longer typing, or frowning in concentration, Reagan looked up. "How're you doing?"

"Better."

"How much better?"

She offered Reagan a hopeful smile. "I've gotten a start."

"That's wonderful! See? We'll take it day by day. Eventually, you'll get there."

A light breeze ruffled Serenity's hair as she slid back in her chair and crossed her legs. Reagan seemed so quiet today. Serenity worried that something was wrong, but Reagan insisted it wasn't. "I can only hope my publisher will be patient. I've asked them to give me to the end of the summer."

"Think they'll go for it?"

Now that she was finally writing, finally feeling as though she might have a chance of regaining her earlier momentum, she was afraid her publisher had already given up hope. "I don't know. I haven't been able to check."

"Why not?"

She raised her eyebrows. "You made me turn off my WiFi, remember?"

The first grin Serenity had seen all morning appeared on Reagan's face. "I remember. We're not letting anything distract us. So, let's hear it."

"Hear what? That you were right? That I needed to sit my butt in a chair, forget everything else and simply write?"

Reagan folded her arms. "No, I want to hear what you've written."

Not only had Reagan made Serenity turn off her WiFi, she'd taken away her cell phone, so that it couldn't be a distraction, told Lorelei to make sure Serenity wasn't interrupted until lunch was ready and started working on her social media pages, introducing herself as "a member of Serenity's team"—as if Serenity had a team—who'd be interacting with them while Serenity dedicated herself to meeting her deadline.

Her real deadline was past, of course, but she and Reagan had decided on a new one—and that was what she'd taken to her publisher. Serenity hoped she'd adequately communicated her renewed commitment to the project in the email she'd sent her editor. Her professional future rested on her publisher's perception of her ability to deliver.

"I need to finish the first chapter and then I'll edit it several times before I read it to anyone," she told Reagan.

"Why not let me see how you've started it? Just the first couple of sentences."

Reagan was being so supportive that Serenity was reluctant to refuse. With a shrug, she complied. "'It was a hot and humid morning in Baton Rouge, Louisiana, when Linda Maynard rolled out of bed on August 2, 1997,'" she read. "'She was looking forward to the end of what had felt like a long summer—a hard summer, considering the setbacks her husband had experienced at work—and planned to spend this Friday shopping for school clothes with her three children.'"

She looked up to find a pained expression on Reagan's face. "What? It's no good?"

"The writing's great. It's just that… I mean… Is this the day he *killed* them?"

Relieved to learn Reagan was reacting to the sadness of the subject matter and not the way Serenity had begun the book, she nodded.

"And no one saw it coming? What kind of man *was* he?"

"Most people say he was quiet, contemplative, private. Seemed harmless."

"That's terrifying!"

"It is. But that's how he's been characterized by his

work associates, neighbors and siblings. So that's how I'm going to portray him."

Lorelei peered out, saw them talking instead of working and opened the door. "Are you two getting hungry?"

Reagan glanced at her watch. "I am. Should we eat outside?"

They agreed that would be ideal. Lorelei said she'd have Lucy help set the table and disappeared back inside.

"*Now* can I have my phone?" Serenity was teasing Reagan, acting as though Reagan had been a grueling taskmaster this morning, but she was grateful that her new sister was helping her focus and move forward.

As soon as Reagan handed it over, Serenity turned on the ringer and checked her email.

"Anything?" Reagan asked.

"Not yet." No answer meant her editor was probably taking the situation to upper management, and they were trying to come to a consensus on how best to proceed—whether they needed to move her book in the production schedule to accommodate the new deadline.

Serenity hated that she was causing other people extra work. But she hoped the credibility she'd established over her previous books would carry her through.

Reagan slid her laptop toward Serenity. "Want to see what I've been working on?"

"I thought you were interacting with the people on my Facebook page."

"I was, for a while. But I also wrote my first post for *Serenity Alston Investigates*."

"You're done? Jeez, if it was that easy, maybe *you* should be the writer."

Reagan chuckled—although not as freely as she normally did—and moved her chair out of the shade so she could turn her face up to the sun. "It only took an hour to go over the various filicide studies and other things I found online. I'm used to scanning for facts and then coming up with something on the spot. Pitching ads trains you to do that. But since I'm used to writing advertising copy, this might be too short for a blog."

"If it's interesting and covers the topic, short is fine. There are no set rules."

"Good, because it's only about three hundred words. I thought I'd finish with a few details about the book you're writing—a teaser of sorts. So let me know if your editor gives you a new release date. Do you have a title yet?"

"I have the one I submitted. My editor seemed to like it, but once marketing weighs in, we might have to change it."

"What's your suggestion?"

"*All Gone.* It works for the people he murdered and the fact that he disappeared for twenty years before being caught."

"That's positively haunting."

"Yeah. This whole case is haunting. I think that's part of the reason I'm struggling to write about it. It's too dark for me right now, since it involves kids and what Sean did involved kids, too. God, what's wrong with people?"

"Damned if I know." Reagan's expression was troubled enough as she stood that Serenity wondered if she was only referring to Mr. Maynard, or if there was something else bothering her.

"Is everything okay?" she asked.

Her smile looked forced. "Fine."

"What's happened? Have you heard from Drew?"

Her shrug didn't come off nearly as careless as she no doubt intended it to. "I spoke to him for a few minutes."

Serenity was surprised she hadn't said anything about the call. "When?"

"This morning."

"And?"

"He was an ass. But none of that matters."

"Of course it matters—"

"No, it doesn't," she broke in. "It doesn't change anything—nothing that makes a difference, anyway. I knew before I let myself call him that I had to cut off all contact. It's hard, though, to have my image of him ruined, too."

"It was that bad?"

"Let's just say I was even a bigger idiot to get involved with him than I thought."

Serenity bit her lip. "I'm sorry."

"Like I said, it doesn't change anything." That same forced smile returned. "I'm going to wash my hands for lunch while you check over my post. If it's not what you're looking for, let me know, and I'll revise. Or you can edit it however you like. Don't worry about hurting my feelings. After working in a New York City advertising firm for ten years, I'm used to constructive criticism—and every other kind of criticism, too," she joked.

"Thanks." Serenity was watching her go, wishing she could do something to make things better, when her phone buzzed.

She looked down at her lap, expecting a text from her mother or someone else in her family. Ever since she'd found those files on Sean's computer, she'd isolated herself from almost everyone else.

But it wasn't anyone in *her* family. It was Sean's mother—someone she'd hoped never to hear from again.

Several of Sean's scrapbooks, from when he was a little boy, are missing. Do you have them?

Why would she have kept those—kept *anything*? She didn't want to be reminded of him, their marriage or how it had ended.

No.

She prayed this interaction would be that short, that simple.

But her ex-mother-in-law wrote back: In the last letter he sent, he told me he put them under the house. Your house. Have you searched there?

Serenity lived in a Bushrod Victorian built in the 1920s in the Berkeley Hills. She'd gone down the narrow, rickety steps leading into the basement and grabbed everything she could find that belonged to Sean. But she hadn't been willing to search through all the boxes that weren't labeled or were buried in the far back. She was uneasy in that dank, dark space—if only because of the spiders that had to be living down there. She'd figured if she still had anything of his, she'd get it to his family when she moved or cleared out the basement completely, whichever came first. It wasn't as if he'd be able to do anything with his belongings until he got out of prison, anyway.

If I run across anything, I'll make sure you get it, she wrote back.

When? That's the question. I'm trying to create a slideshow for our family reunion. Those pictures are important to us and can't be replaced. Will you check? Please?

I'm not at home, Nina.

When will you be?

She knew Nina would freak out if she said September. She'd assume Serenity was just being difficult. When do you need them? she asked instead.

Next weekend.

"Damn it." She didn't want to return to Berkeley so soon, especially for that reason. But she also hated to give Sean's family any more excuses to contact her. If Nina didn't get what she was after, Sean's father, brothers or even sisters-in-law could intervene.

If this was the last thread tying her to them, she was all for cutting it as soon as possible.

I'll text you if I can find them.

You'll check? Really?

Her doubt irritated Serenity. Have I ever lied to you?

You lied plenty of times in court.

Serenity almost wrote back, *It was your son who did all the lying.* But getting into a text war wouldn't do anyone any good. Sean's family steadfastly believed that he'd opened those files on his computer by accident, that he'd had no idea what they contained and just hadn't had the chance to report them to the police before she found them—in spite of the fact that other members of the same pornography ring were busted, too.

Can we look ourselves? Nina asked when Serenity didn't respond. Make sure we have all his stuff?

"Don't you dare show up on my doorstep," she muttered. Once the trial ended, she'd considered changing her phone number, so they couldn't contact her anymore. Sean's brothers had gotten so nasty with her she'd had to get a restraining order against the oldest, who'd left her several threatening voice mail messages and kept driving past her house in an attempt to intimidate her.

But she'd decided it was probably futile to give up her number. She'd had it for years, preferred to keep it if she could. Sean's family knew where she lived, anyway.

No. I'll see if Sawyer will come and help with some of the heavier boxes next weekend.

She couldn't reach the ones Sean had put on the highest shelf and wasn't strong enough to lift them down, even if she bought a ladder.

Sawyer? What's going on between you two? Don't tell me you're together...

No, of course not! He's just the only member of your family I'll allow over. Anyway, if he'll help me, and we find anything that belongs to Sean, I'll see if he'll drop it by your place. If not, you'll have to wait for it to come through the mail.

I don't trust Sawyer any more than I do you, came her response.

Serenity felt bad that Sawyer hadn't been able to make up with the people who'd finished raising him.

Maybe he *had* acted to protect her, to a point, and was still paying the price.

I'll Facetime you the moment we open the basement door so I can show you everything that's left. Will you be happy then? What reason would I have to still keep pictures of someone who let me down in the worst possible way?

You're the one who destroyed my son's life! I'll never forgive you for what you've done.

Serenity jumped to her feet. Nina's accusations were so unfounded. *She* hadn't destroyed Sean; she'd only caught him. What did they expect? For her to turn a blind eye, like they did? Don't start or I'll never answer another text from you, she wrote back.

She waited but didn't receive a response.

She wished she could flip them all off—figuratively, since she didn't plan to see any of them ever again—and be done with the whole family. But if she had pictures of Sean when he was little, she figured she might as well let his mother have them. She didn't want any reminders of him.

Now all she had to do was convince Sawyer to act as intermediary. He wouldn't be happy about it, but she had a feeling he'd do it. After the trial, her mother, Sean's mother and who knew how many other members of both families probably assumed he had a thing for her. It was his support that had carried her through.

But he was the type who would stand behind her on principle.

Or…could they be right? *Was* there something more to it?

* * *

reagan

While she was in the bathroom and no one else could see her, Reagan checked her phone for missed calls, messages and emails. She didn't want to hear from Drew or anyone else at work. And yet she did. The lack of a reaction, the total silence, made her feel so unappreciated.

Surely Drew cared about her more than it had seemed on the phone—or there were moments she was tempted to deceive herself by believing that. It would be easier than facing the truth.

And at least one, if not more, of the managing partners at Edison & Curry had to feel the company was worse off for having lost her. She'd been a rising star, a hard worker who'd produced much more than everyone else. It didn't seem fair that she could care so intensely about Drew *and* her work, and yet, when she walked away, he and everyone else at the agency simply shrugged and moved on.

Tears welled up when she found that all she'd received were emails expressing shock and sadness from various work associates who had no power at Edison & Curry. What bothered her even more was that she suspected at least two of those people were secretly happy to have her gone. An opening in the hierarchy above them provided opportunities for advancement.

No doubt they were already eyeing her office.

"Finn's coming over for lunch."

She heard, through the door, Lorelei tell Serenity that and blinked away her tears. At least she felt needed here.

Serenity had started her book, and Reagan had a small hand in helping her make that happen. She'd enjoyed writing the blog for *Serenity Alston Investigates*, too. It felt good to forget about her own goals and desires and concentrate on something else for a while.

But that "while" would come to an end, and then she'd have to cope with the wreckage she'd left behind.

Reminded of what she'd face when she returned to New York, she decided to call her mother and break the news about her job. At some point, she had to let Rosalind know she'd quit.

Slipping out of the bathroom, she moved as quietly as possible to her bedroom, where she shut the door behind her so no one could overhear her conversation.

She held her breath as the phone began to ring.

"Rosalind Sands International."

"Is Ms. Sands there?" She'd been calling her mother at the same office, the one with prints from the Conde Nast Archives covering the reception area and furniture by Jonathan Adler throughout, as far back as she could remember. But the level of formality never changed. The company didn't respect "non-creatives" as her mother called them, so they didn't pay the receptionist enough to keep the position filled for very long. That meant the voice on the end of the line was just that—a voice.

Today, it was a man's voice. "May I tell Ms. Sands who's calling?"

"Her daughter, Reagan."

A pause ensued, during which Reagan assumed he was checking on her mother's availability. "She has an appointment coming up soon, but I'll see if I can catch her," he said, and with that Pavarotti started singing

"Che gelida manina" from *La Bohème* while she was put on hold.

If her mother was too busy to talk, Reagan would have the perfect excuse to procrastinate a little longer.

But if she didn't get through to her now, Rosalind could call back at a far less convenient time.

It wasn't easy to decide which way she wanted it to go—

"Reagan, is everything okay?"

Apparently, the receptionist had managed to catch Rosalind, who sounded like she always did—in charge. But what she'd said caused Reagan's heart to skip a beat. Why wouldn't everything be okay? Had her mother tried to call her at Edison & Curry and been informed that she no longer worked there?

"It's…fine," she replied tentatively. "Why?"

"You don't usually call me in the middle of a work-day."

Reagan let her breath seep out slowly. She didn't call her mother in the middle of a workday because she knew she'd be interrupting, and she'd been trained as a child *not* to demand her mother's attention when she was trying to accomplish something. "I'm in Califor-nia right now. It's three hours earlier here, lunchtime."

"California! What are you doing there?"

Reagan had planned to say she'd taken a spontane-ous trip across the country with friends. But while she was breaking the bad news, maybe she should go ahead and tell Rosalind about Serenity and Lorelei. Get it all over with at once. The distraction might even put Ro-salind on the defensive for a change. And if she and her sisters wanted answers about how they were related it was entirely possible Reagan would *have* to talk to her mother about it eventually.

Or Serenity would have to ask Charlotte.

Feeling as though broaching the subject was becoming inevitable, Reagan threw back her shoulders and plunged in. "That's kind of a complicated story. Do you have time for it?"

"I'll take the time."

Her mother rarely responded so positively. More often, Reagan heard, "This can't wait until later?"

"After you started having heart problems and your doctors mentioned that you might need an operation, I wondered if I had any genetic weaknesses I should be aware of. I've only got information about one side of my family tree, after all, so I have no idea if I'm susceptible to diabetes or cancer or any other disease on my father's side."

"So..."

"I had my DNA tested."

"You did."

Reagan was listening carefully, trying to detect what her mother was feeling. Fear? Dread? Ambivalence? But it was impossible to determine from so few words. Her mother's voice could sound clipped even when she wasn't upset. "Yes."

"And?"

"Nothing serious came up. Except—"

"Don't tell me you took that test hoping to find your father's family."

Her mother had always been smart. She'd already caught on.

"In a way, I guess I did," Reagan said, although she hadn't cared as much about her father and his family when she took the test as she did now that she was beginning to wonder if her mother had been lying to her all along.

"Why would you do that?" her mother asked. "What's the point?"

"The point is I know nothing about my father and his side of the family. On my birth certificate it gives my birthplace as Cincinnati, so you must've lived there before moving to New York. I'm guessing that's where the two of you met, but you never talk about it."

"That is where we met. It's where I was born, too. But what difference does it make in the here and now?"

It wasn't easy to keep pushing her mother; it was like swimming upstream, against a forceful current. "Why did you decide to leave?"

"After your father died, there was nothing there for me. I wanted to be a fashion designer. Of course I would come here."

"What about his family? Are they still in Cincinnati?"

"How would I know? They've never been supportive—of you or me."

Rosalind hated to talk about these things so much that Reagan couldn't help wondering why. "Is there a reason they weren't?" Had her mother gotten pregnant out of wedlock? Been artificially inseminated so she could have a child on her own? Slept with a married man and never told him she was carrying his baby—the way Reagan would be tempted to do if she was pregnant with Drew's baby? *What?*

"They didn't like me, I guess. After I moved here, we just...drifted apart. I lost contact with them years ago."

Was that the truth—or a cover-up? It was difficult

to tell. "So you have no idea where they live now? Do you have their last known address?"

"Reagan, I've got an appointment. Can we talk about this later?"

When? Reagan got the impression that even if Rosalind wasn't lying she'd be careful to avoid this subject in the future. She expected Reagan to accept what she'd been told without question, simply because that was what Rosalind dictated—and Rosalind *always* called the shots.

But, for once, Reagan wasn't willing to let her have her way. "You asked me why I was in California. You don't want to hear the answer before you go?"

"I already know the answer. You're chasing ghosts."

"Not ghosts, Mom. After I took that DNA test, I received a notice that I have two half sisters. I'm with them—at a cabin in Lake Tahoe."

A tense silence followed. Then her mother said, "So you went to California to find them, without telling me?"

How could Rosalind expect Reagan to confide anything in her? Reagan felt as though she knew her half sisters better than she did her mother—already. "I suspected you wouldn't be supportive."

"Whether you're right about that or not, we should've discussed it before you took off for the opposite coast."

Reagan preferred not to get caught up in a debate about that. She was thirty-five, old enough to do as she pleased. "Who are they, Mom? How is it that they even exist?"

"How should I know? This is as much of a shock to me as it is to you."

"You don't think… I mean, my father wouldn't have…"

"Cheated on me? He must've, right?"

Her mother didn't seem too hurt by the idea. But then, it had been a long time since he'd been around. Did Rosalind no longer care?

"How? When?" Reagan demanded. "Serenity, Lorelei and I are all close in age, and yet we're from different parts of the country. You don't find that strange?"

"Your father sometimes traveled for work."

"You told me he was a commercial real estate broker. Why would that necessitate travel to different states?"

"He had to meet investors."

"That's the answer?"

"What other answer could there be?"

Was her mother being evasive? Why wasn't she more humiliated, embarrassed? A woman as proud and beautiful as Rosalind would hate to admit that her husband had strayed. Rosalind wanted to pretend she was somehow above the foibles that brought suffering to everyone else. "So you didn't know about these other children he might've had."

"No. He didn't make it a point to tell me. Why would he?"

"Wouldn't Serenity's and Lorelei's mothers have demanded child support?"

"Not necessarily. Or maybe he gave them some money here and there, but that sort of thing never came to my attention."

That comment, too, sent out a warning signal. Nothing slipped past Rosalind. But he'd died not quite two years after Reagan was born, so there wasn't a lot of time for anyone to pursue him legally. And maybe Ro-

salind hadn't been as diligent and cautious back then…
"But that means Serenity's mother must have cheated,
too. And Serenity will find that hard to believe. Her
parents have always been madly in love. She was born
into the most perfect family you can imagine."

"More perfect than yours, you mean."

"More…complete," she hedged.

"It's not my fault he died, Reagan."

"I'm not blaming you for that. I'm just saying that
Serenity grew up believing the man who raised her
was her father."

"That doesn't mean anything. Maybe her mother felt
it was better that she not know. Her mother could've
kept it a secret from both of them."

"That's it?"

"What more can I say?"

"You don't seem to be the least bit curious about Serenity and Lorelei."

"I'm not. And if I were you, I wouldn't waste time
worrying about the past."

Reagan, who felt she was always trying to mitigate
her mother's irritation, felt a strong dose of irritation
herself. "I've never had siblings. Now I have two. And
you're acting as if…as if it's no big deal?"

"I have an appointment," she repeated. "I have to go.
We'll talk about it when you get back, okay?"

"I'm not coming back." She spoke quickly to catch
her mother. "Not until the end of August."

There was a long pause. "What about your job?"

Downstairs, she could hear voices, louder than before. Finn must've arrived.

"I don't work at the agency anymore."

"Why not?"

Dropping her head in her hand, she massaged her forehead as she sifted through all the various excuses she'd thought up—that she was tired of working her life away, that the partners at Edison & Curry were suddenly holding her back, that she wanted to do something else with her life.

So she had no idea why she suddenly blurted out the truth. Maybe it was because she was tired of trying not to set her mother off or lose her approval. Or maybe it was that so much of her life was already unraveling she felt a certain reckless abandon—the desire to go ahead and smash the whole damn thing. "Because I had sex with my boss right on his desk. But everyone makes mistakes. Right, Mom?"

She disconnected before she realized she was going to do it. Then, her blood rushing in her ears, she stared down at her phone. She'd never hung up on her mother before.

"Shit," she muttered. Apparently, all kinds of things were changing.

She was changing. And she had no idea if she'd even recognize herself when it was over.

Especially if she was pregnant.

The possibility that she might be expecting a child was the only bombshell she hadn't told Rosalind.

It was also the one that would upset her the most.

17

lorelei

Finn smelled good—woodsy with a hint of…citrus? Lorelei couldn't remember ever finding a scent so appealing. Every time she passed him as they carried the food out to the deck, she wished she could stop, put her nose up against the warm skin at the opening of his polo shirt and breathe deeply.

She was obviously developing a crush on him, which wasn't good. The last thing she needed was more pressure on her marriage. But she couldn't seem to help herself. She loved the timbre of his voice, his ready smile, the twinkle in those unusual amber-colored eyes when someone said something amusing.

And she found the casual way he approached life soothing. Just being around him helped relieve some of the angst that gripped her whenever she thought of Mark or Francine.

So, regardless of anything else, she was glad she'd met Finn. After putting all of her effort and energy exclusively toward her home and family for ten years, she felt as though she'd been digging a tunnel—burrowing a little deeper each day—and she was only now returning to the surface to poke her head out and take a look at the world she'd left behind.

Maybe she should've crawled out of that tunnel sooner. Maybe she could've prevented what'd happened between Mark and Francine if she'd been less concerned with filling a role and more concerned with what her husband was thinking and feeling and doing.

Mark had obviously found his life too unexciting. And as much as she hated to admit it, she could be partly responsible. She'd forgotten to change things up now and then, search out new opportunities, be flexible. If he hadn't done what he'd done—ripped their marriage apart at the seams—it was possible she would've spent the next ten, twenty or even thirty years, if not the rest of her life, continuing to dig that same tunnel.

The weird thing was that she'd considered herself happy.

Now—and this was an uncomfortable thought—she wondered if she'd just felt safe. Safe by itself would be such an improvement over the insecurity she'd felt as a child it was entirely possible she'd believed their relationship was strong simply because there'd never been any real blowups—until Francine.

Was it possible their marriage had gone stagnant, and she'd been too busy doing her part as a good wife and mother to notice?

"His fever is gone?" Serenity was talking to Finn about Davis as they sat down to wait for Reagan.

"Yes. He should be here on Sunday."

Lorelei helped Lucy scoot her chair closer to the table. "That's wonderful."

"It wasn't looking good there for a minute," he admitted. "Instead of him coming here, I thought I'd have to go home, at least for a while. But when he woke up this morning, his temperature was back to normal."

Serenity handed them each a napkin. "Did they give him antibiotics?"

"They did. He was resistant to whichever one they used first, so they switched to a new one."

"Thank God this one is working."

One of the French doors opened and Reagan hurried out onto the deck. "Sorry, I was on the phone."

She seemed flustered.

"Everything okay?" Serenity asked, but Lorelei could plainly see that it wasn't. The way Reagan sank into her chair, as though having it there to catch her came as a relief, suggested she wasn't feeling very steady on her feet.

"I'm not sure."

Lucy eyed her critically. "Are you *crying*, Aunt Reagan?"

"No." The edge to her voice indicated she was on the verge, however. "I like it when you call me Aunt Reagan," she added, attempting a smile. "That makes me feel a lot better."

Lorelei peered more closely at her. "What's going on?"

"I just hung up on my mother."

Serenity, who'd stood and grabbed the pitcher of iced tea as soon as Reagan appeared, waited before actually pouring it into their glasses. "Did you say hung up *on*—or hung up *with*?"

"On," she clarified with a pained expression. "I've now committed the unpardonable sin—which is the

cherry on top of all the other crap I've done to ruin my life in the last two weeks."

"You told her about quitting your job?" Lorelei asked.

"I told her about *everything*."

"Not Drew…" Serenity said.

"Who's Drew?" Finn asked.

"My married boss," Reagan explained before he could ask if Drew was a husband or boyfriend.

"Uh-oh," he said.

"Exactly," Reagan agreed.

"What did you say about Drew?" Lorelei asked.

"I told her I had s-e-x with my boss, quit my job and took a DNA test that revealed I have two half sisters."

"What's s-e-x?" Lucy asked, clearly perplexed.

"Nothing you need to worry about for quite some time, little one," Finn said, jumping in. He gestured at the pasta, salad and garlic bread in the center of the table. "How about all this food. Was your mommy the one who made it?"

"Yes!"

Lucy's enthusiasm for Lorelei's efforts brought Lorelei a warm feeling despite her concern for Reagan.

"And do you think it'll taste as good as it looks?" Finn asked.

When Lorelei's daughter nodded vigorously, he said, "Why don't we see about that?" and scooped up a small serving of pasta for Lucy while Lorelei and Serenity continued to gape at Reagan.

What had gotten into Reagan? Lorelei wondered. With the way she'd dreaded telling her mother about her job, Lorelei hadn't expected her to take the conversation that far. "How did she react?"

"To which part?" Reagan replied morosely.

"Why don't we start with what happened with Drew."

"I didn't give her much of a chance to react to that one. I blurted it out right before I hung up."

Lorelei and Serenity exchanged a glance.

"Sounds like the telephone equivalent of shooting up the place," Serenity mumbled.

"It was," Reagan said. "I don't know what came over me."

"How did she react to hearing about us?" Lorelei asked.

"As if it means nothing, no big deal. Which is probably why I got angry. I wanted her to be transparent, to be real, to just *talk* to me for a change."

Serenity rested the pitcher on the table. "You were hoping for some honesty."

"And I was frustrated that I couldn't get it."

"So what *did* she say?" Lorelei pressed.

"That my father must've been unfaithful."

Serenity scowled. "But that means my mother would have to have known your father. Lorelei's, too."

"Can we say with any certainty that they *didn't* know each other?" Reagan asked. "Maybe they did, and the mystery can be solved that easily."

A look of skepticism appeared on Serenity's face. "Did your father ever live in California or Florida?"

"No, but my mother said he traveled sometimes."

"By himself?"

"I guess. For business. To meet investors for real estate."

"Then I suppose it's possible," Serenity allowed. "But was he in California long enough to get to know my mother? And in what capacity could they have met? We can't say what Lorelei's mother did for a living, but my mother's always been an organic gardener. Organic gardeners don't usually have any reason to meet out-of-town commercial real estate agents."

"They could've met in a restaurant, a bar, a grocery store," Reagan suggested. "Think of all the random strangers you pass each day."

"Just because I pass them doesn't mean I meet them—or go home with them," Serenity said, stubbornly resisting the idea that her mother had cheated.

Lorelei had a huge stake in this conversation. What they found might provide answers to the questions that had plagued her since she could remember. And yet she was slightly distracted by seeing Finn help Lucy get some salad and a piece of garlic bread on her plate. It was thoughtful of him to keep her occupied.

"I can't imagine my mother cheating," Serenity continued, "not when she was happy in her marriage and in love with her husband."

"Could it be that your parents weren't always as in love as they are now?" Lorelei asked.

"Every marriage has its rough patches," Serenity admitted. "Still, where was my father when my mother and your father were potentially together?"

Reagan shrugged. "At work?"

"I'm not buying it. Maybe it's just that I don't want to believe it, but I don't see my mother getting pregnant like that and never telling anyone."

"There are people who'd argue that keeping the pregnancy a secret would be the best way to handle it," Reagan pointed out. "Look at what a happy childhood you had. Who knows what would've happened if she'd told. It's possible your parents would've split up."

"Without DNA testing, Serenity's mother might've

been able to take that secret to her grave," Finn said in agreement. "She had no way of knowing technology would eventually out her. Had she known, she might've made a different choice."

"Finn's right," Reagan said. "It was a whole other world back then. A lot of women might've made the same decision. But I'm not convinced my father slept with both your mothers. My own mother was being evasive. She wanted me to assume my father cheated so I'd believe that was the end of the story and drop it."

"You got the impression she was hiding something?" Serenity asked.

"With her it's hard to tell. But yes. She didn't want to discuss it."

"I hate to play devil's advocate *again*, but it wouldn't be fun to hear that your husband might've cheated on you with two women—who each had a child by him," Finn said. "Maybe it's easier for her not to even consider it—to just continue living her life as she's been doing for years, believing he was true to her and you were his only child."

Reagan's expression didn't clear. "But if she didn't know I have two half sisters until I told her, she would've shown more surprise, more interest and curiosity, wouldn't she? Something beyond, 'I've got to go. We'll talk about it later.'"

"You've mentioned how busy she is," Lorelei said. "Is it possible she really *did* have to go?"

"Yes, but it was still a brush-off."

Serenity finally poured the tea. "What was your father's name again?"

"Stuart Sands."

"Stuart," she repeated. "I'm going to text my mother

and tell her that I ran into someone here in Tahoe who claims to have known her and give her that name."

Reagan's hand stalled as she was bringing her glass to her lips. "What if she says he's dead?"

"Then that'll prove they knew each other," Serenity replied.

After taking a long drink, Reagan put her iced tea back on the table and reached for the pasta. "Yes, it would—and the simplest explanation is often the right one."

* * *

serenity

Would Sawyer even pick up?

Although he'd called her recently, the conversation hadn't gone well. Maybe he was finished with her after making the effort to be friendly and not getting a very warm response. Maybe he'd only rung her in the first place as a final check-in, to make sure she was doing okay after the trial so he could feel that his duty to stand for truth and protect the innocent was done.

She couldn't imagine any other reason he'd be interested in talking to the person who'd once been married to his stepbrother and had driven such a wedge between him and the family who'd taken him in and raised him. Even if that wedge had been the result of Sean's actions and wasn't *her* fault—she knew they both understood that—she was afraid she represented the entire negative experience for him.

She had herself so convinced that Sawyer was frowning when he saw her name pop up on his phone that she almost didn't allow the call to go through.

He answered before she could stop it. "Hello?"

She froze.

"Serenity?"

If she disconnected now, she could pass it off as a pocket dial. She had Nina waiting for those pictures that might be at the house in Berkeley, but she could hire someone to lift the boxes down for her and deliver them to Nina's house herself.

There were ways around getting Sawyer involved; she knew, in her heart, that Nina was just the excuse she was using to call him. This wasn't about Sean's pictures as much as the regret she felt for being so remote with Sawyer when he'd reached out to her the last time.

"Hi." Although she'd hesitated, she hoped it wasn't long enough to reveal her anxiety. She was pacing in her bedroom with the door shut even though Reagan, Lorelei and Finn were gone. When they'd mentioned taking Lucy on a walk after lunch, she'd begged off, saying she had to take care of some emails. She'd wanted privacy to make this call, and she figured she'd have a better chance of enlisting Sawyer to help her this weekend if she gave him some notice.

"Are you okay?" he asked.

His voice was *so* deep. *Everything* about him was different from Sean. Sawyer was tough, mentally and physically. He could be a poster boy for the marines—he'd been a marine before starting his own real estate appraisal business, so that made sense—while Sean had been more talkative and social, and was always looking for the next "fun" thing to plan or do or buy. Serenity had been drawn to his optimistic, happy-go-lucky personality. He loved wine, food, traveling, dinner parties, movies and television.

But then…who wouldn't love those things? Maybe it was just that Sean had always had the luxury of indulging himself. He could take a relaxed approach to life because he came from a place of privilege, having such a devoted family to act as a safety net if anything went wrong.

Sawyer, on the other hand, had sustained considerable loss at a young age, and he'd largely had to fend for himself ever since. Life for him had been a struggle, and he took it more seriously.

Now that *she'd* suffered a serious setback, her first major life blow, she understood Sawyer and his caution far better—and she was sort of embarrassed. She'd suddenly realized that the difference between her and Sean, and Sawyer on the other side, was that Sawyer had grown up a lot sooner than they had.

She wondered if he'd recognized her immaturity, if that was part of the reason they'd always been at odds with each other.

"I'm fine," she replied.

She thought of all the things she wanted to say to him but couldn't decide where to start. Should she tell him how grateful she was for his support? If he hadn't felt the need to protect her, he probably would've been able to avoid creating such a terrible rift with his family. At the very least, his actions wouldn't have been such a focal point during the trial. And she'd never thanked him, never even broached the subject. She'd simply ignored his sacrifice while she tried to cope with all the other emotions that were making her miserable.

She opened her mouth to acknowledge what he'd done but changed her mind. She didn't want to put him on the spot, make him uncomfortable.

He broke the strained silence. "What's up?"

She had to say *something*. "I was… Please don't feel any pressure to say yes, but…"

"But…" he prompted when she didn't finish.

"Never mind. I don't have the right to ask you for anything. I'm sorry I bothered you," she said and disconnected.

"Great. That was just great," she muttered to herself. "Congratulations, Serenity. You're an idiot." What made her think Sawyer would want to gather up the last of his stepbrother's items and deliver them to a stepmother who now hated him?

She obviously hadn't thought that through carefully enough—

Her phone vibrated in her hand; he was calling back. *Damn it.* She had to answer. He knew she was right there, next to her phone—she'd just called him. "Hello?"

"Care to tell me what's going on?" he said.

She stopped moving and spoke while staring at her feet. "Your stepmother texted me last night."

"I'm sure you were happy to hear from her."

The sarcasm was unmistakable. "Yeah, not so much. She claims I have some of Sean's childhood pictures. But if I do, they're on the top shelf in the basement, where I can't reach them. Even if I could, I don't like going down there. There're too many rats and spiders—"

"You want me to come get them for you," he guessed before she could finish.

"If you would."

"No problem. What time?"

She drew a deep, steadying breath. "I'm in Tahoe now. But I was planning to head down the mountain on Saturday morning. So any time on Saturday. If you're free. But don't feel obligated," she quickly added. "I'm sure you've got a million things you'd rather do with your weekend than hang out with your ex-sister-in-law."

"I'll be available around four."

"That would be perfect. It'll be a lot better if you're there with me." She bit her knuckles as soon as those words came out of her mouth. *What* had she just said? It sounded as if she missed him, felt safer when he was around. But she couldn't take it back or clarify without drawing even more attention to her *faux pas*.

"Okay," he said as if she hadn't said anything out of the ordinary. "I'll call you when I'm heading over."

"Thank you."

"See you on Saturday," he said and then he was gone.

Serenity groaned as she fell back on her bed. *It'd be a lot better if you're there with me?*

She tried to tell herself she didn't know where that had come from. But she had to acknowledge that while she'd been navigating the sharp rocks and reefs of Sean's lies, his family's anger at her defection, his lawyers' pressure to change her testimony, the loss of her marriage and, maybe, the hope of ever having a family—not to mention the mounting pressure of being unable to write during the whole ordeal—it was Sawyer showing up at the courthouse each and every day that had been the lighthouse guiding her safely through.

18

lorelei

"**D**id you notice your husband getting a bit too chummy with your best friend before you learned the truth?"

Reagan had taken Lucy down to the water, which left Finn and Lorelei sitting farther up the beach. When they'd set out from the cabin, they hadn't intended to walk clear to Sand Harbor. Lorelei would never have attempted such a distance on her own, not without a stroller. Lucy could easily tire on the way back, which would mean carrying her home.

But with Finn letting Lucy ride on his shoulders, Lorelei didn't have to be so practical. When they got involved in conversation and continued on to the lake, Lorelei hadn't protested or asked to turn back. She was enjoying herself too much.

"Not really," she replied. "Francine and I were so close that she spent a lot of time with Mark, too. She'd hug us both when she arrived or left. Would remember to bake him a cake for his birthday. Would bring over cookies or meals she knew he'd like. Would talk to him about movies or TV shows they both enjoyed. But she did plenty of nice things for me, too, and everyone else she loved. I didn't get the impression she was flirting with him so much as being thoughtful—a good friend to both of us."

She could feel Finn's eyes on her but didn't dare meet his gaze. Every time she looked at him, she felt a flutter in her stomach—an awareness she hadn't experienced in ages, which was crazy. She was avoiding the hard problems in her life by admiring him. Or maybe she was looking for some reassurance that she was desirable in spite of how unattractive Mark had made her feel.

"When do you think it switched to something more?" he asked.

Lorelei stared out over the water. The beach wasn't crowded; it was still too chilly for sunbathing. And it was a Monday. Apparently, many of Tahoe's visitors came only for the weekend now that it was no longer ski season. But with the vivid blue of the lake, the Brunswick green of the tall stands of pine trees that looked as though they'd marched boldly up to the water, and the white-capped mountains rising all around them, it was a beautiful place to be. Lorelei felt as if she was sitting in the middle of a painting, especially with someone as handsome as Finn lounging beside her. Maybe one day Finn *would* paint this place…

"That's the thing," she replied. "I don't know. They joked around and teased each other all the time, but I got the impression it was more like a sister horsing around with a brother-in-law."

He grimaced. "That makes it even worse."

"It does. Obviously, it changed somewhere along the line. I'm not sure exactly when that was or why I didn't notice, but I'll lose my best friend as well as my husband—if I go that way."

Sitting up, he crossed his legs in front of him. "Is that the direction you're leaning?"

She shook her head. "I can't decide. It's so hard to give up on a marriage when you've devoted everything you have to it. Especially when there's a child involved. But how will I ever trust Mark again?" She didn't mention that she believed Mark was taking steps to protect his income should she leave him, because that hurt almost as much as the affair. It revealed a stingy, ungenerous side of her husband, one that was, in the end, ruthlessly practical as well as blatantly unfair. It certainly did little to convince her that he truly cared about her or her well-being.

"Considering the way you grew up, I can understand how important trust is to you."

Finally, she looked at him directly. "Don't you think he should've understood that, too?"

Although he seemed about to agree with her, he deferred at the last second. "Marriages are complicated, Lorelei. I don't want to steer you wrong." He picked up a rock and threw it as far as he could into the water. "Do you have a picture of Mark? And Francine? We've talked so much about them, but I don't even know what they look like."

She pulled her phone from her pocket and thumbed through her photos until she came up with a picture of her husband. Finn glanced at it and nodded. Then she found one of Francine at the baby shower she'd thrown when Lorelei was pregnant with Lucy.

"She's pretty, isn't she," she said as she showed it to him.

She watched as he studied her ex-best friend's image, imagined him taking in the long blond hair, big blue eyes, petite but curvy figure and the dimples that flashed whenever she smiled.

"No prettier than you," he responded and handed her phone back as Lucy came running up the beach.

"Momma, come wade with me!"

"Isn't the water too cold?" Lorelei asked.

"It's *freezing*!" Reagan called from the water's edge.

That didn't deter Lucy. She tugged on Lorelei's hand. "It's *not* too cold," she insisted.

Lorelei laughed. "Okay, okay. Let me get my shoes off."

Finn kicked his flip-flops to the side, got up and pulled her to her feet.

"Thanks," she said, but he caught her by the elbow to stop her before she could follow her daughter down to the water.

"If I'm reading between the lines of our conversation correctly, you're thinking there must be something wrong with you. That you're not attractive enough, or interesting enough, or adventurous enough—or *something*—or your husband wouldn't have gone elsewhere for what you were already providing."

What he said was so accurate, and her self-doubt so severe, that tears sprang to her eyes.

"But don't you believe it," he added and gave her arm a sympathetic squeeze before striding down the beach.

* * *

serenity

The bedroom off the loft that contained the library smelled of old leather, and dust motes floated in the swordlike shafts of sunlight stabbing through the blinds. This place wasn't spooky like the basement in her house in Berkeley. There were no cobwebs or spiders. But it was packed so tightly with storage that it wasn't easy to navigate. There were boxes stacked to the ceiling, some old furniture and an antique lamp shoved into one corner, a standing jewelry box her father had once given her mother but was now out of fashion, extra bedding, a pile of sheet music from when the twins were taking piano lessons and other odds and ends.

Serenity had already burrowed through the box just inside the door—the one filled with toys and games. That was where she'd found the puzzle for Lucy. Serenity had taken a game or two out of that box before. But as far as she was concerned, there'd never been anything else of interest in this room.

Until now.

Before texting Charlotte about Stuart Sands, she'd decided to see what she could find up here. When her parents were moving from Berkeley to San Diego, they sold their house as soon as they put it on the market, months before the new place was finished. Rather than rent an apartment, they'd decided to live at the cabin. And when they finally *did* move to their new home in Southern California, they'd left quite a lot of their belongings behind—anything they wanted to keep but weren't likely to use.

Serenity thought that might include some old scrapbooks, photo albums, files for home purchases and/or other records. After all, the cabin was more enduring than anything else the Curringtons had ever owned. Their cars changed. Their boats changed. Even their main residence had changed. But Serenity knew her parents would never sell the cabin. Too many memories had been formed here. And with their children now grown, they were planning for the next generation.

Even if her mother hadn't left any family photographs or birth certificates behind, there could be *something* here that would shed a bit of light on what her parents' lives had been like in the early years of their marriage, before Serenity was born. A journal chronicling the years in question. A picture of her mother with another man from about the time Serenity was conceived. Keepsakes. Mementos. Love letters.

She went through the boxes first. They contained the twins' college textbooks, some handmade Raggedy Ann and Andy dolls from when they were small—and old prom dresses. Why Charlotte was hanging on to those, Serenity couldn't say. She supposed her mother was saving them for grandchildren, so they could play dress-up.

Other boxes included various things Beau had made in Boy Scouts or at school. Her mother had kept a lot of their schoolwork and other projects.

Disappointed by what she'd found, she moved on to the closet but had no better luck. The clothes there were so dated they had to have belonged to her parents way back when they were in college.

When she was finished with even the drawers of the

tallboy dresser—which she'd only been able to reach by pushing and pulling and heaving the other furniture out of the way—she turned in a slow circle, wondering if there could be something she'd missed.

Had she spent her afternoon on a wild-goose chase? It felt that way.

"Damn."

Her phone buzzed in her pocket.

She took it out to see that Reagan had texted a picture. They were at Sand Harbor. Finn had Lucy on his shoulders and was standing to one side of Lorelei. Reagan was on the other side with the water glistening behind them.

Serenity was tempted to forward it to Mark. Although Reagan was in the picture, too, it looked like Finn was Lucy's father—that Finn, Lorelei and Lucy were a family. And going by the way they were smiling, they seemed happy.

If Mark wasn't careful, maybe Finn really *would* step in and replace him...

But it was the fact that Reagan had looped her arm casually through Lorelei's that made Serenity stop and study the picture. How was it that they were becoming so close already? Not too long ago, they'd barely known each other and yet...

There was something powerful and meaningful there. Something beyond friendship. She felt it, too. A defensiveness toward those who weren't treating her sisters right. A hope that they could overcome their struggles. The desire to help them do so.

If that wasn't a testament to genetics, Serenity didn't know what was.

With a flicker of regret for not accompanying them—

especially since she hadn't found anything of interest in the cabin while they were gone—she wrote Reagan back. Glad you made it to the lake. Beautiful, isn't it?

Spectacular. Now I see what I've been missing spending all my time in a New York City high-rise.

Maybe what happened between you and Drew—what sent you on this course—was meant to be. Your life was out of balance.

I have to grant you that. But forced change is never easy.

As long as it's worth it in the end?

Fingers crossed.

When will you three be back?

We're starting back now.

If you get too tired, give me a call. I can pick you up.

We've got Finn with us, so we should be fine. There's no way Lorelei or I could carry Lucy that far, but he seems to have no trouble.

Serenity scrolled up to take another look at the picture she'd received before responding. Lorelei really likes Finn.

From what I can tell, he likes her too.

How much?

I guess we'll see. ;)

It would serve Mark right if Lorelei fell in love with
Finn. But she supposed that was the sisterly defensiveness she'd noticed creeping in again. Reagan was right
when she said they shouldn't judge Mark too soon. Serenity needed to remember how hard it was to evaluate a
situation accurately when she was only looking in from
the outside—but it wasn't easy to be that fair-minded.

She put her parents' storage back the way she'd found
it and meandered into the library. If her mother had a
cache of love letters or an old journal, she hadn't come
across it. There was nothing left to do but text Charlotte about Stuart Sands.

But that could tip her mother off and might bring
Charlotte rushing to Tahoe to either explain or justify
the past. And considering how things were going with
Lorelei and Reagan, Serenity wasn't convinced that
would be a good idea. Yes, they wanted to discover
how they were related. But they also wanted to get to
know each other.

Which was more important?

They could have both, if they were patient.

Still hoping for some other way to find the information they were looking for, she sat in of one of two soft
leather chairs, rested her head on the back and tried to
put herself in her mother's shoes. Where would Charlotte hide something she wanted to keep secret—from
her kids *and* her husband?

She stared at the three walls filled with bookshelves.
Between the pages of a book?

No, that would be too risky. Someone might pull that particular book from the shelves and chance upon the information. Charlotte wouldn't leave herself that vulnerable to being exposed. But maybe there was a hidey-hole behind the books...

She stood up, intending to take every single volume off the shelves so she could see what might be behind it, when a new thought sent her hurrying back into the storage room.

When she was a child, her mother had given her a jewelry box that had a false bottom. Serenity had loved having somewhere secret to hide the notes and trinkets she received from friends and boys as she got older.

Could it be that the standing jewelry box her mother had used years ago also had a false bottom?

And, if so, what might be inside it?

* * *

reagan

Reagan stared at her calendar. She'd spoken to Rally twice since that initial texting session and told him they'd go out once she got home. But now that she was staying in Tahoe she had to let him know she couldn't make their dinner date.

Would putting him off until September kill the relationship?

She thought it probably would—and was strangely reluctant to do that. Although they hardly knew each other, Rally seemed different than the other men she'd met—more mature, steady, balanced. But she had no business going out with him or anyone else until she had her life together.

What if she was pregnant?

She needed to buy a pregnancy test. But the mere thought of that filled her with dread. Until she saw a positive result, she could continue to hope for a negative one. That was the reason she hadn't yet made a concerted effort.

Still, she couldn't ignore the possibility indefinitely. Should she get up early tomorrow and drive to the store? They'd returned the rental car, but Serenity would let her take the X5. She could make up an excuse about needing something else—tampons or face cream or gum.

A negative test result would be *such* a relief.

She closed her eyes as she imagined it, longed for it. Problem was, it could easily go the other way. So while she longed for relief, fear stood in her way.

She rubbed her forehead as she rested on the pillows she'd propped against her headboard. The house was quiet; she assumed Serenity, Lucy and Lorelei were asleep. As late as it was, she should be asleep, too. But the worry she'd been trying to ignore burned like acid in her stomach.

If she was going to have a baby, what would she do? Work until she delivered, and then take maternity leave? What if she was stricken with morning sickness and couldn't handle the demanding routine and stress of working in a top-tier advertising firm? If she admitted to being pregnant, would anyone hire her even if she could handle the job?

Edison & Curry would never take on a pregnant

woman—not if they could avoid it—so how could she expect anything different from their competitors?

She supposed she could scrimp on money and wait until after she had the baby to return to work…

But once the child was born, what then? Would she put the baby up for adoption? Or would she try to keep him or her?

And if she did…

She stopped her mind from wandering to childcare, how her mother would react, whether she'd be the kind of parent a child deserved. Her whole life would change. She'd have to make so many decisions, not the least of which would be whether or not to tell Drew.

Did he have a right to know?

He wouldn't be happy about it. He'd dismissed their encounter as though it had no meaning whatsoever and made clear that he'd never let his relationship with her interfere with his family. But if he had a child by her that would definitely interfere. The repercussions might even tear his marriage apart. Look at Lorelei and Mark… She wasn't Sally's best friend, but still.

"What a mess," she muttered and tried, once again, to compose a text to Rally. Since it was later in New York, nearly three thirty in the morning, she expected him to be asleep. That meant she probably wouldn't hear back from him until morning. But that was part of the reason she'd chosen this particular time. He'd see her text when he woke up, shrug it off with a *call me when you finally return*, which she wouldn't, and that would be that.

Hey, I hate to do this, but I'm going to have to break our dinner date. I thought I was coming home on Friday, but my sisters and I have decided to spend the summer in Tahoe. I'll let you know when I'm back in town, in case you're still interested. Maybe we can grab a drink then.

She hit Send and got up to turn off the light. Even if she wasn't pregnant, she wasn't going to rush back to New York. With the number of men she'd dated in the past, none of whom had worked out, what were the chances that Rally would be the exception? This could be the only opportunity she'd ever have to spend an entire summer with her sisters. And, as odd as it felt to make a decision based on siblings—since she'd never had any before—Reagan was going to take advantage of it.

19

serenity

The first thing Serenity saw when she woke up was the letter she'd found in her mother's jewelry box. It had also been the last thing she'd seen before falling asleep the night before, since it was sitting on the nightstand. She'd even dreamed about what it contained—had a terrible nightmare in which she'd caught her mother dancing with Uncle Vance, laughing with him, agreeing to meet him secretly here at the cabin.

Earlier, when Serenity had been on the phone with her mother and Charlotte had mentioned what a womanizer Uncle Vance had always been, Serenity had rejected the idea that he could be the link tying her to Lorelei and Reagan. While she'd briefly considered the genetics, the possibility that he might've been with her mother hadn't even crossed her mind. She'd assumed that, if he was somehow involved, she would be a cousin to Lorelei and Reagan, not a sister. Anyway, her mother was a wonderful person; she would never have an affair with her husband's brother.

But the letter in that old jewelry box seemed to indicate otherwise. And, as Mark had recently proved to Lorelei, those kinds of indiscretions, between a husband and a wife's best friend or even a brother and a sister-in-law, *did* occasionally happen.

Had her mother been temporarily dazzled by Uncle Vance's good looks and huge personality? Was it his flattery, his unfailing smile, his good-natured teasing?

Was Uncle Vance Serenity's *father*? Lorelei's and Reagan's, too?

Your uncle Vance is always in a new relationship. I don't even pay attention anymore. He's never been with the same woman for more than three years.

Serenity wished she could decide if it was bitterness instead of simple disgust she'd heard in her mother's voice. If Uncle Vance had caused her to break her marriage vows to a good man, a man who was everything Uncle Vance was not, she could understand why Charlotte might hold some resentment toward him.

But Serenity had seen Uncle Vance at various dinners and other family functions through the years. If he was her father, wouldn't her mother have avoided going to any events where she knew he'd be present?

Not necessarily, she decided. Perhaps Charlotte had feared that would create suspicion.

In any case, if Charlotte had been uncomfortable when he was around, Serenity hadn't picked up on it.

And what about Uncle Vance's relationship with Serenity's father? Did Chuck give his brother money whenever Vance was down and out because he was afraid Vance might say something to Serenity or someone else in the family?

That would be blackmail! Assuming her father knew,

of course. The letter suggested he didn't. In that case, what would it do to him to find out?

What would it do to everyone else in the family?

Uncertainty and worry congealed in the pit of Serenity's stomach like a lump of bacon grease. She should've left this alone, steered clear of it entirely. After the past eighteen months, she was already disillusioned when it came to love and trust. She didn't want to become as bitter and uncertain about her mother as she was about her ex-husband.

She also didn't want to feel that her father had any reason to love her less than her siblings, or that Beau and the twins would no longer consider their relationship with her to be as important to them as their relationship to each other. Would learning she belonged to Uncle Vance suddenly push her outside the safe, warm circle of familial support she'd always taken for granted? Make her an outsider?

The letter she'd found raised so many questions. As difficult as it had been to learn, when Lorelei first contacted her, that her father might not be her biological father, it was even more difficult to imagine Vance taking his place. Vance wasn't anyone she could respect. He was someone everyone else murmured about and discounted because he couldn't keep his shit together. And he was part of their extended family, no less, making it all the more scandalous.

"Thank God I didn't say anything," she said aloud. If she'd mentioned her two half sisters to her parents, her mother's secret—if there *was* a secret—would have been out. And although the secret was as old as Serenity, the sheer magnitude of such a lie could cause all kinds of problems. A divorce. Doubt and insecurity that persisted well into the future. Barriers and estrangement—not only between Chuck and Charlotte, or Serenity and Chuck and Charlotte, but between Serenity and the siblings she'd grown up with. It didn't necessarily matter who'd been in the right and who'd been in the wrong thirty-five years ago. The twins or Beau could easily take their mother's side. Loyalty was a strange thing. Who could say *exactly* how they'd interpret the situation? They could claim everyone made mistakes, that Charlotte had been an amazing mother. That was true. They could also argue that their father must've done something to leave her vulnerable to their uncle's advances, or it would never have happened.

If it came to a split between her parents, and they were each grappling for support, whose side would *she* be on? Serenity wondered. Given what her mother might've done, Charlotte wasn't the obvious choice, but it would be weird to take her father's side if he wasn't even her father.

"This just gets better and better," she muttered.

"What, Aunt Serenity?"

Serenity lifted her head to see Lucy standing in her room. "You're up?" Serenity hadn't heard the door open.

"Yeah," she said.

Serenity couldn't help feeling slightly irritated. "Where's your mother? Is she still sleeping?"

Lucy seemed slightly confused by Serenity's tone and expression, which wasn't welcoming, but she didn't leave. "She's in the shower…"

If Lorelei was in the shower she obviously wasn't going to step into the room and lead Lucy away, not immediately.

Serenity nearly told her niece to go out and close

the door and let her sleep. She'd had a terrible night, and she was having a terrible morning. The more she thought about her mother and Uncle Vance together, the more upset she became. Her two new sisters were putting the family she'd always had at risk, and it was hard not to resent them for it. After all, if Lorelei had never contacted her, Serenity would still be blissfully unaware of the whole thing.

But as soon as she opened her mouth to send Lucy away, she noticed that her niece was carrying something—a book. "What do you have there?" she asked.

Lucy turned it to show Serenity the cover. It was the copy of *Are You My Mother?* Serenity had read to her before.

The sight of it washed away Serenity's irritation and brought a wave of guilt. She couldn't blame Lorelei for reaching out to her, searching for family. In a world where it was so easy to become anonymous, invisible, just another face in the crowd, wouldn't anyone crave those bonds? Have the desire to feel a bit more important to at least a small group of people?

It wasn't Lorelei's fault—or Reagan's or Lucy's, either—that they were in this position, and as difficult as things might get, Serenity needed to remember that.

Lifting the bedcovers, she patted the mattress beside her, and that was all the invitation Lucy needed. Her dimples flashed as she scampered over and climbed in beside Serenity, careful to help her cover them both before settling back and handing over the book.

Serenity read *Are You My Mother?* four times before Lucy had had enough. They were deep in a discussion about whether the gulls at the lake had mothers, too, when Lorelei called for her daughter.

"I have to go," Lucy said as though she knew she was somewhere she wasn't supposed to be. But she allowed Serenity to pull her in for a quick hug and a kiss before she scrambled out of bed and hurried down the hall.

"I'm here," Serenity heard her call back.

When she was gone, Serenity got up and put the letter she'd found in her purse. She hadn't told Lorelei or Reagan about it. She was afraid that speaking the words would somehow make them true.

* * *

lorelei

I miss you. Will you come home? Please?

Lorelei was with Finn when that text from Mark popped up on her phone. She glanced at it, then lifted the light-weight, oversize sweater she was wearing and put her phone back in the pocket of her yoga pants.

Serenity and Reagan worked in the mornings—Serenity on her book and Reagan on Serenity's social media—but Finn usually painted in the afternoon. That left him available after breakfast, so he and Lorelei had started taking Lucy on a walk each morning around ten.

A few days ago they'd gone into town to see what they could find there. That had been fun but not quite as enjoyable as the beach, especially to Lucy. Since then they'd spent most of their mornings at Sand Harbor, and today they were meandering in that direction, too.

Tahoe hadn't quite made the transition to summer,

so while there were a few boats on the water when they arrived, there weren't a lot of people on shore. It was Friday, so Lorelei supposed more enthusiasts would come later, as the day warmed and the weekenders arrived, but she preferred this quieter time.

As Lucy started to hunt for the flat, smooth pebbles Finn had taught her he needed to be able to skip rocks, Lorelei removed her tennis shoes and dug her toes into the cool, gritty sand. This place was beginning to feel like an old friend. She was always eager to return, especially with Finn. Being out in the mellow sun and the breeze felt wonderful, and the beauty she encountered never got old. But the conversation was the best part. When she and Finn were together, they talked about all kinds of things.

She was most interested in hearing about his work. That he could be so masterful at something so difficult inspired her. She asked him what he hoped to achieve in his career; he said it would be incredible if he could get his paintings into some of the most exclusive galleries around the world, but he'd be happy if he could just earn enough to support himself doing what he loved. She asked what served as his inspiration; this had been harder for him to define—he said almost anything could inspire a painting. Something had to agitate his imagination in such a way that he was excited about re-creating it. And how long did it take him to complete a painting? Anywhere from one to six months, depending on the size, the level of detail and the level of difficulty.

She got the impression the walks they took were research for him. He'd decided that he wanted to do a nature scene. So he was trying to gain a true sense of this place, to become acquainted with it well enough to paint it, which was why they'd also driven around the lake last night with Serenity and Reagan. Painting something was an intimate experience, he'd explained. He couldn't capture the true essence of any subject from a distance.

"You have to be *inside* it to really bring it to life," he'd said earnestly.

Lorelei wasn't sure exactly what he meant by that, but he was so animated when he spoke about his work that she loved engaging him on the subject. He was unlike anyone she'd ever met—a dreamer, someone who viewed life from an entirely different perspective. One she found unique and refreshing.

Occasionally, he stopped to take a photograph, but she didn't get the impression that he'd settled on the scene he wanted to create quite yet. He was still searching. She could tell by the way he measured everything with his eyes.

"When are we going to Hidden Cove?" he asked as they stood on several rocks jutting out into the lake and gazed at the sunshine reflecting off the water.

Lucy was farther up the beach. She'd found a beetle and was crouched over it, watching it make its way slowly across the sand.

"I don't know," she said and averted her face so he couldn't realize she wasn't planning to go to Hidden Cove, after all. When the subject of the nude beach had first come up, visiting it had seemed innocuous. People went to nude beaches all the time. It didn't make them any worse than anyone else. But Finn had been a stranger to her when that idea was born, someone who held no real significance in her life.

Now…things had changed. She'd become too aware of him on a sexual level. Going to a nude beach with

Finn would make her feel a little predatory—because she'd no longer be going just to prove that she was capable of stepping out of the confines of her former life and *living* a little. She'd be going because she wanted to see what he'd reveal when he tossed aside his clothes.

"You're not interested anymore?" he asked.

"I don't think so."

His eyebrows furrowed. "Why not? You were pretty gung ho last week."

She was even more interested *this* week. But for all the wrong reasons. That was the problem.

"Has something changed?" he asked.

"Not really, no." She suspected he knew what was happening and that he was trying to get her to say it, but she couldn't ruin a perfectly good friendship by admitting that her feelings for him were growing out of control. That when he spoke, she sometimes watched his lips and imagined them on her body, moving over her breasts, down her stomach—lower.

Feeling her face heat, she jumped off the rock and began to wade in the cold water up to her ankles. No matter what happened in Tahoe, she had to return to Florida eventually. Had to deal with her marriage— or her divorce—and what she was going to do for a living. She'd decided, either way, she was reentering the job market and would no longer rely on Mark or anyone else to provide her living. Lucy was almost in school; she could manage, especially because the second child she and Mark had been discussing wasn't a possibility anymore—now that he was having a baby with someone else.

Anyway, she'd have to leave this idyllic place soon enough. She wasn't going to ruin the time she did have here. She'd promised herself *one* precious summer, and she was going to have it.

"Have you heard from Mark lately?" he pressed, following her.

She thought of her husband's text message of a few minutes ago. She hadn't said anything to Finn, but she guessed he'd noticed the way she'd glanced at her phone and returned it to her pocket. "That was who just messaged me."

"What'd he say?"

She took out her phone to show him.

"Do you believe him?" he asked when he handed it back.

"I don't know what to believe. I got a text from Francine last night, imploring me to have a conversation with her. When I didn't respond, she said, 'What do you want me to do? Abort this baby? Give it up for adoption?'"

"*Is* that what you want?" he asked.

"Part of me does," she admitted. "She doesn't deserve a child, not considering how she got it. But that's the jealousy and anger speaking. The better part of me, when I allow that part to take control, has to acknowledge that the child didn't do anything. I don't want this baby to be raised the way I was raised. I wouldn't wish that on my worst enemy."

He shoved his hands in the pockets of his linen shorts. "So what's the answer?"

She toed a smooth, flat rock and pulled it out of the water for Lucy, knowing her daughter would eventually forget about the beetle and come ask Finn to skip rocks. "I'm not even going to think about it," she said. "Not until September."

* * *

reagan

Reagan had bought three pregnancy tests—a selection, since she didn't know which one was the most reliable, and this was something she needed to trust. She'd told Serenity that she had to pick up some lip balm and a few other toiletries and borrowed the X5. She'd made the request when Serenity was writing and Lucy and Lorelei were out walking with Finn, so she wouldn't be in danger of anyone asking to accompany her, and that had worked out perfectly.

Except, even after she'd purchased the tests, she'd found one excuse after another to avoid actually taking one. She didn't want to do it even now. But with Serenity hard at work out on the deck and Lucy and Lorelei once again walking with Finn, she had the privacy. And with the weekend coming on, and Davis and Nolan arriving on Sunday, she didn't want this hanging over her head, ruining any fun she might have.

Her phone dinged with a text from Rally. Did you do it?

Not yet, she wrote back.

Take a deep breath and get it over with. You have to find out at some point.

Easy for you to say.

If you are pregnant, it won't be the end of the world.

Oddly enough, after she'd broken her date with him, Rally had continued to text her. They'd even spoken on the phone twice—late, after Lorelei and Serenity had gone to bed. One of those phone calls had lasted for over an hour, the next for forty-three minutes. Since she was going to be gone for so long and had no expectation of a romantic relationship with him, it'd been easy to fall into a friendship—and that had encouraged her to tell him everything, the whole sordid story.

She'd thought he might quit contacting her. The facts didn't make her look good. But he'd remained in touch, had been kind, supportive, even willing to offer some advice.

It felt *so* comforting to have someone to confide in.

Of course, he was probably counting his blessings that the truth of her situation had been revealed before they'd ever gone out. But she could only care about so many things right now, and being self-conscious with him about her predicament wasn't one of them. That was why she'd confided in him. He was so removed from the situation it felt safe.

Would you pee on it already? he wrote.

God, you're pushy, she wrote back.

You could be going through hell for nothing. Stand up and take it like a man.

Ha, ha! Funny...

I have my moments.

Too bad you're not facing this instead of me.

Spoken like a true narcissist.

She sent him a horrified emoji.

Kidding. Anyway, if you don't want the baby, I'll take it.

She stared at those words. *What?*

Never mind. You'll want it. It'll be the best thing that ever happened to you.

How could that be true? She had no job. The father of the child would be furious. Just telling him would create a battle she'd have to fight for the next eighteen years. Her mother would be appalled. She herself would never be able to forget how the baby was conceived so this child would be a constant reminder of her naiveté and stupidity.

Need she go on?

You'll see, he added when she didn't respond.

"I hope I *don't* see," she mumbled. You're supposed to be rooting for the opposite.

I am. So put us both out of our misery and take the damn test.

She didn't want him pressuring her. And yet…without *some* pressure, she knew she might chicken out again. "What the heck," she said. Doing it now.

As she opened the package that looked the most promising—the one that seemed to imply the best chance of a negative result—she thought of Drew, of that heated encounter, and was embarrassed. How had she done what she'd done at *work* of all places? On his desk? And, he, a married man?

She groaned. Somehow she'd gotten so caught up in the excitement and the attraction—in looking for him around every corner, in listening for his voice, in that rush of awareness when she found him watching her—she hadn't realized how tawdry and ridiculous her actions were. She'd believed he cared about her. That she was in love with him. That they were somehow different from all other couples who'd had in-office affairs.

How foolish!

The more days that passed without any word from him, the more she began to realize he couldn't ever have cared about her. He was just spoiled and rich and bored; he'd used her as entertainment. And if he wasn't the man she'd thought he was, how could she be in love with him?

She was in love with the romanticized version of him she'd created in her own mind—that was all.

"Bastard," she muttered as she unwrapped the applicator and moved to the toilet.

At first, she was so nervous she couldn't release her bladder. After she managed to squeeze out a few drops, her hand shook as she held the receptacle. A plus would indicate she was pregnant; a minus that she wasn't.

"Minus, minus, minus," she chanted as she paced the length of the bathroom.

But what eventually appeared was what she'd known in her heart—what some sixth sense had already told her. Her worst nightmare was coming true; she was going to have Drew's baby.

"No!" she cried and dropped the tester as though it had burned her.

Bending over, she put her hands on her knees and

gasped for air so she wouldn't pass out. This couldn't be real. There had to be some mistake.

She grabbed the sack that held the other two kits. She'd take them all and pray that one or both of the last two tests would indicate she wasn't pregnant. That would at least allow her to *hope* there'd been a mistake.

But there was no mistake. All three showed the same thing.

Tears rolled down her cheeks and dripped off her chin as her phone went off. Somewhere in the back of her mind, she heard the chimes of rapid-fire texts, but she ignored them. She couldn't focus on her phone when she was wallowing in the depths of misery.

The insistence of the person, who then called, hung up and called again, finally forced her to look at her screen.

It was Rally, of course. He was expecting to hear the results.

She let the call transfer to voice mail. She couldn't answer because she couldn't speak. The terror roiling in her gut wasn't just making her eyes water, it was clogging her throat, causing her to tremble, turning her bones to rubber.

How could she have destroyed her life—for "fifteen minutes of panting and one good climax" as Drew had put it?

More ringing.

Rally wouldn't give up.

Eventually, she hit Accept.

"Reagan?"

Any response she might've given lodged in her throat and refused to rise any higher.

When he heard nothing, his voice grew gentle. "I'm sorry. But it's going to be okay."

"How could…anybody…be so stupid?" she managed to respond, hiccuping through her tears.

"You were lonely. You were working too many hours. You had no social life or other outlet. And you believed what he told you."

"But I'm a…a smart woman. All it would've taken was a condom!"

"It happened at the office. You weren't planning on having sex with him or you would've been prepared."

"I was so stupid. How am I going to deal with this?"

"You'll find the strength. It's not as though you're still in high school. You're an adult. You can care for a child, if that's what you want. And if that isn't what you want…there are other options."

She didn't sense any judgment in that statement. Rally was one of those people who saw the many gray areas of life, and she really liked that about him. "No *good* ones," she complained. She'd thought of them all. Gone over them ad nauseam when she couldn't sleep for fear she'd find herself in this exact situation.

"You'll have time to think it over and decide."

She dashed a hand across her cheek. "It's karma. I deserve this."

"No, you don't. The universe isn't out to punish you. It's just one of those things. Unplanned pregnancies happen."

She imagined telling her mother she was expecting with no potential husband—not even a significant other—to help support the baby and felt nauseous. Her mother had preached and preached about birth control, about the difficulty of raising a child alone.

And their relationship was already so rocky. Although Rosalind had tried to call once since Reagan had told her she'd quit her job, Reagan hadn't answered.

Anyway, what was she going to say? She'd always been careful not to get on her mother's bad side. She knew how long her mother withheld her love and support as punishment.

Reagan supposed she'd have to apologize to Rosalind eventually, figured she should get the punishment cycle started by allowing her mother to criticize her actions until she'd exhausted her anger.

But Reagan couldn't bring herself to do it; she wasn't ready for that yet.

"Do I tell Drew?"

"I think he should be held responsible, don't you?"

"I don't want him in my life."

"You do have the option to leave him out of it, but it'll cost you a bit more."

"It's not just about finances. Wouldn't my child deserve to know her father?"

"In a perfect world, yes. But in my opinion, no father is better than a bad father—if the child has a good mother. And this one will."

Reagan clung to her phone as she stared at herself in the mirror. Her eyes, big and hollow, looked like a stranger's—a panicked stranger. She'd been raised without a father, didn't want the same thing for her child. But maybe, as Rally had said, it would've been different if she'd had a more sensitive and caring mother. If Rosalind hadn't been so strict and busy all the time, Reagan wouldn't have longed for someone else.

Would *she* be a loving parent? Or would she resent

her child, see him or her as a nuisance, dead weight she had to carry, the way her own mother had?

Taking a deep breath, she tried to pull herself together. "Why are you even talking to me, Rally?" she asked. "You barely know me. It would be easy for you to walk away. Any other guy would."

"Reagan, if I only chose people who have no problems to be my friends, I'd have no friends."

He was being so kind. She wished she could allow his words to comfort her. But she was afraid to rely on them—on him. She knew from experience that she had to rely on herself.

"Thanks. Listen, I hear Lucy so Lorelei must be back," she lied. "I'd better go."

"I'll call you later?" he said.

"You don't have to," she replied and disconnected. Then she stuffed the packaging from her tests back in the brown paper sack, which she scrunched up so it'd look empty, and threw it away.

She didn't want her sisters to know. She had a lot of decisions to make before she told anyone else.

20

serenity

The drive to Berkeley had been quick and easy. The weather was pleasant, the roads clear. There wouldn't be heavy traffic on Westbound 80 until Sunday night, when the visitors from Sacramento and the Bay Area had to return for work on Monday. Then it could get backed up for miles.

In an effort to keep her mind off seeing Sawyer again, she listened to a podcast on writing the entire way. She knew Reagan, Lorelei and Lucy would've been happy to tag along and keep her company. They'd expressed an interest in seeing her house, and she planned to show it to them. But since they'd be with her all summer—meaning there'd be other chances—she hadn't invited them on this particular trip. She'd made it sound as though she had to take care of some business so she could meet Sawyer alone. She preferred her sisters not be around when he arrived. Seeing him was going to be awkward enough without having to introduce two family members he never knew she had, especially since she couldn't explain where they'd come from.

She decided she wouldn't mention them at all. She'd find those pictures of Sean for her ex-mother-in-law, get them returned and, in the process, say what she felt she needed to say to Sawyer. Then she'd drive back to the cabin, where she'd show Reagan and Lorelei the letter she'd discovered in her mother's old jewelry box.

She'd been putting that off, hadn't wanted them to immediately assume she'd found the answer. It wasn't an answer she was happy to accept. But this was the only lead they had, and if Uncle Vance was really her father, she figured she might as well face it. Solving the mystery might lead to greater problems, but at least they'd understand how they were connected and could go from there.

"Really, though? *Uncle Vance?*" she muttered but managed to rein in her disgust when her mother called. Her father got on the phone after Charlotte to say hello and tell her he missed her, and she felt she did an admirable job of acting as though nothing had changed. She had good parents; she couldn't deny that. So how Lorelei and Reagan could've appeared out of nowhere didn't make any sense.

Maybe after she'd taken care of Sean's pictures and Sawyer was gone, she'd call her uncle while she was at the Berkeley house alone and try to devise a clever way to get some information out of him—if he had any information to give. She supposed it was possible he didn't know they were more closely related than niece and uncle. For that matter, it was possible even her mother didn't know. If Charlotte had been sleeping with both men at the same time, how would she?

Maybe that was how Charlotte had been able to distance herself from Vance. It could be that she'd slipped up once or twice, regretted her actions and refused to even consider the possibility that her pregnancy could be the result of those encounters when she'd been with her husband much more often.

The whole thing turns my stomach.

After she parked, she checked the time on her phone before climbing out and grabbing her overnight bag. She hadn't left the cabin as early as she'd intended. Lucy had asked for pancakes, so she'd stayed to make them for her. She'd wanted to let Lorelei sleep in for a change. And Reagan wasn't feeling well, so she couldn't help with breakfast. Last night she'd said she had a terrible headache—hadn't even gone to Finn's when Serenity, Lucy and Lorelei headed over with dinner.

Serenity was glad she'd spent that time with her niece. It had been a nice morning. But now she had only a few hours until Sawyer arrived, and she planned to do some cleaning and organizing. She'd been so stressed about missing her deadline, and so depressed in the aftermath of Sean's trial and all it had cost her financially and emotionally, that for all those months, she'd made herself stay on her computer instead of doing anything else, even though the words wouldn't come, and she'd invariably switch over to social media to feel she was being productive.

As she opened the door to her little Victorian on Cedar Street, she was glad she'd given herself time to get it straightened up. Her former self would never have left it in such a mess. But going to Tahoe—staying there—had already done her a world of good. She was writing again. The relief that brought could not be overstated. Her editor had replied just this morning with a terse message letting her know that the publisher had agreed to move the release of *All Gone* to the following June, one year away.

She had the second chance she'd been hoping for. She planned to make the most of it, cling to that opportunity to the exclusion of all else, if necessary. She had to get back to building her career, find the confident, successful person she used to be and become that person once again.

Maybe she should sell this house, she thought as she put down her bag and closed the door. There were too many memories associated with it. None of Sean's belongings were here anymore, with the possible exception of that childhood stuff Nina was going on about. Sawyer had boxed them up and taken them away. But Sean had been the one to find this place. They'd purchased and furnished it together. She'd never forget how excited they'd been when their offer was accepted and how they'd celebrated their first night in their new home. It was only a few years after that, once they'd felt more settled in their careers, that they'd started talking about having kids.

Had he already been viewing and selling child pornography at that point?

She tried to think back five years, when they'd bought the house—and came up empty. There was nothing to indicate anything out of the ordinary. But if it hadn't started then, when *had* it started? And why? What could've transformed someone who'd seemed to be such a warm and caring person into the worst kind of predator?

Sean had been so intent on denying that he'd ever

done anything wrong he wouldn't answer the questions that burned uppermost in her mind—how, when and why. Not honestly, anyway.

Most criminals didn't care that they left their loved ones in turmoil, with no closure, the detective who'd investigated Sean's case had told her. And Sean had proved him right. No matter how many times Serenity had implored her husband to *talk* to her, to help her understand, he'd just continued to deny it. He'd also tried to make her feel he was innocent and her insistence that he wasn't cut him more deeply than she could imagine.

It was all about *his* suffering, not the suffering he'd caused. According to the detective, narcissism was another trait common among pedophiles. Dealing with Sean had made Serenity a believer.

With a heartfelt sigh, she went around the house, opening the windows. It was a gorgeous day—mild and breezy—and the house needed to be aired out. She didn't want Sawyer to realize how badly off she'd been, that depression had taken such deep root she'd barely been able to pull her laptop into bed with her in the mornings.

She dusted and vacuumed, changed the linens on her bed and washed all the blankets. Sawyer wouldn't see her room—there was nothing of Sean's left in there— but knowing she had a clean house to return to might make it easier to face coming home after the summer.

Or maybe she'd take some photographs before heading back to the cabin in the morning. They'd be helpful if she decided to put the house up for sale while she was away. She didn't need to be around in order to do that; it would actually be easier if she wasn't. A Realtor could deal with all the showings. Then she could find a different house in Berkeley, or maybe even San Francisco, and start over. The only thing she knew for sure was that she wouldn't move too far from Tahoe. Going there meant too much to her.

After she'd finished cleaning, she went out to buy a few groceries. The least she could do was feed Sawyer while he was over. She didn't cook often, but her mother was excellent in the kitchen and had taught her a few meals she prepared whenever she entertained. She made excellent baba ghanoush—her mother had always grown eggplant. With pita bread for dipping, it would make a delicious starter, after which she'd serve a vegetable and tofu stir-fry. Paired with a nice wine and followed by a ready-made peach tart from Whole Foods, the meal should be a good one—a modest thank-you for Sawyer's time. After tonight, she'd feel she'd done at least *one* small thing to repay him for everything he did during the trial.

She jumped into the shower after she received a text saying he'd be over by four.

Dressed in a pair of flowing, wide-legged pants with a short midriff-bearing sweater, she was stirring the tofu to make sure each piece was getting covered by the marinade when she heard his knock.

He was here. Her pulse quickened at the thought. She had no idea why. She hadn't seen him for a while, but why would that make any difference?

She quickly covered the dish and went to the door.

He had his back to her when she first saw him through the window. He was leaning up against the pillar of her porch, gazing out at the rest of the neighborhood, and he was dressed far more casually than she was in a T-shirt and pair of faded jeans.

She realized she might've overdressed, but it was too late to change now.

Hearing the bolt move, he turned, and she caught her breath. Although she'd never allowed herself to acknowledge how attractive he was while she was married to Sean, she couldn't help acknowledging it now. She saw that he'd just showered; his blond hair was slightly damp and curling around his ears and at the nape of his neck, and she could smell a hint of cologne.

"Hello," she said.

His eyes lowered, studying her slowly, before rising to her face. "You look good," he responded, as direct as ever.

"So do you," she admitted.

She held the door as an invitation for him to come in, and he turned sideways to slip past her without knocking into her. "You're doing well, then?" he asked.

"I'm doing better. I've managed to start writing again."

He peered at her more closely. "I didn't realize that had become a problem."

"Not a *big* problem," she lied. "Like I said, I'm back at it now. My publisher has agreed to move my latest book to June of next year, so…that's lucky." Why was she saying too much?

There was just something about him that unnerved her. And because he didn't fill the silence, she ended up revealing far more than she intended.

"You missed your deadline?"

She opened her mouth to deny it—to make her job situation sound less dire—but ultimately figured there was no point in pretending. "Basically," she admitted with a shrug.

"Why?"

"I don't know. I just…couldn't function properly. If I'm not careful, Sean will cost me my career along with everything else. But, like I said, this week has been better," she quickly added.

"This *week*," he repeated.

"Yeah."

"It's been eighteen months since you found those files."

"But only six since he was sentenced," she said, feeling a bit defensive.

He continued to study her. "Is he in touch with you?"

"I hear from him now and then."

"Email?"

"Snail mail."

"What does he say?"

"I quit reading his letters months ago. In the last one I read, he was begging me to remarry him—said there'd never be anyone like me."

His upper lip curled. "I hope you weren't tempted."

"Not in the least. I wish I'd never married him in the first place."

"Did you tell him that?"

"I haven't bothered to write him back. What's the point? I don't want to become pen pals. I don't want anything to do with him ever again."

He grunted but didn't look away. She could tell he was trying to determine how committed she was to that statement.

She cleared her throat. "Do you ever hear from him?"

"Nope. Hasn't written me once."

"He blames you for our divorce. You know that, right?"

He reared back in surprise. *"Me?"*

"He thinks he would've been able to convince me he was innocent, if not for your support."

"I didn't do anything."

She clasped her hands tightly in front of her. "Actually, you did. I wouldn't have gotten through the trial without you. I know I've never admitted that, but... I want to thank you."

Their eyes met and, for a moment, Serenity couldn't breathe. She told herself it was profound gratitude that was causing her to react to him the way she was. He'd always believed her, from the beginning. His faith had never wavered. When everyone else was drilling her or trying to make her look unreliable or out to get Sean, he simply stood behind her.

"Why did you make that choice?" she asked. "Why did you remain so firm and steadfast? It obviously wasn't a good thing for you, considering how your family reacted."

"You mean *his* family?"

"They're your family, too. The only family you have."

A muscle moved in his cheek. "I knew you wouldn't lie about something like that."

"His parents didn't believe me. Your other brothers didn't believe me. They all blame me for ruining his life."

"He ruined his own life."

"It's been futile trying to convince them of that. I'm surprised you don't hate me, too. After all, I'm the one who found those pictures on Sean's computer. I'm the one who contacted the police. I started the whole thing."

"You did. And you wouldn't let it go, no matter how

much pressure he, his family and his lawyers put on you. You hung in there and refuted all his lies, and you didn't let your love for him or fear of being alone or anything else blind you. As far as I'm concerned, that makes you one of the bravest people I know."

She wanted to slip her arms around his waist and rest her cheek against his solid chest. He seemed strong enough to carry the entire world on his shoulders. Maybe that was why she'd always been so careful to keep her distance. He tempted her to lean on him, which frightened her at the same time as it appealed to her. "Even though it cost us both so much?"

"It got a predator off the streets, didn't it? Fighting that sort of thing is a battle, which means some people are going to get hurt. We can't always expect it to be someone else."

She nodded. "Right. I look at it that way, too. When I can," she added lamely.

He glanced around the house. "Have you started dating again?"

"No. Much to my mother's disappointment, since it means I can't give her any grandchildren. But I'm not ready for that yet."

His gaze swept over her again. "Really? Because this sort of looks like a date." He leaned closer, his nose almost touching her neck. "Smells like a date, too."

She felt herself flush with embarrassment. She'd *definitely* overprepared to see him. "What? It's not a date—"

"Because you're still in love with Sean?"

"No! Because I'm still too burned by him. Trust has become a big issue for me."

"Not all men are like Sean, Serenity."

"But how to tell the difference. That's the thing."

He stepped closer, watching her the whole time as if daring her to hold her ground. "You trust me, don't you?"

She didn't retreat, but she narrowed her eyes, feigning skepticism. "In what way?"

"I would hope in *every* way," he replied and lifted her chin with one finger as he lowered his head.

He was going to kiss her. Serenity felt a moment of panic. She hadn't been touched by a man in a year and a half, since before she found those stomach-churning files on Sean's computer. And this was Sawyer, Sean's *stepbrother*. He was off-limits, wasn't he?

Or…maybe her mother was right. Maybe he wasn't off-limits anymore. After what Sean had done to her, she didn't owe him anything. She didn't owe Sean's family anything, either.

She was divorced, a free woman.

She assumed Sawyer was unattached, too, or he wouldn't be doing this.

Still, she was afraid it would be weird—until his mouth covered hers and all she could think about was the delicious taste of him. He'd always been so determined and tough and demanding. That was the perception she'd had of him, anyway.

But he wasn't the least bit overbearing right now. In fact, she felt him tremble slightly as he pressed his hand against the bare skin at the small of her back. And his kiss… God, it was good. There was no force behind it. It was an *invitation*, a sample of what he was willing to offer.

As his lips moved over hers lightly, gently, she got the impression that he was being careful not to spook her. He was giving her just enough physicality to determine whether she'd accept and respond.

So when she slid her arms around his neck and clenched her hands in his hair, she could tell he was surprised—but not unpleasantly so. She heard him groan as she opened her mouth and their tongues met, turning the kiss into something far more powerful and satisfying.

Several seconds later, as they both gasped for breath, he pulled her up against him again. And this time she could feel his rock-hard erection.

"I—I made dinner," she managed to say.

It was her one and only attempt to turn the world right-side-up again. But that didn't deter him.

She would've been disappointed if it had. She was so aroused all she could think of was how desperately she wanted to feel him push inside her—to fill her completely and, if only for a moment, stop the ache of loneliness and heartbreak that had pursued her for so long.

"I have everything I want right here," he said and slid his hand up under her sweater.

As soon as he touched her, she let her head drop back and closed her eyes. It was then that she realized why she'd left Lorelei, Lucy and Reagan behind and gone to so much work before he arrived.

She'd wanted this all along.

* * *

lorelei

Finn was away for the night. He'd driven around to the south side of the lake to meet a friend who'd moved from LA to Sacramento last year. He'd invited her and

Reagan, but Lorelei knew that they were planning to go to a casino, which wasn't any place she could take a child. And Reagan wasn't feeling well. She hadn't been throwing up, but she'd been sleeping all day and, when Lorelei went to check on her, she refused to eat.

"Can I get you anything?" Lorelei asked, still holding the rejected tray of soup and crackers she'd brought to Reagan's room.

"No, I'll be okay," Reagan mumbled without lifting her head. "I just need some rest."

With the blinds drawn so tightly, the room was pitch-black even though the sun hadn't yet gone down. "But you've been sleeping since before Serenity and I went over to Finn's last night, and I don't think you've eaten anything. Should you see a doctor?"

"There's nothing a doctor can do."

"How do you know? What are your symptoms?"

After a slight hesitation, she said, "It's just…"

"A migraine?" Lorelei guessed when Reagan couldn't seem to come up with a good description of what was wrong.

"Yeah. A migraine," she replied, seemingly relieved that Lorelei had made the answer easy for her.

"Those can be terrible. One of Mark's sisters is bedridden for days whenever she gets one. Are you sure you don't need a painkiller or something?"

Reagan responded but her words were so muffled Lorelei couldn't make them out.

"What was that?"

"Already took some," she repeated, her voice louder and more distinct.

"Oh. Okay. I'll let you rest, then."

After closing the door behind her, Lorelei carried the tray of food back to the kitchen, where Lucy was coloring at the table. "Where's Aunt Reagan?" she asked as though she'd expected Lorelei to bring Reagan back with her.

"In bed."

"Why?"

"She has a headache."

"Where's Aunt Serenity?"

"She's at her other house."

"What other house?"

"The one she normally lives in. This house is just a place where she comes for vacation, remember?"

Lucy put down the blue marker and picked up the red one. "When is she coming back?"

"Tomorrow."

Lorelei was about to offer to let Lucy watch a movie when she was distracted by a text from Finn.

Reagan feeling any better?

Lorelei sank into the seat next to Lucy while she answered. Not really.

What's wrong with her?

Migraine.

That sucks.

Have you met your friend yet?

Just waiting for him to arrive.

She wished she could've gone. She missed Finn already. Although they'd only known each other for a week, they'd spent a lot of time together. He was so easy to be around.

When will Davis be here tomorrow? she wrote.

Nolan isn't exactly an early riser, he responded. Not unless he has to be. I'm guessing they won't make it until dinner.

I'll cook for everyone.

You don't have to do that. I can manage.

You're out tonight. It'll be easier for me. And that will give you a good excuse to bring him over, so we can meet him.

I doubt he'll be willing to leave the house. Can you all come to my place? If you'll make the meal, I'll get the wine and the dessert.

Sounds good.

She was sliding her phone back into her pocket when it buzzed with a text from Francine.

Why she hadn't blocked the woman, she didn't know. She should've done it the second she learned Francine was pregnant with Mark's baby. She'd wanted to. But if she took Mark back, she'd essentially be taking Francine back, too, because of the baby. She supposed that was why she hadn't bothered. She still hadn't fully decided what she was going to do.

Are you really seeing someone else?

Mark had obviously been talking to her. Why wouldn't he? Lorelei had told him he could see her. She'd even suggested Francine move into the house with him.

Had she?

Are you living with Mark now? she wrote back.

No, of course not. Why would I be living with Mark? You live there!

I told him it was fine with me if you moved in. Just box up my stuff and put it in the garage.

It was the first time she'd responded, no matter what Francine had sent, but waiting so long didn't seem to be making the situation any easier. She wasn't over anything. Her initial shock had just turned to red-hot anger. She wanted to strike out, to hurt Francine the way Francine had hurt her.

I'm not going to move in with your husband, came the reply.

So that would be going too far?

Francine ignored Lorelei's sarcasm and came back with, He loves you. And so do I.

Lorelei's chest grew tight. This had been her best friend. She'd trusted Francine with all her secrets. When she was frustrated with Mark and needed to vent, she'd turned to Francine.

Now she felt that Francine had exploited any weakness she'd revealed in their marriage. Bullshit, Lorelei wrote.

It's true, Lorelei. We didn't mean for this to happen.

Her phone rang; Francine was calling. But Lorelei wasn't about to answer. She knew she'd only hear the same excuses Francine had already left via several messages on her voice mail. Besides, Lorelei had no idea how she might respond. She didn't want Lucy to overhear a conversation that was bound to turn ugly.

Lucy is here, she texted after rejecting the call.

What does that mean?

I can't talk to you. I'd rather she didn't hear what I have to say.

Which is...what? You hate me now? :(

Lorelei felt zero empathy for Francine despite that frowny face. Hate isn't nearly a strong enough word for what I feel toward you.

Ouch, Lorelei!

It's true.

No, you can't mean it. We've been best friends since college. Let's not let this cost all of us more than it has to!

You should've thought of that before you climbed into bed with my husband.

If you'll just come back, we can work it out.

She sounded like Mark. I'm not coming back.

Ever? What about Lucy? You can't take her from her father. I can't believe you'd even consider breaking up your marriage.

Almost any wife would consider breaking up her marriage if her husband was fucking her best friend, don't you think?

"Mommy, what's wrong?"

Lorelei glanced up to see her daughter watching her in confusion and smoothed her expression. "Nothing, honey."

"Is it Daddy?" Lucy asked, unconvinced and worried.

"No, it's not Daddy." Attempting a smile, Lorelei touched her daughter's cheek. A second later, her phone buzzed again.

You think being crude and hating me is going to help the situation?

Francine had become very religious lately. Obviously, she didn't approve of Lorelei's language, which was pretty ironic considering what *she'd* done, but Lorelei didn't point that out. There were more important things that needed to be said. No, nothing is going to help the situation. You betrayed me in the worst possible way, and we can't fix it now.

So that's it? You're just going to write me off? Our friendship is over?

Lorelei's heart pounded as she stared down at those words. *Was* it over? Did she dare make that declaration?

She was tempted to do it, to reject these people who'd hurt her so badly. But the ramifications would be huge, and she knew it. She'd be on her own again for the first time since she'd met Mark—and this time she'd have a kid to take care of.

She'd be facing her worst fears—what she'd faced in some ways, as a child—trying to forge a good life with no family. She had two sisters now, but she'd only known them for a short while. While she liked them, she didn't dare rely on the hope that they'd be there for her like regular sisters.

She had to make the decision assuming she'd face the worst-case scenario, not the best.

It would be terrifying for her. For years Mark had been her bulwarks against the world. But after so much had happened, would she be any happier going back to him than striking out on her own?

No.

It is over, she wrote.

You don't mean that, Francine replied.

Actually, I do.

What about your marriage?

Lorelei stared at this question for so long Lucy climbed off the chair and started tugging on her arm to go into the living room and put on a movie. But after telling her daughter to give her a moment, she drew a deep breath, set her jaw and typed, That's over, too. Mark's all yours now. I hope you'll both be happy.

The response didn't come immediately. Lorelei sat with her heart in her throat for a full three minutes, which felt more like three hours. Was Francine not going to respond?

We could never be happy without you, her ex-best friend finally wrote.

The lump in Lorelei's throat grew until it threatened to choke her. You've made it impossible for me to be happy with you, she wrote back. Then she slid her phone in her pocket and watched Lucy, who'd given up on a movie and gone back to coloring, while waiting for the avalanche of pain and regret she expected to sweep over her.

Had she done the right thing? Would she regret taking this turn in life? What would it mean for Lucy?

She had no answers, but she suspected her newfound determination to end her marriage might have as much to do with Finn as it did Francine.

21

serenity

Sawyer made love as expertly as he did everything else. Serenity had to admit there was nothing lazy or selfish about him. She liked the way he touched her so much she spent hours in bed with him before suggesting they eat. Even after they polished off the dinner she'd prepared—at almost three o'clock in the morning—they went right back to her room.

Although she'd ignored her attraction to him, tried to pretend it didn't exist in the first place, there'd been so much sexual tension between them during the past year, maybe even longer, she supposed it was bound to come to this eventually.

But now what?

She hoped he'd make this morning easy on both of them and just get up, find that box of Sean's pictures in the basement and leave. Then she wouldn't have to think about what they'd done. Through all the years Serenity had known Sawyer, he'd only ever had one steady girlfriend, and he hadn't seemed particularly committed, even to her. Serenity doubted it would trouble him to say thanks for a fun night and walk away.

But he didn't seem to be in any hurry.

"Hey," he said, nudging her.

Pretending she hadn't been lying awake thinking for the past fifteen minutes or so, she acted slightly befuddled when she rolled over and looked up at him. His hair was mussed, and he had a shadow of beard growth covering his jaw, but he'd never been more appealing to her.

Somehow that didn't help.

She resisted the urge to draw his mouth back to hers; she had to put an end to this at some point. "Morning."

"It's getting late," he said.

She covered a yawn. "How late?"

"Ten thirty. I texted my mother—Sean's mother—that I'd have those pictures to her last night." He checked his phone, which he'd put on the nightstand at some point. "She's blowing up my phone because I didn't come by."

"Do you need to go? I can scramble some eggs really fast so you don't leave hungry."

"That's okay. We didn't get much sleep last night. You stay in bed. I just wanted to say goodbye."

"I don't mind getting up." She held the sheet to her chest as she searched the floor for her underwear, but she remembered that they, along with her other clothes, were in the living room, where she'd kicked them off.

She glanced at the dresser, gauging the distance. She hadn't minded Sawyer seeing her naked last night. They'd even eaten naked—or mostly naked; she'd pulled on his T-shirt for warmth—and then showered together. But for some reason, she was more self-conscious about her nudity this morning. Sex was one thing. She could relegate a heated sexual encounter to its own folder in her brain. Other forms of intimacy were more frightening because they lasted much longer and impacted the world she dealt with every day.

His forehead creased as he watched her deliberate. "You're acting distant this morning," he pointed out. "Is there a reason?"

"I'm not being distant," she said, "just *polite*. There's nothing wrong with polite, is there?"

"Coming from you? Yes. You've never been polite to me," he said dryly.

"Because you're always challenging me," she retorted.

His teeth flashed in the smartass smile she remembered seeing now and then over the years. "You like it when I challenge you."

"No, I'd like to be able to beat you at something," she corrected. "But you're too damn good, doesn't matter what we try."

She expected him to keep the banter going. She liked it; it prevented the conversation from getting too serious. But he sobered. "Is that so?" he said. "Because I think you have me at a disadvantage right now."

She scoffed as she looked over at him. "In what way?"

"I'd like to see you again," he said simply, honestly.

Serenity forced herself to get out of bed, even though he was still there. "Last night was the first time I've been touched by a man in eighteen months, Sawyer," she said as she took a pair of panties from her drawer. "That it was my ex-husband's *brother*, someone so familiar with the recent past and all the terrible memories associated with it, isn't something I really want to acknowledge."

He studied her for several seconds.

"You're not going to respond?" she said.

"What can I say? Sean caused those memories, not me. But you already know that. And I'm *not* related to him. You know that, too."

"In a way you are. He's how we met."

"Don't let that hang you up."

"It's not only that." She pulled on a sweatshirt that fell just below her panties. "I'm in the middle of another problem, and it could turn out to be as devastating as what I went through with Sean. So I can't take any chances right now. I need to be cautious, smart."

He got out of bed, too, completely unconcerned with his nudity, went to the living room and came back with his clothes. "Are you talking about having trouble writing?"

"No, but I'm not out of the woods there, either."

"So what is it?"

"It involves my family."

He put on his boxers. "You won't tell me what's going on?"

She sat on the edge of the bed and pulled her knees into her chest as she watched him stuff his legs into his jeans.

"Serenity?" he prompted as he buttoned his fly.

Should she tell him? She couldn't see any harm in it. He didn't have any contact with her parents or siblings, and she felt fairly confident he wouldn't tell anyone in Sean's family. Why would he? None of them were speaking to him; the rift might well turn out to be a permanent one. "I took a DNA test not too long ago, just to see how it all works—for my writing—and got a big surprise."

He froze. "Don't tell me you were adopted…"

She rested her chin on her knees. "It's possible. I don't know yet. All I know right now is that I was contacted by a woman only two years younger than me who lives in Florida, claiming to be my half sister."

"Have you checked out her story? Is it true?"

"It is. And that's not all."

He sat down next to her. "What else could there be?"

"We have another sister—this one only six months younger than me. She lives in New York."

"*Two* sisters? That's…hard to believe. I've met your parents. They seem so open, honest. Have you talked to them about these women?"

"Not yet. I'm afraid I've stumbled on a deep, dark secret, one that might end their marriage."

He took her hand and straightened her rings as he spoke. "Neither your mother nor your father has ever mentioned having other children?"

His fingers looked so big and brown next to hers. "No. That's how I know it must be a secret. But if my father cheated, and my mother learns about these other children… Or if my mother cheated…"

"You said one of these sisters is only six months younger than you. How could your mother have been the one?"

She went out to get her purse and handed him Uncle Vance's letter when she returned.

"What's this?" he asked.

She gestured for him to read it.

After he did, he looked up. "Who's Vance?"

"My uncle."

"Holy shit."

"See what I mean?"

"Have you mentioned him to these new sisters? Tried to determine if they have a connection with him, too?"

"No. I just found this letter not too long ago and I've been trying to wrap my mind around it ever since. I'll probably tell them, though. I sort of have to, don't I?"

"Have you met them?" he asked. "Do you even know what they're like?"

"They've been staying with me for over a week. They're at the cabin in Tahoe right now, waiting for me to come back. We're planning to spend the rest of the summer together."

"What are they like?"

"Normal people. Good people. Smart. One has a daughter who's four. Lucy. She's sweet."

He let go of her hand and stood up to finish dressing. "Can't they shed some light on the past?"

She'd liked sitting there on the bed with him, her hand in his. It had felt reassuring, comforting. But she couldn't attempt to have a relationship right now, especially with Sawyer. "Unfortunately not. Lorelei was either abandoned or lost as a toddler. She was found in the middle of a busy intersection in Orlando and raised in foster care. The other one—Reagan—was raised as an only child in New York City. Her mother is a successful clothing designer who claims her father died when she wasn't quite two."

His head came through his T-shirt. "*Claims?* You think her father might be your uncle Vance?"

"After reading that letter, don't you?"

Before he could answer, there was a loud banging at the door.

"Sawyer? I know you're in there, damn it! I drove by last night and your truck hasn't moved. You'd better open up and give me those pictures of Sean, or I'm calling the police to tell them Serenity's trying to steal his property!"

"It's Nina." Serenity's heart began to pound as she hopped up and started digging through her drawers for a pair of yoga pants.

Fortunately, Sawyer was already dressed, but his hair was standing up on one side and with that beard growth on his face, Serenity wasn't optimistic that Nina would believe he'd just arrived. Nina had already said she'd seen Sawyer's truck outside last night and it hadn't moved.

"Shit," she muttered.

He shot her a look that told her to calm down. "We haven't done anything wrong. Doesn't matter what they think," he insisted and went out to answer the door.

Although Serenity remained in the bedroom, she could hear everything Nina said. Sean's mother accused him of all kinds of terrible things—that he'd probably planted those pictures on Sean's computer to frame him and steal his wife, that he'd been jealous of Sean his whole life, that he didn't have an ounce of loyalty in him.

He responded with admirable restraint—tried to keep his voice low and talk some sense into her—so when Nina screamed that he was no better than a parasite and they should never have taken him in, Serenity threw down the yoga pants she'd been shaking too badly to put on and marched out of the bedroom in her underwear and sweatshirt.

"Get off my porch right now," she said, pointing toward Nina's car at the curb, "or I'll be the one to call the police. And don't you *ever* contact me or come to my house again. Do you understand? I don't care what excuse you think up. If I find something of your son's— your *pedophile* son who's in prison for his crimes—I'll mail it to you. But I'll never speak to you again."

A neighbor had just come home from the grocery store. He stood near his vehicle with several bags in each hand, gaping at them as Nina screamed, "So you've ruined Sean's life, put an innocent man in prison and now you're spreading your legs for his *brother*?"

So embarrassed she wished she could crawl under a rock somewhere, Serenity was preoccupied with looking at her neighbor and would've been caught unawares when Nina reached out to grab her hair or slap her or... something. But Sawyer grabbed his mother's hand.

"You need to go home, Mom," he said, keeping a tight hold on her wrist. "Your love for Sean has made you blind."

She wrenched her hand away, then jabbed a finger in his chest. "Don't you call me Mom! Don't you ever call me Mom again, you ungrateful bastard! You sack of shit! You, you—"

Serenity yanked him back, out of the way, so she could slam the door. Then they both stood there as the house shook and the reverberation echoed around them.

"She's vile," Serenity said, her voice barely above a whisper. "As if what Sean did wasn't bad enough."

Sawyer rubbed his forehead as though he had a headache. "She's hurt, too," he pointed out. "No one wants to believe their child could be that kind of person. You know what they say about a mother's love."

A mother's love was something he'd been denied, at

least for many years. And yet he was far more deserving than Sean had ever been. Sometimes there didn't seem to be any justice in the world. But Serenity couldn't help being impressed that Sawyer could look at the situation that objectively, especially after the hurtful things Nina had said to him.

"I'll get the pictures from the basement and leave them on her porch," he said. "Then we should be done with her."

We? Serenity shook her head. She should never have asked Sawyer to come over. She didn't want anything to do with Sean or his family, didn't need to be reminded of everything that'd happened. "There's cereal in the cupboard, and I bought milk yesterday. Feel free to have some breakfast before you go," she said. "But if you'll excuse me, I have to get back to Tahoe."

"Serenity…" he started, but she pushed past him to the bathroom. She had too much going on, couldn't risk inviting more drama into her life.

When she got out of the shower, he was gone.

* * *

lorelei

When Lorelei went to Finn's on Sunday with the dinner she'd prepared, Lucy was her only companion. Serenity had returned from Berkeley, but she'd excused herself by saying she hadn't slept well the night before, that she'd meet Davis tomorrow. And even though Reagan had come out of her room for a while earlier, she said she still wasn't feeling well enough.

Lorelei had been tempted to cancel with Finn, but she'd already made some cheese and herb polenta and chicken with fig sauce, and she was eager to see him. It hadn't been all that long since they were together, but it felt like an eternity. She was also looking forward to meeting his brothers. They'd talked about Nolan and Davis all week.

Finn met her at the door and helped her carry in the food. He said Davis and Nolan were showering.

When they finally emerged, she could see that Davis wasn't quite as tall as Finn or Nolan, and the pallor of his face—as well as the way his clothes hung on his frame—made it plain he'd lost a lot of weight recently. But even so, he was attractive. He had the same chiseled features and striking eyes as Finn, although his were brown.

He greeted her with a polite dip of his head when Finn introduced them, but his "nice to meet you" was clipped enough to let her know he wasn't interested in much social interaction.

Nolan had tattoo sleeves on both arms and darker hair than either of his brothers, which he wore long. He hung out with her and Finn in the kitchen while she put the finishing touches on the meal. As they talked and laughed, Davis sat morosely in front of the TV and kept to himself—or attempted to. Despite the fact that Lorelei had tried to prepare Lucy to meet Finn's injured brother, Lucy had never come into such close contact with someone who'd lost a limb, and she was absolutely transfixed by the empty sleeve pinned to his shirt.

No matter how many times Lorelei drew her away

from him, as soon as she got distracted with something Finn or Nolan said, she'd find Lucy near Davis again, staring at his missing arm. And, much to Lorelei's mortification, at one point she came out and asked, "What happened to your arm?"

He told her he was in a motorcycle accident, but that only inspired more questions.

"The motorcycle cut off your arm?" she asked.

"Lucy," Lorelei called, but Lucy ignored her in favor of getting an answer.

"The motorcycle smashed it and the doctor cut it off," Davis explained woodenly.

This answer seemed to horrify Lucy so much that she again ignored Lorelei when she tried to get her attention. "When will it grow back?" she asked Davis.

"It won't," he said simply.

"Then how are you going to tie your shoes?"

Since Lucy wasn't listening, Lorelei crossed the living room and grabbed Lucy's arm, forcing her daughter to look up at her at last. "It's time to eat," Lorelei said and walked her over to the table.

Lucy continued to stare at Davis while they ate, so dragging her away hadn't made any difference.

When Davis had difficulty cutting his chicken, Lorelei glanced at Finn, her expression asking if she should cut it for him. But Finn gave her a subtle shake of his head, signaling that she should leave Davis to his own devices, so they all cringed when Lucy piped up with the offer instead.

"Want me to help you?"

Davis pretended he didn't hear her. He stabbed his chicken breast with his fork and bit off pieces instead of trying to cut it. Lorelei was so afraid Lucy would continue singling him out and asking about his recent injury that she stayed only two hours before saying she had to go home to give Lucy a bath and put her to bed.

Finn walked them out. As soon as he closed the door behind them, Lorelei lowered her voice and whispered, "I'm so sorry."

"It's okay," he said. "He's going to have to get used to that sort of thing."

"But it's so soon!" She frowned at Lucy. "I don't know what got into her. I told her it wasn't kind to stare, warned her not to ask him any questions about his missing arm. But all of that went out the window as soon as she saw him."

He smoothed Lucy's hair out of her eyes. "She didn't mean any harm, did you, little one?"

Lucy looked from him to her. "Are you mad at me, Mommy?"

Finn spoke up before Lorelei could. "No. No one's mad at you. It's perfectly natural to be curious."

Lorelei rubbed Lucy's back to reassure her but spoke to Finn. "You wanted our help to make things better, but I feel we've only made them worse."

"Davis will be fine," he insisted.

"Okay. I'll see you tomorrow." She started to leave, but he caught her elbow.

Surprised, she turned to see him looking at her left hand. "Why don't you come back after Lucy's asleep?"

Reagan and Serenity would be at the cabin, if, for some reason, Lucy woke up. They could alert Lorelei to any problem, not that she expected one. But Lorelei knew what would probably happen if she returned to Finn's alone.

She'd removed her wedding ring after that exchange

with Francine, and Finn had obviously noticed. He was taking that as a sign.

"I don't know..." she said, feeling conflicted.

His gaze lifted to her face. "You don't want to?"

"That isn't it."

He lowered his voice. "Then come."

She gestured toward the cabin. "You've got your brothers here now."

"It's different with guys. They won't care."

She let go of a long sigh. After what she'd told Francine, Mark had been trying even more frantically to get hold of her, but she hadn't answered his calls or texts. She refused to let him or anything else continue to intrude. This was *her* summer. She had three months to spend with her sisters. Three months in which she could forget about the mess she'd left in Florida, with Francine and the baby. Three months to revel in the smell of the forest, the cushion of pine needles beneath her feet and the reflection of the sun on the lake before returning to real life.

"Lorelei?"

Her heart began to race as she looked up. "Okay, I'll come back."

22

serenity

She'd left Berkeley before taking any photographs of the house so she could list it for sale. She should've stayed and cleaned it up again so she could put it on the market. She'd had the time. But she'd been afraid Sawyer would come back. He hadn't liked the way their night had ended. She could tell he wanted to talk about it, but she didn't. She didn't know what to say. She wasn't in the right frame of mind to start a relationship, especially with him. She couldn't imagine they'd be able to make it work.

But when she'd gone into the kitchen to fill the dishwasher before leaving for Tahoe, she'd found a vase from her own cupboard filled with purple hydrangeas. He hadn't left a note or anything else, just the flowers, but seeing them had hit her hard. She'd stood there, staring at the delicate periwinkle-edged blooms for several minutes.

She had a big hydrangea bush in the backyard. He must've cut the flowers from there. It wasn't that they'd been hard to come by—because they hadn't been—that held her so transfixed. It was the thoughtfulness of the gesture. She had several rosebushes right outside her front door and yet he'd chosen the hydrangeas, which meant he must've remembered that they were her favorite.

She tried to recall ever having mentioned it to him, but no snippet of conversation about flowers came to mind. Had he overheard her talking to someone else? If so, it was even more impressive that he'd remembered. It wasn't as though he'd ever paid her a great deal of attention. In the years before she found those files on Sean's computer, he'd baited and teased her on occasion, been an absolute pain in the ass if there was anything competitive going on, but he'd never acted as though he was taking notes on what she did or didn't like. Most of the time he hadn't shown up at the family parties she and Sean attended. And if he was there, as long as they weren't playing any sort of game, he gave her a wide berth.

As she prepared for bed at the cabin that night, she thought of those hydrangeas and the man who'd gone to the trouble of bringing them in for her. Now that Nina knew Sawyer had spent the night, she'd tell the rest of the family. Serenity was afraid she'd get hate texts from Sean's other two brothers, like she had during the trial. Felix had been particularly mean, which was why she'd had to get a restraining order against him. But Thomas had been a jerk, too. Either one of them could start bothering her again.

Even with the threat of that hanging over her head, however, she couldn't regret her time with Sawyer. He'd made the night everything she'd wanted it to be—and then some.

She checked her phone as she'd been checking it all day. She hadn't heard from him. Fortunately, she hadn't heard from Nina or the rest of Sean's family, either. Had Sawyer found the photographs while she was in the shower? Dropped them off after he left her place? If so, how did it go with Nina after that embarrassing scene at her front door?

Or did he simply put the box on the porch and leave?

While she wondered about those things, she spent even more time wondering about something else: Was what had sparked between them over as quickly as it had begun?

She doubted Sawyer would ever lack for female company. He could have just about any woman he wanted, so why would he choose *Sean's* ex-wife?

"Hey, you have a minute?"

Serenity looked up to find Reagan standing in the doorway. She could hear Lorelei talking to Lucy down the hall, getting her ready for bed.

"Sure. What's going on?" Serenity put down her phone. "Sorry I didn't say hello when I got home. Lorelei told me you were sick, so I didn't want to wake you."

"I'm not sick."

Serenity blinked at her. "Then what's wrong?"

Reagan opened her mouth to answer, but covered her face instead.

"Reagan?"

"I'm pregnant," she said, the words coming out as though they were wrenched from her.

A jolt of surprise brought Serenity's hand to her chest. "Are you… Are you sure?"

She dropped her hands and cocked one eyebrow. "I've taken three home pregnancy tests so far, hoping I'll get a different reading. Do you think I should take another one?"

"No. Three should be enough. But…how did it happen?"

She rolled her eyes and groaned in apparent self-loathing. "Don't ask."

"You didn't use any birth control…"

"We didn't plan on having sex in the first place! It was…unexpected and…and we did what we could but apparently it wasn't enough."

Meaning they'd used the withdrawal method. Serenity's mind immediately reverted to last night. Thank God Sawyer had had condoms. He'd had to go out to his truck to get more after they'd used the one in his wallet, but at least they hadn't risked a pregnancy. "I'm sorry. I can tell you're not happy about it."

"I'm *not*. I'm mad at myself. I'm mad at Drew. I'm even mad at the baby growing inside me—which is cruel, of course, and makes me hate myself even more."

A year and a half ago, Serenity had *wanted* a baby. She'd pictured her life going in a completely different direction, would never have guessed what was just around the corner. But if she'd learned she was pregnant *after* she found those files, she knew she would've been as distraught as Reagan was. She couldn't help feeling she'd dodged a bullet—the same bullet that had hit Reagan right between the eyes. "What you're feeling toward the baby will change," she said. Serenity wasn't positive that was true, but she was hoping to offer some encouragement. "You'll see."

"If it doesn't, I'll have to give the baby up for adoption," she stated with anguished honesty. "I can't approach parenting with the same attitude my mother did. I always felt she saw me as a burden."

"I can't believe she really felt that way about you."

"I think she did. She wasn't cut out to be a mother," Reagan insisted. "She's big on responsibility, on being strong and getting the job done—whatever needs to be done. But she's not good with kindness, understanding, nurturing. She probably only raised me because she was faced with something like this, something she thought she couldn't get out of."

Serenity slid across and patted the bed beside her. "Come sit down."

Reagan walked over and slumped onto the mattress.

"Are you going to tell Drew?"

"What do you think he'd rather I did? Leave him out of it completely? Or give him a chance to be part of the child's life?"

Serenity stiffened. "Why do we care what *he'd* prefer?"

"If he doesn't want the child, I don't see how forcing him into fatherhood will do me or the baby any good."

"It'll mean he'll have to pay his share of the expenses."

"I'd rather cover all the costs myself if it means I don't have to take him into account. I'd settle for that in a heartbeat. I'm just not sure it's fair to the child, not if there's a possibility Drew might want to be involved."

"What if he wants to be involved to the point of raising the child himself?" Serenity asked. "Will you give it up to him?"

"I can't imagine that would ever be an option. When he grabbed me that day in his office, he wasn't in it for…

this. Think about it. His wife would be in the same position as Lorelei, and we know how unhappy she's been."

Serenity couldn't believe Reagan's luck. "These are not easy decisions."

"Something strange, something like this, must've occurred in the lives of our mothers before we were born—or we wouldn't be related. Do you think they felt the same panic and fear I'm feeling now?" she asked.

It wasn't pleasant to consider that their mothers were mortified to be pregnant, but it was a reasonable possibility. "Maybe."

"Will we ever find out what happened?"

Serenity thought of the letter in her purse. She'd tried to reach Uncle Vance on the drive back to Tahoe, but he hadn't picked up, and he hadn't returned her call. From what she'd heard about him, that wasn't unusual, though. He was a lot easier to reach when *he* wanted something.

"Serenity?" Reagan said when she didn't reply.

After getting up to retrieve her purse, Serenity handed Reagan the letter she'd discovered in her mother's jewelry box.

"Where did this come from?"

"I found it here in the cabin while you, Lorelei and Lucy were out on a walk with Finn."

Reagan's gaze immediately skipped to the bottom of the page. "Who's Vance?"

"My father's brother."

"I don't understand. What's this about?"

"Read it."

Frowning, she started to read out loud. "'Dear Charlotte, I'm sorry I stood you up last night. Chuck dropped in unexpectedly. At first I thought he knew about the baby, that you must've broken down and told him. But he didn't say anything about that. You understand why you can't, right? Please promise me you'll never tell him. Love, Vance.'" Reagan dropped the letter in her lap and looked up. *"Damn."*

"Sounds like they were having an affair, doesn't it? There's no date on that note, but the fact that it refers to a baby, and it's so old and yellow, makes me think he was talking about me."

"Where did you find this again?"

"Here in the cabin—in my mother's old jewelry box."

"Why would she leave it there, where your father could possibly come across it?"

"It has a false bottom. He'd never suspect that. I only thought to look because I had a similar jewelry box as a kid, and I loved the secret compartment."

"Still. She should've *burned* this letter!"

Serenity grimaced. "The fact that she didn't makes me believe his declaration of undying love might have meant something to her."

Reagan paused to read the letter again. "This has to be upsetting for you."

"It is. But it might solve the mystery of how we're related."

"How would he have known my mother and Lorelei's?"

"From what I've heard, he's lived in many places."

"Cincinnati? Florida?"

Serenity took the letter back. "I can't say for sure. I only know that he's moved around."

Reagan stood. "How can we find out more?"

"I've called him. He didn't pick up, but he might call me back."

"What will you say when he does? You're not going to tell him you found this letter, are you?"

"No. My mom thinks he lives in Vegas. I was going to tell him I'm coming to Vegas for a few days, see if he might be able to have dinner with me."

"And if he agrees? What will you say then?"

Serenity folded the letter and returned it to her purse. "I won't say anything in particular. I'll make small talk until he leaves the restaurant, and then I'll take his glass and swab it for DNA."

"Of course! Smart."

"We should tell Lorelei," Serenity said. The house had fallen quiet; she guessed Lorelei had finally gotten Lucy to sleep.

"Not *my* news," Reagan protested. "I'm not ready to face how it's bound to make her feel."

Serenity touched Reagan's elbow. "Just about the letter, then."

She got up but Lorelei appeared in the doorway before Serenity could take more than a few steps.

"Is there any way you two would mind watching Lucy?" she asked. "I mean, she's asleep and I'm pretty sure she won't get up, so it shouldn't be any trouble. But I wanted you to know I won't be here, in case."

"Where are you going?" Reagan asked.

"Next door to watch a movie with Finn and his brothers."

Serenity had noticed that Lorelei had stopped wearing her wedding ring. And right now her eyes were bright, her cheeks flushed. Her level of happiness had changed a lot in the last few days. Serenity hated to interfere with that, but she didn't want Lorelei to end up in an even worse situation. Maybe one like Reagan's. "Are you sure you want to get involved with Finn, Lorelei?"

"We're just going to watch a movie," she said as though Serenity was crazy to be worried, and after what Serenity had done last night, she didn't feel in any position to preach.

"Okay. I'll watch Lucy."

"I'm glad to see you're feeling better," Lorelei told Reagan and hurried off before Reagan could respond.

"I'm worried for her," Reagan murmured once they were alone. "She's falling too hard and too fast for Finn. She hasn't even taken time to get over Mark."

Serenity blew out a sigh. "I know."

* * *

lorelei

Davis went to bed almost as soon as Lorelei returned, but Nolan stayed up with them to watch a Marvel movie. Lorelei was actually grateful for Nolan's presence; having him in the room kept things from moving too fast with Finn. She was excited about being with him without having to worry about how Lucy might be perceiving their relationship, but she was also supremely aware that the man she was lying beside on the couch was not her husband. She hadn't been intimate with anyone else since meeting Mark twelve years ago.

Once the movie ended, Nolan said good-night, but Lorelei knew by then that she wouldn't be staying. It wasn't a question of not being interested in Finn; it was just too soon.

Finn seemed to understand, because he didn't press her. When she said she needed to get back, he grabbed his coat—the weather had chilled off since she'd come over—and insisted on walking her home.

"Thanks for dinner tonight," he said as they meandered back to Serenity's cabin. "It was really good."

Now that she was sure she wasn't going to do anything she might regret, she was in no hurry to say goodnight. "You're welcome."

He kept his hands in his pockets the whole way and they talked about how much she liked Nolan and how angry Davis was—and whether he'd get over it.

Once they reached the front porch and she turned to say goodbye, however, he caught her hand. "You're not wearing your wedding ring anymore."

She welcomed the warmth of his touch. "I told Francine that I'm not going back to Mark."

His eyebrows shot up. "You finally spoke to her?"

"It was via text. She tried to call, but I wouldn't pick up."

"Do you mean what you said to her? That it's over between you and Mark?"

She hesitated. "At times I mean it," she allowed.

His hands were now holding hers. "And other times?"

"I think of Lucy and how this will affect her."

"Mark was a good father?"

"He was—if you can call him a good father after he did something so obviously against her best interests," she said with a shiver.

"You're cold. Come here." Pulling her inside his coat,

he wrapped his arms around her. "What did Francine say?"

She savored the smell of him, which was so unique to Finn. "She was shocked. I think she expected me to forgive them both—that I'd somehow welcome her back as my best friend and accept her child. But that's too weird for me. Every time I start telling myself I need to forgive them, that we can all go back to being happy again, I consider their baby and feel so betrayed. I doubt I'll ever get over it."

"There's no need to make a quick decision—not when it's this important."

His voice seemed to reverberate in his chest. "I only know a few things for sure," she said.

"And they are…"

"One, I want to stay for the summer."

"I'm glad about that."

"Two, I'm happy I met you."

She felt a change in him, knew that if the situation was different, he'd be kissing her by now.

"I'm glad about that, too."

"And three, I want to get a job—"

He let her go. "Get a job?"

"I have to do something to make money. Mark will cut me off if I don't go back."

The wind whipped at his hair. "He would really leave you and Lucy with no money?"

"He hasn't yet, but I'm pretty sure he would."

"What about child support, if not alimony?"

"He'll owe that. I should get half the equity in our house, too, not that it'll amount to much. But it will take time for the divorce and all those matters to be decided and settled. I have to be able to survive until then."

"You mean there'll be nothing making him pay beforehand."

"Exactly. And he'll feel completely justified in cutting me off because I have a choice, right? I won't be in dire financial straits if I go back. He feels that I'm being unnecessarily difficult, and maybe unfair."

"How could he ever accuse *you* of being unfair?"

"I'm withholding, being too harsh, whatever."

Finn looked angry. "Wow, I want to punch him in the face and I've never even met him." He shook his head. "What kind of job are you hoping to get?"

"It'll only be for the summer, so I'd be satisfied if I could work as a waitress or in the front office of a motel or something. I only need grocery and spending money."

"Maybe Nolan can get you a job as a waitress at the bar where he's working this summer."

"But you said that's a half-hour commute. I need to get something close by, so that I can take the bus or walk."

"You can borrow my car."

"I don't want to lean on you."

"I work at home."

"Still, I can take an Uber, if it's close enough."

"What if you helped *us* out this summer? Then you wouldn't have to pay for an Uber or find someone to watch Lucy. I'm sure I can get my father to pay you for looking after Davis—have you wash and fold his clothes, make his meals, do his dishes, drive him around if he wants to go somewhere. We were considering getting someone to do those things, anyway. He's so proud, it would be harder for him to accept our help. We're the guys he's had to compete with his whole life, right?"

She was about to decline. She didn't want him to ask his father to pay her if Davis didn't truly need her.

But she'd seen Davis. Until he got used to living with only one arm, he'd need someone to help him dress, hang up his clothes, cut his meat—or make sure what he was served didn't need to be cut at the table in the first place. She wished she'd thought about that tonight but somehow it never occurred to her.

"Do you think Davis could tolerate Lucy's questions?"

"Once she spends enough time around him she won't have questions. Someone innocent and sweet like Lucy would be good for him. You'd both be great."

She smiled. "Well, if it turns out that he does need someone, talk to him about me and Lucy before you ask your father. I want to be sure he won't mind that it's us."

"He won't care who it is—or even if there *is* someone. He doesn't care about anything right now. That's the problem. We need to make him care again. And who wouldn't fall in love with you and Lucy?"

She hadn't planned on kissing him, but the next thing she knew, she rose up on her tiptoes and pressed her mouth to his.

But then he parted his lips to deepen the kiss and she felt a moment of panic.

Just before she could pull away on her own, the door opened behind her and they broke apart.

"I thought I heard voices." It was Reagan.

"Is Lucy okay?" she asked.

"She hasn't stirred."

"Good. Well—" Lorelei cleared her throat "—I'd better go in. Thanks for walking me home."

Finn didn't rush off, didn't act self-conscious or

embarrassed in the least. Reagan said something she couldn't hear, and he responded as Lorelei hurried to her room. Part of her was sad that Reagan had interrupted them. She was excited about Finn. But another part was relieved.

She had no business jumping right into another relationship—especially one that had so little chance of working out. She had a daughter to think of, and in order to take the best possible care of Lucy, she had to protect her own heart.

23

reagan

She had to come to grips with being pregnant. She couldn't mope around all day, couldn't feel sorry for herself forever. After all, she had no one to blame but herself.

Well, she could blame Drew, she supposed. He'd played an equal role in screwing up her life. What she was battling with was whether to tell him what had resulted from that "fifteen minutes of panting and one good climax" on his desk.

The next couple of weeks were filled with days when she believed it was wrong to deny her child access to her father. And other days when she was certain her child would be better off if he or she didn't know. Different parenting styles could have an adverse effect on a child, and Drew had no good reason to cooperate with her. She'd have no leverage, and that frightened her.

So did the whole aspect of having to contend with his wife. She didn't want to subject her child to someone who would have such a good reason to resent him or her.

Shouldn't she simply parent alone?

She'd turned out okay—and she was raised by a woman much less empathetic than she was.

But she hadn't had an easy childhood...

"What are you thinking about?"

She glanced up from her computer to see Serenity watching her. They were on the deck writing while Lorelei went over to Finn's. Lorelei had started working for Finn's brother Davis, who was so moody and pissed at the world that Reagan thought Lorelei deserved a medal just for putting up with him.

But Lorelei was falling in love with Finn, so Reagan figured being around Davis's brother was the real reward. That went beyond the $100/day Davis's father was paying her. She and Lucy were beginning to spend *a lot* of time next door, even when Lorelei wasn't working. And Reagan had interrupted that kiss. She also saw the way Finn and Lorelei looked at each other when they thought no one was watching.

"You're supposed to be writing," she said to Serenity.

"I *was* writing, but when I glanced up the expression on your face was so pathetic, I couldn't help feeling sorry for you."

Reagan chuckled. "You *should* feel sorry for me. You and Lorelei both have the chance to heal from what you've been through and move on. Your wreckage is behind you. I, on the other hand, have to live with the consequences of my actions—"

"You act like having a baby is a death sentence," she broke in.

"It's not a *death* sentence, it's a *life* sentence."

Serenity lowered her voice. "Have you told Lorelei you're pregnant?"

"No. I don't want to. I don't want to tell my mother, either."

"You can wait to tell your mother until you get back to New York, but you need to tell Lorelei much sooner. If she feels you kept it from her—and yet you told me—she'll be hurt. Why not be up front with her? You don't think she'll decide you're not worthy of her love, do you?"

"No. It's more that I don't want to make her sympathetic to Francine just because she's sympathetic to me and my situation."

"Your situation isn't exactly the same. You weren't best friends with Drew's wife."

"I'm still the other woman, and I'm pregnant. That's going to be hard for Lorelei to swallow. And if she forgives me for what I did—which I feel she will since it doesn't affect her directly—she'll feel she has to do the same for Mark and Francine."

"Maybe she *should* forgive them. Maybe that's what's best for Lucy."

A bird trilling in the closest tree drew Reagan's attention. It was going to be hard to leave this place when the time came… "If I felt Mark and Francine were truly penitent, I'd agree with you. But you heard what Mark did yesterday, didn't you? He took her name off their joint bank account, cut her off completely."

"He did? Then she was right. She said he'd do it eventually."

"After living with him for so long, she knew what he'd do. But he's the one who screwed up their marriage in the first place."

"I bet he's afraid she's moving on and is trying to limit the damage to himself."

"See what I mean? That's looking out for number one—not being sorry you hurt someone else. Is he with Francine now?"

"Claims he isn't."

Reagan started to go back to commenting on Serenity's Facebook page—she'd posted a photo of Serenity writing in Tahoe that was going over well—but since Serenity had stopped working, she decided to ask about Vance. "Any word from your uncle?"

"None."

"Is he out of the country or what? What could take him so long to get back to you?"

"I'm beginning to think he has good reason for not calling me. Maybe he knows what I want to talk about."

"How could he?"

Serenity took a sip of the coffee at her elbow. "He can't *know*, but he might wonder, might worry, which makes him nervous to talk to me."

"I've been thinking... If he won't even call you back, it won't do you any good to go to Vegas. What if we tried a different approach?"

"To get his DNA?"

"No, this wouldn't give us his DNA, but it might tell us if you should pursue a trip to Vegas."

Serenity pushed her computer away and leaned back in her chair. "What are you suggesting?"

"We use my phone to call him. He's never heard my voice, doesn't know me from Adam. Or Eve." She grinned briefly. "I impersonate my mother, tell him that my daughter's found a sister in Florida and that this sister, who was discovered wandering in the streets as a toddler, must be his, too. See how he reacts. If he doesn't know my mother, says I couldn't possibly be his—and neither could this child from Florida—we know we're chasing the wrong guy and move on."

Serenity frowned as she considered the suggestion. "But that might give away what *I've* been calling about. It's not as if I usually contact him."

"Even if it does, a call from a different number, a number he doesn't recognize, might get him to pick up the phone. Maybe if we can just reach him we'll end up with more to go on. We have to take some chances, or we might never figure this out."

"What if he's remained in contact with your mother? What if he recognizes that it's not her voice?"

"He hasn't. My mother might've made the mistake of getting involved with him when she was young, but if he didn't step up, she would've washed her hands of him. She doesn't mess around. That's why she's been single ever since. She can't put up with anyone."

"I suppose it's worth a try," Serenity said. "If he suspects, he may say something to my mom—that I've been calling and he got this other weird call—but he wouldn't involve my dad, because that might give away their secret. It should be safe."

"I doubt he'd tell your mother he heard from another woman he also impregnated back in the day. That would only make her feel worse toward him—and she might try to stop your father from ever helping him again."

"That's true, I guess."

"Then should I do it?"

"What about Lorelei? I told her about Vance. Shouldn't she have a say in how we proceed?"

"Why would she care if we try to get information this way? She has nothing to lose."

"I just think she should be here."

"She's always with Finn these days. If we wait until she gets home, it'll be too late in New York, where I'm supposedly calling from."

"True."

"So?"

Serenity got out of her seat and began to walk around the deck. Obviously deep in thought, she went over to the railing and gazed toward the lake. "Yeah, do it," she said when she turned around.

* * *

lorelei

Mark was calling her again, but she ignored the ring. His calls had gotten ugly—accusing, nasty, punishing.

Although Lorelei worried about what taking Lucy's father away might do to their daughter, wouldn't it be worse to grow up in a house where Mommy and Daddy were constantly bickering? Slamming doors? Not speaking?

And now she had Finn to consider. She hadn't slept with him, but she wanted to. He'd backed off after that night he'd walked her home. She was pretty sure he was trying to give her time, that he knew it was too soon. But he kissed her now and then—when Lucy wasn't watching—and she thought about sex more and more.

That certainly told her she was starting to have feelings for him and wanted to be with him even if it meant putting up with the dour Davis, who rarely spoke—and acted as though she didn't exist. He even managed to ignore Lucy, something Lorelei would previously have considered impossible. Whenever he was sitting on the couch, watching TV—which was about all he did— Lucy thought he was available to play. He wasn't working or anything else that looked important, so that was generally when she approached him. But if she asked him to color or do anything else, he scowled at her so darkly she quickly moved away.

If it wasn't for Finn, Lorelei might've tried to find a new job. Davis was *that* sullen. It wasn't easy to be around someone who was desperately unhappy. But because of Finn, she kept hanging on—and kept explaining to Lucy that Davis was going through a hard time and was "mean" because he was struggling to heal from the loss of his arm.

"Is that Mark?"

She looked up to see Finn standing in the doorway. She hadn't realized he'd entered the kitchen, where she was preparing lunch. He'd gone down to paint a little earlier than usual. Normally when he started work, he didn't emerge for several hours. She'd expected to bring him a sandwich. "Yeah."

She hit Ignore yet again and slid her phone into her pocket.

"Have you told him you have a job?"

"I told him I'm working for a neighbor, yes."

"Good. Then he knows you don't need his money."

"For now. Things will change after the summer's over, of course, but I refuse to think beyond August. Not when it's still June."

He came up behind her. Lucy was playing on the floor in the living room and couldn't see them above the couch as Finn slid his hands around her waist. "Does he know about me?" he murmured in her ear.

She felt a wave of desire. Her sexuality had been as crushed as her heart but, thanks to Finn, it seemed to be reviving. She was more comfortable now with letting him touch her—she *wanted* him to touch her. "Lucy mentioned you to him."

"So he knows I'm the neighbor you work for?"

"I didn't specify that, but he guessed, and it's driving him mad."

He pressed his lips to her neck as her phone went off for the fourth time in a row. She had no doubt it was her husband. She wasn't even going to check, but Finn pulled her phone from her pocket.

"He won't leave you alone," he said when he saw all the missed calls. "This is getting obsessive."

"It's because I won't answer. We've been doing nothing but fighting."

"No wonder. First he gets your best friend pregnant, then he cuts you off financially."

She felt slightly defensive of Mark, which was strange, since she was angrier with him than anyone else had reason to be. "He's trying to force me to come home. That's all. In his mind, if I run out of money, I'll have no choice."

"Shouldn't he care more about whether you *want* to be with him? Whether he deserves a woman like you?"

"He thinks he can convince me how good things were when we were together if I'll just come home, that everything will go back to the way it was."

"Were things *that* good?"

"Before the affair." Or maybe she didn't know any differently. She hadn't met anyone like Finn, hadn't known she had sisters. Her perception of everything was changing.

He looked uncertain. "Do you want to get back together with him?"

She shook her head. "It's hard to even think about that—when there's you."

His gaze lowered to her lips, but he didn't kiss her. Lucy's voice, coming from the living room, interrupted them.

"So what if a motorcycle cut off your stupid arm? You have another one, don't you?" they heard her yell, and then something crashed.

"Lucy!" Lorelei rushed around the island to find Davis standing about three feet from her, breathing hard, a lamp broken against the wall behind her. "What happened?" she asked.

"I've had it with her—with everyone!" Davis snapped and stalked out of the room.

"I'm sorry, Mommy," Lucy said and ran to her.

"You need to apologize to Davis, not me," Lorelei said as she scooped up her daughter. "Why did you say that to him?"

"Because he's mean!" she said and started to cry.

"I'd better go talk to him," Finn said, but Lorelei thought it was time *she* said something. Finn had been running interference for her and Lucy for two weeks. It wasn't fair that he had to be the one to constantly smooth things over.

"Can I?" she asked. "If Davis and I don't start getting along, this arrangement will never work. Right now he resents me and Lucy, even though I'm here to help him."

"He really likes kids. Having a child around should cheer him up. He's just…in a bad place."

"I understand that. But Lucy's right. He needs to quit feeling sorry for himself. It might sound harsh, but babying him isn't doing him any good. He's not the only person in the world who's ever suffered."

Finn studied her for a moment. "You're going to tell him that?"

"Maybe." If she managed to summon the nerve. His brothers wouldn't do it because they felt too sorry for him. They treated him like an invalid, and that was part of the problem. The loss of his arm would be a real challenge, but it didn't have to destroy the rest of his life. Maybe he needed to hear a few harsh realities, or he'd never recover.

She gave her daughter a hug and passed her off to Finn. "Can you keep an eye on Lucy for a few minutes? Stop her from getting into the glass?"

Nolan appeared at the top of the stairs. He worked until two, so he often slept late. "What's going on?" he asked. "What was that noise?" He was standing in nothing except his boxers, raking the sleep-mussed hair from his face. She spent enough time in the house that none of them bothered to be particularly modest.

"Your oldest brother is throwing a tantrum." She motioned to the broken lamp he'd thrown against the wall.

He pinched his neck as though he had a crick. "He's...not himself."

She was tired of their excuses. "I don't care. He can't behave like that. What if a piece of glass had shot out and hit Lucy? Someone has to put a stop to his bullshit."

"And you're going to be the one?" Nolan asked.

"Why not?" she replied.

Nolan looked to Finn. "You think that's what's best?"

Finn hesitated as though he might stop her, but then he shrugged and wiped Lucy's tears. "I guess we'll find out," he told Nolan.

24

serenity

Serenity watched as Reagan dialed her uncle. She didn't expect him to pick up, especially right away, so she was surprised when he said hello.

She wrung her hands as she listened to their conversation, which Reagan had on speaker so she could hear and help interpret the way her uncle said certain things—or didn't say certain things. She was, after all, the one who knew him.

"This is Rosalind," Reagan said.

He hesitated. "Rosalind. Rosalind who?"

"Sands. Don't you remember me?"

Reagan was talking boldly, confidently, impersonating her mother in a no-nonsense, brisk voice.

"No. I've never heard of you before," he started but caught himself a second later and reversed his answer. "Wait. You took me off guard is all. Of course I remember you. How could I ever forget? It wasn't every day that… Never mind. It's been years and years. Why are you calling me?"

Serenity's heart sank. They'd guessed right—they'd figured it out. Rosalind knew Vance. Charlotte must've had an affair with him, and he must've slept with Reagan's mother and Lorelei's, too.

Serenity felt nauseous. She doubted Reagan was any happier with this information. Reagan believed her father to have been a good man who'd died when she was very young; it wouldn't be pleasant to learn he was alive and well—and yet not part of her life. That meant either he'd let her down or her mother had lied to her.

Lorelei was the only one who might be pleased. At least she'd know where she came from, and maybe Vance could shed some light on who her mother was.

Even though they'd expected to receive confirmation of what they'd already found, Reagan seemed as stunned as she was. But Serenity didn't want to tip him off that something was up. She made a rolling motion with her hand, indicating that Reagan needed to hold it together long enough to finish the conversation.

"Hello? Are you still there?" he said.

She cleared her throat. "My daughter—*our* daughter—took one of those DNA tests," Reagan said.

Although she sounded less certain, Serenity hoped Vance wouldn't notice.

"What are you talking about? *Our* daughter? She's not mine!"

"I'm talking about *Reagan.*"

"I know who you're talking about, but you understood—" Suddenly, he fell silent. Then his voice changed, grew suspicious instead of indignant. "Wait—what's going on?" he said tentatively. "Who is this?"

Reagan's eyes flew wide.

"Damn it! Tell me who you are!" he said when she didn't respond.

Reagan nearly dropped the phone in her hurry to hang up.

After she did, they gaped at each other.

"What the hell?" Reagan set her phone on the table as if she didn't dare touch it any longer and walked to the railing and back, trying to calm down. "He said he wasn't my father," she reiterated as if Serenity hadn't heard for herself. "And he sounded pretty damn certain of it."

"But he *has* to be your father," Serenity insisted. "He has to be mine and Lorelei's, too. That's the only explanation that makes sense."

"He acted as if there was some *other* explanation— and that my mother should know it."

"If there is another one, she probably does! But will she tell you?"

"Not if it reflects poorly on her. My mother seems to believe she's never made a mistake in her life."

"If I could get a DNA sample from him, we'd know for sure."

"It'll be a waste of time to go to Vegas. He acted shocked that I—or Rosalind—would say such a thing, as if I must've lost my mind."

He had. Reagan was right. "But he obviously knew about you. He recognized your name."

Reagan returned to the railing and looked pensively through the tall trees that surrounded them. "What if you got a DNA sample from your father instead? Wouldn't that be easier? If we're all related to him, we'll have our answer—or at least good reason to continue pursuing Vance. We'll know then that your uncle must be lying."

"He's *got* to be lying. We have that letter."

"Just because he had an affair with your mother doesn't mean he had an affair with mine, or that any of us are his."

"He mentions a baby!"

"Still. I say we get your father's DNA and go from there."

Serenity hadn't seen her parents for several months, and she knew her mother felt she'd been acting distant lately. She *had* been acting distant.

"Why not?" Reagan asked. "Or wait until you finish your book. I don't want anything getting in the way of that—not even this. We don't have to know *now*, I guess."

"It takes six to eight weeks to get the DNA results. If we're going that route, we should start pretty soon. Then we might know by the end of summer."

"That would be good," Reagan agreed.

"Okay. I'll go this weekend or next, whenever I can get a flight for a decent price."

"What reason will you give your folks for coming?"

"I'll just say I'm visiting for a few days. We're close enough that I don't need a reason. It's probably stranger that I *haven't* come home for so long. She's been bugging me to."

"But will you be able to spend time with your parents without giving us away?"

Lorelei and Reagan were becoming an integral part of her life—and she shared *everything* with her mother. To be keeping this secret not only felt strange, it felt duplicitous.

"I'll manage." Serenity spoke with more confidence than she felt. She was afraid to return home for fear she'd act strange, and they'd call her on it.

She was, however, eager to return to the Bay area;

from there she'd fly to San Diego. Maybe she'd allow herself to see Sawyer the night before her flight. She hadn't heard from anyone in Sean's family, which helped her stop worrying about Nina's having found them together. And she couldn't stop thinking about Sawyer, about the way he kissed her, the way he touched her, the way he felt inside her—or those flowers he'd left on the counter. He hadn't called, but she believed he'd left those hydrangeas as an invitation to contact him again.

And the longer she waited, the harder it became not to.

* * *

lorelei

When Lorelei knocked on Davis's door, he didn't answer.

"Davis?" she called through the panel. "I need to talk to you. Will you give me a minute?"

"Go away," he said.

She set her jaw. "I *won't* go away. It's time we had a heart-to-heart."

"I don't have to talk to you. I don't even know you. You have no right to be here."

She curved her nails into her palms. "Your father is paying me to be here. But if you don't think I'm making your life easier, maybe this isn't the best arrangement."

"I don't need you," came his response. "I don't need anyone."

"I agree," she said. "You could do what I'm doing if you really wanted to. It would just take some determination and practice. Why don't you start making yourself do a little more each day?"

No answer.

"Either way, while you *do* have help, would it kill you to be kind? And to show a little gratitude to your father and your brothers, who are trying so hard to be supportive?"

"What's happening to me is none of your business," he snapped. "I don't have to listen to you."

"No one forced you to get on that motorcycle," she said. "*You* made that choice, and when you ride a motorcycle, you have to accept the risks that go along with it. I'm sure you knew it could be dangerous, so you don't get to treat everyone like shit just because you had an accident. It's unfortunate, and I feel bad about it, but you've had enough time to grieve. It's been nearly two months, and you haven't shown any signs of improvement—you're actually getting worse! It's starting to turn into a pity party."

The door swung open and banged against the inside wall as he stood in the doorway. "Did you say *pity party*?"

She was intimidated by his stance, the anger in his eyes and the vein that throbbed in his throat, but she was already in too deep to back out. She lifted her chin to show her own resolution. "Yes. You're so busy feeling sorry for yourself that you've forgotten to be grateful for all the things you *do* have. It could be worse, you know. You could've been killed. You could've broken your back or your neck and become a quadriplegic. You could've bashed your head in and ruined all hope of becoming an actor. You could've lost one or both legs. If you'll change your attitude, you can overcome this and still live a good life, especially once you get a prosthetic, which your father is rich enough to provide! How lucky is that!"

"I don't know who the hell you think you are!" he cried.

Maybe she'd gone too far—and maybe what she'd said should've come from someone else. But the people who loved him couldn't bear to tell him what he needed to hear. "Lucy and I have been nothing but nice to you," she said, speaking in a much calmer voice, in hopes that he would, too. "You don't have to be a jerk, even if you have lost an arm."

Her calm voice did little good. "Get out of here," he yelled pointing at the door. "Get out and don't come back. I don't ever want to see you or your daughter again!"

Tears sprang to Lorelei's eyes. This was more than she'd bargained for. And it was her fault. She was angry and frustrated by life, too. There'd always been things she wished she had—like a family, a different past, the knowledge of who she was and where she came from. And now she was mourning the loss of her trust and belief in Mark, the person she'd expected to spend the rest of her life with.

But she couldn't sit around feeling sorry for herself. She needed to get beyond her challenges, and so did he. "Fine, Lucy isn't safe around a two-hundred-pound baby, anyway."

"Lorelei…" Finn had carried Lucy to where they were and she could hear Nolan's feet pounding down the stairs as he hurried to join them. She guessed they wanted her to stop, but she wasn't in full control of her emotions. She was feeling her way through each day, just trying to keep things together and figure out a future. She didn't need someone like Davis to make her life any more difficult. She was only earning about fifteen dollars an hour. Surely, she could find something else that paid that much.

"I'm leaving and I'm not coming back," she told Finn. "But I think you and Nolan should tell your brother that he needs to be the one to clean up the lamp he broke." She shot Davis a disapproving look. "He should also be the one to pay for it."

With that, she grabbed Lucy and stormed out of the house.

* * *

reagan

Serenity was right. Reagan needed to tell Lorelei about the baby. She'd just convinced herself she'd do that at the next opportunity when Lorelei came stomping into the cabin, handed her Lucy and started to her room.

"Uh-oh," she murmured to Serenity, who walked out to see what was going on.

"What's the matter?" she asked Lorelei, but Lorelei was already halfway to her room.

It was Lucy who answered. "Mommy's crying."

Reagan had been able to see that for herself. She bent her head to peer into the little girl's face. "Why?"

"Davis."

"What did he do?"

"He threw the lamp," she said, wide-eyed.

"At who?" Serenity asked. "He didn't hit her, did he?"

"No. It broke."

"It doesn't sound like things are going too well next door," Reagan murmured. "Here, take Lucy. I'll go check on Lorelei."

She was about to start up the stairs when there was

a quick knock at the door and, before she could answer, Finn opened it. "Can I talk to Lorelei?" he asked.

He didn't look as though he'd take no for an answer, so Reagan motioned him past her. "She's in her room. Third one on the right."

He took the stairs two at a time, and she heard the door shut as he went in.

"Why is your mommy upset?" she asked, returning to Lucy.

Serenity answered for her. "She just mumbled something about Davis and Lorelei getting into a fight."

Reagan scowled. "Over what?"

"I haven't been able to figure that out." Serenity caught Lucy's eye. "What were they fighting about?"

"The lamp," she said with a sniff as though reliving it was upsetting her again.

"Why did he throw it?" Reagan asked.

She stared down at her dangling feet. "I said something bad."

Reagan took her hand. "What? What did you say?"

"I don't remember," she said and turned into Serenity's shoulder as she started to cry.

Serenity hugged her close. "I'm sure it'll be okay."

"That lamp better not have hit anyone," Reagan said.

"I'm sure it didn't," Serenity responded. "Finn would never allow it to go that far."

"I wonder what Finn's saying to her now," Reagan said.

Serenity motioned at the table. "Let's eat. Maybe after he leaves, she'll tell us."

A text came in as Reagan was pulling up her chair. It was from Rally. *How are you feeling?*

"It's Rally again," Reagan said. "He won't leave me alone."

Serenity slid a piece of avocado toast onto her plate. "Have you *asked* him to leave you alone?"

"No, but I haven't responded. I'm trying to do him a favor, trying to make sure he doesn't get caught up in a mess. Who wants to date a woman who's pregnant with someone else's child?"

"*He* does, apparently. If he minded, he wouldn't still be talking to you." Serenity dumped some chips in a bowl. "He might be the real deal, Reagan. Maybe you should answer him—before he does give up."

Reagan looked at Lucy. "What do you think?" she said conspiratorially, in an attempt to distract the little girl and cheer her up.

"You should talk to him," she said and smiled at Serenity to show solidarity.

"Then I will. After all, you're the boss," she said with a wink.

* * *

lorelei

Finn sat on the edge of Lorelei's bed. "I'm sorry about Davis."

"I shouldn't have tried to talk to him." She gave him a defiant look. "But I still believe he needed to hear what I had to say."

"That's probably true," Finn conceded. "But you were a little rough on him, don't you think?"

"*Rough on him?* That lamp he threw could've hurt Lucy." But it wasn't just that. Davis's attitude had been wearing on her. Biting her tongue when she was dying to tell him how she really felt had been getting harder and harder, especially because she was struggling herself. He wasn't the only one suffering; his problems were just a little more obvious.

"But it *didn't* hurt Lucy." He tried to take her hand, but she wouldn't let him. She was too upset. "He lost his arm, Lorelei. Give him some time."

"How long do we let him sulk? What if he throws something else and he *does* hurt Lucy? He's getting worse instead of better."

He briefly covered his face before dropping his hands. "Look, I didn't come to fight with you."

"Then why *did* you come?"

"Why do you think?" he countered with a scowl.

"I can't keep working for your father if Davis doesn't want me around."

"If he doesn't have you to do things for him, he'll *have* to learn to do them himself. Maybe you did what you were trying to do—but not in the way you intended. Not every change comes about peaceably, even changes that are for the best."

She considered that, but it was hard to feel much better. Because of what had just happened between her and Davis, she'd still have to find other work. And it wouldn't have had to be like that. If only he'd co-operated—since she was trying to do something useful, something that was supposed to help him—they could've had a nice summer.

Or…maybe finding another job was for the best. She was falling in love with Finn. While it felt good, she was afraid it was clouding her judgment. Why do the hard work of forgiving Mark and Francine when there was a golden boy keeping her company, helping her forget?

She couldn't imagine it was a good idea to gamble

on a younger man she'd met only weeks ago, regardless—especially when she had a child to consider. For all she knew, he'd let her down just as badly, or in a different way. There were no guarantees, nothing to say he'd love her better or longer or be more loyal.

"You're right," she said. "Maybe this was meant to be." Closing her eyes, she took a deep breath. "I have no business being at your place so often when I need to be thinking about my daughter and my future."

He narrowed his eyes. "What's that supposed to mean?"

"I don't think we should see each other anymore."

"Because of something my *brother* did?" he said, now angry himself.

"Because I'm still married, and I'm in a mess and you're only making it worse!"

"*I'm* making it worse?"

"It's true."

"Fine," he said and stood up. "You want me to go, you got it."

She almost stopped him as he walked out. She *didn't* want him to go. But she had to choose, and it would only hurt more to make that choice later.

Was it a mistake to end her marriage? No matter what Mark had done, she had a twelve-year history with him, they had a legal responsibility to each other, she used his name, his family had become her family, they shared a house—and he was the father of her daughter.

One summer couldn't erase all of that and set her on a completely different course.

Could it?

25

serenity

They told Lorelei about their call with Vance. Serenity thought it might help her feel better to focus on something else. But it didn't seem to make much difference. Lorelei muttered that she agreed with having Serenity get her father's DNA, but she didn't seem captivated by the mystery, as Serenity had expected. Lorelei seemed to have bigger things to worry about.

After Serenity made a plane reservation for San Diego and told her parents she was coming on July 2 and would be staying for the Fourth, she convinced Lorelei and Reagan to go shopping with her. She thought it might cheer them both up to get out of the cabin.

But neither one of them showed any interest in the pretty things they saw. Reagan frowned every time she came across a dress or something she would have considered purchasing if she weren't pregnant. And Lorelei, who still didn't know about the baby, spent most of her time looking for businesses that were hiring.

Reagan bought an alpaca teddy bear for Lucy from

a tourist shop. Lucy smiled and hugged it to her chest, but even Lucy didn't seem to be herself. She kept glancing at her mom; she understood Lorelei was still upset.

"Are you going to be okay?" Serenity asked Lorelei while Reagan used the restroom and they were waiting for their dinner at Hubby's Barbecue. Hubby's served delicious mac and cheese and offered pulled pork as a mix-in, which was what they'd ordered for Lucy.

Lorelei took a drink of her IPA. "I'm fine. I was stupid to let myself get so—" she checked to see if her daughter was tracking the conversation and paused to choose a word that wouldn't give away too much "—attached."

Reagan rejoined them in time to hear Lorelei's response. "It could happen to anyone," she said, jumping right back into the discussion. "The...um...*man* you're talking about is incredibly handsome and smart and empathetic and—"

"You're not helping," Lorelei broke in.

"Is it Finn, Mommy?" Lucy guessed.

When all three of them said no at once, Serenity had to laugh. So much for watching what they said in front of Lucy.

After dinner, they wandered through a few more shops. Serenity held Lucy's hand and kept her occupied so Lorelei wouldn't have to worry about her and could relax, and Reagan did her part by looping her arm through Lorelei's and pointing out different things they saw, but she couldn't get much of a reaction.

They returned to the cabin shortly after. Lorelei said she wanted to put Lucy to bed early, since Lucy had missed her nap, and Reagan wanted to watch a movie.

Ever since she'd made her plane reservation, Serenity had been dying to text Sawyer. She'd been trying to distract herself as much as she was trying to distract her sisters when she'd insisted they go shopping today, but it didn't really change anything for her, either—it just postponed the inevitable. She wasn't going to text him when she was with Reagan and Lorelei in case he responded and they happened to see the exchange. She wasn't ready to talk to them or anyone else about Sawyer; she still wasn't sure what she was doing where he was concerned, and as long as she didn't tell anyone, it didn't feel serious.

It *wasn't* serious, she told herself. And yet as soon as she was alone, while Lorelei was busy giving Lucy her bath and Reagan was watching her movie, she pulled out her phone.

Should she start by explaining why he hadn't heard from her for so long? Ask how things had gone with Nina? Ask why *he* hadn't contacted *her*?

Maybe he wasn't interested in seeing her again.

That possibility made her pace in agitation—until she broke down. In the end, she swallowed her pride and skipped all the stuff that was going on inside her head, except what was simple and true. I want to see you again.

She held her breath as she waited. Would he respond? If she were him, she probably wouldn't. A relationship with almost any other woman had to be less complicated.

But it was only a moment before she got a response and, fortunately, like her, he didn't bother with lengthy explanations, accusations or anything that would make her think too deeply.

When?

I'll be in Berkeley on the first.

Text me when you get there.

She closed her eyes after she read those six words. She'd promised herself she'd let whatever had started between them go.

Too bad she couldn't.

* * *

lorelei

It was three hours later in Florida—almost eleven. Lorelei was afraid she might wake Mark. He had to work early in the morning. But she had to call him, had to stop their marriage from unraveling any further before it was too late. She was beginning to wonder if she was partially to blame for how bad things had gotten, because she hadn't been entirely focused on her husband or healing. She'd been distracted by her handsome, young neighbor and maybe that had changed how she would normally have reacted to the situation.

Maybe Finn had been a catalyst in their rapidly disintegrating relationship as much as Francine had.

Well, not as much as Francine. But definitely part of the problem. Lorelei had to consider the possibility that she hadn't done much to put things back together, and she owed the past twelve years of her life, Lucy, the man Mark had been and all they'd established so far enough to give it an honest effort.

So after Lucy fell asleep, she went back to her own room, closed her door and dialed his number.

He answered right away, but she was pretty sure she'd awakened him. "Lorelei?" he said.

"Yeah, it's me."

"What's going on?"

She couldn't answer. Tears had welled up. Would she ever get over the pain of his betrayal? Just hearing his voice felt like another twenty lashes on an already lacerated heart.

"Babe? Are you okay? Is Lucy okay?"

The endearment made things even worse. "She's fine. I don't know if I am."

"Has something happened?"

"I just wish we could go back in time—to when we were happy."

"I'm sorry. I didn't mean to do this to us. I don't know how I did."

She wiped her cheeks. "I keep trying to forgive you. I really do. But whenever I think of you holding Francine's baby, or doing anything with her, something inside me rebels."

"I know. It's hard. But will you please come home? We can't deal with this long distance."

"How will I even get home?" she said. "You've cut off all the money."

"You said you were working."

She refused to let him know that she'd left her job. "I am, but I don't make much. Just enough for incidentals."

"*I'll* buy the plane ticket. You know I will. Should I go online in the morning?"

She was about to say yes. But then it struck her. He was talking softly, his voice so subdued. And why would he suggest doing it in the morning? If he was already awake, why not do it now?

Was Francine there? Was she in bed with him, and he was trying not to wake her?

Lorelei would have no reason to fault him if she was.

She'd told him he could be with her. But that he'd taken her up on that offer so readily made her feel as though his disappointment over losing her couldn't be as sincere as he said.

"Is Francine there?" she asked.

He hesitated just long enough that she didn't believe him when he said, "No. No, of course not."

"Send me a picture of our bed. Right now."

"Lorelei, it's late. I have to work in the morning."

"Send me a picture," she insisted.

"This is ridiculous."

"It's not ridiculous if you won't do it. There has to be a reason."

His voice grew more strident. "You told me we could be together! You practically shoved her at me! What am I supposed to do? Lose both of you? Then I wouldn't be a full-time father to either of my children!"

Lorelei covered her mouth so she wouldn't sob aloud and pressed End.

* * *

serenity

The lake, as still and smooth as glass, reflected the rays of the early-morning sun. Gliding through it would feel like a hot knife slicing through butter.

Serenity couldn't wait as she took her kayak off the rack on her SUV and carried it down the beach. After tossing and turning for most of the night, she'd decided to go out as soon as it was light and before either of her sisters was awake. It wasn't that she didn't want them to come—she owed Lucy a ride and planned to give her one—but she figured they could join her once they'd had breakfast. Or she could bring them another time. This was her first chance to get out on the water, and she felt a bit nostalgic about it. Kayaking almost every weekend was how she'd maintained her sanity last summer, when the trial was going on.

She wasn't really looking at the people who were getting their boats on the water at the same time. She didn't expect to run into anyone she knew, not this early. So she was surprised when she noticed a lone man walking along the shore. A man who looked sort of familiar.

Who was he? He was far enough away that she almost shrugged off the sense of recognition. What did it matter?

But as she drew closer and he turned, she could see that he had only one arm.

Davis.

What was Finn's brother doing here? Did Finn or Nolan even know he wasn't in his room?

She knew they were trying to look out for him, but he was an adult, so she also figured it was up to him where he went and whether he told anyone.

She was angry with him about the way he'd treated Lorelei and Lucy yesterday, so she'd rather not speak to him. But when he caught sight of her, her natural sympathy for his situation prompted her to wave.

He hadn't shaved for what looked like several days and his hair stood up as though he'd come straight from bed. Maybe he hadn't showered for a while, either. Lorelei had mentioned that he didn't seem to have any interest in taking care of himself. He was in too deep a depression.

But Serenity had just gotten out of bed herself. Most everyone here probably had. The dark circles beneath his eyes told her he hadn't slept any better than she had last night.

He responded to her wave with a nod of acknowledgment, somewhat grudgingly, then put his head down and kept walking.

Obviously, he didn't expect her to speak to him. She doubted he even *wanted* her to speak to him. And that was okay with her. So she wasn't sure why she spontaneously called out, asking him if he'd like to go kayaking with her.

She was positive he'd say no, and yet…she could see him wrestling with himself. "I won't say a word while we're out there, if that's what you're worried about," she added.

"How am I supposed to help you paddle?" he asked.

"You still have one arm, don't you?"

When he scowled as if he couldn't do anything with one arm, she shrugged and climbed in to show that she was fine going without him.

She was just getting her kayak ready to launch when he spoke. It startled her to find him so close.

"I'll go. If I'm a dead weight, you'll have to propel us both."

"You can do your part. It's not that hard. I'll be right back," she said and handed him one of the oars she'd brought down.

She got another oar from her X5 and trudged back to the water's edge.

"You came prepared," he said.

"I left a note for Lorelei to bring Lucy down once she wakes up, but they don't normally get up until eight. You can use it till then."

"You're going to be out that long?"

"Probably not. It was just in case."

"Fine."

She held the kayak and motioned for him to get in.

After a pause that let her know he wasn't sure he should've accepted her invitation, he did as she said and took the front seat, since it was the back person who had to steer.

They were a little unsteady when they first launched. Serenity wasn't used to having so much extra weight in the kayak. It'd been a while since she'd gone out with Sean, and he hadn't joined her that often, anyway. Getting up early had never been his thing.

But once they got out away from the beach, they were fine. They didn't talk while they were paddling—other than when she gave him directions.

He did better than she thought he would, especially because they weren't worried about speed. They were only out to enjoy the beauty of nature, to heal and find balance.

At one point, she closed her eyes, turned her face up to the sun and let the kayak drift. She wasn't sure whether he minded, but he respected her privacy and said nothing while she meditated for several minutes.

By the time they were done on the lake, there was still no sign of her sisters and Lucy, and she was glad. She thought this had worked out the way it was supposed to. Even though Davis couldn't paddle that well yet, he'd been the easiest person she'd ever gone out with. He didn't ruin the solitude; he needed it just as badly.

Once they'd pulled the boat onto the shore, he followed her lead and put his oar in the kayak. "Thank you," he said and started up the beach.

"I'll be here, same time, tomorrow morning," she called after him.

He turned to look at her. He'd heard, but he didn't say whether he'd be back. So she was slightly surprised to find him at the beach the next day, the day after that and the day after that. Soon, he was waiting for her every morning where she parked the SUV so he could help carry the kayak to the water.

She didn't mention the change. She acted as if he *should* be there to do his part.

She brought Lucy out in the afternoon occasionally, after the girl's nap when it was much warmer, but she never mentioned kayaking with Davis. Somehow that felt private—an hour they stole from each day that didn't need to be discussed.

She was fairly certain he hadn't mentioned it to his brothers, either, because she had no doubt they'd come along or make sure he had his own kayak with a mounted paddle frame so he could paddle on his own. They had the money, after all. If they thought going out on the water was helping him recover, they'd gladly supply the boat and any type of oar he might need.

But she suspected that doing it together was somehow part of its appeal. The hour they spent on the lake helped them both welcome and be grateful for each new day. They didn't speak much, never mentioned Lorelei or what'd happened, whether he was recovering, his brothers and what they thought or anything else. It was the silent support they both craved—the silent support and the ability to share the incredible beauty of Tahoe with another human being. Somehow that enhanced the experience.

"I'll be leaving tomorrow for Berkeley, early, and I won't be back for five days," she told him on the last day of June. "Would you like me to put the kayak somewhere you can take it out by yourself?"

He'd just climbed out. He studied her for a few seconds but ultimately shook his head. "No, I don't have a vehicle for it."

His brothers did, though, which confirmed that they *didn't* know he was coming out every morning. He didn't even want to tell them so he could use the car.

"I'll be here on Monday."

With a nod of acknowledgment, he helped her carry the kayak to the Beamer.

"Would you like a ride?" she asked once they had it loaded.

"I'd rather walk," he said, which was what he'd told her every other time she'd offered.

She drove away as he started out, but when she parked in the garage of her own cabin and was about to go into the house, a vehicle pulled up at the curb.

Who could be coming to visit this early? she asked herself. It was barely seven o'clock.

But as soon as she spotted the man who got out, she knew before he could even mention his name.

* * *

reagan

Reagan was awake because Rally had been messaging her. Although they talked many times during the day, he'd started wishing her a good morning every day right at seven. His greeting made waking up easier, and she was pretty sure that was his intention. After that she typically allowed herself to drift off for another half hour or so before climbing out of bed to have breakfast and begin working on Serenity's social media.

In many respects, she'd never had such a fun and relaxing summer. Despite the stress of the pregnancy and the many life questions that still loomed large in her mind, she was enjoying her sisters—making them real in her life, part of the fabric of it, and that felt significant to her despite everything else.

Besides doing Serenity's social media, she'd been watching Lucy from eleven to three the past four days and would continue through August. Lorelei had managed to get a job waiting tables at a nearby restaurant but only worked the lunch shift. She didn't make a lot of money, but since she refused to speak to Mark—had cut him off completely—she couldn't expect any financial help from him, not until she forced the issue legally. And she wasn't talking to Finn, either. She didn't want what she felt for him to confuse her, didn't want to open her heart to any more hurt.

So working at the restaurant gave Lorelei something to do as well as bringing in some much-needed cash.

Reagan was worried about her, though. She had no idea what Lorelei was going to do after the summer, but if she was going to divorce her husband, Reagan thought she should get started on it. Although Reagan had mentioned it a time or two, Lorelei refused to do anything that might ruin her last two months in Tahoe. She said she'd face September when it arrived, but she was going to reserve this time for herself. This was *their* time—their sister time.

Which was why Reagan hadn't been able to bring herself to tell her about the pregnancy. She knew she needed to, and she'd been looking for the right opportunity, but Lorelei was enjoying herself in spite of what she was going through, and Reagan didn't want to ruin that by giving her something else she'd have to make allowances for. Reagan didn't want to risk ruining the close and easy friendship that was developing between them, either.

She was enjoying Serenity, Lorelei and Lucy too much to want to change *anything*—that concerned them, anyway. After Lorelei left for work in the mornings at eleven, Reagan finished whatever she was doing for Serenity, fed Lucy lunch and then they walked down to the lake. She let Lucy play in the sand, or Serenity took her out in the kayak, and then brought her back to the cabin for a nap. She'd thought babysitting, because she'd never been responsible for a child before, might be difficult, but it wasn't. Those four hours went fast.

With a yawn, Reagan stretched out her arms and couldn't help noticing how brown her skin was getting. They were all starting to tan, even Lorelei, who hadn't been out in the sun as often.

Reagan was considering buying them each a gold ankle bracelet. She had to watch her bank account, since she wasn't sure she'd be able to find work when she returned to New York until after the baby came, but she thought they should each have something to remember this summer by, and she'd spotted what she felt was *just* the thing at a local jewelry shop—a dainty chainlike ankle bracelet with tiny diamonds at regular intervals.

She was trying to decide if she could allow herself to splurge enough to go back and buy three—Lucy was too young for a keepsake like that—when she heard a commotion downstairs.

"What are you doing here?"

Reagan sat up. That was Lorelei's shocked voice. But she had no idea who she was talking to until Lucy cried, "Daddy!"

26

lorelei

Lorelei couldn't believe it. Mark was standing in the living room. Apparently, he'd taken off from work and flown to Reno, where he must've rented a car.

Her first thought was that she should never have given him the address of the cabin.

But she'd done that way back when she, Serenity and Reagan were first planning to meet, so he'd have the information and be able to reach her in case of emergencies.

Her second thought was, *Where's Francine?*

She didn't ask. She didn't want Lucy to hear the jealousy and bitterness that was bound to accompany that question. She was feeling conflicted again, watching her daughter hug her daddy as though it had been forever since she'd seen him.

In a small child's mind, five weeks *was* a very long time.

Had Lorelei been wrong to stay here?

Regardless, she'd had to stay. Having a safe place, a

place where she could grapple with the loss of her marriage while enjoying the support of her two sisters, was what had kept her going.

"Look at you!" He pulled back to peer into Lucy's face. "I hardly recognize you! Your hair has gold streaks from the sun, and you're getting a few freckles."

She gave him an affronted look. "What are freckles?"

He laughed. "The cute little dots on your nose."

He kissed and hugged her before setting her down and returning his attention to Lorelei. "I'm sorry to show up out of nowhere, but you blocked me. Since I can't call or text you, I had no way of notifying you."

"The fact that I blocked you should've told you I… I didn't want to do this."

"We *have* to talk, Lorelei. We can't let what we have slip away just because I was stupid enough to do what I did."

She glanced at Reagan, who was standing barefoot in yoga pants and a T-shirt, hair mussed, on the stairs. Serenity was on the other side, by the kitchen, dressed in a short-sleeved wetsuit that had the legs cut off. Reagan had just gotten out of bed, but where had Serenity come from? Had she already been out on the lake?

"I decided to go kayaking," Serenity explained, apparently responding to the confusion in her face. "I do that if I get up before you two."

"You do." Lorelei hadn't realized she'd been leaving, but it was usually eight or so when she and Lucy rolled out of bed.

She was focusing on the mundane, on things that didn't matter. She had to say something to Mark, but she had no idea what. Should she introduce him to her sisters?

No. That would be far too polite for this situation. She'd decided she had to end her marriage.

"Why don't I get Lucy some breakfast?" Serenity offered. "Are you hungry, sweetheart?"

Lucy seemed reluctant to leave her father. "Will you stay?" she asked Mark.

"I'll be here," he promised and then looked at Lorelei. "Can we take a walk, though, just you and I?"

"Can't I go with you?" Lucy's little eyebrows gathered in worry.

"You have to eat, honey," Lorelei said.

"But you'll walk with me?" Mark asked.

"I have to get dressed," Lorelei said dully.

He nodded. "I'll wait for you."

"What about me, Momma?" Lucy wasn't convinced she should eat instead. But as much as Lorelei hated to disappoint her, if Lucy was with them, all the things that needed to be said wouldn't get said.

She motioned her daughter over to her. "Come get dressed. You can eat with your aunts, and then after that, Daddy and I will take you down to the lake, okay?"

"Okay," she said, obviously relieved that they weren't going to disappear on her.

Reagan caught Lorelei's arm as she and Lucy passed her on the stairs. "You go ahead." She took Lucy's hand. "I've got her."

With a nod, Lorelei relinquished her daughter and finished hurrying up the stairs.

Once she'd put on some clothes, she washed her face, brushed her teeth and tied her hair back before heading down the stairs. It made her feel slightly better that she could hear Reagan making a game out of getting Lucy dressed. Reagan was purposely drawing it out, using up as much time as possible, and Lorelei was grateful.

Mark looked up as she descended the stairs, and she wondered what he was thinking. Why had he come?

As soon as she'd realized Francine was sleeping in her bed, she'd blocked them both. She'd told herself she was done with them forever, but because she had a legal tie to Mark, she knew she'd have to deal with him at some point, if only to divvy up their assets and figure out visitation and custody of Lucy.

She wasn't expecting to have to deal with him quite this soon, however. "I only have a couple of hours," she told him as they stepped outside. "I have to get ready for work at ten, and I promised we'd take Lucy to the lake before that."

"Can't you call your boss—Finn or whatever his name is? Tell him you need some extra time today?"

"I work at a restaurant now. The pay's better."

"Got it." He seemed relieved, was probably hoping something had come between them. "This shouldn't take too long. I just… I had to see you."

"Why?"

"I've been worried about you."

"I'm fine."

"What about the nightmares? Are you still having those?"

He'd known about the nightmares because they had started up again while she was home. "I've had only one since I've been here. I'm hoping I won't have another."

"Why do you think they're back?"

She slanted him an accusing look. "I wonder," she

said sarcastically and stopped to face him. "Why are you really here, Mark?"

He grabbed her hand beseechingly. "Because I still love you, and I need you to know that. *You're* the one I want."

She yanked her hand away. "How could that be true? Everything you've done says otherwise."

"Not *everything*—"

"Francine was in bed with you when I called you the last time!"

He pressed three fingers to his forehead. "I know. And I regret that. I was angry. If you weren't willing to forgive me, I was going to move on without you. I realize now how stupid I was, that I only made things worse."

Although they were supposed to be walking, their conversation was too animated for that. They stood out by the road a short distance from the house, but at least they could talk without worrying about anyone overhearing them.

"Mark, I can't believe you love me, and if I can't believe it, it doesn't matter if you do. That's what kept me going all the years we were married. I believed you cared about me and Lucy and would never hurt us."

A pained expression settled on his face. "Haven't you ever made such a big mistake that you freaked out and made things even worse? I'm just as upset by Francine's pregnancy as you are. And now she's at me all the time, demanding this and that, claiming I cost her her best friend. I'm torn in two! Don't you understand? There's no way I can keep you both happy!"

"That's just it," she said. "Now we have to take her into consideration and we'll have to do that forever. It breaks my heart to stay with you, and it breaks my heart to give up on our marriage."

"Come here." He pulled her to him as though he'd longed to have her in his arms again. "Please. Can't we get beyond this?"

She tried to allow the embrace, tried to let it soothe the hurt. Was she willing to make the concessions that staying with Mark would require? Was she *capable* of making those concessions?

The only way it could work was if she welcomed Francine back into her life, loved her as she had before and accepted her baby.

But every time she tried to talk herself into going in that direction, some elemental part of her rebelled. It was futile. She couldn't fix what he'd broken, no matter how hard she tried. If she'd learned anything from coming to Tahoe this summer, it was that.

She was trying to figure out the best way to explain. She didn't want to be unnecessarily hurtful, not when Mark had come so far. Although she'd never cheated on him, she understood what it was like to make mistakes, to feel regret.

Before she could find the words she wanted to use, however, she heard a car engine and looked over to see Finn behind the wheel of his Jeep. He was just about to pull into the driveway of the cabin next door, but instead of doing that, he stopped in the middle of the road the instant he saw them.

"Is that him?" Mark asked. "The guy you've been seeing?"

Finn finally looked away and drove into the garage. As she heard the door go down, she said, "I haven't been seeing him. We're…friends, that's all."

"Do you think he'll make a better husband than me?"

"I don't think that would be hard," she said dryly.

He winced. "It was *one* mistake."

"But it was a catastrophic mistake," she said. "I can't get past it."

"You can," he insisted. "You love Francine and you love me. You don't mean what you're saying."

She closed her eyes as she tried to feel her way through this morass of pain and regret. She imagined going to the restaurant, as she'd been doing the past four days, thought about how hard it would be to get back into the job market and tried to imagine what her future would entail if she let go of the past. The restaurant was slammed almost every day, especially on the weekends. It was a stressful place to be, and they didn't pay her very well.

But she liked the idea of having her own money, of not having to justify what she spent it on, of the freedom working would allow. There was no good path to take from here, but she hoped she could live without the anger and doubt she felt now, if she decided to go it alone. "I wish I didn't," she said at length. "But I'm afraid that you came all this way for nothing. I'm sorry."

She must've sounded resolute, far more resolute than she actually felt, because tears appeared in his eyes. "And Lucy?"

"I'll do whatever I can to facilitate your relationship with her. You know how much I love her. I would never do *anything* that would hurt her."

"You mean like I did," he said.

At least *she* hadn't pointed that out. "I don't know how you got involved with Francine in the first place. I can't even pretend to understand. Maybe you were just caught up in something you couldn't get out of, and a bigger person could take it in stride and keep our family together. But I can't. So now we have to figure out how to go on from here."

"When you called, I thought… I thought I had a second chance."

"I thought so, too, but…" She shook her head. That call had severed the last of her loyalty and hope; that was when she knew they'd never get back together, that the past had slipped through her fingers and she had to face the future alone, had to weather the blow and march on. "At least you've got Francine."

"She'll never mean as much to me as you do," he said sadly.

* * *

serenity

The next few days were going to be awkward. Serenity was glad she wouldn't be around. Mark insisted on staying in town even though Lorelei had told him it was over between them. He said he wouldn't leave until he'd spent some time with Lucy, that he'd taken a week off of work. So when he left to get a motel room, he took Lucy with him while Lorelei hurried to get ready for work.

Serenity guessed he was hoping he'd be able to change his wife's mind while he was in town. He was on his best behavior, was being friendly and cooperative and oh-so-likable. Serenity wondered if he'd be this nice once Lorelei filed for divorce. The worst often came out in people during a divorce. She said as much to Reagan after Lorelei left for work, while Reagan sat on her bed, watching her pack.

Reagan's eyebrows lifted as she considered Serenity's words. "I know you're right, but Lucy is *so* excited to have her daddy around. Lorelei wants to let them be together as long as he's here."

"Well, keep an eye on the situation while I'm gone. Her generosity might turn around and bite her in the ass, poor thing."

"I will," Reagan said.

"When are you going to tell her you're pregnant?" Serenity asked.

"Not while he's here, that's for sure." She smoothed out the comforter. "Are you nervous about seeing your folks?"

"A little," Serenity admitted. "I *want* to see them, but I'm such a bad liar. I'm afraid I'll say something that'll drag this whole thing into the open, and it'll damage their marriage."

"You know what's at stake. You'll be careful. Text me once you have his DNA."

"I will. I don't know how I'm going to get him to spit in the tube, but I'll figure something out. I'll send it off right away, too, so that we don't have to wait any longer than necessary."

"Great. This has to lead us to the answer."

Serenity paused while putting her hair spray into her makeup carrier. "I hope so. But my mind keeps going back to that call with Vance. He sounded sincere. Why would he try to deny that he's your father if he thought he was talking to the one woman who would know?"

She fell back onto her elbows. "I can't quite work that out myself, but we can't explain away that letter."

"True." Even if Vance wasn't their father, it would be too coincidental for him to have mentioned a baby in that letter. And how would he know Reagan's mother? Reagan's name? He was the only person linking Serenity to Reagan—he *had* to be involved in some way.

That was likely why he wasn't calling Serenity back. But she planned to use her mother's phone to try to reach him again while she was in San Diego. She couldn't impersonate Charlotte the way Reagan had tried to impersonate Rosalind, but at least she might be able to get him to pick up.

* * *

lorelei

Lorelei was so harried at the restaurant she didn't really look at the three men who walked in right at the peak of the lunch rush. In her peripheral vision she saw them speak to the hostess. Then the hostess seated them at Lorelei's only open table, which surprised her because she was new and some of the more experienced waitresses weren't quite as busy.

She didn't know it was Finn and his brothers until she approached the table to bring them water. Even if she'd been paying closer attention, she wasn't sure she would've realized sooner. She never would've guessed that Davis would come out in public. When she was working at their place, she could barely get him to leave his *room*.

She froze as soon as she recognized them.

When Finn looked up, he nudged Davis.

She glanced behind her, wondering if she could get someone else to pick up this table, but the Hatch brothers had spoken to the hostess, so they must've requested her. That was why they were seated at one of her tables, even though she was the least capable of handling a full section.

Remembering the unhappy expression on Finn's face when he saw her standing on the street with Mark earlier, she took a deep breath, manufactured a smile and approached as though they were total strangers. "Here's your water. Can I get you anything else to drink while you look over the menu?"

Nolan cleared his throat. "Not for me. Water's good."

Finn and Davis declined, too.

"Okay. I'll be back in a few minutes to get your order."

She started to walk away, but Finn called her name. "Davis has something he wants to say to you," he said when she turned.

Davis studied her for a moment. Then she saw his Adam's apple move as he swallowed. "I was out of line. I'm sorry."

She couldn't tell if it was said grudgingly or not. Maybe Finn had coerced him into an apology. But it would take a lot for a proud man like Davis to apologize, and he was struggling, so she wasn't going to make his life any harder. "Thanks. I shouldn't have said what I did, either. It wasn't my place."

"It needed to be said, and if you didn't say it, who would?" he responded.

Surprised, she flashed him a more genuine smile before hurrying off to take care of her other tables. From there, it was all she could do to stay on top of everything; she didn't want to look as though she couldn't handle her new job. She didn't have much time to talk to Finn and his brothers—she was too busy—and was sad when they left without saying goodbye.

She still had two tables to serve, so she told herself she'd think about Davis's apology later. But the young man who bussed her tables caught up with her in the back. "Hey, you should see the size of the tip those three guys left you!"

She hadn't even considered what they'd leave her. "How much is it?"

"I don't know exactly. I didn't touch it. But you should get out there and grab it before someone else does."

Why did they leave her such a big tip? They'd already paid her what they'd owed her for working for them. Finn, or someone else, had left an envelope with her name on it in the mailbox the day after she and Davis had that falling out.

She double-checked that the brothers were really gone before she went over. She didn't want to look greedy or too interested in the money. But she was curious.

Seeing a stack of bills, she grabbed the money and ducked into the back to count it.

It came to nearly $100—far more than she could allow herself to keep.

27

serenity

Serenity had been obsessed with the mystery surrounding her sisters. She'd been worried about the pregnancy that Reagan hadn't yet divulged to anyone else. And now she was worried about Lorelei having to deal with Mark, especially while she was in San Diego. She was even concerned with how she'd handle herself when she got there. But all those things melted into the background as she drove to Berkeley. Then all she could think about was Sawyer.

Was it a mistake to see him again?

Possibly. But she'd never felt so compelled to be with someone.

Was he going to come?

She kept taking out her phone to text him. But, again and again, she forced herself to hold off. She didn't want to look overeager. She'd probably be better off if he *didn't* come. So she was far more relieved than she should've been when *he* texted *her*.

You still going to be in Berkeley tonight?

She pulled over so she could reply. I am. Are you coming over?

What time will you be there?

I've got another twenty minutes on the drive.

I'll come over after I finish the two appraisals I have to do today.

It was barely noon on a Wednesday. She'd been so anxious about seeing him that she'd taken off right after breakfast. She hated that she had to wait until evening for him to arrive, but she'd expected as much. She planned to get her nails done and buy a new dress or something.

Her phone rang.

Because she'd just been texting with Sawyer, she thought maybe it was him. Her heart started to beat faster until her Bluetooth announced that it was her mother.

She told it to answer and then greeted Charlotte.

"Hi, honey," her mother said. "I'm just calling to confirm that you'll be spending the weekend with us."

"My flight leaves at eight tomorrow morning, so I'll arrive at the airport shortly after nine."

"We'll be there to get you. Where are you leaving from?"

"Oakland."

"I thought you were spending the summer in Tahoe so I thought maybe you'd fly out of Reno."

"I'm driving home now."

"Got it. Can't wait to see you."

"I'm looking forward to it, too." She was about to get off the phone, but her mother stopped her before she could say goodbye.

"You know… I didn't say anything because I didn't want to upset you, but maybe that was the wrong decision."

"What are you talking about?"

"Nina called us not too long ago."

Serenity tensed. "What did she have to say?"

"She told me that you never really loved her son, that you were having an affair with Sawyer all along, and that's why you put those pictures on Sean's computer and called the police."

"She's claiming I set him up?" she cried.

"Yes! Isn't that the craziest thing you ever heard?"

Now that she'd slept with Sawyer, it didn't sound quite as crazy to her as it would have otherwise—at least, the affair part. She was afraid she'd been attracted to Sawyer all along. But that hadn't been something she could control. She'd never acted on it; she'd never even acknowledged it until now.

"What did you say?" she asked.

"I told her she must be drunk. Nothing has ever happened between you and Sawyer."

Visions of making love with him in her bed, in the shower and in the kitchen played on the stage of Serenity's mind. She wanted to say, "Not while I was married," but qualifying it would reveal too much. "She wanted some pictures I had of Sean's, and Sawyer came over to pick them up. She happened to stop by while he was there, so she saw him at my place, but she's really stretching it to say I must've set Sean up. Sean was the author of his own destruction."

"I know. I told her she'd better leave you alone—that I never wanted to hear from her again—and hung up."

"I hope *I* never hear from her again, either. I don't need her starting trouble. If she riles up her other two boys—"

"We'll go to the police."

Serenity wondered if her mother would ask if she was seeing Sawyer. Charlotte had already said she thought Sawyer had a thing for her. And Serenity had no idea how much Nina had told Charlotte about what she'd seen.

It must not have been much, though, because Charlotte didn't seem to know or even suspect. Nina had probably led with her ugly accusation, so Charlotte hadn't been willing to listen to anything after that. And Serenity wasn't going to tell her. She had no idea what she was doing with Sawyer, or whether it would last. Why would she bring her mother into it?

"How's Sawyer doing, anyway?" Charlotte asked.

"Seemed good," she said with an indifferent tone, as though their encounter had been far less intimate than it was—as though she wasn't going to see him again tonight.

"I've always liked him," Charlotte said.

Serenity stiffened. "I didn't realize you really knew him."

"I don't know him *well*. But we attended some of the same family gatherings, remember? And the way he used to stand off by himself—I felt sorry for him. I got the impression he was lonely."

Not only was Sawyer particularly attractive, he had

sex appeal. And he didn't always stand off by himself. There were those moments when she'd glance up and be surprised that he was watching her with a strange sort of far-off look. That didn't occur very often, but it was a little disconcerting when it did. More often he was trying to beat her at whatever they were doing, or he ignored her entirely. "He could be with just about any woman he wants, Mom. There's no need to feel sorry for him."

"Maybe he seemed restless, then."

Serenity was nearing her house. "I can see that. Anyway, I've got to go. I'll talk to you when I get to San Diego tomorrow."

"See you soon!"

When Serenity disconnected, she breathed out a long sigh. She couldn't believe Nina had called her mother.

Good thing Charlotte had taken offense and hung up on her.

After she pulled into the driveway, she gathered her bags and slid out of the X5. She was trying not to be excited about having Sawyer come over, especially after what had happened last time. But she would've risked just about anything to see him again.

And that scared the hell out of her.

* * *

lorelei

Lorelei hadn't had a chance to return the money that Finn and his brothers had left for her at the restaurant. Because Mark intended to spend as much time with

Lucy as possible while he was in town, he was keeping her with him. But after Lorelei got off work yesterday, he'd insisted it would be less traumatic for Lucy if they acted friendly toward each other and asked her to join them for dinner.

She'd agreed because she also believed in making their split as amicable as possible, and it turned out fine. He hadn't talked about Francine or the baby or whether she and Lucy would come back to Florida before the end of the summer. He hadn't brought up anything that might cause an argument. So it had been pleasant—a chance to pretend, if only for a short while, that their whole world hadn't collapsed.

She wished they didn't have to go through what lay ahead. She was under no illusions; she knew it wouldn't be easy. As soon as she filed for divorce and the court ordered Mark to give her half his assets, or however much he'd have to share, he'd get angry again. That was why she considered this brief time to be such a blessing.

He'd asked her to have dinner with them again tonight. She got the impression that he was hoping to include her in their activities as much as possible. But she saw the danger in trying *too* hard to accommodate him. Since he was on his best behavior, she could easily get sucked in again—get her hopes up that they could put their marriage back together—only to face the immovable problems that had come between them. And with Serenity gone, she didn't think it would be polite to leave Reagan on her own.

So she'd declined by saying she was too tired.

She *was* tired. Bone-weary. Her new job was kicking her butt. She was used to taking care of Lucy all day, but taking care of Lucy wasn't the same as running frantically around a restaurant for four hours. What with the stress of her new job and having Mark in town, she wanted to crawl into bed and sleep.

It was nice to have someone who loved Lucy as much as she did step in for a while, though. She couldn't claim she wasn't enjoying the support. Pretending everything was okay for their daughter's sake had been taxing, almost overwhelming at times. Right now she didn't have to put on that show, and it was a wonderful release.

Maybe that was another reason she was so exhausted. For weeks she'd been pushing herself to act as normal as possible. Now that she had a chance to put down that burden, she was crashing.

So when Reagan asked if she was interested in going out to eat, she almost declined that invitation, too.

In the end, however, she couldn't bring herself to say no. She wanted to be close with her new sisters, was here to get to know them, and because she had Lucy and a job that took her out of the cabin every day, she was already unable to spend as much time with them as they spent with each other.

After summoning the energy, she put on a pair of jeans and a pretty top with a lightweight jacket, since it cooled off quite a bit at night, with a strappy pair of heeled sandals, and they took an Uber to an Italian restaurant.

"How are things going with Mark?" Reagan asked after the waitress had brought them some water and they were trying to decide what to order.

The smell of pizza cooking in wood-fired ovens made Lorelei's mouth water. She was hungrier than she'd realized. "He's on his best behavior, so things are going fine."

A skeptical expression appeared on Reagan's face. She was obviously leery of Mark's behavior. "You know why, don't you?"

"I do." Having decided to order the barbecue chicken pizza with a side salad, she put down the dinner menu and picked up the wine list. "Should we have a glass of chardonnay?"

Reagan looked uncomfortable.

"Reagan?"

"I don't want to drink tonight," she said and stuck her nose in the menu.

Slightly surprised by the abruptness of her response, Lorelei set the wine list aside. "You never want a drink these days. I'd think you don't drink, except you had a glass of wine the first night we arrived. Does it give you a headache or something?"

"No."

"Then why don't you want some?"

"I'm not in the mood," Reagan said. "But you should go ahead."

"That's okay. I don't need one, either." Reagan was acting odd, but Lorelei would've shrugged it off—she wasn't all that invested in having a drink—if Reagan hadn't closed her menu and sighed.

"I have something to tell you," she announced.

Judging by her tone, it wasn't good news. Lorelei was so raw from her own problems that she didn't feel very resilient. Her stomach muscles tightened. "What is it? Do you know how we're related? Have you and Serenity figured it out?"

"No. Serenity's going home to get her father's DNA. Nothing's changed there. This is more of a…a personal problem."

Lorelei relaxed slightly, even though she was still concerned. "It's not about Rally, is it? You two seem to be getting along well. He texts you all the time." She bent closer to the table. "Or is that it? Are you leaving Tahoe and going back to New York right away?"

"No."

The waitress approached, and Reagan indicated they'd talk after they ordered. But once the waitress left, it didn't seem to be any easier for her to say what was on her mind. "Maybe it would be smarter for me to tell you after Mark leaves. I was trying to wait, but…"

Now Lorelei was confused. Reagan had said it was a personal problem. "What does Mark have to do with it?"

"Nothing *directly*." She took a sip of water. "Oh, what the hell," she said as she set down her glass. "I'm just going to tell you—I'm pregnant, Lorelei."

She blinked several times. This was the last thing she'd expected. *"What?"*

"Drew and I didn't use any birth control. As you know, we weren't planning on…on doing what we did, so we weren't prepared. I know it was stupid, but par for the course, I suppose. What I did was stupid in the first place—shortsighted, selfish. The list could go on."

Lorelei straightened her silverware. "Don't beat yourself up. You've already done enough of that. But when did you find out?"

"Not too long ago."

"Does he know?"

"He doesn't."

"Are you going to tell him?"

"I haven't decided, to be honest. I don't know what to do. I don't even know if I should keep the baby."

Lorelei drank some of her water, not because she was

thirsty but because she needed a second to decide how to respond. As the wife of an unfaithful husband, she couldn't excuse Reagan's actions. She wasn't in the best position to offer sympathy, either. And yet she knew that sometimes even good people made bad choices. Mark wasn't evil. She wasn't leaving him because she thought he was. It was more about being unable to live with the consequences of his actions than trying to punish him.

But did she feel the same about Francine? Francine had broken up her family. Francine had known when she slept with Mark that she could cause a divorce, cost Lucy her father. She *had* to know. And yet she'd done it anyway.

Still, Francine had been acting out of her own need, a deep-seated desire that drove her beyond her ability to resist. She wanted to be loved, fulfilled. That was what everyone wanted. And she'd perceived Mark as being a good husband, a good father. She'd also been miserable in her own marriage and was even more miserable after her divorce, feeling she'd never have the family she craved. So she'd been needy when she did what she did—hadn't been acting from a position of strength.

That didn't mean Lorelei could be friends with her again, but it did mean that she could at least try to understand how Francine had done such a terrible thing.

"I'm sorry," she said when she put her glass back down. "That would be so hard."

Reagan sat taller. "You're not upset?"

"Not really. I know you regret what happened, that you didn't intend to do what you did. Have you already told Serenity?"

"I have. I've told Rally, too. I didn't want to hide such a nasty surprise. But I hesitated to tell you because..."

"Because of Mark and Francine," she finished.

"Yes. With what you're going through, I didn't want you to be faced with trying to decide whether you can forgive me for doing the same thing your best friend did. I'd hate it if that came between us. I also didn't want you to feel you had to forgive Mark if you decided to forgive me." She looked miserable when she added, "I felt it would put you in an awkward situation, I guess."

Lorelei nibbled on her bottom lip. "You're sorry for what you did. And like I said, you didn't do it on purpose or plan to have his child."

"I didn't," she said. "I'm not ready to start a family. And I definitely don't want to do it alone."

Lorelei scooted closer to the table. "Lucy has been the best thing to ever happen to me." Not every mother felt that way. It was possible she hadn't meant anything to *her* mother—and that fact was tough to ignore since they were talking about maternal love and fulfillment. But Lorelei was getting to know Reagan well enough to believe Reagan *would* love her child and enjoy being a mother, no matter how the pregnancy had come about.

Reagan offered her a determined smile. "I hope I feel the same way."

"So you're going to keep it?"

Reagan paused before answering. "I'll be honest about this, too. I don't know. That's another reason I've hesitated to tell you. I understand why you'd be particularly sensitive to decisions like the one I have to make. But I might not be able to make a commitment one way or another for several months. So much about my life is up in the air right now. But if I waited until I decided what I was going to do about the baby to tell you, I could be showing, and I'm hoping you'll be such a big part of my life that not telling you until then wouldn't be an option."

The last part of what she said made Lorelei smile. Maybe it would be tricky to navigate this pregnancy as close sisters, but if Reagan couldn't use a close sister now, when could she?

Lorelei needed Reagan, too. They'd both be severing old ties and embarking on a new life—new jobs, new personal relationships.

"I will be," she said confidently.

They purposely discussed other things during dinner. It was almost as if they'd made a silent pact to steer clear of Mark, Francine and Drew for the rest of the meal. But Serenity and Rally were safe subjects. They talked about what Serenity might find out in San Diego with her family, about how much they were enjoying Tahoe and about the fact that Rally hadn't backed off, despite the pregnancy.

"You're really going to go all summer without seeing him?" Lorelei asked as they had a cup of coffee with some tiramisu after the waitress had taken away their dinner plates.

"I'm afraid to see him," Reagan admitted. "Everything's going so well between us right now. I'm worried that any kind of change might burst the fragile bubble in which we're currently living—that maybe if he sees me he'll realize how crazy it is to be talking to a woman who's pregnant with another man's baby."

"Don't sell him short," Lorelei said. "He's aware of the situation. He knows what he's doing."

"We'll see."

The waitress brought their check. As they left, Lorelei couldn't help being glad she'd made the effort to join Reagan tonight instead of caving in and going to bed. She felt bad about what Reagan was facing. Having Drew's baby wouldn't be any easier for her to cope with than it would be for Lorelei to go through a divorce. But the support they offered each other made everything easier.

"What are you going to do about Finn?" Reagan asked as they drove home.

"I'm not going to do anything about him."

"I know you have feelings for him, Lorelei."

Lorelei had been trying not to think about their neighbors. She couldn't believe Finn was all that interested, anyway. She was still married, about to go through a divorce, and she had a child. Not only that, she lived in Florida and wouldn't be able to leave the state. If she did, Lucy and Mark wouldn't get to see each other very often.

She couldn't imagine Finn would be willing to move clear across the country, not when his family was here in California. "Meeting Finn was good for me. It showed me that I might find someone else one day and be happy again, even though, in my darker moments, it doesn't feel like that will ever happen."

"You never know," Reagan said.

As soon as they returned to the cabin, she told Reagan she was going to bed. It was early yet, but she expected to fall right asleep. She figured she should use this time when she didn't have Lucy to build some reserves for when Mark went home.

So she had no idea why she texted Finn. Can you meet me outside?

She told herself it was just so she could give him back the money. But she knew she could've returned that another time, when they wouldn't have the chance to be alone.

28

serenity

Serenity made dinner again. She wore the new dress she'd bought, too. She knew Sawyer would see it for what it was—another attempt to please and attract him; he noticed *every* detail. But she'd already admitted that she wanted to see him. What good would it do to play games?

She was hoping he'd pull her into his arms the second he crossed the threshold. That they wouldn't have to talk. She preferred he take her straight to bed, where she could work out her anxiety and satisfy her desire for him.

But he didn't touch her. After she let him in, he watched her as though he wasn't quite sure what to expect.

"Are you hungry?" she asked. "I made some pasta. I found a recipe online—it has olives, feta cheese and garlic olive oil. I didn't know if it would turn out, but I tasted it and it's delicious."

"Sounds good." He was still in the chinos and button-down shirt he must've worn for work. He looked tired but as attractive as ever. Her hands itched to take off his shirt and feel his smooth, warm chest, to delve into the silky strands of his hair…

"Hard day?" she asked as she led him into the kitchen.

"Busy. Had to be up early."

"Your business must be doing well."

"The real estate market is booming."

"That's nice—except it means you're working long hours. You can go home right after dinner if you'd rather hit the sack early tonight." She hadn't taken his work schedule into consideration when she'd planned to see him, and she should have.

He paused instead of sitting down. "Whether I leave after dinner or not depends on you, Serenity."

She grabbed the hot pads so she could put the pasta in a bowl. "On *me*?"

He came over and took the pan out of her grasp, putting it back on the burner. "What am I doing here?"

"What do you mean?"

"Is this all about sex? Or are you willing to care about me?"

Serenity's mouth went dry. "I—I don't know," she stammered. "Do we have to make that decision now? I mean…as long as we enjoy each other—"

"No," he said, adamant. "We've known each other too many years for that. If you don't agree to give me a fair chance from the get-go, I'm not convinced you'll ever open your heart."

She was tempted to step away from him, but he had her wedged between his six-four frame and the stove.

"I'm not out to hurt you, if that's what you're intimating."

"I know that. I wouldn't be interested if I thought you were that type of person."

"How can you be interested in me at all?" she asked.

His eyes widened. "Are you kidding? I've wanted you since the first moment I laid eyes on you. You're all Sean's ever had that's made me envious."

Her mind raced as she sifted through her memories. "You never even gave me a second look."

"Because you were married. But you're not anymore. I want a real chance with you, but I don't want to be sleeping with you while you look for someone else, someone you deem more…fitting or whatever."

She could feel her heart thudding in her ears. She'd never expected Sawyer to be so direct. But as intense as their lovemaking had been, she could see why he might've expected their relationship to change, and why he was probably confused that it hadn't. "We had sex three times in one night," she pointed out.

"Believe me, I remember."

"Well, obviously I'm attracted to you."

"That's not the same thing. I thought you'd call, but you didn't."

"I texted you."

"Weeks later."

"You could've called me," she countered.

He shook his head. "No. You needed to be the one. I'd already told you I wanted to see you again. You had to decide whether you felt the same."

She said nothing.

"And now here we are," he went on. "Is this a repeat of last time—or the start of something new?"

Turning back to the pasta, Serenity went ahead and put it in a bowl.

"Serenity?"

"I'm not sure I can get over the fact that you're Sean's brother."

"Why? What's that got to do with anything?"

"It's…weird, awkward."

"Even though Sean and I aren't actually related?"

"His family is your family! How will I explain that to anyone? What will *my* family think?" She refused to admit that her mother had suggested Sawyer as a possible match for her; there were more people in her family than Charlotte. "What will the Alstons think?" she added. "You saw how Nina reacted."

"So others might think badly of us. What does it matter if we haven't done anything wrong? Are you going to let other people get in the way of what we feel?"

She faced him again. "You say we haven't done anything wrong, but I feel I *must* be doing something wrong, just because of who you are. And I don't want any more ties to the Alstons."

"I would never ask you to be around them. I know they haven't treated you well. I doubt they'll ever forgive me, anyway."

And *she* doubted it would be that cut and dried. They were all the family he had. Surely he'd miss them and want to repair his relationship with them eventually. What would she do then? If she'd learned anything about becoming a couple, it was that staying together required compromise. And extended family *did* matter.

They were certainly a bigger part of the equation than she'd realized when she married Sean. If she got with Sawyer, she'd have Sean's family in her life—

would possibly have *Sean* in her life once he got out of prison, which was an even more horrific thought.

Would that drive her and Sawyer apart in the end?

Why take the risk? There were plenty of other men out there. Why did she have to choose *this* one?

"It's not that simple," she said.

"It is to me."

"Sean will be out of prison soon."

"What does that mean?"

"I don't ever want to see him again—not as long as I live."

He grasped her shoulders. "Serenity, he and I are not a package deal. I would never put you in that position."

"It's not just that. Getting into a relationship with you, especially so soon, would make me doubt myself."

"In what way?"

She tried to articulate her confusing thoughts and emotions. "I'm afraid I'd wonder if I ever really loved my husband, or if *you* were the one I wanted all along."

"Is that true?" he asked.

She squeezed her eyes shut. "No. I loved him. I'm sure I did. But then I met you and…and as much as I fought it, and refused to acknowledge it, there were times when…"

He leaned in closer—until she could smell the familiar scent of his skin, which only weakened her resolve. "When…"

"I dreamed about you." She shook her head. "God, I can't believe I'm even admitting that."

"Why?" he said. "It's exactly what I need to hear." He pulled her up against him. "I don't know where this will go, Serenity. All I'm asking is that you don't rule me out from the beginning."

"After what I've been through, another relationship, especially with you, is too scary."

He rested his forehead against hers. "I understand that. But at least I also understand what it was like for you in a way most other people couldn't. Part of the reason I admire you is that you're one tough chick."

When she chuckled at his response, he held her face in his hands. "I also think you're beautiful as well as brave."

As soon as he kissed her, in a very different way from before—sweeter and with more meaning—she could hardly regret her decision. She and Sean had had a good marriage before he did what he did. It had been pleasant and companionable and fine. She'd been satisfied. Had he been as decent as she'd thought, they would've made it.

But she'd never experienced the kind of raw passion Sawyer evoked. There was something to be said for that, too.

Maybe she was heading straight from the frying pan into the fire, as the cliché went, but what a way to go.

* * *

lorelei

Lorelei shivered in spite of her jacket. It wasn't that cold, but she was nervous. Other than when Finn had brought his brothers to the restaurant so Davis could apologize, she hadn't seen him. He hadn't called, and he hadn't come over, so she didn't really know how he was feeling toward her.

She was already waiting by the tree where she'd told him to meet her when he walked up. He had his hands jammed into the pockets of his jeans, but he wasn't wearing anything over his polo shirt.

"Don't you need a coat?" she asked as he approached.

He shrugged. "I'm fine."

She pulled the money they'd left at the restaurant out of her jacket. "This is way too much, Finn. I appreciate the gesture, but…no."

He made no move to take it. "We want you to have it."

"I can't. Really. It's too much. But thank you." Since he still had his hands in his pockets, she tried to force the money in around them.

When it fell out, he bent down to pick it up. "So… was that Mark I saw you with yesterday?"

She nodded.

Hunching forward again, he nudged a pinecone from one foot to the other. "How long will he be here?"

"A week."

He continued to move the pinecone. "Are you returning to Florida with him?"

She wasn't surprised he'd assume that. Mark had been hugging her when Finn came upon them. "No."

His head snapped up. "No?"

"What you saw yesterday… Mark and I have a lot of history together, Finn. And we're in a difficult situation right now. So any kindness between us is welcome. Well, not *any* kindness, but you know what I mean."

"I *don't* know what you mean. Not really." He tilted his head as he looked at her. "Are you staying with him?"

"No. I can't save our marriage. He's still hoping I'll change my mind, but it won't happen."

A relieved smile appeared as he started messing with that pinecone again. "So…what are your plans?"

"I'll finish out the summer here. I like it, like the reprieve it's giving me. But once August is over, I'll go back to Florida, where I'll file for divorce. Then we'll have to work out the separation of our assets, visitation, custody—all of that. I'm not looking forward to it," she added.

"Will you have to face Francine?" he asked with a grimace.

"I doubt I'll be able to avoid it."

"Doesn't seem fair."

"It's not. That's where a lot of my anger comes from. I don't feel I did anything to deserve what he did—and what she did—but I have to deal with it, anyway. So I'll just keep putting one foot in front of the other, until I outdistance the wreckage. It'll take time, but if I stay with him, I'll never break free."

He scratched the back of his neck. "I'm sorry. I'm also sorry that things went the way they did when you were working for us. Davis was out of line—"

"He apologized," she interrupted. "It doesn't matter anymore. How's he doing, anyway?"

"Seems a bit better—although Nolan and I aren't very good cooks. We don't clean up after him, either. So I bet he regrets losing you. If we don't order food from a restaurant, he eats peanut butter sandwiches, and he makes them by taking a bite of bread with a spoonful of peanut butter. He'd probably like some jelly, too, but he can't spread it, and I'm not going to wait on him. He had help. He's the one who screwed it up."

"Tough love might be the best approach with him.

It'll be slow going, but if he has to figure things out for himself, he will."

"Right." His chest lifted as he drew a deep breath. "About us…"

She bit her lip. "Is there an us, Finn?"

His expression grew sorrowful. "That's what I'm wondering. I hate not spending time with you and Lucy anymore."

"I've missed you, too," she admitted. But she had a child to consider and couldn't stay in California, even if there was some way to arrange it. As attracted as she was to Finn, this was simply the wrong time and place to start another relationship. "But I don't see how we can have a future together."

"I know," he admitted. "I keep coming to the same conclusion. That's why I haven't contacted you. But we're friends, aren't we? I care about you. Do we have to let that go, too—just because we can't be more?"

She blinked quickly to ward off tears. "No. We don't have to let that go," she said and slipped her arms around his waist so she could rest her cheek against his broad chest. She needed to feel the warmth and support of this man—who'd been so kind to her when she needed it most—just one more time.

* * *

serenity

Serenity had to get up early, but she didn't want to sleep, not while Sawyer was with her. What he'd said earlier, the fact that he'd made her commit to being open-minded, had changed how she viewed him. Now she was trying to make it work instead of focusing on all the obstacles that stood in their way.

She feared her new perspective might crumble in the light of day, but while they were alone together, while he was curled around her in bed, being with him felt perfectly natural and right.

"I've never asked you this before, so all I know is what Sean told me," she said. "But…what happened to your father?"

She'd thought maybe he'd fallen asleep, but when he let go of her and rolled onto his back, she knew he hadn't. Was this too difficult a subject, especially this early in the relationship?

"What'd Sean tell you?"

She plumped her pillow. "Would you rather we not talk about it?"

"No, it's okay."

Although he said the words, she wasn't sure whether to believe him. She could feel a sudden tension in him that hadn't existed before. But how was she supposed to get to know him in a different way—a more intimate way—if they couldn't talk about the most important events in his life?

"Sean said he drowned in a river when you were just a kid," she told him. "But I've always wondered how it happened."

When he took a moment to respond, she decided she was too happy right now to risk probing any more. "Never mind. We can talk about it another time."

"No, it's fine," he insisted. "He and his friend were fishing in Alaska. He loved to fish. It was his dream to go there. But there was a lot of flooding that spring and, somehow, his buddy fell into the river. My dad jumped in to pull the guy out, but the current and the cold were too much for both of them."

She winced. "I'm so sorry. How old were you?"

"Nine."

She could barely see his profile in the darkness, but she could tell his face was filled with sadness. "That must've been devastating."

"I'll never forget the day my mother showed up at school to tell me. It felt like my whole world had come crashing down, especially because it killed me to witness *her* grief."

"She must've taken it hard."

"Very."

"So how did she meet Sean's father?"

"She was a teller at a bank, and he walked in one day."

"How long was this after your father died?"

"About two years."

"What made Cody leave Nina—do you know?" He'd married Nina right out of college. They'd had Sean and Felix and divorced. Then Cody had met and married Sawyer's mother. After she died, he went back to Nina and they had Thomas. Knowing that they'd been divorced for a while had always made Serenity wonder why they couldn't make it the first time.

"No clue. They never talked about the divorce, but sometimes I could tell Nina resented me."

She was certainly quick to turn on him. Maybe she resented his inclusion in the life she could've had with her husband and her own sons had Cody never met Sawyer's mother. "Was she with someone else, too, during that period?"

"When Cody married my mother? My mother wasn't around for very long, and then they got back together, so I doubt it." He fell silent, seemed to be reliving the loss of his mother. But then he said, "I think she knew she had cancer when she married him. I think she did it because she believed he was the kind of man who'd take care of me after she was gone."

"Oh, wow," Serenity said. "And she was right."

"Yeah."

Suddenly Serenity had a great deal more respect for Cody Alston. She'd always thought it generous of him to raise a son who wasn't his, especially since Sawyer's mother died so soon after they were married, but this drove it all home. Also, that Sawyer had taken a stand against Sean suddenly seemed to be an even greater sacrifice than it had before. "How do you feel about Cody?"

"For the most part, I respect him," he said. "He did his best to be fair, so I'm grateful."

"But the trial…"

"Parents are blind when it comes to their kids. Especially their own blood."

"Meaning you don't think Cody would've stood behind you in the same way?"

"Maybe he would have. He's a loyal guy. But I've never been under the illusion that if he had to choose between me and Sean, he'd ever pick me."

"Why didn't you stay out of it, try to salvage your relationship?"

"And put who knows how many children at risk because I was afraid of what it might do to *me*? No."

He hadn't been able to contribute anything that would help get Sean convicted. Only she'd been able to do that. But he'd supported her so she could withstand the onslaught of Sean's lawyers and Sean's family and the stress, embarrassment and shame and do what had to be done. Now that she understood this, she had to admire him for making that decision.

She slid closer and he shifted so he could wrap his arm around her. "I don't want to come between you and the Alstons," she murmured. "I don't want to cost you your family."

"That's the thing. It was Sean who came between us, not you."

"But if we get together…"

"I'd rather have you in my life than anyone else."

She kissed his collarbone, his neck, his jaw. "Will you feel the same in five, ten years? Maybe longer?"

"Wow. Now you're talking *really* long-term," he joked.

She leaned up on one elbow. *"And you're not?"*

"I wouldn't have started this if I didn't think it could be serious," he said.

"And you won't change your mind about Sean and the Alstons and begin to resent me?"

"Of course not."

She thought about that for several seconds. Then she said, "I'm afraid of what you make me feel."

He pulled her on top of him. "Good. That makes two of us."

29

lorelei

When Lorelei woke up, she listened for Lucy only to realize that she'd agreed to let Lucy stay with her father at the motel. He'd promised to take her out for strawberry waffles this morning.

It felt strange not to have her daughter at the cabin with her, especially at this time of day, but she'd have to get used to Lucy being with Mark. She'd probably be with him every other weekend, if not more often since she still had another year before she started kindergarten.

Lorelei would have to plan some activities for when she was alone, so she wouldn't feel forlorn, she decided. Or now that she was working, it was possible she'd welcome a few days off.

She covered a yawn and was just considering getting out of bed to make breakfast when her phone buzzed. She assumed it was Mark, calling to tell her how Lucy had fared during her first night away, but it was Mercedes.

She hesitated before answering. She was going through such a difficult time right now; she wasn't sure she had anything to offer Mercedes. And it often felt awkward, trying to dodge her many conversion attempts.

In the end, however, she couldn't ignore the call. What if Mercedes needed her? Maybe they'd wound up being very different people, in very different situations, but they'd both started in that lonely foster home. She would always be there for Mercedes, no matter what. "Hello?"

"Hey, where are you?" Mercedes asked. "I've driven over to your house three days in a row, and no one's ever home. Are you guys on vacation or something?"

A wave of sadness washed over her. She and Mark would never be on vacation together again. "No. I'm in Tahoe. So is Mark, but he'll be back after the Fourth."

"You're staying? What for?"

"Thanks to DNA testing, I've found two sisters in my family tree."

"No kidding? You always talked about finding your parents."

"I'm still working on that," she said. "But at least I've found *some* family."

"These sisters can't tell you more about your mom and dad?"

"Unfortunately not. They were shocked *I* even existed. But we're trying to figure it out."

"When will you be back in Florida?"

"At the end of August."

"But Mark's coming back before then?"

Lorelei sat up taller. "We're breaking up, Mercedes." She gasped. "Are you serious?"

Lorelei could hardly believe it herself. She would never have dreamed their marriage would crumble the way it had. "I am."

"*Why?* What happened?"

She considered lying to try to cover for Mark. No matter how angry she felt, he was Lucy's father. And he and Mercedes had never really liked each other. She didn't want Mercedes to be glad that their marriage had failed. But with Francine pregnant, there would be no hiding the truth, not for long. Lorelei figured she might as well get used to telling everyone the same thing. "Because Francine is going to have Mark's baby."

"Francine, your best friend? *That* Francine?"

"Yes."

"No way! Oh, honey! I'm so sorry! When did you find out?"

Her sympathy brought a lump to Lorelei's throat. She'd never felt like crying as often as she had in the past two months. "The beginning of May."

"Why didn't you call me?"

She couldn't call Mercedes or Osha. Neither one of them could do anything to help. "You've been pretty busy with the church, so... I didn't want to bother you," she finished lamely.

"But that's the thing! Oh, my gosh! You and Lucy should come and live here. You would *love* it. That's why I was calling—to invite you to visit the compound. It'll be friends and family day a week from Saturday, so you could see for yourself how wonderful it is, how peaceful and loving."

Lorelei wasn't even tempted. She'd seen how much Mercedes had changed, and she didn't think it was for the better. These days Mercedes insisted that aliens were going to come and kill everyone except those who belonged to her church. They, of course, would be saved and repopulate the Earth.

"I'm afraid I won't be home in time," she said.

"That's okay. You can always come when you get back. I'll talk to the head disciple and set up a tour for you whenever you want. If you'd just give Brother William a chance, I know he'd be able to help you."

"That's okay, Mercedes, I'm going to be fine on my own," Lorelei insisted and when they hung up, she was more determined than ever to make it true.

* * *

finn

"Can we talk?"

Finn looked up from his easel to find Davis standing in the doorway of the room he'd turned into his studio. Since he was no longer spending his mornings with Lorelei, most days he started work right when he woke up. "About what?"

"You've been so quiet lately. What's wrong?"

"With *me*?" Finn said. "You're the one who's always in a bad mood, bro."

Davis lifted his stump. "I have a reason. You don't."

This was partially true. Finn had it pretty good. At least he hadn't lost an arm. But he hadn't been himself since the rift with Lorelei, and he couldn't figure out why. He'd known from the beginning that she wasn't the best fit for him, and yet he'd let what he felt move beyond friendship.

Last night hearing what she had to say only made it worse.

Davis came into the room and dropped onto the bed Finn had pushed against one wall to give him more space. "You still mooning over our next-door neighbor?"

"I can't believe you'd say a word about her. You're the one who screwed things up for me."

Davis grimaced. "I feel terrible about that. But I apologized. What more can I do?"

Finn stood back to scrutinize the shade of blue he'd chosen for the lake. Although it had taken him several weeks, he finally knew what he wanted to paint. Although he wasn't quite finished, he'd set his other project aside so he could create this nature scene while he was actually here to view it in person. "Nothing. What's done is done."

"Anyway, *I* couldn't have screwed anything up. She's married, so it's not like you could have her anyway."

"She's getting divorced."

"She told you that?"

He studied the photograph he had pinned to his easel. "She did."

"When?"

"Last night."

"You saw her?"

He dabbed his brush into the paint again. "Briefly."

"Damn. I'm sorry I was such a dick when she worked here."

Finn didn't say anything. He was glad that Davis was

acting more like himself, but things had been going well with Lorelei until he threw that lamp.

"What about Michelle Radkin?" Davis asked. "I always figured you two would get married. I think she sort of figures that, too."

Because Finn kept going back to her, even though they weren't quite right for each other. On the face of it, they should've made the perfect couple. She was a nice girl, they lived in the same area and they'd dated— on and off—since they were in high school. Even *he'd* thought he'd probably marry her.

But he hadn't missed her at all since he'd met Lorelei. "I'm over Michelle."

His brother suddenly looked uncomfortable. "You don't mean that."

"I do."

"You two have broken up plenty of times before."

"I know, but this time I'm not going back to her."

"Uh-oh."

Finn stopped painting. "What is it?"

A sheepish expression descended on Davis's face. "I invited her to the cabin, dude, hoping it would cheer you up. She's coming to surprise you for the Fourth. She'll be here tomorrow."

* * *

reagan

Even though Serenity was gone, Reagan sat out on the deck like she did almost every morning. She had to keep up with Serenity's social media. She put up a new post and did some commenting. Then, while Lorelei was inside making breakfast—thank goodness she liked to cook because Reagan certainly didn't—she clicked over to a book site and bought *What to Expect When You're Expecting.*

She was in over her head. She needed a manual.

She felt nervous as she checked out online. This made the pregnancy so real. She was preparing for a baby, *her* baby.

And Drew's—which wasn't such a pleasant thought.

I just bought "What to Expect When You're Expecting," she wrote to Rally. I think I'm starting to wrap my mind around this. Or at least I'm starting to accept that this is my new reality, and I'm getting prepared.

He didn't respond right away. He was at work and might not have seen her text, so she interacted with people on Serenity's Facebook page until she heard her phone ding.

Good for you! You know what I have to say about the pregnancy—you'll love being a mother, and you'll be a great one.

She smiled. Even if they never dated, she'd be grateful to him. He was coaching her through a very difficult time, and she'd grown to like and respect him a great deal.

I'm trying to take your word for it.

You'll see. Once he or she arrives, you'll never love anyone else as much.

Her phone rang while she was reading his text. She was surprised to see that the call was coming from Edison & Curry. Assuming it was Flo Cook, the office manager, asking when she was going to come in and pick up her stuff so they could clear out the storage room, she answered. "Hello?"

"Reagan?"

She stiffened. It wasn't Flo; it was Drew. "What do you want?"

"Gary just hired your replacement."

Did he have to twist the knife? "What am I supposed to say to that?" She could say, *What the hell took him so long?* It had been weeks. But she didn't bother.

"Nothing. I only hope you're missing us as badly as we're missing you. It's so hard to pass your office and see someone else in there. I can't believe you're not coming back."

"It's been over a month since we last talked, Drew. And you're just now missing me?"

"I've been trying to get over you, but it's not easy. This new girl—she could never replace you, not in a million years."

Reagan didn't know how to take that. The "new girl" couldn't serve as a replacement for Drew's extracurricular affairs? Or she couldn't cut it in advertising? "Why? Because she's too old or unattractive?" Reagan asked dryly.

"Ouch! I'm wounded that you'd accuse me of being so shallow. Especially since I really cared about you."

She nearly laughed aloud when he used the past tense. To her mind, that gave him away. "You couldn't have cared too much if you got over me in a matter of weeks. But that's fine. I realized I'd been taken for a fool almost as soon as it happened. And I have a completely different perspective on you these days, too."

"I didn't mean for what happened to happen, Reagan." He'd lowered his voice in an obvious attempt to sound distraught and sincere, but she couldn't buy it. He'd pursued her for months, and she'd been stupid enough to fall for the flattery and attention.

"That's easy for you to say," she responded. "You still have your wife and kids—and your job. You've been able to go on as if it never happened."

"You didn't *have* to quit. I told you not to!"

"I was trying to do the right thing—to be sure we didn't wreck your family." She hadn't known at the time that *she* was more concerned about his family than he was.

He didn't respond to her comment about his wife and kids. "Why don't you come back?" he asked instead. "I can talk Gary into it."

She got up and walked over to the railing. Considering how resolute and angry Gary had been in his response to her resignation, this came as a surprise. She wished she could believe Drew missed her and wanted her back for that reason, but she knew it was her pride and vanity speaking. It was much more likely Gary had hired someone else who'd lasted only a few weeks, and Drew had realized that not just anyone could replace her. "Sorry, I'm happy where I am."

"Which is…"

"Lake Tahoe."

"Still? When will you be coming back to New York?"

"Not until the first of September."

"You're staying all summer? What are you doing for work?"

She thought of the social media and blog she was doing for Serenity. "Nothing much. Just some volunteer stuff here and there."

"You can't live off volunteer work, Reagan. Come back in the fall. We'll take you on whenever you get here."

He was acting as if he was trying to do her a favor, but she suspected Edison & Curry needed her more than they'd realized. She'd worked so hard, done so much for the firm.

Feeling slightly vindicated that they were feeling her absence, after all, she stiffened her spine. "That's okay. I'll find something that suits me better."

"Like what? Where will you go?"

"I haven't decided yet." She wouldn't tell him, anyway. He was well-connected in the advertising community; she wouldn't put it past him to submarine her, if he could.

"Gary takes that non-compete pretty seriously."

She couldn't help bristling at the threat. "Fine. He can spend a lot of money trying to sue me for getting another job if he wants to, but I'm not convinced that non-compete will hold up in a court of law—not unless I'm doing something that directly threatens his business."

"We taught you everything you know. Just working for someone else will reveal our trade secrets."

"That's bull."

"I'm just telling you how he'll see it."

No, Drew would be on Gary's side. She needed to come across as strong as possible, put them both on notice that she wouldn't be that easy to bully. "Then I guess it'll be up to a judge to decide, won't it?"

She was gambling, hoping if she *did* start with one

of their competitors, Gary would decide it wasn't worth the money to try to screw things up for her. The non-compete was more of a scare tactic than anything else. Whether or not it had any teeth would depend on the outcome of any litigation that ensued. She couldn't believe they could really stop her from earning a living at the only profession she knew.

"I never thought it would end like this," he said when she didn't back down.

She put a hand to her stomach. "I didn't, either. But we're a little premature in worrying about the non-compete. I have to decide what to do about this baby before I can work anywhere."

Dead silence. "*What* baby?"

Gripping her phone more tightly, she said, "I'm pregnant, Drew."

There was another long pause in which she could easily sense his panic. "You're not saying the baby is *mine*…"

"I'm not saying that, no—not if you don't want to hear it," she added.

"What do you mean? What kind of answer is that?"

"An open-ended one. Why don't I send you an agreement where you can waive your parental rights? Then no one will have to know, it won't cost you a cent and you'll never have to hear from me again."

She hadn't yet committed herself to telling Drew, wasn't sure why she'd gone ahead with it, but she guessed it was because she didn't want to be blamed for her child's lack of a father. As long as she gave him the opportunity to stand up and accept responsibility, she'd be able to live with herself and look her child in the eye.

She held her breath as she awaited his response.

"How'd it happen?" he finally asked.

"Oh, come on," she said. "You know how it happened."

"But...we only did it once!"

"Unfortunately for me, once was all it took."

He seemed to be at a loss for words, and she could understand why. It had taken some time for her to recover from the news, too. "It's easy enough for you to fix," she went on. "I'm the only one who's really stuck. All you have to do is sign the form I send you. Will you do that?"

Once again, he lowered his voice. "You sound *eager* for me to sign it."

She was. If she didn't have Drew in her life, she could raise her child whichever way she felt was best, and he would have no say. Her mother preached about how difficult it was to be a single parent, but in this case, Reagan felt doing it alone would be better than the alternative. "I'm trying to save you from having to tell your wife." She felt it was safe to spin it in that direction, since he'd spun everything he'd said so far to fit *his* purposes.

"I can't believe this," he muttered.

"Should I send it, just in case?" she asked.

Nothing.

"Drew?"

"Yeah. Send it. But can I have a few days to think it over?"

"I guess. I'll give you my address so you can send it back after you've had it notarized. I'll need the hard copy."

"Fine, I will—*if* I decide to go that way," he clarified.

"Breakfast is ready!" Lorelei emerged onto the deck using a cookie sheet as a tray. "I invited Finn and his brothers over. I hope you don't mind."

Reagan put up a hand to let her know she couldn't respond until she got off the phone. "I've got to go," she said into her cell.

Drew didn't even answer.

30

serenity

Her parents were there to pick her up. Serenity hated that things felt different. But how could they be normal? She was harboring two half sisters in Tahoe—two women they probably didn't even know existed.

At the very minimum, they didn't know *she* knew they existed.

"There you are!" her mother cried when Serenity emerged from Baggage Claim.

Charlotte pulled her into a tight embrace, and Serenity buried her face in her mother's neck, breathing in the familiar scent of Dolce & Gabbana's Light Blue. She was so torn. She owed this woman her utmost loyalty. And yet she had her father to consider—and Lorelei and Reagan. Somehow, she needed to be fair to all of them.

"Hi, honey." Her father jumped out of the car, which he left running at the curb, to get her bag.

"How come you're off work?" she asked, surprised to see him midmorning on a Thursday.

"Are you kidding?" He put her suitcase in the trunk.

"I couldn't go to the office today. My girl was coming to town." He gave her a hug before holding her in front of him. "We've been worried about you, but you look good."

She couldn't believe she looked *too* good. It seemed as though her wake up call had come as soon as she and Sawyer had fallen asleep. They'd barely had a chance to shower before Sawyer, who'd convinced her to cancel her Uber, drove her to the airport.

But she was happier than her parents had seen her in a while, so there was that. "You're kidding, right? I didn't even bother to put on any makeup."

"You don't need makeup," he said.

She climbed into the back seat.

"How's your writing going?" her mother asked as they put on their seat belts.

The stereo was playing a Top 40 station as her father shifted into Drive and started looking for a break in the traffic. The San Diego airport was always busy. But she knew he was listening.

"Better," she said. "*Much* better."

"That's wonderful news! I told you you'd get back in the groove."

She'd only done it with Reagan's help but, of course, she couldn't give her the credit. "If I can hit my new deadline, I *might* be able to pull out of this nosedive. I have almost a third of the book done, and the ending always goes faster than the beginning."

"You'll make it. Even if you don't, they'd be foolish to let you go."

Spoken with the typical bias of a loving parent. Serenity hid a smile. "I'm the one who missed my deadline. If I miss it again, there's no way I can blame them."

"You'll make the next one."

Serenity hoped their confidence wasn't misplaced. She was starting to feel some interest in the case again, which helped. Although it *was* sad, and nothing would ever make it less sad, it was the puzzle aspect of solving a crime that had always appealed to her, and this one had required plenty of sleuthing. That Mr. Maynard had managed to start over and leave his past behind—as though he'd never had another family and never done what he'd done—shocked and amazed her. So did the fact that he'd been able to hide for so long. If not for a TV series that spotlighted cold cases and asked for tips, he might never have been apprehended. Fortunately, a woman he'd once dated recognized his likeness when she saw it on TV.

"What about the young men who are staying next door?" her mother asked. "How are things going with them?"

"We see them quite a bit," Serenity replied.

"We?"

Serenity's heart leaped into her throat. *Shit.* "Me and my kayaking friends," she said. "Sometimes the Hatch brothers go out on the lake with us."

Her father glanced into his rearview mirror. "You should take them out in the boat. That's got to be more fun than a kayak."

"It's a different kind of fun. But I've been meaning to. Maybe we'll do that when I get back."

"Do you like one of the Hatch brothers a little more than the others?" her mother asked, her voice hopeful.

Thank God Charlotte seemed to accept her answer on that "we." Her parents trusted her and probably couldn't imagine she'd have any reason to lie about something like that, anyway. "They're all nice," she said as the alarm receded.

Charlotte turned down the radio. "What about the boy who lost his arm? How's he doing?"

Much to her surprise, Serenity was beginning to look forward to seeing Davis every morning. That first day he'd been so angry at the world she hadn't liked him much, and was put off by the way he'd treated Lorelei. But she felt he was beginning to have moments when he was glad to be alive, and the more the dark cloud hanging over him lifted, and she could see what he was really like, the easier it was to forgive him. The last time they'd gone out on the water had felt almost…companionable. "He's healing," she said.

"I'm so glad."

"It's tragic what happened to him," her father added.

Serenity gazed out at the traffic. Driving in San Diego was never easy, and today was no exception. "It is, but at least he's going to be okay."

"It's nice of you to befriend him, honey," her mother said. "But I'll admit I was keeping my fingers crossed that you'd feel a little more—if not for him then for one of his brothers."

"We're just friends. But I'll meet someone eventually," she mumbled, feeling self-conscious about having spent the night with Sawyer. She would've told her parents about him. She knew they wouldn't think badly of her. But she was afraid her mother might mention him to Beau or the twins, or someone else in the family, and she didn't want to go through all the explanations, as well as the discomfort of admitting who he was, especially if the relationship wasn't going to last.

Fortunately, Charlotte changed the subject before

Serenity could break down and tell her. "What would you like to do for the Fourth? Beau is coming home, so I thought we'd have a barbecue, and I'd make my s'mores bars. Are you interested in watching the fireworks?"

"I'm open to anything." She wasn't concerned with how they'd celebrate. She only cared about getting her father's DNA. She'd thought of swabbing his glass, like the police might do so they could get DNA without a suspect's knowing it. But she didn't have a full-service lab at her disposal. And why make it hard when it could be easy? If her father wasn't aware of her half siblings, he might be willing to take the test simply to learn about his heritage and genetic makeup. His birthday was coming up at the end of August, so she'd give him the test as a present, have him take it while she was there and then send it off herself.

She didn't see how he could refuse, unless he had a good reason to. If he did balk, she was willing to bet she could get Beau to spit in a tube under the same pretense. If Beau wasn't related to Lorelei and Reagan, she'd be able to rule out Uncle Vance, and that was what she was hoping to do.

But if Vance wasn't her father, and Reagan's and Lorelei's, too, how was it that he knew Reagan's mother? What else could explain the letter Serenity had in her purse?

"We could go to Big Bay Boom and watch the fireworks. We haven't done that since we've lived here. Or we could go to Sea World or Ocean Beach. They have shows."

"I'm fine with whatever," she said. "Honestly. It doesn't matter to me."

"Then we'll let Beau decide."

"When will he be home?"

"Tomorrow."

"Too bad the twins can't be here." She suddenly felt as though she was in danger of losing Tara, Tia and Beau and missed them all terribly.

"They're too busy," Charlotte explained.

"But your uncle Vance will be here," her father piped up.

Suddenly feeling asphyxiated by her seat belt, Serenity pulled it away from her body. *"What?"*

Her father signaled to get into the other lane. "Uncle Vance called this morning. He'll be in town, too."

What were the chances? Vegas was only about a five-hour drive from San Diego. She knew he came to visit her parents every now and then, but he'd be joining them while she was there?

At first she thought it was a lucky coincidence— or it would be if this thing didn't blow up in her face.

Then she began to wonder if Reagan impersonating Rosalind could have anything to do with Vance's decision to come. It was the Fourth of July—not an odd time to visit family—but it hadn't been that long since she and Reagan had contacted him. Was he hoping to have a chance to speak to Charlotte in private, to make sure she'd continue to keep quiet about *the baby*?

"How long will he be staying?" she asked.

Another driver was kind enough to let her father in, even though the freeway was jam-packed. "He didn't say."

"What brings him to San Diego?"

"He's probably hoping to borrow some more money," her mother grumbled before her father could respond.

Her father shot her mother a dark look. "I don't think so, Charlotte. I just gave him some."

"Then he has another business idea he's hoping you'll back." Charlotte obviously wasn't willing to assume Vance was coming simply because he cared about them and wanted to see them.

"Does he know I'm going to be here?" Serenity broke in before her father could get upset that her mother had made another negative remark about his brother.

"I didn't tell him," her father said. "Why do you ask?"

"Just wondering if he realizes you'll already have company."

Wearing an *oh, come on* expression, Chuck turned around to look at her. They were stopped in traffic, anyway. "You and Beau aren't company. You're *family*."

That was true. But were she and Vance more closely related than Chuck realized?

"It'll be good to see him again," she murmured, but her mind was no longer on the conversation. She was thinking of the letter in her purse: *Please promise me you'll never tell.*

Would she finally be able to figure out what Vance and her mother were hiding?

And if she could, would she be sorry she did?

* * *

reagan

She'd told Drew about the baby. After all the thought and deliberation she'd put into the question of whether she should or shouldn't, she'd pulled the trigger—and now she was afraid the bullet she'd fired would rico-chet and hit her instead.

She'd emailed him a Voluntary Relinquishment of Parental Rights, a form she'd downloaded from the in-ternet for free, almost as soon as they'd hung up. She'd told herself it needed to get into his inbox immediately, that she'd have the best chance of having him walk away if he made the decision while he was frightened for his marriage.

But she hadn't heard from him and was no longer convinced she should pressure him to sign it.

If he relinquished his rights so easily, she'd feel as though she'd never meant anything to him to begin with. She'd been trying to cope with that ever since she'd spo-ken to him from the cabin that first time. This would soften the blow, make it easier to forgive her own fool-ishness. If he cared, even a little, then she hadn't been duped quite so completely.

If he didn't sign it, however—if he decided to be their child's father—he'd play a big role in her life. And his wife and other children might expect to be involved, too. That could prove difficult to cope with, especially as her life moved on. What kind of wrinkles would it cause when she fell in love again and possibly had other children?

But if Drew accepted the responsibility, she might be able to respect him enough to make it work, for their child's sake.

Her mind kept going back and forth like that as she tried to decide what to hope for. Problem was, what would be best for the child might not be the best thing for her—it probably wasn't, in all honesty—so she felt even more torn.

She heard a creak and turned from the window in the living room, where she'd been staring pensively out at the lake, watching the sunrise. Lorelei was coming down the stairs, but as soon as she saw Reagan in the semi-dark, she yelped and nearly fell.

"God, you scared me," she cried as she caught hold of the banister. "What are you doing up so early?"

"Sorry. Couldn't sleep." Tired of all the tossing and turning, she'd finally climbed out of bed and had been wandering through the cabin ever since, trying to calm her heart and mind.

"What's going on? Have you heard from Drew?"

"Not yet."

Lorelei came up beside her and gazed out at the lake, too.

"Why are *you* up so early?" Reagan asked.

She shoved her sleep-tousled hair out of her face. "I couldn't sleep, either."

"What's wrong?"

"I'm not used to having Lucy gone, I guess."

"Mark's acting as though he's completely devoted to her."

She rubbed her arms. "He is devoted to her. Just not as much as I am."

"Does it sway you at all to see how hard he's trying? Are you tempted to go back to him to keep your family together?"

"The temptation is constantly there," she admitted.

"So…will you change your mind?"

Lorelei shook her head. "I can't imagine a future like the one I'll have if I go back. That isn't what I ever envisioned for my life, and I've told him so."

"But he's not convinced."

"Not yet. He's still trying to prove he's contrite, believes that'll make me soften."

"I'm surprised it's not working."

"I am, too," she said. "I've always loved him. I still do. If he'd cheated with anyone else, I might've been able to forgive him. But the fact that it was Francine…"

"I understand." Reagan put an arm around her. "I'm sorry."

"So am I," she said softly but her eyes remained dry and that told Reagan, more than anything else, that she'd already made her decision.

"When does Mark go home?" Reagan asked.

"On Sunday."

"So he'll be here tomorrow night for the Fourth."

"He's heard that the Lights on the Lake in South Shore is one of the best fireworks shows in the country, so he's planning on taking me and Lucy." She tucked her hair behind her ears. "You can come with us, if you'd like."

"Mark won't want me there, not when he's trying to win you back. I'll see if Finn and his brothers feel like going." She left the window and the fabulous view. "Will you tell him you're filing for divorce after he goes back, then?"

"No. I need to be confident and brave enough to do it in person."

"When?"

"I've agreed to have dinner with him tonight. Would you mind watching Lucy so we can be alone?"

"Not at all." Reagan studied Lorelei's face. She looked tired, drawn, all right. Reagan didn't know how her sister would manage at work today. "Somehow we'll both get through the next year and put our worlds back together."

"It'll be a lot easier now that I have you and Serenity in my corner," she said.

* * *

lorelei

By the time she got off work, Lorelei was dragging, and she still had to get home. She'd ridden a bike that had been in the garage, since Serenity had taken the X5, but the restaurant wasn't that far away. It shouldn't have been a big deal to cycle there and back, and wouldn't have been, except that she'd gone to work so tired in the first place.

She could barely turn the crank as she pedaled home. She planned to take a nap before Mark came to drop off Lucy and pick her up for dinner. When she'd texted him that Reagan had agreed to watch their daughter, he'd been eager to have some time alone with her. He probably felt he'd proven himself this week and would be able to convince her to come back to him.

She wasn't looking forward to disabusing him of that notion. One week of good behavior didn't change anything. She doubted he'd be quite as amiable after she delivered that message.

As she struggled to climb the hill to the cabin, she came upon the place Finn and his brothers were renting and slowed to a pace that made her wobble. She couldn't help looking over to see what the Hatch brothers might be up to. She checked for any sight of Finn whenever she passed. Although she usually kept going, today she came to a stop.

There was a car she didn't recognize parked in the driveway.

Had their father come to town? Finn had mentioned that Mr. Hatch and his wife planned to visit, but he hadn't said when. Maybe they'd come to Tahoe for the holiday weekend.

Except this car didn't look like anything a wealthy man, much less the owner of several car dealerships, would drive. It was old and inexpensive, and it needed some bodywork.

So whose was it? Finn and his brothers didn't know anyone in Tahoe. Could this be the friend who lived in Sacramento, the one he'd met at South Shore a while back?

"Lorelei!"

She glanced up to see Reagan standing in the road outside Serenity's family cabin, waving her on.

Taking a deep breath, she forced herself to start pedaling again. "What is it?" she asked when she reached her sister. "Have you heard from Serenity?"

"Not yet. I just..."

"What?" she prompted when Reagan faltered.

"I didn't want you to stop at Finn's house."

"Why not?"

Reagan looked pained when she replied. "I went over there a little while ago to see if they were interested in watching the fireworks at South Shore tomorrow night."

"And?"

"And a woman answered the door. She said she was Finn's girlfriend."

"His *girlfriend*?" Lorelei repeated.

"She told me she drove up from LA and would be staying for the weekend."

This came as a complete shock. Lorelei didn't even know how to respond.

"Are you okay?" Reagan asked, her voice filled with concern.

She nodded.

"Are you sure?"

She nodded again. It was only because she was so tired that she felt like throwing up, she told herself. What Finn did was none of her business.

"This doesn't change anything, does it?" Reagan asked.

As much as Lorelei wished she could say no—she'd been so sure just a moment before—it shook her confidence. She'd already agreed that she and Finn would be friends; that had been *her* choice. And yet this made her doubt Finn had been as sincere as he'd seemed, and that made her fear she'd never find anyone else to love her, which tempted her to go back to Mark, to accept what was familiar instead of striking out on her own. As someone who'd had no family until she'd found Serenity and Reagan, she'd clung even harder to the one she'd created with Mark.

But she'd decided she wouldn't allow herself to return for the wrong reasons. She couldn't use her marriage as a crutch. Doing that would ultimately keep her from building a more fulfilling life, one in which she wouldn't be subjected to the constant reminder of Mark and Francine's betrayal.

She was right to divorce Mark. And to stay out of the way and let Finn move on. But when she imagined telling Mark to go home without her, she wasn't convinced she could do it, after all. Maybe she'd been foolish to think she ever could.

"I don't know," she admitted.

31

serenity

Uncle Vance didn't seem surprised to see her—at least not that Serenity could tell. She didn't mention that she'd left him three messages, all of which he'd ignored, and neither did he. He proved as unruffled, jovial and easygoing as ever.

When the five of them, including her brother Beau, who'd arrived only an hour before Vance, sat down for dinner, Serenity was eager for a taste of her mother's cooking, but her anxiety made it hard to enjoy the meal.

At least when Vance was around, it was easy to forgive him for whatever character flaws he possessed. In these more social moments, it didn't seem to matter that he couldn't keep a job and often needed financial help. He told one funny story after another and always had something interesting to contribute when someone else was talking. Even Serenity's mother softened toward him. By the time they were on dessert, she was laughing as much as anyone, and treating Vance in a much friendlier way than Serenity would've expected given what she'd said about him in the car.

While Serenity listened, she surreptitiously watched Charlotte and her uncle. Not even once did Vance look at her mother strangely, touch her in an inappropriate way, whisper in her ear or do anything else that might suggest they shared a romantic past.

Serenity might've talked herself out of what she'd come to accomplish. Her family seemed fine, just as they'd always been. All she had to do was leave them alone.

But Reagan and Lorelei were proof that *something* wasn't right—or hadn't been thirty-five years ago—and Vance had to be involved in some way.

"Hey, why are you so quiet tonight?"

Startled by Beau's voice, which came from behind her, Serenity whirled around. She hadn't realized her brother had followed her into the kitchen. He stopped to fill his water glass while she covered the carrot cake she'd just served. "I'm tired, I guess."

"Mom says you're spending the summer in Tahoe."

"Yeah. It's been nice."

"I can't wait to get out of school. Maybe I'll be able to use the cabin next summer."

She was glad he wasn't coming *this* summer. If he did, she'd need some notice or she'd have a lot of explaining to do. "I bet you'd enjoy it." She nudged him aside so she could put the cake in the fridge. "How're your classes going?"

"I'm…managing."

Was he, though? She knew their mother was worried about him. His grades had dropped and Charlotte had said he rarely came home these days. "Everything okay?"

"Absolutely."

He answered with conviction, but something was off; she could tell. "Beau?"

He stared at his feet for several seconds before lifting his gaze. "Everything's fine, Serenity. Really."

Then why had there been such a marked change in him? "I'm glad to hear that." She studied his face, searching for clues. "So…what's the latest? What's going on?"

Although she sensed he was somewhat reluctant, he let his breath go in an audible sigh and said, "I might as well tell you. I'm getting married."

She stepped back. "Wow! Are you kidding? Since when? Do Mom and Dad know?" And why the hell was he so somber about it?

"Not yet. I'm looking for the right time to tell them. I was going to do it tonight—" he hooked his thumb over his shoulder and lowered his voice "—until Uncle Vance showed up."

"Your engagement must've happened fast. The last time I talked to you, you said you weren't dating anyone. Who's the lucky girl? How long have you known her?"

He shifted uncomfortably.

"What is it?"

"His name's Trevor," he said. "I met him last year at Coachella, so I *was* dating someone when you asked me before. We've been together for months."

Stunned, she took a moment to process this information. "But…you never… My God, Beau, you're twenty-four years old. Why didn't you tell me before now?"

"I don't know." His hair fell over one eye as he

hunched forward and shoved his hands in his pockets. "As great as Mom and Dad have always been, I'm the only boy in the family. I was afraid they'd be disappointed, even if they wouldn't admit it."

"You obviously don't know how much they love you—how much we *all* love you. Why would we care who you marry? We just want you to be happy."

He looked up at her. "I hope that's true, because I am happy now—happier than I've ever been."

So *that* was why his grades had fallen. His attention had shifted. He was hiding a secret of his own— and maybe missing too many classes so he could hang out with his new love interest. "When's the big day?"

"We haven't set a date. Trevor came out when he was young. His parents are cool with it. But he wants to wait until I tell Mom and Dad, so both families can be on board."

"And you've decided not to do that tonight?"

"It'll be hard enough without having someone outside our immediate family listening in. I'd rather not put them on the spot."

"I understand." She gave him a hug. "You're sweet to be so empathetic. You've always been special. Trevor is a lucky man, and I can't wait to meet him."

He flipped his hair out of his eyes as he smiled. "Thanks. Let's go out for a drink after Mom and Dad go to bed tomorrow night."

"Why not tonight?"

"I'm supposed to meet up with some old friends."

"No problem," she said. "Tomorrow it is, then."

He started to walk back to the dining room, where their mother and father were still talking and laughing with Vance while finishing their coffee, but she caught his arm. "What do you think of Vance, by the way?"

"Forgive and forget," he replied earnestly. "Start over with a clean slate. Get counseling."

She nodded. She agreed that saving their marriage would require exactly those things. But that wasn't all. He'd have to navigate this tricky situation perfectly—treat her in a way that wouldn't leave her writhing in jealousy whenever he fulfilled his obligations to Francine and their child. And she didn't believe that was possible. Even if he started out as he was now—humble, patient, solicitous—which might make the situation bearable, before too long he'd get complacent, frustrated or tired and begin to expect her to be more understanding and flexible. To give him more time with Francine's child. To watch the child when he had to go somewhere or do something. To provide more money than the court stipulated or help Francine get into a house or whatever. And what if she didn't want to—or simply couldn't bring herself to agree?

They'd argue and everything would go to hell.

"You might think that other guy, Finn, is a better option," he said. "But you barely know him. You've only seen the best of him. You have no idea what he might *really* be like."

She thought of the woman who'd identified herself as Finn's girlfriend. Maybe she *hadn't* seen the worst of Finn. He hadn't had the chance to do anything like Mark had—but he certainly didn't seem too sad about the fact that she was going back to Florida at the end of the summer.

And yet…what else did she want? For him to suffer? No. Definitely not.

Mark took her hand as they entered the restaurant. Rather than embarrass him by pulling away, she allowed it.

She didn't pay much attention while he spoke softly

to the maître d'. She was too busy formulating what she'd say to him later. But when it seemed to be taking a long time to get a table, she tuned in to see why, and heard him mention privacy.

He was setting up something special, which made her slightly uncomfortable. What could he have planned that required privacy?

She hoped he wasn't going to do anything too sentimental, like present her with a new ring or a bouquet of roses and ask her to marry him again. She didn't want any grand gestures. She just wanted him to make it as easy as possible for her to pick up the pieces of her life and move on.

The maître d' led them to the far back corner.

"This table seats four," Lorelei said when the man was gone. "Are you sure we should sit here? Maybe a bigger party will come in."

"It's fine," Mark said dismissively.

It wasn't fine to her; it was impolite. There was no need to make the restaurant give up the seating if they didn't need to. She was about to insist they make a change.

But then she saw *why* he'd requested this particular table—and her stomach dropped.

* * *

reagan

While Lucy ate some apple slices and a peanut butter sandwich, Reagan tried to call Serenity but got her voice mail. When Serenity had arrived in San Diego yesterday, she'd sent a text to say that her uncle Vance was going to be there, so Reagan was dying to see how that was going. If she were Serenity, she'd pull him aside and ask about the past. He had to know something about what had happened—he was familiar with Rosalind, after all—and Reagan was becoming more and more convinced that they couldn't solve the mystery without help. But she had to be patient. Serenity was in a difficult situation, had to be careful about her parents' marriage.

When she didn't pick up, Reagan sent her a message. Anything?

Serenity didn't respond to that, either, so Reagan assumed she didn't have her phone with her. Rally was with his son; they'd gone to a Yankees game together. Lorelei was out to dinner with Mark. Finn had his "girl-friend" over. Nolan was in Truckee at work, and she didn't have a relationship with Davis that was separate from the one she had with Finn.

Which left her on her own with Lucy for a couple of hours until Lucy went to bed.

Since Lucy didn't need her at the moment, she considered calling her mother. They'd finally spoken a few times, just recently. But neither she nor her mother had mentioned her father again. Each conversation had been brief and perfunctory.

Her mother had stopped asking about her job—thank God—but the subtext of "What the hell are you doing with your life?" was always there, just below the surface. Reagan hated that Rosalind wouldn't let down her guard and simply be approachable and transparent, but she'd been dealing with that same frustration her whole life and wasn't interested in running into the brick wall that stood between them yet again.

As soon as she finished her dinner, Lucy began to

play with a stuffed bear she'd brought from home, and Reagan took her into the living room, where the TV was, and got on her computer. She did a bit more work on Serenity's social media, in between helping Lucy put a little dress and some shoes on her bear. Then a cartoon on TV caught Lucy's interest, and Reagan opened Google. Even though she'd searched her father's name—well, Stuart Sands, who might or might not have been her father—several times in the past and nothing of interest had come up, she hadn't done the same for Vance Currington. Because Serenity knew him, it hadn't occurred to her that there might be more information about him online than Serenity already possessed. But since she was bored and growing impatient with the mystery, she typed "Vance Currington" into the search engine and was surprised by the number of links that popped up.

Most were the obituaries of men with the same name or a similar one, possibly relatives. Other listings were paid for by companies trying to sell background checks.

Reagan thought it might be wise to pay for a background check or even hire a private investigator. If they could find some proof that Vance had once lived in Cincinnati or discover a connection to Florida, where Lorelei was found, it might be worth it. Lorelei couldn't spend the money, and Serenity would be worried that having someone poking around in the past might threaten her mother. But Reagan could probably handle the entire expense herself and tell the PI to be discreet.

She was considering that possibility while she clicked the more obscure links that were several pages into her search. She didn't expect to find anything of note, but when she visited a site that mentioned education and job history for someone named Edward Vance Currington, she saw a long list of previous employers.

This could be the right Vance Currington—Serenity had mentioned that he couldn't keep a job.

Most of the companies she didn't recognize. None of them were in Cincinnati, anyway.

Assuming she'd hit another dead end, she moved the cursor back to the search box and typed in, "How to find a good private investigator." But just before she hit the enter key, something jumped out at her.

It was the name of an adoption agency.

32

serenity

What's your uncle's full name? It's not *Edward* Vance Currington, is it?

Serenity didn't receive Reagan's message until after she'd finished the dishes and said good-night. Her parents were still talking to Vance in the living room, but Beau had left, and as much fun as Vance was, Serenity wasn't interested in hearing about how he might be moving to Southern California to sell energy-efficient HVAC systems to the owners of large commercial buildings. She was much more intent on learning what he'd been doing thirty-five years ago.

Yes. He was named after my grandfather, why? she replied.

Reagan answered right away. Has anyone in the family ever mentioned an adoption agency called My Sweet Angel?

Serenity's blood ran cold. Instead of texting back,

she called Reagan. "What's going on? What makes you ask about an adoption agency?"

"You recognize the name?"

"No. I've never heard of it, but the fact that it's an adoption agency makes me uneasy."

"From what I can tell, your uncle used to work there—or he was associated with it in some way."

"What makes you think so?"

"I found it when I did a Google search of his name."

"*When* did he work there? Was it right before we were born?"

"I can't find any dates. The information isn't complete. I only discovered it because I read everything that came up."

Serenity shoved some pillows behind her back and leaned up against the headboard. "So maybe Vance *didn't* have an affair with our mothers. Maybe we were all adopted."

"That's what it looks like now."

She felt an avalanche of relief to hear something that suggested her mother *hadn't* cheated with her husband's brother. She felt she could take any other answer as long as it wasn't *that*. "But why would your mother adopt a child? You've said again and again that she's never been interested in kids, that she didn't really want you."

"I have no clue."

"And why wouldn't they tell us we were adopted? That's why we ruled it out. What reason could they have had to hide it?"

"I wish I knew," she said. "Can you read Vance's letter to me again?"

Serenity pulled it out of her purse. "'Dear Charlotte, I'm sorry I stood you up last night. Chuck dropped in unexpectedly. At first I thought he knew about the baby, that you must've broken down and told him. But he didn't say anything about it. You understand why you can't, right? Please promise me you'll never tell. Love, Vance.'"

"Now that I hear it again, it could be that he facilitated the adoption," Reagan mused.

"But if I was adopted, surely my father would know. So what could my uncle be referring to? What isn't my mother supposed to tell him?"

"Where Vance got you from?"

Serenity felt her pulse quicken. Here she was, trying to get a DNA test from her father, her brother and/or Uncle Vance. But maybe she didn't need it. If Vance had merely arranged for her parents to adopt a baby, a DNA test would only confirm that she came from two people who weren't Chuck or Charlotte—something she felt fairly safe assuming now that she knew Vance had worked for an adoption agency.

"That would mean I'm more related to you and Lorelei than I am to Beau and the twins," she said. "Or even my parents."

"And it would mean I'm not technically related to my mother."

"Wow." Serenity swallowed against a dry throat as she tried to absorb the implications.

"Are you still there?" Reagan asked when she didn't speak.

She sighed. "Yeah, I'm here. Have you done a search for My Sweet Angel?"

"I have. They're a private agency located in Atherton, California."

Atherton was an affluent area—and it was where her father and uncle had been raised. That had to be more than a coincidence. "They're still in business?"

"They are. Says here they've been around for forty-five years."

"Lucky for us. Maybe we'll be able to confirm that Vance once worked for them."

"I doubt they'll disclose that type of thing. Legally, I bet they can't."

"We could pretend he's applying for a job and that he used them as a reference."

"It's been too long. They may not even have employment records going back that far. Why would they?"

"True."

"Why don't you just *ask* him, Serenity?"

There had to be a reason this had been such a well-kept secret, a reason Uncle Vance had pleaded with her mother not to tell her father about "the baby." She was afraid to alert Vance to the fact that she was digging around in the past for fear he and her mother would close ranks and do what Rosalind had done—offer an alternate explanation, one she couldn't quite believe.

But he was probably already aware that the secret he'd been guarding was under attack. No doubt they'd tipped him off when Reagan had impersonated Rosalind on that call.

* * *

lorelei

A white-hot rage filled Lorelei as Francine approached the table. She was wearing a conciliatory expression, a pitiful expression in Lorelei's opinion, and her best dress.

She glanced uncertainly at Mark the second she saw

Lorelei's anger. Clearly she'd caught on that this was a mistake, but Mark beckoned her forward.

"I can't believe you'd blindside me like this," Lorelei said between clenched teeth as she turned to him.

"I'm not blindsiding you, I'm just trying—"

"Yes, you are," she broke in, "and you're doing it in a public place so I won't cause a scene."

"No, wait. You're getting it all wrong. Just hear me out." He raised his hands in a defensive gesture. "I would've told you she was coming, but I knew you wouldn't see her if I did. I spent a lot of money on her plane ticket, and she dropped everything to come here. We did it so we could *both* tell you that we love you and want to make this right."

"It doesn't matter how much you spent. There *is* no way to make it right." Lorelei stood up to leave, but Mark jumped up, too, and cut her off.

"Lorelei, *please*."

"I'm sorry, Lorelei, I really am," Francine said. "Before you go, think about what you're throwing away."

"What I'm *throwing away*?" Lorelei echoed. "I'm not throwing anything away. This was your doing, not mine. You destroyed my marriage, broke up my family and killed our friendship in one fell swoop. I can't think of anything my worst enemy could do that would be worse."

Francine flinched. "It was a stupid mistake—" she started, but Mark was speaking, too, and his voice was louder.

"I know she's a big part of why you won't come back to Florida right away," he said, "but we'll never be able to save our marriage, not if you can't forgive us both.

That's why I had her come—so you can see and hear for yourself how terrible she feels."

"I don't care how terrible she feels!" Lorelei retorted. "Don't you get it? I don't ever want to speak to her again. And I'm done with you, too. I will be the best ex-wife I can be. I'll let you see Lucy whenever I can manage it, and I'll be fair when it comes to splitting up our assets. But I won't stay married to you while you have a baby with the one person I trusted more than anyone else, other than you."

Tears rolled down Francine's face as Lorelei shoved past Mark and nearly bumped into the waiter who was coming to bring them water. But the claustrophobia that had plagued her since Mark told her about Francine was gone. So was all the questioning and the agonizing and the attempts to make herself accept what was, for her, unacceptable.

She did not have to let someone force her into an existence in which she'd be miserable. She would break free. And maybe she wouldn't have the future she'd always imagined—that was already gone—but at least she'd live on her own terms.

* * *

reagan

When Reagan spotted Lorelei on the side of the road, she expected her to be standing in a puddle of tears. She knew Francine had shown up without warning at the restaurant where Mark had taken her for dinner.

When Lorelei had called to tell her she'd walked out on them, she hadn't been gone from the cabin for long. That said it all.

But when Reagan pulled over in Finn's Jeep to pick her up, she found her sister dry-eyed.

"You're driving Finn's car?" Lorelei asked in surprise.

"He wasn't going anywhere tonight, so I asked if he'd mind. It made more sense than to pay for Ubers to take me to you, then take us to wherever we're going to have dinner and then take us back home. Especially because you might want to get wasted—and I wouldn't blame you—but I can't touch a drop, so I'm a great designated driver."

Lorelei climbed in and looked into the back seat. "Where's Lucy?"

"Finn insisted I leave her with him. I hope you don't mind. She's already had dinner, and I thought you'd be upset, so… I decided it would be better for her not to see you."

Lorelei closed her eyes as she leaned her head back. "I'm okay, but that was nice of you—and Finn."

Reagan hesitated before pulling back onto the road. Where were the tears? Why wasn't Lorelei falling apart? "Are you *sure* you're okay?"

Lorelei gave her a weary smile. "Yeah. Things aren't perfect, of course. But I'm better than I've been, and that's good enough for me."

"I'm blown away that you're handling this so well."

"Getting upset will only make it harder." She adjusted her seat belt as Reagan pulled back onto the road. "What was Finn doing tonight?"

Reagan thought she detected a trace of jealousy in Lorelei's voice. "Not much of anything. Nolan's at work. Davis is practicing tying his shoes—something Lucy is very interested in helping him with. That's what they were doing when I left."

"Davis doesn't mind Lucy's help?"

Reagan shrugged. "He's the one who asked for it."

They drove a few blocks before Lorelei said, "What about Finn's girlfriend? Hard to believe *she's* okay with Finn lending us his Jeep and taking care of my daughter."

"I have to admit she didn't seem pleased, but Finn didn't ask for her permission. I don't get the impression she has much say over what he does."

"And yet she's his girlfriend?"

Finn had treated Michelle more like an old friend when Reagan was there, despite the label Michelle had given their relationship. "My interpretation is that she'd *like* to be his girlfriend, but he wouldn't have shown so much concern over what was happening to you if he was in a relationship with her."

"I can see why she'd want him."

While they were stopped at the traffic light in the middle of town, Reagan peered at her sister more closely. "Do *you* want him?"

"Of course I do. But I can't have him. There are too many things working against us right now."

It was the maturity of that comment and the resolution she sensed in her sister that told Reagan Lorelei was going to recover. The next year would be hard; divorce was never easy. But Lorelei was making wise choices—for her and for Lucy. "Finn is special, and you never know. Maybe in a year or two things will work out," she said. "Now let's go eat some tacos and forget about our problems for an hour or so."

And when they were done? She'd tell Lorelei about My Sweet Angel and Vance Currington.

* * *

serenity

Serenity couldn't help dwelling on what she'd learned about the adoption agency. When everyone else was watching fireworks at the pier on Ocean Beach, which was where they'd ended up going to celebrate the Fourth, she was thinking how it might change their family if Beau and the twins found out she was adopted. It shouldn't have mattered to her. She was an adult. But rewriting the story of her life was difficult even at this age.

She would've let it stay a secret—let the past go and tried to forget about it. She'd known all along that she was holding a hand grenade, and she didn't want it to blow up in her face and hurt her family. But what she could potentially discover was Lorelei's best bet of plugging the gaping holes in her early life. Serenity couldn't just…stop.

Besides, she wanted to know why. Why she'd been adopted if her parents could have children. Why she'd been available for adoption in the first place. Why Chuck and Charlotte had decided not to tell her. Who her biological parents were. And how she and Reagan could come from the same father and be only six months apart. Physically that was possible, of course, but impregnating two different women in such a short span of time was still odd enough to make her wonder how it had all gone down.

There were still so many unanswered questions. Even the adoption agency lead hadn't been confirmed. It just made sense in light of everything else.

At one point, she asked Vance to tell her about some of the jobs he'd had over the years, and he'd mentioned a few, but he hadn't said anything about an adoption agency. If Chuck and Charlotte hadn't been around, Serenity might've been more direct, but he didn't give her the opportunity to get him alone. He visited with her parents the entire time he was in town. Then he left very early on Sunday morning, before the rest of them were up.

"You've sure been on your phone a lot this weekend," her mother complained while making breakfast.

Serenity *had* been texting quite a bit—with Reagan, Lorelei and Sawyer. They all wanted to know what was going on, if she'd learned anything. So far, she had nothing to tell them, but now that she could safely assume her mother hadn't been unfaithful to her father, she was willing to overcome her reservations and ask Charlotte for the truth.

Unfortunately, however, this wasn't a good time. She couldn't cause a big emotional scene right before Beau shared his news. Like her, he was leaving later today, so this would be his only chance, and she knew he didn't want to put it off any longer. Trevor was expecting to set a date. "Sorry," she said.

"No need to apologize. Who've you been talking to?" This was the perfect lead-in to tell Charlotte everything. But Beau walked into the kitchen, freshly showered and shaved and looking nervous as he poured himself a cup of coffee.

"Where's Dad?" he asked.

"In the shower," Charlotte said. "He'll be down in a minute."

The smell of bacon permeated the house. Her mother had cooked it in the microwave and was now frying eggs on the stove.

"Uncle Vance is gone?" Beau said.

Charlotte took a piece of toast out of the toaster and buttered it. "Yeah. He left a couple of hours ago."

Beau shot Serenity a look that said, *This is it*, and Serenity smiled. She knew her parents wouldn't care that he was gay, but it would come as a shock. He'd hidden it so well, had never let on.

"Morning," her father said when he finally joined them.

"Morning," Serenity replied and nudged Beau with her foot.

He put down his coffee. "Dad? Mom? Can you come over and sit down for a second?" he asked. "There's something I'd like to tell you."

* * *

lorelei

After a busy and emotional weekend, Lorelei was relieved to have Monday off. It hadn't been easy to get used to working again, but she was grateful to have a job. Earning a paycheck gave her a degree of independence, and that would be important, especially after what happened on Friday night. Mark had finally accepted that she wasn't coming back to him, but it had made him even angrier than she'd expected. Although she'd unblocked his number when he came to Tahoe so they could make arrangements for Lucy and so that she'd be accessible if anything went wrong, she'd had to block him again.

On Saturday, she and Lucy went with Reagan to see the fireworks instead of going with him because he'd sent a string of vile texts claiming she was the most unforgiving bitch he'd ever met and he'd make it as difficult as possible for her to get anything out of the divorce—as if she hadn't contributed to their marriage at all and was trying to steal something she didn't deserve.

Whether or not he could back up his threat of leaving her penniless, she didn't know. It was upsetting to think she could spend twelve years with him and it would come down to this. When he swung by to tell Lucy goodbye yesterday morning, he wouldn't even speak to her.

But Lorelei had expected her divorce to be a painful journey; she couldn't let the very first step cause her to falter. She was doing her best to cope with the fallout and to be grateful for what she *did* have. Lucy was the light of her life, and her two sisters were quickly becoming her best friends.

You'll survive, she told herself. He was gone now, which brought some relief, and Serenity was back. She hadn't been able to get a DNA sample from her father while she was in San Diego. Although she'd mentioned that it would be interesting for him to learn about his ancestors and could be helpful from a medical perspective, he'd told her he was concerned about the amount of information such places were accumulating and what they might do with it, which was an objection she hadn't been able to overcome. She *had*, however, convinced her brother to take one, in case it provided *some* information that might turn out to be pertinent. She'd mailed it off before leaving San Diego, which meant they'd have the results in early September.

At least that was hopeful. And spending the day with Lucy and her sisters on the beach was proving therapeutic.

"This is *so* relaxing," she murmured as the sun warmed her skin. They'd played in the water when they first arrived—had attempted to skip rocks even though they weren't nearly as good at it as Finn—and then Lucy had fallen asleep on a towel under their beach umbrella, which gave them a chance to lie out in the sun.

"I'll always remember this summer," Reagan said.

From the first, Lorelei had admired Reagan's beauty, but with all the time off work, the rest, the sun—maybe even the pregnancy—she looked healthy and vibrant as well as beautiful.

So did Serenity, even though she wasn't pregnant.

Raising herself up on one elbow, Serenity lifted her sunglasses as she scanned the horizon. "I'll never forget it, either."

Lorelei smiled. They'd all arrived with significant problems. Some of those problems lingered. Reagan didn't know how Drew was going to respond about the baby. They hadn't figured out how they'd come to be related and Lorelei still didn't know anything about her parents. But *everyone* had problems. Their time here had been a godsend. They'd gotten to know each

other on a level they couldn't have any other way—
had become real sisters—while staying in this beautiful place.

She wondered if she would've had the strength to
leave Mark had she not made the decision to spend the
summer here with Reagan and Serenity...

"We have a month and a half left," she said, determined not to face the end before she absolutely had to.

Reagan straightened her towel. "But it'll go fast, and
then we'll have to return to the real world."

Serenity put her sunglasses back in place and
dropped languidly onto the sand. "That'll be okay, because we will *always* be there for each other, no matter
where we are or what we're doing."

Lorelei tucked that promise away, knew she'd need
it to soothe the anxiety and fear that would inevitably
come later.

"And maybe we'll get invited to Beau's wedding,"
Reagan joked.

"I wouldn't rule it out," Serenity said. "Once my
parents learn about you, I know they'll be welcoming."

Lorelei's phone buzzed. She checked it to make sure
the restaurant wasn't shorthanded and texting her to
come in. But it wasn't from work. "Finn's asking if we'd
like to have dinner over at their place tonight. He's planning on making rice and teriyaki kabobs—steak for us
and tofu for you," she told Serenity.

"Will his girlfriend be there?" Reagan asked before
Serenity could respond.

"You mean his *ex*-girlfriend?" Lorelei said. "When
we were texting last night about how things were going
with Mark, he told me he's not with her and hasn't been
for a while." Maybe that was why she was feeling so

good today in spite of everything. She didn't have a future with Finn, but at least she knew he'd been sincere.

Reagan covered her eyes with one arm. "He might want to remind *her* of that."

"I'm sure she's gotten the point."

"So *will* she be there tonight?" Serenity asked.

"No, he told me she was leaving this morning. My guess is she's already gone."

Reagan sat up to put on another layer of sunblock. "That still leaves Davis."

"He's okay," Lorelei said. "I'm over what happened, and so is he."

"He's doing *so* much better these days," Serenity said. "When he met me to go kayaking early this morning, he was actually smiling. Smiling! *Davis!* And after we got back he thanked me for taking him out."

Lorelei removed the straw hat she'd been using to shade her face and sat up. "You took Davis kayaking this morning?"

"I've been taking him every morning. It wasn't anything I intended to do, but when I saw him out here one day I asked if he wanted to join me, and now he waits for me at dawn. It's gives us a chance to meditate before all the noise of living interrupts."

"Why didn't you mention it before?" Lorelei asked.

"I felt I'd be doing him a disservice if I told anyone. He was so fragile and skittish I was afraid he'd stop coming. And I could tell he needed it—that it was a kind of therapy for him. Now that I'm more confident he'll be okay, it seems safe to talk about it." She chuckled at herself. "Listen to me. I'm probably making too big a deal out of it, but...that's why I didn't say anything until now."

"What do you guys talk about?" Reagan asked, her curiosity obviously piqued.

Serenity's smile stretched wide below her big sunglasses as she turned her face back toward the sun. "That's just it. We don't talk about anything."

33

reagan

"Any word?"

Startled, Reagan glanced up to see Serenity coming out onto the deck where she was already sitting with her laptop. She hadn't been expecting Serenity to join her for another hour. She'd headed down a little earlier than usual because they were taking the boat out with the Hatch brothers as soon as Lorelei got off work, and she wanted to create and schedule several posts for Serenity's Facebook page before she had to watch Lucy.

"Not yet." She knew Serenity was asking about Drew. She'd been checking her email obsessively ever since she'd sent him that Voluntary Relinquishment of Parental Rights. Over the weekend, she'd told herself to be patient. He was probably celebrating the Fourth of July with his family and wouldn't respond until Monday.

But it was Tuesday morning and she still hadn't received any word from him. Why not? What was he waiting for? "What do you think his silence means?" she asked.

"That he's struggling with the decision."

"Or he's going to hang on to his rights."

"If he does, his wife is bound to find out."

Reagan tried to picture him as he usually was, clean-shaven and wearing an expensive suit and plenty of cologne. She'd always liked the touch of gray at his temples; it made him look distinguished. "True. He's probably feeling sorry for himself, even though I'm in a much worse position."

"You'd be better off if he walked away, Reagan," Serenity said. "I'm really hoping that's what he'll do."

Both options had a precipitous downside. "I'd just like to know one way or the other," she said. "I can't take the waiting. Should I call him?"

Serenity seemed to contemplate her answer as she set up her workstation. "I don't see why not," she finally said. "You don't have anything to lose."

As soon as she called his cell, Reagan felt so jittery she couldn't sit still. She'd been dealing with this situation for weeks, was beginning to accept the fact that she was going to have a child. At times, she even felt a little excited about it. It wasn't as though she was getting any younger. Maybe she'd be glad to have a baby. Maybe she'd love her child as much as Lorelei loved Lucy. While her sisters were sleeping and no one was around to see her, she often browsed ideas for nurseries online.

But she'd expected to hear from Drew by now, and the fact that she hadn't put her on edge. Was he in or was he out? It would help to know before she told her mother about the pregnancy. Breaking the news would be much easier if she had answers for the many questions Rosalind was bound to ask.

He answered as soon as the phone started to ring, and she closed her eyes. She didn't want to feel anything. Part of her hated him now. But there was still that inexplicable attraction. She'd felt it from the first moment they'd met.

She'd been beating herself up ever since she'd made the mistake that had put her in this position, but maybe it was fate. Maybe she'd been doomed from the start. "It's Reagan."

"I know."

"I haven't received the Voluntary Relinquishment of Parental Rights from you."

"Because I don't want to sign it."

She caught her breath. Did that mean what she thought it meant? "You're going to claim this child? Help me support him or her? Set up visitation? The whole nine yards?"

"Look, I don't see why it has to be all or nothing. I care about you, or we wouldn't be in this situation. Can't we work something out?"

That made her dubious. What wasn't he saying? "Like what?"

"Why don't we wait until you get back to New York? Then we can talk about our options."

"But I don't see how our options will change. Either you want to be a father to this baby or you don't. How is waiting until I come back to New York going to benefit either of us?"

He lowered his voice. "It's not that simple, Reagan. I already have a family."

"That's exactly why I sent you the release, Drew. I'm giving you an out. I'm willing to take full responsibility."

He sighed audibly. "Look, I can't talk right now. You know how crazy it is here at the office. Can I call you later?"

"When? Tonight, when you're at home with your wife?"

"Why do you have to make everything so difficult? I still want to be with you! I've told you that. I'm just trying to figure out how to make it work."

"Unless you get a divorce, there is no way to make it work."

"Why not? There's still a lot we could be to each other. You'd have a better life with me in it. Like I told you before, I'd be generous and…and not too restrictive, since you'd have to be flexible with me."

Flexible. She stiffened. "I won't be the other woman. I've told you that. Either you claim this child, which means your wife will find out about the baby—only fair, since your money is her money, too, and you'll have to pay child support—or you sign that paper I sent you and mail it back to me so you can go on your merry way."

"You don't understand what's at stake. You're asking me to walk away from my child, which I can't do. And I can't let her know about the baby, or she'll leave me and take half of everything I have. We're not talking pocket change here, Reagan. That's a couple of million dollars!"

Stunned, Reagan shook her head. He wasn't worried about anyone's happiness—not hers or his wife's, and certainly not that of his children. He was worried about the money a divorce would cost him. "Just sign it," she said flatly.

"I want to see you again first. If you still feel the same way afterward, *then* I'll sign it."

He thought he could break her down; he thought he was so irresistible that she'd soften with a little pressure. "Sign it and email it to me to show me that you have, then mail the hard copy to me or I'm calling your wife."

"You wouldn't…" he said.

"Try me," she responded. "You've got an hour."

Serenity was watching her with wide eyes when she hung up. "Yikes. That didn't go well."

Reagan no longer felt weak and shaky. She was too angry. "It's okay. I think it *did* go well."

"What do you mean?"

"He isn't half the man Rally is, and I'm lucky to be figuring that out early on."

"I agree. But…will you really call his wife if he doesn't email you the release?"

"If I have to."

The door opened and Lorelei stepped out. "What's going on?"

"I just talked to Drew."

Her expression changed from curiosity to concern. "And? Is he going to sign the paper?"

Reagan rubbed her forehead. "I'm giving him until after breakfast. And then we'll see."

"That's ominous."

"At least the waiting will be over."

"Would you like an omelet?" she asked. "The one thing I can do to make someone feel better is cook."

Reagan surprised herself by smiling. "And you're good at it. Where's Lucy?"

"She isn't awake yet. I came down to get a drink and saw the two of you out here wearing such intense expressions it scared me."

"If that offer stands for me, too, I'll take an omelet," Serenity told her.

Reagan was too nervous to eat. "Nothing for me," she said and paced around the deck the entire time Lorelei was in the kitchen.

When Lorelei appeared with two omelets, Reagan waited by the railing while they ate. Then as soon as her phone indicated it had been an hour, she checked her email.

"Anything?" Lorelei asked.

Reagan covered her mouth the second she saw her inbox.

"Is it there?" Serenity pressed.

Dropping her hand, Reagan nodded. "He signed it."

* * *

serenity

When Sawyer called her that night, Serenity slipped out of the living room, where Reagan and Lorelei were binge-watching a series on Netflix, and hurried up the stairs. She didn't want her sisters to hear her talking. She still hadn't told them she was seeing Sawyer. At first she'd held back because she wasn't sure she and Sawyer would ever really get together. And then, after she'd seen him right before she left for San Diego and again when he'd picked her up from the airport and taken her to lunch as she came back through, she'd kept her mouth shut because she was afraid she'd jinx the most wonderful thing to happen to her in a long time.

She wouldn't be able to keep their relationship a secret for much longer, though—not from Lorelei and Reagan. He was coming to the cabin on Friday. He wanted to see her, and she definitely wanted to see him.

"What are you doing tonight?" she asked as soon as she reached her room and closed the door.

"I just got my mail."

"Isn't that like telling someone you just washed your hair?" she joked, but he didn't laugh.

"Where does your mail go?" he asked. "Is it forwarded to you in Tahoe while you're away?"

"I'm having it forwarded, but I haven't checked it in a week. Almost everything comes via email these days, so I keep forgetting. Why?"

"I got a letter from Sean."

A prickle of foreboding ran down her spine. She'd finally stopped thinking about her ex-husband and didn't want to be reminded of him. "What does he have to say?"

"Nina must've told him she found me at your house, because he's accusing me of stealing his wife, and he's telling me I'd better leave you alone."

"Or…?"

"He doesn't say what he'll do if I don't go along with that."

She sank onto the bed. "Are you going to listen?"

"Hell, no."

"Maybe you should."

"I can handle it," he said. "I'm not afraid of Sean. I just don't want him harassing *you*."

Even if he felt he could handle it, it had to be upsetting to get a letter like that from a brother. "If he wrote me, I don't have it yet, but it could be waiting out in the mailbox."

"If there *is* a letter from him, don't open it. I'll open it this weekend when I get there."

"Why don't I just throw it away? Then neither of us has to see it."

"Because we should keep his letters. If he goes too far, I'll take them to the police."

Sawyer had been looking out for her ever since she'd had to turn Sean in. She felt such gratitude for that—and she was starting to feel a lot more. "Have you heard from anyone else in the family?"

"I got a call from Felix. He was pissed off, too. But that was right after Nina showed up at your place, which means it's been a while."

"Why didn't you tell me?"

"You hadn't called, and I didn't know if you would. I thought it might be a moot point."

Dropping back onto the bed, she stared up at the ceiling. "What if they won't leave us alone, Sawyer?"

"They will," he said confidently. "They just need to get used to the idea. Then it won't be news anymore. Everything will be okay."

She massaged her forehead while she tried to come up with the best approach to the rest of her life. "This is costing you so much. Are you sure I'm worth it? It's not too late if you'd rather back out."

"I'm not backing out."

"Because…"

"Because I've never felt like this about anyone else."

He wasn't the type of man who'd normally reveal something like that. Those words, spoken in his deep voice, felt like a caress. "Okay, that makes it all better."

"Are you being sarcastic?"

"Not at all."

"Then that was easy," he said with a laugh. "What are you and your sisters doing tonight?"

"Watching TV."

"Have you called your mom? Asked her about that adoption agency?"

"I haven't. My brother just told them he's getting married. I can't come crashing into the most exciting time of Beau's life like a wrecking ball."

"So how long will you wait? Until after the wedding?"

She pictured her brother's face—how relieved and excited he'd been when her parents had immediately hugged him and reassured him that he couldn't disappoint them simply by marrying the person he loved, regardless of that person's gender. "I might have to. We'll see, once they set the date."

"I guess you've waited this long…"

"Now that I'm so happy, I'm tempted to leave well enough alone." This was something she could admit to him but not to her sisters, which was why she let herself say it. But she should've anticipated his response.

"Why are you so happy?"

She almost made up some pretext to avoid having to tell him the truth. But he was largely the reason; he deserved the credit. "Because of you."

There was a brief silence. Then he said, "I'm going to marry you one day. You know that, right?"

After what she'd been through, this declaration should've terrified her. But it didn't. A wave of excitement rushed through her. "We just started dating. How can you be sure?"

"I've known since I first saw you sitting in that courtroom wearing that black dress and looking broken and terrified but *so* determined."

She closed her eyes, wishing she was in his arms right now. He'd believed Sean was guilty, yes, but now she knew her mother had been right—that wasn't the only reason Sawyer had been sitting behind her day in and day out during the trial. "I'm glad you're finally letting me in on the secret," she said.

After they hung up, she went back downstairs to tell her sisters.

She was starting to trust Sawyer—to trust her feelings for him and his feelings for her.

That was what she'd needed; now she was ready to break the news.

* * *

lorelei

The rest of July and the first week of August passed in a summery haze of working, boating, rock-skipping, talking, laughing, making meals (since she liked to cook more than anyone else, she did most of the cooking), eating, playing board games and taking long walks, hikes or scenic drives with her sisters. Sawyer came up every weekend and usually at least one Hatch brother was over at the cabin or joined them no matter what they were doing.

Ironically, as close as she'd become to Finn when she first arrived in Tahoe, Lorelei had gotten to know Davis and Nolan and loved them every bit as much. She felt like she'd not only gained two sisters but three brothers as well, and despite the difficulty of dealing with Mark, who'd informed her that he was going to marry Francine as soon as their divorce was final, she was happier than she'd ever been, even though she hoped to find someone else one day herself.

Even if that didn't happen, she knew Reagan and Serenity would stand behind her in good times and bad in a way that poor Osha and Mercedes weren't capable of doing, and she'd be lifelong friends with Finn, Nolan and even Davis, who was beginning to impress them all with what he could accomplish using only one hand.

All six of them were talking about coming back next summer—and Sawyer had agreed that he'd be there on weekends. Lorelei had no idea how she'd get the time off, since she had to find a job as soon as she returned to Orlando and would presumably be working, or what she'd have to concede to Mark, but this summer had been so precious—valuable in a way few things were. She wasn't going to miss the chance to spend another three months with these people and to get to know Reagan's baby.

She'd found her family—although, as the days passed she couldn't stop wondering if she'd been adopted when she was born. If she was tied to Serenity's uncle Vance, and he was connected to an adoption agency, there was certainly the possibility. And if that was the case, maybe it was her adopted mother who'd lost or abandoned her and her birth mother was still out there.

Would it be possible to find her? Would she be interested in meeting?

And if an adoption had occurred, where was the

woman who'd taken her in? Where had she gone? What happened when Lorelei was two?

As grateful as Lorelei was to have found her sisters, her new best friends, those questions nagged at her. She'd drifted about like a tumbleweed, blown this way and that, her whole life—until Mark, and then he'd sent her tumbling again with a mighty shove. She craved roots, or at least knowledge, so she could fill in the blanks. And while Serenity couldn't bother her family during the preparations for her brother's wedding, which was at the end of September, there was no reason Lorelei couldn't visit My Sweet Angel Adoption Agency herself—while she still had time in California—to see if she couldn't find a thread of truth that would unravel the whole mystery.

"Serenity tried calling them. They can't give out any information, remember?" Reagan barely looked up from her computer when Lorelei presented the idea to her early on a Friday morning. Lucy had gotten up as soon as the sun started to rise and dragged them out of bed. She was watching cartoons in the living room and Serenity was out kayaking with Davis. The two of them still did that most mornings.

"I remember, but I'm not planning to ask them for the name of my birth mother. I know they won't give me that. I'm planning to ask them for the name of my *adoptive* mother."

Reagan, who'd been shopping for baby clothes and furniture—something she'd begun to do openly when she wasn't talking on the phone or texting with Rally— closed her computer. "Of course! Why wouldn't they give you *that*? Your adoptive mother shouldn't be a secret."

"Exactly."

"Except… I'm guessing they won't even be able to admit that you were adopted through their agency."

Maybe she hadn't been adopted at all. They were guessing at all this, trying to piece it together.

Still, it made sense as a possibility and was worth a shot. "Technically, they probably shouldn't. But it's a business run by *people*, right? Surely they'll see that my situation is unique—and have some empathy, for God's sake. And if we can confirm they handled *my* adoption, chances are really high they handled yours and Serenity's, too."

"True. But even if they do have some empathy, they might not be willing to break the rules. They might be too afraid of getting in trouble—losing their license or whatever."

"This isn't a recent adoption we're talking about. It's been so long—for all of us. I can't imagine they'd have to guard the information so fiercely after that much time. Anyway, it's worth a try. We only have three weeks left of summer. If I'm going to pursue this, I need to get on it, and I happen to have the day off. I'm going down there. Any chance you'd like to go with me? I bet Serenity would let us take her Beamer."

"What about Lucy? We can't leave her with Serenity—she's got to meet her writing quota for the day."

"I'm thinking of asking Davis. I really don't think he'd mind. They've become so close lately." Davis played with Lucy whenever they were together.

"Okay. Serenity can take over when she's done. But Sawyer will be coming up tonight. It's Friday."

"We should be back by then. Even if we're not, I

doubt it would bother him to have Lucy with them for a short while."

They both looked up as Serenity walked in from outside wearing her cutoff wetsuit. "What are you two doing up so early?"

"Lucy woke us at the crack of dawn," Reagan said.

A sheepish expression descended on Serenity's face. "Sorry. Maybe I was too loud when I went out."

"It doesn't matter. It's good that we're getting an early start," Lorelei said and told her about their plans.

"Do you think it's worth the drive?" Reagan asked Serenity when Lorelei was finished.

"I do," Serenity replied. "If you don't try, you'll always wonder. I'm happy to take over for Davis and watch Lucy after lunch, and you can take the X5."

"I'll wait in the car while she goes in," Reagan said. "It'll be less threatening and more sympathetic if she's alone. I'm just going to keep her company."

"Fingers crossed," Serenity said. Then Reagan smiled conspiratorially and Lorelei couldn't help laughing.

"Let's do this." She got to her feet, but before she could head up to shower and dress, Serenity caught her by the wrist.

"Even if you never find the answers you're searching for, you'll always have us," she said.

34

reagan

It was a total bust, Reagan wrote to Rally as she rode with Lorelei back up a winding Interstate 80 to the turn-off for Incline Village.

What happened?

Nothing. Lorelei went in, but they claimed they didn't have records going that far back, that they couldn't help her. She tried to plead her case, but they just gave her a list of resources for adopted children who are seeking their birth parents.

You don't believe them?

No. I think they get hit up a lot, and they have a standard response, which they give to protect their business.

Is she upset?

Disappointed. So am I.

What's next?

We wait for the DNA results, and if they don't tell us anything, Serenity talks to her mother after the wedding. I might try to approach mine again, too, once I'm home. I can tell her I've been doing some research and hit her with Vance's name and the name of the adoption agency. Maybe she'll break down and tell me the truth if she thinks I'm going to find it on my own, anyway.

The way you've described your mother? I wouldn't bet you could break her down that easily.

She chuckled, and Lorelei, who was behind the wheel, glanced over at her. "What's Rally saying?"

"He feels bad that we couldn't get what we were hoping for, but he doesn't think my mother will ever provide any solid information."

"Do you?" she asked.

"I'm not optimistic about it, but I'm willing to give it a try. If the DNA doesn't turn up anything, and Serenity and I can't get anywhere, maybe we should consider hiring a private investigator."

She frowned. "I can't afford that. Mark is already giving me fits, and I can't even begin to guess what kind of job I'll be able to find when I return to Florida."

With her own job situation up in the air, Reagan realized it probably wasn't wise for her to pay an investigator, either. She needed her money to last a year, until the baby was a few months old. She couldn't really attack the job market before then. "It's an option, anyway. For the future. I mean...who knows? You've been talking about creating your own cookbook. Maybe you'll do that, and you'll make millions."

"You never know," she said, but Reagan could tell she wasn't too optimistic.

"How are you feeling toward Mark these days?"

She took a moment before responding. "I try to remember that he has his good points."

"But you're not getting along with him or Francine?"

"Not right now. She's turned on me, too."

"Let them have each other. I doubt it'll last, even if they get married."

"I suspect they're already living together."

"Because Mark's a cheap bastard," Reagan said. "He probably wanted her to help make the mortgage payment."

"I wouldn't put it past him," Lorelei said. Then they talked about Rally and how much Reagan was coming to like him.

"It's going to feel weird when I finally see him again," she said.

"Why?"

"I've only ever seen him once."

"But you've come to know each other so well."

"I like that we started our relationship this way. We really have gotten to know each other." She put a piece of gum in her mouth. "But I'll be showing a month or two after I get home. You don't think it'll be weird to be dating while I'm pregnant?"

"If Rally doesn't mind, why would you?"

"I guess you're right."

Lorelei turned down the air-conditioning. "You're getting excited about the baby. I can tell."

A smile tugged at Reagan's lips. "Yeah. I can't imagine what it'll be like to have a baby come into my life, to care for someone so fragile and beautiful, someone who'll be completely dependent on me. It scares me and feels kind of cool at the same time."

"Wait until you've gained forty pounds and your feet start to swell," Lorelei said.

"Gee, thanks—buzzkill."

They laughed and the conversation moved on to the Hatch brothers, how lucky they were to have met them and then how perfect Sawyer was for Serenity. She never even mentioned Sean anymore.

"Thanks for going with me today," Lorelei said as they pulled into the garage.

They were both in a good mood, despite having wasted their entire day. "No problem. It was fun."

Because they'd been held up by traffic and returned much later than they'd planned, Serenity had texted Lorelei to let her know she was going out to dinner with Sawyer and had taken Lucy back to Finn's.

Since Lorelei went to get Lucy, Reagan was alone when she went inside. Sawyer's truck was parked out front, so she knew he and Serenity hadn't left yet. She expected to see them, but she wasn't expecting to interrupt such a highly charged conversation.

"I don't think we should open it," Serenity was saying. "Why let him upset us?"

Reagan put down her purse and glanced between them. "What's going on?"

They looked over, and Sawyer lifted an envelope he held in one hand. "I went out to get the mail, and this was there."

"It's from Sean," Serenity said.

Reagan could see there wasn't a return address on it. "How do you know?"

"She *thinks* it must be Sean, because he's been writing me," Sawyer said. "But if it was, there'd be a stamp to indicate it came from a correctional institution."

"It could be from Thomas or Felix—or even Sean's mother," Serenity said. "It doesn't *have* to be from Sean in order to upset us."

"It's addressed to you," Sawyer said. "So I won't read it if you don't want me to. But I wish you'd let me. If this is another one of his threats, I plan to take care of it."

"I can't stand the idea of pitting you against your family again," she said. "They're being such assholes. Why allow them to ruin our weekend?"

When he hesitated in spite of what she'd said, she walked over and kissed him. "Please?" she said softly. "I've been looking forward to having you here all week. Don't give them any power."

"Okay," he said, but with obvious reluctance.

Serenity took the letter and tossed it in the garbage can, but as soon as they left, Reagan couldn't resist fishing it out. She was thinking it had better *not* be from anyone in Sean's family, and they'd better not be threatening Serenity or Sawyer. She was going to insist on getting the police involved, if they had.

When she opened the envelope and pulled out the letter, she was assuming she'd feel angry and defensive. Then she'd get rid of it so that Serenity wouldn't have to see it, since she didn't want to know what it said.

But what she read wasn't anything like she'd expected. "Holy shit," she murmured as soon as she realized what it was and what it meant.

Her hand was shaking so badly she almost dropped her phone when she called Serenity. "Can you come back?"

"What's wrong?" Obviously Serenity had heard the breathless quality in Reagan's voice; Reagan's heart was racing so fast she could barely speak.

"You have to see this," she said. "You and Lorelei both."

* * *

serenity

Serenity could feel Sawyer beside her as she stared down at the photocopy of an old newspaper clipping Reagan had handed her. "What's this?"

"It's what was in that envelope."

"You opened the letter from Sean?"

"I have no clue who sent it, but I'm guessing it wasn't Sean."

Lorelei had arrived. Serenity could hear her urging Lucy to hurry up the stairs. "But this is old news. It's from—" she checked the date on the article; she had that even though she could see only a few letters of the newspaper's name "—thirty years ago. Why would—"

The headline sank in, and she fell silent. "Priest Gets Forty Years for Sex Crimes."

"What's going on?" Lorelei asked as she came into the room. "What's the emergency?"

Serenity's tongue felt like sandpaper against the roof of her mouth. "Someone sent me a copy of this newspaper article. It's about a priest—a Father Greenstone—convicted of having sexual relationships with the young women in his parish. In one instance the girl was only fifteen, another two were seventeen and one was eighteen. There's a quote in here from one of the victims, although the reporter doesn't give her name. She said she loved him, expected him to leave the priesthood and marry her."

Lorelei looked confused. "He abused his position, took advantage of these young girls while he was pretending to be a man of God. How tragic. But what does that have to do with us?"

"Possibly everything."

"What?" Lorelei said.

Serenity held up her hand as she read the article. "He was in the Bay Area, but when the church started receiving complaints about him, they sent him to Cincinnati."

"Oh, my God!" Lorelei cried.

Serenity looked from Lorelei to Reagan. "This son of a bitch priest must be our father—or someone thinks he is."

They gaped at each other for several seconds, too shocked to speak.

"When you're done, let me see it," Sawyer murmured and Serenity handed him the paper with the article as she sank into a chair at the kitchen table. Her legs had gone rubbery; she was afraid she'd fall.

"It doesn't say anything about Florida," he pointed out as though that might leave some hope.

Serenity struggled to gather her splintered thoughts. "That doesn't mean anything. We don't know that Lorelei was *conceived* in Florida, or even born in Florida—only that she was found there."

Sawyer still seemed skeptical. "But your uncle handled the adoptions for an agency here in California."

"So?"

"So how could Reagan be adopted in Cincinnati?"

At first Serenity thought he had a point. She assumed what she was piecing together *couldn't* be the truth. But when she considered how desperate the church would've been to bury the scandal, she changed her mind. "If I was the church, I'd work with only one agency. The fewer people who know, the better."

"That's true," Sawyer agreed. "I guess he could've called an agency in Cincinnati and worked with them to place Reagan. He could easily have done the same with Lorelei."

"So this…priest, Father Greenstone, who had sex with those young girls in his parish—you think he got some of them pregnant?" Lorelei said. "That you, Reagan and I are the result of those pregnancies?"

Serenity was so busy examining the puzzle from all angles, trying to determine if the picture coming together in her mind was actually possible, it took her a moment to respond. "That's what this indicates to me."

Sawyer spoke up again. "The timing is right. This says he was convicted thirty years ago, which means he was free the years before that to prey on the young women he came into contact with. And instead of calling the authorities, the church moved him. That's what they did back then, to avoid the publicity."

"But Lorelei's two years younger than we are," Reagan said. "Moving him didn't help. He must've done the same thing at least once more."

"And the church probably paid off the mothers and got rid of the babies," Sawyer said. "Vance must've known who his client was, and he told your mother."

Reagan's forehead creased. "That's what I don't get. Why would he tell her?"

"She could've demanded more information," Sawyer replied. "Or he thought he could confide in her. It would be pretty scandalous news, and let's face it—scandalous news is always the hardest to keep a lid on. Once he opened his mouth, maybe he regretted it. Hence the letter."

"If word got out, it would've cost him his job," Serenity said.

"But he'd be more likely to tell his brother, wouldn't he?" Lorelei asked.

Serenity shook her head. "My father would've gone to the police or the press. I know him—and so does Vance. I can see why he didn't do that."

"If this is all true, we're the product of...what? Rape?" Lorelei was still trying to grasp it all.

"This doesn't read like it was forced," Sawyer replied. "Father Greenstone got into relationships with these girls."

"So it was statutory rape."

"Looks that way."

Lorelei's eyebrows slid up. "*That's* what connects us?"

Serenity touched her arm. As shocked and sad as she was for herself, she felt worse for Lorelei. Lorelei hadn't had a Chuck and Charlotte to take over and raise her. She hadn't even had a Rosalind. "It does explain everything—why Reagan's mother never told her she was adopted, and why my mother didn't tell me."

"A lot of children know they were adopted and don't know anything about their birth parents," Lorelei said.

"Maybe my mother didn't know," Reagan said. "My father could've arranged it."

"That's possible," Serenity allowed. "But even if she did know, I'm betting she couldn't tell you. So many adopted children try to find their birth parents. If I was the church, I'd make non-disclosure a stipulation."

Lorelei took the paper that had the copy of the newspaper article. "But…who could've sent this?"

Serenity showed her the envelope. "According to the cancellation on the stamp it was mailed from San Francisco last week. That was what made me think it came from the Alstons and must be an attack on Sawyer and me. They live in the Bay Area."

"Maybe your uncle Vance sent it to you," Reagan said.

"What would he be doing in the Bay Area?" Lorelei asked.

Serenity was about to say she didn't know, when the answer hit her so hard she jumped out of her chair. "My father!"

"Your father?" Lorelei echoed. "What would make you think it was him?"

"He was in the Bay Area on business last week. His office used to be in San Francisco. My mother mentioned that he went up to meet with an old client, but it was just for the day, so he never said anything about it himself. He probably doesn't even know I was aware of the trip."

"You asked your father to take a DNA test. Could he have begun to suspect that you know you're not his?" Sawyer asked.

Lorelei looked confused. "Wait. I thought he didn't know about the secret to begin with."

"He must've figured it out," Serenity said. "Or my mother finally told him, possibly years later, after Greenstone was already in prison."

"That makes sense," Sawyer said. "Your parents have been together for a long time. He must know by now. And

I can't imagine he'd want you to find out that you were adopted without having you understand why they didn't tell you—that they were keeping the terms of their agreement while also trying to protect you from the stigma."

"But he doesn't want to start a big thing in the family right now, with my brother's wedding coming up," Serenity agreed.

"Yes. Think about it," Reagan said. "This leaves the knowledge in your hands. You can decide if you want to tell Beau and the twins or not. Hard as it is to learn that we came from such a terrible set of circumstances, the way your father handled it is very classy. He knew you were beginning to question, and he relieved your need to know without involving anyone else, without opening a dialogue that could tear your whole family apart."

"But why wouldn't he just pull you aside and have a talk with you?" Lorelei asked.

"In case I'm *not* questioning. If I didn't know, I wouldn't understand what this article means. I'd toss it, and that would be the end of it. It's not as if I came out and asked him. I acted as though nothing had changed."

"Maybe it's not him," Sawyer said.

Tears gathered in Serenity's eyes, making it difficult to read when she pulled out her phone and scrolled down her list of favorites for her dad's name. She knew in her heart it *was* him, but she had to be sure.

"What are you doing?" Lorelei asked in alarm.

She sniffed as she struggled to hold back her emotions. "Double-checking."

They all watched with worried expressions, as though she was disarming a bomb. She supposed she *was* disarming a bomb—an emotional one. But she had to know if the answers they'd come up with were the truth.

Thank you for the article, she texted.

She could tell they were all holding their breath as they awaited his response.

When it came, the tears filling Serenity's eyes spilled down her cheeks. Her father didn't say a word about the article or why he'd done what he'd done. He said: I have always loved you, and I will always love you. How you came into my life means nothing to me. I'm just glad you're here.

After a few seconds, she said, "It *was* the priest. We are the result of three different women being victimized by the same man."

Reagan plopped down on the couch. "Shit."

"Wow. We knew so little for so long. And now…" Lorelei shook her head. "I have no idea how to feel."

"Neither do I," Serenity said. "It wasn't the answer we were hoping for, but at least we know." She felt Sawyer rubbing her back as her sisters came over to embrace her.

* * *

lorelei

The last weeks of summer were spent accepting the most probable story she could construct of her birth and adjusting to that knowledge. She'd wanted to know where she came from, even if it was hard to hear, and now she felt she did. There was a certain peace in having even a small amount of resolution. But she still wondered what'd happened to the poor girl who'd been her birth mother, whether the priest who'd gotten into a relationship with her was still in prison, and who had adopted her. If her story was the same as Reagan's and Serenity's, where were her adoptive parents when she'd been found wandering in the street?

She was tempted to go back to the adoption agency and demand they give her more information. If she'd been adopted and it had happened through that agency, they must have an entire file on her.

But she doubted it would do her any good. When she'd driven down the last time, they'd been polite but immovable. And she was so busy working, taking care of Lucy and enjoying Tahoe—while dreading the moment she would have to return to Florida and confront Mark and Francine and her divorce—that she didn't want to spend the last of her time being unsatisfied.

She promised herself she would hire a private detective as soon as she had the money and find out for sure. Now that she could provide a PI with a likely place to start, he or she should be able find out more.

But right now she'd be grateful for what she had— *some* information and the love and support of her two sisters. At least they'd figured out how they'd come to be related. She'd be able to unravel the rest with time— she hoped. Maybe she'd find out she had even *more* siblings. She, Reagan and Serenity had certainly discussed the possibility.

On her last day of work, she was eager to pick up Lucy and head to the lake. She hated that she had to fly home on Sunday—only three days from now—but it was time.

The manager and the other employees at the Blue Bayou had purchased a farewell cake and some balloons to let her know they were going to miss her. That was so thoughtful, she was still smiling and thinking about how much she hated to leave this place and everyone she'd met here when she walked out of the restaurant.

She'd been riding Serenity's bike to avoid tying up their only car, so she was surprised to see the X5 idling in the parking lot with both Serenity and Reagan inside it.

"What's going on?" she asked the second she opened the back door.

"Throw your bike on the rack," Serenity said. "We're taking you to dinner."

"Where's Lucy?"

Reagan rolled down her window. "She's swimming with Finn, so she's in good hands."

"But… I'm in my uniform. If we're going out, shouldn't I go home and change?"

"This isn't that kind of night. We have something we want to talk to you about. We were thinking we'd just get a burger and a shake at The Burger Shack. Do you mind going in your uniform?"

"Not to The Burger Shack." Feeling slightly anxious about what her sisters might have to say, she loaded her bike and climbed into the back seat. "What do you want to talk about?"

Neither Serenity nor Reagan spoke right away. "We'll tackle that when we get there, okay?" Serenity said at length.

Lorelei's excitement over the party her coworkers

had thrown her dimmed as they drove to The Burger Shack, placed their order and found an outdoor table that was well away from where anyone else was sitting. "You two are so somber," she said. "You're scaring me."

Reagan scooted forward. "I'm sorry. We don't mean to scare you. It's just…well, we tried to do something nice for you and…we were successful, in a way. But we aren't quite sure how you'll react."

"The last thing we want to do is make anything worse for you," Serenity added.

"I believe that," Lorelei said. "So what's this about?"

Reagan nudged Serenity. "You explain."

"It's about your adoptive mother," Serenity said.

Lorelei sat up straighter. "Don't tell me you've found her!"

They exchanged another glance. Again, it was Serenity who spoke. "We have. Sort of."

"How?"

"I asked my father to talk to Vance."

"And—"

"That was a dead end. Vance didn't handle your adoption. He couldn't tell us anything. But it made my father eager to help, and he hired a private investigator who's uncovered a few key pieces of information."

"You're kidding! That's so kind of you. I don't even know what to say."

"We're happy to help. But…about what he found."

"What is it?" she asked.

Reagan jumped back in. "Only eighteen months after Bernard Greenstone—the priest who…did what he did to our birth mothers—was sent to Cincinnati, the church relocated him again."

"Not to Florida…"

"No, they sent him to Mississippi, where he was finally arrested. That's where he used his position to prey on the youngest of his victims."

Lorelei's whole body began to tingle. "Which means… what?"

"It means that he impregnated another girl while he was there. It might even have been her parents who blew the whistle on him, although we haven't been able to verify that."

"So *was* I adopted? Is that where it happened?" Lorelei asked, grasping at the hope this information implied.

"Yes," Serenity said. "And the PI my father hired managed to get the names of your adoptive parents."

"No way!"

Serenity had won the lottery with her parents. Lorelei couldn't believe how lucky she'd been—but at least Lorelei had won the lottery when it came to sisters. "Who were my adoptive parents?"

"Their names were Mitch and Sarah Ryan."

Names! Information, at last! "And? Do you know anything about them?"

"A little," Serenity replied. "They divorced thirty-one years ago, only a year or so after they adopted you. The PI can't find your father. He thinks he returned to Canada, where he was from."

The burgers, fries and shakes were ready, but Lorelei could barely hear the teenager calling out, "Alston?" Serenity and Reagan didn't react, either, so he brought the food to them.

Ignoring the interruption, Serenity caught Lorelei's hands and held them tight. "Your adoptive mother was murdered, Lorelei. The PI found an article about her body being discovered by a nature enthusiast in a swamp in Florida."

Murdered... It sounded like something that could only happen on TV. "Who killed her?"

"No one knows," Reagan said. "The case has never been solved."

"But why couldn't they—the cops—ever connect me to her?"

"She'd just moved there. She was so new no one realized she had a child. When she was murdered, you must've gotten out of the house somehow. The killer might even have let you out. That's why you were found wandering in the street, and why your mother and father never searched for you."

Lorelei sat in stunned silence. "Didn't I have grandparents?" she asked when she could speak.

"We don't know yet," Serenity said. "But I'm guessing you didn't—at least not grandparents who were alive and well or invested in their daughter's life at that point."

"The police claim they did what they could to find your mother's killer, but there were no good leads," Reagan said.

"Her body wasn't found until you would've been six," Serenity added, picking up from there. "By then there were just bones. It's no wonder the two incidents—a lost child and a murdered woman—were never connected."

Lorelei sat numbly. Her mother hadn't abandoned her? That thought brought such tremendous relief, and an upwelling of warmth, as though someone had wrapped her in a blanket.

But she was shocked and hurt that some stranger could rob her of the life she might've had.

It wasn't until a tear dropped off her chin that she realized she was crying.

"I bet she loved you as much as you love Lucy."

When Reagan said that, Lorelei closed her eyes and let those words soothe the hurt. "I was lucky to have survived," she said. "My poor mother."

"It's so sad, what happened to her," Reagan agreed.

"How did the private investigator find what he did?" Lorelei asked.

"He wrote a letter to Father Greenstone, for one."

"The priest is still alive?"

"He's still in prison but—and this is a chilling thought—he's scheduled to get out next year."

"I can't say I'm looking forward to knowing he's out there, walking around. Will either of you go see him?"

"Not me," Reagan said.

Serenity shook her head. "I have nothing to say to him, either."

"What about your father?" Reagan asked. "Will you try to find him?"

She took a moment to mull it over, to imagine what it might be like to locate Mitch Ryan. Would it even be possible? Was he still in Canada? Would he be happy to hear from her? He'd been part of her life for such a short time. But he might be able to tell her more about Sarah, and her thirst for answers was still strong. "I might."

"Maybe he'll give you information if nothing else," Serenity said as though reading her mind.

"Yes." The smell of the food finally registered, and Lorelei stuffed a French fry in her mouth. "It's good to know all this," she said once she'd swallowed. "What you've both done—and your father, too, Serenity. That you'd all go to so much trouble and expense is beyond generous." Although her voice softened with emotion, she tried to keep it as strident as possible. "Thank you."

Reagan's eyes grew glassy from unshed tears. "You're worth it," she mumbled.

"I'm just sorry we couldn't learn more," Serenity added. "But at least this is a start."

Reagan pulled her burger in front of her. "There's one more thing…"

Lorelei, hungrier than she'd realized, grabbed her burger, too. "What is it?"

"Do you want to tell her?" Reagan asked Serenity.

Serenity took a drink of her shake before meeting Lorelei's eyes. "With your permission, I'd like to write our story."

"Seriously? You mean like…it'll be your next book?"

"If you're okay with that. I already talked to my editor, and she was very interested, because I'd have such a unique perspective."

"And since you just turned in *All Gone*, you're available."

"Exactly."

"That's wonderful! Of course it's fine with me. Maybe…maybe you'll be able to dig up more." The few details she'd learned answered questions she'd had her whole life, but they also raised more.

"That's what I'm hoping, too. I know how much you must want to know what really happened to your mother. I can't promise my involvement will amount to a whole lot, but I'll do everything I can to convince the police to reopen the file. Who knows? Maybe with the advances they've made in DNA testing, they'll be able to find your adoptive mother's killer one day."

Although Lorelei was happy, she was also close to tears. "Just hearing you say that gives me goose bumps."

epilogue

reagan

It was a cold, snowy day in New York when Reagan's water broke. The baby was coming, but she was ready. She had her nursery all prepared, and both Serenity and Lorelei had come to town for the birth—Serenity from Berkeley, although she'd sold her house there and now lived with Sawyer, and Lorelei from Florida. Mark had Lucy this week, so Reagan wouldn't get to see her little niece, whom she missed so much, but she figured that was for the best since it would've been hard to have Lucy at the hospital.

"Are you doing okay?" Serenity fed her ice chips. The doctor wouldn't allow her to have anything else.

"No," she said bluntly. The labor pains were getting stronger. She was beginning to understand just how difficult this process was going to be. "Tell me again that it'll all be over soon," she said to Lorelei.

Lorelei stood on the other side of the bed and held her hand. "It *will* all be over soon," she repeated dutifully. "You're doing great."

"I'm not doing anything but suffering," she said. "Can I really take credit for that?"

"It's just one of the encouraging things people say," Lorelei told her. "But now that you mention it, that does sound pretty lame. The truth is it's going to be rough for a little while, but then you'll have your beautiful baby in your arms and all the pain will be forgotten. Is that better?"

"I don't think so," she admitted, and they laughed.

"Then focus on the baby."

An ultrasound a few months ago had revealed she was having a girl, and she already had a name picked out. Summer.

"Where's Rally?" Reagan asked.

"Out in the waiting room with Sawyer," Serenity replied. "Do you want me to get him?"

Reagan cared about Rally. It wasn't the same as what she'd felt for Drew—wasn't an all-consuming sexual rush. But what they had was far deeper. It was solid, supportive, kind and filled with genuine respect. She wasn't sure they'd end up married. They hadn't talked about that yet. But she knew that even if they didn't get married, they'd be friends for life. Rally was *that* kind of man. "No, he can meet Summer once she arrives. I've got the two of you. That's all I need."

Reagan saw Lorelei wince as she looked over at Serenity.

"What is it?" she said. "Why'd you give her that look?"

"Your mother is on her way," Lorelei said. "She texted me a few minutes ago."

It was difficult to be around her mother. Although Rosalind had taken the news of the pregnancy far better than Reagan had anticipated—mostly because she liked Rally so much and assumed they'd both raise Summer—Reagan wasn't looking forward to coping with her mother's presence while she felt so vulnerable.

But she would've been hurt had Rosalind *not* made the effort. So she nodded. "That's nice of her."

"I can run interference for you if you don't want her here," Serenity offered.

Reagan shook her head. "No. I want her here."

"Are you sure?" Lorelei asked.

"I'm sure." Maybe her mother wasn't the most nurturing woman on the planet, but Reagan knew all too well that sometimes taking on the role of parent wasn't easy. After confronting Rosalind with what she'd learned about her birth, Rosalind had finally admitted that it was her father, Stuart Sands, who'd been behind her adoption. Rosalind had gone along with it. And then, when he died, she'd been left with the responsibility of raising the child *he'd* wanted more than she had.

At least Rosalind had kept Reagan. At least she'd tried to fulfill her commitment. In Rosalind's own mind, she'd been a good mother. So Reagan had decided to simply be grateful that she'd had a mother and that her mother had done her best, and leave it at that. There was no guarantee she'd do any better with Summer, but she'd promised herself she was going to try.

"What are you talking about? I don't care if there're already two people in the room. I'm her mother!"

When they heard Rosalind barking at the nurses in the hall, they started to laugh.

"There she is," Reagan said, but then another contraction came, and she gritted her teeth to be able to bear it.

Her mother had nudged Serenity out of the way and was at Reagan's side by the time the contraction ended. "Reagan, I'm here now. How are you doing?"

"At this moment? I can't believe I got myself into this," she said honestly.

"You'll get through it. You just need to let nature take its course." While her words were kind enough, she couldn't help sounding more like a drill sergeant than a concerned parent, and Reagan managed a wobbly smile.

"Thanks, Mom. I know I'll get through it now that you're here."

She meant what she'd said, but long after it was over, and she held her child in her arms late that night, when Rosalind and even Rally had left, it was her two sisters who were still with her.

"I think you're right," Reagan said as her daughter's tiny hand curled around her finger.

They were all tired. Serenity had fallen asleep in the recliner not far from Reagan's bed. Lorelei was sitting next to her, awake, but barely so. "Right about what?"

The beauty and perfection of her daughter nearly moved her to tears. For the first time, she felt sorry for Drew, that he'd miss out on Summer's life. "I'm already in love."

* * * * *

Questions for Discussion

1. Have you ever taken a DNA ancestry test before? Were you surprised at the results?

2. Serenity, Reagan and Lorelei came together at a time when they were all facing a crossroads. How did they help each other through their individual challenges?

3. Serenity was shocked and horrified to learn of her ex-husband's crimes. She feels guilty that she didn't catch him sooner. Do you think it's possible for someone to miss signs that their spouse is leading a double life?

4. Part of Lorelei healing from her husband cheating on her with her best friend is letting herself enjoy a romance with Finn. Did you think Lorelei and Finn were right for each other long-term, or was it a good idea for them to split when they did?

5. If you were Lorelei, do you think you would have given Mark another chance? How about Francine— do you think you could restore a friendship with her?

6. When Reagan learns she's pregnant with Drew's child, she questions whether she should tell him or not. Do you feel Drew has a right to know, no matter their relationship? Or do you feel he relinquished his right to know with the way he behaved?

7. How do you feel Lucy's character added to the story?

8. Could you identify with any one of the three women more than the others? If so, who and why?

9. If you were making a movie of this book, which actors would you cast?

10. What do you think the future holds for each of the characters?

A Conversation
with the Author

What inspired you to write this story?

My best friend had just found a "secret" sister through DNA testing. She was talking about having met her previously unknown sibling and telling me what the woman was like. Then one of my family members found a "secret" sister—a close family member—which came as a shock to me. I was fascinated by all the "what ifs" the people involved faced, and I was seeing this type of thing pop up so much in the media that I wanted to explore it through the pages of a novel.

What kind of research went into writing this novel?

Fortunately, the internet provides writers with so many tools. I was able to do a lot of research online, but my husband was kind enough to actually have his DNA tested so I could see exactly how it worked. The family member who found a "secret" sister also shared the process with me. It was really interesting!

What was the most challenging part of writing this novel, and what was the most enjoyable?

The most challenging part was probably trying not to veer too far into the lives of Finn and his brothers, the men staying next door. I really liked them and what they contributed to the story, especially Finn's brother, Davis, who had just lost an arm. I can't imagine how difficult that would be to cope with, so I was fascinated with how he might react and loved watching his inner strength come through as he fought to recover from this tragic setback.

What I loved most was helping each of the women overcome their challenges. Since I live close to Lake Tahoe, which is an incredibly beautiful place, I also really enjoyed setting the book there.

You wrote from the perspective of four different characters—Serenity, Reagan, Lorelei and Finn. Did you have a favorite character, and why?

I think I identified with them all to a certain degree. But I especially love Reagan's budding romantic relationship, and the friendship Finn offers Lorelei. So maybe a tie between the two of them.

You've written more than sixty novels in your career. How was this book different than any other?

I had a much bigger canvas to work with and fewer conventions to follow. Many of my books have been in the romance genre, in which the two love interests must wind up together in the end. In a book like this, that isn't necessarily the case. It more closely resembles real life, so it was fun to widen the parameters and have my characters take on and overcome challenges they may or may not fully conquer by the end. This book was different in that I had to face my own challenge of weaving all these story lines together, too.

What kind of books do you like to read, and do you find that they affect what you write?

I'm such an eclectic reader! My favorite genre is probably women's fiction, followed closely by historical novels à la Philippa Gregory, then contemporary romance and psychological suspense. (See? I'm naming almost all of them!) Maybe I should mention what I typically *don't* read, and that would be sci-fi and fantasy, although I loved, *loved* the Game of Thrones series as well as Harry Potter. I also read a lot of nonfiction, usually on the subjects of the universe, evolution, religion or physics. The only magazine I subscribe to is *National Geographic*, so that tells you a little about my nonfiction reading tastes.

Everything I read and experience informs my writing. I just never know beforehand when certain things will manifest themselves.

What is your writing process like?

I write five days a week, although the hours are certainly a little longer than if I held a regular day job, especially because I travel quite a bit, too. I don't outline my books in advance. If I do, I feel as though I've already told the story and quickly grow bored with it. It also results in a lot of flat, emotionless telling—maybe because I'm trying to force the characters to do what I want them to instead of what they would naturally do. An advance outline also gets me in trouble because I tend to reveal all the surprises in the story way too soon (I guess I can't keep a secret!). So I have to let the plot grow out of the characters and be surprised as the reader would be. Every writer has their own process, and this is the one that works for me.

If you enjoyed this story,
visit www.brendanovak.com to receive
a FREE digital follow-up novella called
Pieces of Perfect, *which carries on the*
story of Serenity, Reagan and Lorelei.

Don't miss New York Times *bestselling author Brenda Novak's newest stand-alone novel,* Summer on the Island.

A summer of healing, friendship, love...and a secret that could change everything.

After the death of her US senator father, Marlow Madsen travels to the small island off the coast of Florida where she spent summers growing up to help her mother settle the family estate. For Marlow, the trip is a chance to reconnect after too long apart. It's also the perfect escape to help her feel grounded again—one she's happy to share with friends Aida and Claire, who are hoping to reset their lives, too.

A leisurely beachfront summer promises the trio of women the opportunity to take deep healing breaths and explore new paths. But when her father's will reveals an earth-shattering secret that tarnishes his impeccable reputation and everything she thought she knew about her family, Marlow finds herself questioning her entire childhood—and aspects of her future. Fortunately, her friends, and the most unlikely love interest she could imagine, prove that happiness can be found no matter what—as long as the right people are by your side.

Available now wherever books are sold!